A VAALBARA NOVEL

VISIONS & SHADOWS

USA TODAYS BEST SELLING AUTHOR

MICHELLE HEARD

Cover Designer: Cormar Covers
Map: Meryl, PixelMagic
Formatter: Image Ink Designs
Editor: Sheena Taylor

DEDICATION

It took fifteen years to have enough faith in myself to publish
Visions & Shadows.
I'm so proud of myself for never giving up.

Songlist

Fire on the Mountain – Rob Thomas
Amanda's Song – Jason Koiter
Man in the Mirror – J2, Cameron the Public
Don't Fear the Reaper – The Spiritual Machines
Hold on for your life – Sam Tinnesz
Journey On – Elms District
Soft Dark Nothing – Lily Kershaw
Stand By Me – Ki:Theory
Forever Young – Lily Kershaw
Such Great Heights – MILCK

Author Note

Visions & Shadows
Vaalbara - Book 1

**The character list and noteworthy details regarding
Vaalbara are at the back of the book.**
This book contains subject matter that may be sensitive for some
readers. There is triggering content between these pages.

18+ only.
Please read responsibly.

SYNOPSIS

A week before my eighteenth birthday, the guy I'm catching feelings for legit tosses me through a waterfall, only for me to find out everything I thought I knew is nothing but a lie.

My name is Alchera, and five years ago, my people wiped my memories and abandoned me at a waterfall so I'd learn what it's like to be human. Turns out I have the destiny of saving humankind and a hotter-than-hell guardian to help me through the nightmare I have to face.

Adapting to a life of brutal training was not on my list of things to do after graduating. But the ten chosen ones depend on me, and I have no choice but to suck it up and do everything I'm told.

Trying to survive the new world I've been thrown into, I have to cope with my guardian, who can hear my every thought. Besides that, people are out to torture me for information about the visions I receive.

I'm not so sure I'm cut out for this.

"Hope is the heartbeat of the soul."
Michelle Heard

PROLOGUE

RAIGHNE

I am her guardian, and she is my charge.
She's the only being who matters to me.
I vow to protect her.
I'll live and die for her.
I'll sacrifice everything I am for Alchera.

"We have to bring Alchera home. She needs to train, and we're running out of time," Janak, our elder, says. "Awo has spoken the words, and we must abide by them. We can send Griffith to retrieve her from Earth."

"No, Janak." Queen Mya shakes her head. "Griffith is the King's guardian. I will not hear of it."

Standing in the throne room, tension fills the air. My eyes flick between King Eryon and Queen Mya, and I notice the tired lines on their faces. The long years without Alchera must've been hard on them.

It's been excruciating for me.

The Queen's voice is drenched with fear when she continues, "We can't leave the King unprotected."

I glance at my father, who's been King Eryon's guardian for as long as I can remember.

"We shouldn't have sent her away," King Eryon mutters, drawing my attention to him. "Alchera's been alone and probably very confused. Now we're going to snatch her up again and bring her back to a world she'll hardly remember."

"As Your Highness knows, we had to send her away," Janak says. "She had to experience what it's like to be human and live like they do. She has the most difficult task ahead of her, having to save the chosen ten. The future of humankind depends on her."

I suck in a deep breath while crossing my arms over my chest.

I should've been allowed to go with Alchera. It's been pure hell knowing she's alone on Earth.

"We can't forget that we needed to hide Alchera from Adeth, who has the power to kill an immortalis," Queen Mya murmurs, her tone still trembling with fear.

I glance at my father, who's a large man and the best fighter our realm has ever seen. I should know. I've landed flat on my back plenty of times while sparring with him.

Dad meets my gaze, his eyes filled with pride as he nods at me. His deep blue irises are sprinkled with golden flecks, a sign of the great power he wields that keeps many automatically at a distance.

My father is the most powerful when it comes to the guardians due to the bond he shares with King Eryon.

The closer you grow to your charge, the more powers you attain.

Taking a step forward, my voice is filled with strength and determination as I say, "I will go. Alchera is *my* charge."

All eyes snap to me and King Eryon stares at me for a moment before he says, "It's only right that you go, Raighne. Like you said, you're her guardian."

Janak takes a couple of steps closer to me. "You'll have three weeks at most to find Alchera and bring her home. The visions of the chosen ten can start at any time once she turns twenty-one. I shouldn't have to remind you of the severity of the consequences should you fail."

"I won't fail," I state confidently.

Queen Mya rises from the throne she's sitting on, and as she walks toward me, her features tighten with emotion. Coming to stand in front of me, she says, "Please, be gentle with my daughter. She won't remember our ways and will think she's an eighteen-year-old human girl because of the spell that was cast on her." Giving me a pleading look, she adds, "Keep her safe."

"I will," I promise. "I'll protect Alchera with my life."

When Queen Mya returns to take her seat beside King Eryon, I suck in a deep breath.

This is it. The moment I've trained for.

Soon, I'll be by Alchera's side, and nothing will ever separate us again for all eternity.

I glance down at the small vial of elixir in the palm of my hand before I tuck it into my pocket. I'll need to drink it the moment I reach Earth. It will make me look more like a human teenager and less immortalis-like.

Also, it will change my eyes so I don't freak out the humans.

My father holds an envelope out to me. "It's the money they use where Alchera is. It should last you three weeks."

Taking the envelope, I nod while shoving it into my other pocket. "Thank you."

He lets out a heavy sigh. "Be careful. Never let your guard down."

I nod again.

"Remember, she'll have no memory of us until Janak and Aster reverse the spell. Even though you are bonded to her as her guardian, you are a stranger to Alchera. She'll be very confused. So even though she's twenty on Vaalbara, she thinks she's a seventeen-year-old girl on Earth."

"I know, Father."

The last time I saw Alchera was the day Adeth attacked, and Janak and Aster had to cast a spell on Alchera so she'd forget her life here on Vaalbara.

I only got to hold her when I carried her away from danger and took her through the Virtutes Waterfall to leave her on Earth.

Before that day, I was training and didn't get to see her.

My father takes a step closer to me, and putting his hand on my shoulder, he says, "We don't know what Adeth has planned or where she is, so we have to be vigilant at all times."

"I'll be careful," I mutter the words to appease him.

For a moment, emotion tightens Father's features. "You look so much like your mother. She would've been proud of you."

I have my mother's dark brown hair, and before I became Alchera's guardian, I had Mother's light blue eyes. Due to the bond I've formed with Alchera, my eyes are now purple – as is every guardian's when the initial bond is created. Only when we grow stronger does the color change again.

"I won't disappoint you, Father. I'll bring her back safely."

We stare at each other for a brief second before I walk out of my house and into the cool afternoon air.

As I make my way toward the Virtutes Waterfall, I glance over the hills and planes of grass.

I see a rider steer his horse in the direction of the training grounds, where I know men are assembling tents at this very moment for the coming training season. It's almost a full day's ride to get to the camps.

During the hour-long trek toward my destination, my thoughts are filled with Alchera. I'll have to find a way to make her comfortable with me before bringing her home.

I hear the rush of water, and as I reach the top of a hill, the Virtutes Waterfall comes into view. Like always, when I see the spectacular sight, I pause for a moment to take in its splendor.

The waterfall flows over the side of a cliff, the rocks and ground on either side of it a rich brown, which is in stark contrast to the blue-green pool below.

There are majestic trees with the deepest green leaves and trunks covered in soft moss where the pool feeds into a gentle stream. It meanders all the way to the village, supplying our people with fresh water.

The Virtutes Waterfall is the heart of Vaalbara – a planet clothed in its original splendor, just as when Earth took its first breath.

Moving closer, I look up to where I know Kalin and Raker, the guards of the entrance to Vaalbara, are watching me from a ledge behind the curtain.

Kalin, who's not much older than me, is the first to appear, shouting so I'll hear him above the roar of water, "Peace be. State your business, friend."

"Peace be," I call out, greeting him in the way that's our custom. "I seek permission from Raker and yourself to shift to Earth."

At the mention of his name, Raker appears next to Kalin on the ledge. "Peace be. Why do you seek to shift, Raighne?"

"I've been ordered by the head of the guards, the king, and our elder, Janak, to go to Earth to acquire something."

I know better than to divulge the true reason. Who knows if there are ears hiding around us, listening in on our conversation on behalf of Adeth or Void.

There's a moment where we can only hear the rushing of water before Raker nods. "May Awo keep you safe."

Sucking in a deep breath of air, I step into the pool and wade my way closer to the curtain.

This is it.

I'm coming, Alchera.

Droplets of water hit my face and body, and when I'm standing in front of the curtain, I take another deep breath. I clear my thoughts of everything but Alchera before stepping beneath the spray.

The world starts to blur around me as I leave the only home I've ever known.

Not even a minute later, I move out from under the curtain of the waterfall nearest to Alchera.

My sight is still blurry for a moment, and I wipe the drops from my face. Glancing around me, I take in all the trees around the waterfall. The forest is more overgrown than I remember from when I left Alchera here.

I make my way to the embankment, where I pull myself out of the pool. Reaching into my pocket, I take the vial out and quickly drink the bitter elixir. I feel the change wash over me, transforming me from immortalis to a teenage human boy.

Just as I'm about to look at my reflection in the pool, I hear twigs snap.

Someone's coming!

Glancing around, I rush toward the nearest large tree and take cover behind it.

When a girl comes walking down an overgrown trail, every muscle in my body tenses and a breath explodes over my lips.

Her dark brown hair hangs down her shoulders, and her green eyes seem to be filled with loneliness.

Alchera.

My entire being shudders at finally laying eyes on my charge.

Once she's back on Vaalbara, her hair will be as black as a raven's wing, and her eyes will sparkle like emeralds.

I watch as she sits down near the pool and stares at the water. Her features grow sad, then I hear her thoughts as if they're my own.

"I can't wait to leave this town."

Soon, my charge. Soon.

CHAPTER 1

JANE / ALCHERA

Waking up, I let out a groan.

Ugh, I'm so not in the mood for school.

I hit the snooze button on my alarm before snuggling back into my pillow.

Minutes later, when the incessant alarm goes off again, I'm a second away from flinging the damn cell phone out of the window.

Get up, or your butt is walking to school. It's freezing, and you need the ride.

Forcing myself to sit up in bed, I rub the sleep from my eyes.

"Just five more months, then you're done with school," I mutter before yawning. "Ugh. Five months too long. God help me."

Climbing out of bed, I yawn again as I walk to the bathroom. While I'm busy with my morning routine, my thoughts turn to the dream I had for the eleventh day in a row.

It always starts with the same beautiful waterfall. There are lights flickering beneath the blue-green water, and old trees hug the pool where a man is wading through the water toward the curtain.

The man.

I stop brushing my teeth as I get lost in my thoughts.

In every dream, I only see him from behind. He's dressed in leather pants that span tightly around his muscled thighs and a matching shirt that clings to his broad shoulders.

I never see his face, but if he looks that hot from behind, the front can't be all that bad.

It's weird, though. Why do I keep having the same dream, over and over?

Yeah, I love spending time at Fish Creek Falls, but it can't be the reason for the weird dream.

I finish brushing my teeth then rinse out my mouth before walking back to my bedroom.

Opening the closet, I wonder what I should wear. Most of my clothes are hand-me-downs from my adoptive sister, Molly. I don't mind, seeing as nine out of ten times, the clothes still have their tags on because she got a size too small.

Molly has an unhealthy addiction to buying clothes, but at least the girl has great taste.

I pick a pair of faded black jeans, a blue sweater, and a gray jacket. After pairing the outfit with my favorite boots, I quickly grab my bag and cell phone.

When I walk into the foyer of the mansion, there's no sign of Molly.

Molly and Patrick are Mayor and Mrs. Calder's biological children.

I'm the same age as Molly. Seventeen. When I was found at a waterfall nearly five years ago, they had to guess my age because I couldn't remember anything about my past.

How I ended up at the waterfall remains a mystery because the police couldn't find out anything about me.

They started calling me Jane, as in 'Jane Doe,' and the name stuck when Mayor Calder was kind enough to take me in.

Of course, his act of kindness was to boost his status in the small town of Steamboat Springs. At least I benefited from it and appreciate everything the Calders have done for me.

The house is quiet and I wonder if Molly is even awake. Patrick always leaves early for work and only returns late so we hardly see him.

I head to the kitchen and quickly make a cup of coffee. While I drink the much-needed caffeine, I scroll through my social media accounts.

Every other post is something Molly shared about the football team or cheerleaders. Letting out a sigh, I drink the last of my coffee while putting my phone away.

I'm socially awkward and haven't been able to make any friends at school. Honestly, the loneliness is really starting to get to me, especially when I see other students having fun together.

I have Molly, though. I wouldn't say we're friends, but more like acquaintances because we don't have a lot in common. We're complete opposites.

After I rinse my cup, I head back to the foyer, and when there's still no sign of Molly, I yell, "We're going to be late for school."

With Mayor and Mrs. Calder away for the next two weeks, Molly's probably going to oversleep every day. They finally decided to take the trip to Greece they've been planning for over three years, and I love the photos they send us every day.

"I'm coming," Molly shouts, but the second she appears at the top of the stairs, she turns around. "Crap, I forgot my lipstick."

She's the last girl on the planet who needs more lipstick. All the boys trail behind her like lap dogs, and I doubt it's because of her intense makeup regimen.

"Well, don't just stand there. Let's go." Molly rushes by me and is out the door in a blur, leaving behind a whiff of perfume that's going to have me sneezing all the way to school.

Great. By the time we get to school, I'll look like Rudolph the Red-Nosed Reindeer.

Not even seconds after I climb into the car, I start to sneeze.

Molly digs a tissue out of her bag and shoves it into my hand before she starts the engine.

"Thanks," I mutter, cranking the window open an inch so we can get fresh air into the car.

"No," she snaps. "Shut it. It's freezing."

"Your perfume's killing me," I grumble.

Luckily, it's only a ten-minute drive, and the instant the car is parked in its regular spot, I shove the door open and suck in deep breaths of fresh air.

"Come on," I tell Molly. "We're late."

"Yeah-yeah," she mutters while checking her makeup in the rearview mirror.

Not waiting for her, I hurry toward the entrance of the main building. The hallways are already empty, and I make it to class in the nick of time.

While Mr. Brady, our history teacher, writes something on the board, I let out a relieved sigh as I quickly walk to my desk at the back of the class.

Luckily, Mr. Brady is chill and doesn't get angry if we're a minute or two late. If it were Freezo's class, I'd be standing up front trying to solve an equation from hell.

In every class, I sit alone in the corner, where I can go as unnoticed as possible. I keep my grades at a satisfactory level, and the teachers don't pick on me.

Some of the students and town folk think I'm weird because

of the unsolved mystery of how I was found by Fish Creek Falls. It has them keeping their distance from me, and it's part of the reason why it's so hard for me to make friends.

While I dig my sketchpad and pencil out of my bag, I feel the atmosphere change, and hushed voices start to fill the air.

"Oh my," Wendy murmurs from where she's seated in front of me.

"Damn, he's hot," Megan, the head cheerleader, says.

When I glance at Megan, it's to see her teeth tugging at her bottom lip while she drools at whoever's got her attention.

I follow her line of sight to see what's got everyone talking, and then my heart skips one hell of a beat.

Holy shit. Megan's not wrong. He's hot as hell.

There's a guy up front talking to Mr. Brady, and when he gives our teacher a lopsided grin, a couple of the girls sigh dreamily.

The new guy's hair is dark brown and a little on the longer side. His face is flawless, his chin square and strong. Just as I look at his dark eyebrows, his eyes flick to me.

Pale blue eyes any girl can get lost in.

Damn, he's good-looking.

Then it registers that the new guy is watching me stare at him, and my face goes up in flames.

Oh my God. Kill me now.

I try to look away, but then he ends his conversation with Mr. Brady, and when he starts to walk down the aisle in my direction, my heart beats faster and faster.

He's probably going to sit next to Wendy.

The new guy walks with so much confidence every pair of eyes in class is focused on him.

Damn, I wish I had his confidence.

Molly sneaks into class as the new guy glances at the other

students.

When his gaze locks on me again, I have to suppress the urge to swallow hard. By the time he reaches my desk, my heart is beating a mile a minute.

Stay calm. Don't say something stupid.

Ugh, he probably won't even talk to me.

I feel like squirming in my chair and glance down at my white knuckles where I'm clutching my favorite pencil.

I can barely restrain myself from looking at him again.

When the drop-dead gorgeous guy takes a seat right next to me, I try to forcefully keep myself from stealing another glance, but my eyes have a mind of their own. Slowly, I turn my head, and I take in the cargo pants that hug his thighs just right.

Dear God, have mercy on my hormones.

I can't resist and let my eyes slide up his body to his broad chest. He's wearing a dark blue button-up shirt, the top two buttons undone. His sleeves are rolled up to his elbows, exposing his forearms and tanned skin.

Then my eyes land on his hands and the veins snaking beneath his skin, and my heart skips another beat.

Lost in the attractive guy beside me, my eyes drift upward, pausing at his totally kissable lips.

The corner of his mouth curves up, and I'm just about to get entirely lost in him when our eyes meet.

Well, actually, it's more like he catches me gawking at him.

My soul almost ups and leaves my body, and I practically give myself whiplash when I turn my head away to look out the window.

Ugh. Embarrassing!

My heart hammers in my chest while a wave of mortification hits me hard.

Every drop of blood in my body rushes to my face, and

lifting a hand, I rest my elbow on the table and cover my eyes.

Now's a good time for the ground to open up and swallow me whole.

I get a whiff of his aftershave, and of course, it has to smell incredible – fresh and masculine with a hint of rain. And something spicy and addictive.

I suck in a deep breath of air, then open my sketchpad to the page with the waterfall.

"That's really good," he says suddenly, his voice low and deep. "You like drawing?"

To my absolute horror, I snort before awkward laughter bursts over my lips.

Dear God.

I clear my throat and nod. "Yeah."

"Where have you seen that waterfall?" he asks.

The last thing I expected today was a hot guy walking into school and asking me about my drawing.

A slight frown forms on my forehead, and turning my head, I look at him. "It's from a dream I had."

His eyes take mine captive. "That must've been quite some dream." A smile tugs at his mouth, then he adds, "I'm Ryan Jackson."

Somehow, I manage to smile while I murmur, "I'm Jane. Welcome to Steamboat Springs."

His smile grows warm and friendly, making him a million times hotter. "Thank you."

"Did you say your name's Ryan?" Megan asks from the desk next to ours. "I'm Megan, the head cheerleader. Just say if you need someone to show you around."

Ryan nods at her. "I'm good. Thanks."

When he turns his attention back to me, my jaw drops open. No one dismisses Megan, especially not to talk to me.

"I haven't had time to get any books. Mind sharing?" he asks.

"Ah..." I nod quickly while digging the history book out of my bag. "Sure."

My tongue darts out to wet my lips as I open the book between us.

While I wait for Mr. Brady to start, I focus on my drawing, not trying to make it obvious I'm affected by my new neighbor.

As the lesson begins, I desperately try to focus on what Mr. Brady is saying, but it's of no use. The Titanic could be sinking beside me, and I wouldn't even notice right now.

I'm super aware of the hot guy sitting only inches away from me, and all I can smell is his amazing cologne.

Ryan shifts in his chair as he turns the page in the textbook, and his arm presses against mine. When he doesn't move again, my stomach free-falls into oblivion and tingles explode over my body.

I clear my throat and try to control my breathing while my palms grow sweaty. My sole focus is glued to the spot where our arms are touching.

When the bell finally rings, relief floods my body. Gathering my sketchbook and pencil, I grab my bag before darting up from my chair. I squeeze past Ryan's seat and rush for the door as if hellhounds are nipping at my heels.

Holy shit. Sitting next to Ryan was intense.

Sucking in deep breaths of air, I try to calm my racing heart as I head to the next class.

Walking into English Lit, I take my usual seat at the back, and as I set my sketchpad down on the desk, Molly takes a seat in front of me. It's not her usual seat, so she has to have an ulterior motive for sitting close to me.

"Why did you take off like a bat out of hell after history?" she asks.

"I didn't." Molly keeps staring at me so I add, "I'm just excited about our poem reading today."

I hate speaking in public, and the poem I wrote sucks ass.

"Sure, and I'm a unicorn," Molly smirks at me. "I saw the new guy talking to you. What did he say?" Scooting her chair closer, she rests her elbows on my desk, looking like she's about to explode with excitement.

"He just commented on my drawing." She keeps staring at me. I can see she wants way more information. "Really. That's all."

"Then why did you run out of class like that?"

Like a dog with a bone, Molly's not about to let this go.

"I just wanted to read over my poem again. I'm nervous. Aren't you?"

She shakes her head. "Nope." Her eyes light up with interest. "You're so lucky he sat next to you. What's his name?" She glances over her shoulder, then lets out an excited shriek. "Here he comes."

I have to force my eyes to stay down so I don't go making a fool of myself again.

Molly gives a nervous giggle. "He's heading our way."

She's supposed to be madly in love with Robert-the-douchebag, and he'll be one unhappy puppy if he hears how excited his girlfriend is about Ryan.

There are a few desks with open seats, so I'm totally surprised when the chair next to mine scrapes across the floor.

He's sitting beside me again? Why?

I look at Ryan as he takes a seat. It's only a split-second glance before I come to my senses and snap my eyes back to my poem.

Don't stare at him.

I try to look unaffected by his presence while pretending to

16

read my poem, my heart beating a crazy rhythm against my ribs.

"You forgot your textbook," Ryan says as he holds it out to me.

"Oh..." I keep my eyes down while I take the book and quickly shove it into my bag. "Thanks."

The class starts, and soon, we hit a monotonous tone with one student after the other reading their poems, and I allow my mind to wander to the seat beside me.

I wonder where Ryan's from and why he changed schools in the middle of his senior year.

He'll probably join the popular crowd. I glance at the other students and notice how Megan keeps staring at Ryan.

Yep, they'll be a couple before the end of the week.

What Megan wants, Megan gets.

At least she'll leave Robert alone, which will be good for Molly.

Poor Ryan, though. Megan's the biggest bitch in school.

As if Ryan can hear my thoughts, he slightly turns his head in my direction.

When the bell rings, I thank my lucky stars I didn't have to recite my poem. I grab my bag, but before I can dart past Ryan, he gets up, and I'm forced to walk behind him.

Not that it's a problem because he looks all kinds of fine from behind.

When we enter our math class and Ryan heads straight for the seat beside mine, I frown. I glance at the other open seats and notice everyone in class is staring at us.

Great. This will be all over school before lunch.

As I take my seat, Mr. Frost, who everybody calls Freezo behind his back, begins to rattle on like he always does and hands out quizzes that have everyone groaning.

Math is a hated subject by most students. Half the students' eyes are already glazed over, and the other half have a permanent confused look as soon as they walk into the class.

The hour feels endlessly long, and there are a couple of times I have to suppress a yawn. When the bell rings it sounds like my favorite song playing.

Just one more class before lunch.

Walking into the hallway, I look at my watch to check the time as I head to my locker. I need to offload a couple of books and grab the one for social studies.

After I've swapped books, I close my locker. I'm just about to turn around when a hand comes from out of nowhere and slams into the metal right beside my head, narrowly missing my cheek. My whole body jerks with fright, and air explodes over my lips.

"Asshole," I mutter as I turn around, but when I see it's Robert, my heart sinks.

Not again.

"What do we have here?" He shoves me against the locker, a cocky smirk plastered on his face.

When the lock presses hard into my back, I have to grind on my teeth not to wince.

I can't stand him touching me, and he knows it. He's a bully, and he thinks he's better than everyone else. Where most of the girls think he's hot, the guy gives me the creeps.

I lift my chin, not caring that he's easily twice my size.

"Back off, Robert. I have a class to go to." I try to sound as bored as possible to hit his ego hard and bring him down a notch.

I won't give him the pleasure of seeing me upset because I know it's what the bastard wants.

Robert glares at me because I'm not showing the desired interest in him, and I can see my words hit the spot I was aiming for.

When I attempt to shove past him, he moves to block my way, laughing in my face while shaking his head. "Why the hurry, sweetling? I've noticed you're real friendly with my new friend. Why not spare me some of that kindness?"

Ugh! I'd rather slam my head against the wall. Repeatedly.

I have a bad temper and little control over it when it comes to this jerk, and hearing he's already friends with Ryan is disappointing as hell.

"You're not worth my time, let alone my kindness," I mutter. "Why don't you go crawl back down that hole you just came out of and leave me the hell alone."

I shove past him and breathe a sigh of relief when I actually get away.

Still aggravated about the unwelcome run-in with Robert, I make it to class in the nick of time.

I'm not even surprised to find Ryan sitting in the seat next to mine.

When I place the book down between us, I notice my hands are still trembling. Taking my seat, I can feel Ryan looking at me.

After a while, I can't stop myself and dare a fleeting look at him. Seeing concern tightening his features, I'm surprised.

"Are you okay?" he asks.

I nod while sucking in a deep breath, then open the textbook and try to focus on social studies.

CHAPTER 2

JANE / ALCHERA

The shrill bell finally signals the long-awaited lunch hour that I'm in desperate need of.

Finally, I can recharge my batteries.

When I stand up, my phone beeps with an incoming message, and preoccupied with reading the text Molly sent, I move toward the aisle.

Molly: I'm going shopping with the girls after school.

Why am I not surprised?

Unfortunately, Ryan picks that exact second to step to his left. The next thing I know, I plow face-first into his chest. He grabs hold of my shoulders, his touch downright electric.

"Crap…uhm…" Muffled words are all I can get out between my nervous breaths. "Sorry."

That's when it hits me. I'm practically standing in Ryan's arms.

My hands are on his chest.

Holy shit.

My eyes dart wildly through the classroom to see if anyone is watching, and it's in time to see Robert laughing at us before he steps out into the hallway.

A wave of embarrassment washes over me, and it doesn't take my face long to reach the darkest shade of burgundy known to mankind.

When I turn my attention back to Ryan and our eyes meet, he loosens his grip on me while asking, "You okay?"

"Yeah...sure," I reply, my fast breaths making the words come out in a rush.

Ryan is friends with Robert.

An uneasy feeling trickles into my chest.

"I'm okay." I'm relieved to hear I at least sound somewhat normal.

My eyes lower to where my hands are still plastered against his chest. I yank them away, feeling like a total idiot, and it makes my cheeks burn even hotter.

"Ahh...yeah...so..." I keep stammering, making an even bigger ass of myself. My shoulders slump and giving up on trying to explain, I stay quiet and simply look up at him.

"Would you like to grab something to eat with me?" he asks. "Or we can just sit somewhere."

Slowly, a frown forms on my forehead, then a realization knocks the wind from me.

Fuck my life.

This is probably some sort of initiation thing for him. Robert and his friends like to make guys carry out dares in order to become one of the group. They've done this to me before and Robert mentioned Ryan's his new friend.

Anger ignites in my chest, and the longer I stare at Ryan, the more it makes sense why he's been sitting next to me in every class.

It upsets me more than it should.

I let out a harsh breath and shake my head at him. "No,

thanks. I have things to do and places to be. I'm sure your friends are waiting for you outside." Giving him a glare, I shove past him. "Enjoy lunch."

I don't stick around to hear his response. I rush for the door as fast as I can and head toward the cafeteria.

"Jane," I hear Ryan call. "Wait up."

"Not going to fall for the trick," I shout, not even glancing over my shoulder. "Leave me alone."

"Dammit," I hear him snap.

He can *dammit* all he likes. I don't care. Not when I'm sure this is some sort of prank the guys are playing on me.

Jesus, you'd think they'd stop with the stupid pranks our senior year, but no.

Immature assholes.

Walking straight through the cafeteria and outside, where there's an outdoor seating area, I make a beeline for the corner where I always spend my breaks.

When I reach my spot, I sit down and refuse to think of Ryan and Robert again.

Taking out my sketchbook, I work on my drawing until the lunch hour is almost over. I lift my head and glance through the windows into the cafeteria, where groups of students are talking and laughing.

Letting out a sigh, I pack up and hoist the strap of my bag over my shoulder. I don't glance around me as I walk to the restroom, and my day takes a turn for the worse when I find Megan and her friends in front of the mirrors where they're touching up their makeup.

"Well, well, well," Megan sneers, "if it isn't *Jane Doe*."

I decide it's better not to say anything and squeeze by the future silicone squad to get to a stall.

"The freak can't speak," I hear Megan's best friend, Kate,

laugh while I relieve my bladder.

After flushing, I ignore the group of girls while I wash my hands, but before I can leave, Megan steps in front of me.

"What's the deal with you and Ryan?"

Rolling my eyes, I push past her and leave the restroom.

"Don't ignore me," she snaps as she follows after me.

"Get a life, Megan," I mutter, heading toward the next class.

I slip into Art Theory, and when I walk toward my table in the corner, Ryan's already there looking directly at me.

Ugh. Ryan and his friends can all go screw themselves.

I take my seat next to him and slam my bag down on the desk.

"Jane—"

I drag my chair forward, scraping it across the floor to cut off whatever he wants to say.

I can feel his gaze on me as he continues, "Please, could you just—"

Grabbing the textbook from my bag, I place it in front of him, figuring I'll have to share anyway.

"I just want—" He tries again.

"Do me a favor," I snap. "If you're going to insist on sitting next to me in every damn class, will you please not talk to me?"

He stares at me with a frown, and I can see he's struggling not to say anything else.

I glance away, not wanting to have any more contact with him unless it's absolutely necessary.

I haven't had a bad day like this in a while and can't wait for it to end.

My day doesn't get any better, and as we move from one class to the next and Ryan keeps sitting next to me, my frustration continues to grow.

Maybe his initiation is an all-day thing? It sucks ass.

By the time school ends, I'm exhausted from all the tension I've experienced today.

When I leave the building with all the other students, I'm slapped in the face by an icy wind. I pull my jacket tighter around me and begin the five-mile walk to Fish Creek Falls, where I prefer to spend my afternoons.

I seriously hope tomorrow's not a repeat of today.

When I'm a few minutes away from the forest, I hear a car coming down the road. I cut into the thick bushes and trees to make myself scarce.

A brown truck passes by, and when I recognize Ryan behind the steering wheel, my heart falters for the zillionth time today.

I thought he'd hang out with Robert. What's he doing all the way out here?

Shaking my head, I enter the forest, taking an overgrown trail people hardly use until I reach the waterfall.

I sit down and pull my knees up to my chest before wrapping my arms around my shins.

A sigh escapes me as I replay the whole messed-up day over and over in my head.

God, I hope tomorrow is better.

RYAN / RAIGHNE

Today didn't go as planned, and I'm frustrated as hell.

I don't know where I went wrong and why Alchera's upset with me. It's taking a lot of self-control not to enter her mind so I can find out why she's angry.

When I walk toward my truck, a group of guys and girls catch up to me.

"Hey, man," one of the guys calls out, "hold up."

In a hurry to leave, I give the group an impatient look.

"I'm Robert," the leader of the group says, "and these are my friends." He throws his arm around Megan, who introduced herself to me this morning.

Megan stares at me with a seductive smile while she leans into Robert's side.

I don't have time for this shit.

"Hey," I mutter, sticking to the way they like to talk on Earth.

"Aren't you going to introduce yourself?" Robert asks.

"Ryan Jackson," I reply, my tone brisk.

Giving them a chin lift, I continue to walk toward my truck.

"Don't you want to hang with us?" Megan calls out.

"No." Not sparing them another second of my precious time, I open the driver's side door and climb in behind the steering wheel.

"Did he just do that?" I hear Megan gasp.

"His loss, baby," Robert mutters.

When I glance at them, I see Robert's features tighten with an arrogant look, anger simmering in his eyes as if he thinks he actually stands a chance against me.

I almost let out a chuckle. I haven't lived over two hundred years to be bothered by a bunch of teenagers. I have much bigger worries.

Like finding a way to get Alchera to feel comfortable with me so I can take her home before her visions of the chosen ones start.

Steering my truck away from school, I quickly forget about Robert and his friends, and my thoughts turn to my charge, who gave me the cold shoulder today. At first, I thought I was making progress, but she suddenly changed toward me, and I'm not sure why.

I know she likes to spend most of her free time by the

waterfall, but I can't just show up because it will look creepy.

I stop by a diner and order a burger and fries to go, which I eat in my truck. Once I'm done with the way too greasy meal, I start the engine again.

My thoughts revolve around Alchera during the drive out of town, and I come to the conclusion that I'll have to win her friendship before approaching her about going home.

Home. I've only been on Earth three days, and I'm ready to return to Vaalbara.

Everything is different here. The fast pace. The processed food. The filthy air. The people who don't give a shit about each other. The list is endlessly long.

Everyone keeps staring at their phones and hardly pays attention to what's happening around them.

To make matters worse, I'm staying at a motel just on the outskirts of the town. It's flea-infested and makes me long for my own house every time I enter the room.

Why was Alchera angry with me today?

Once again, the thought pops into my head as I turn up a road, and I'm tempted to enter her mind for the answer.

During all the years I've trained with my father, I've learned a lot. He taught me how to fight. How to not invade my charge's privacy by intruding on her thoughts, but to focus more on her feelings. Only when I sense distress from her, is it acceptable to enter her mind.

It's the only reason I didn't listen in on her thoughts when she told me to leave her alone.

Fuck, it would make everything so much easier, though.

No. She might feel you in her mind, and it will freak her out.

Now that I'm here on Earth with Alchera, it's clear as daylight she's far from happy. Not once have I seen her smile, and she doesn't interact much with any of the other students.

I actually get the feeling she's hiding, trying to blend in with her surroundings.

It doesn't sit well with me. It makes me want to wrap my arms around Alchera so she'll feel safe, but I'm pretty sure she'll lose her shit if I try that right now.

I let out a sigh as I turn the truck up another road, and ahead, I see Alchera duck into some bushes.

Shaking my head, I drive past her before turning onto a dirt road. I park the truck behind two large trees, and climbing out, I jog back toward the trail Alchera takes to get to the waterfall.

When I get close and hear rushing water, I deviate from the path, and finding the large tree I hid behind after I arrived on Earth, I see Alchera near the pool.

She's sitting with her legs pulled up and her arms wrapped around her shins, looking more fragile than the strong immortalis I know she is.

I focus on her emotions, and feeling she's much calmer than when she was at school, I let out a breath of relief.

My eyes drift over her face, and I take a moment to drink in her beauty. She'll be downright exquisite once the glamor from the elixir is removed and her human mask falls away. She'll also look a little older because she's turning twenty-one soon, and not eighteen like she thinks.

Fuck, there's a lot she's going to have to adjust to.

I wish I could go to her to explain everything and tell her about our bond.

Instead, I settle for watching over her until night starts to fall around us.

When Alchera gets up and lets out a heavy sigh, my arms ache to hold her so I can offer her comfort and strength.

27

JANE / ALCHERA

When I wake up, I almost have a heart attack.

"What the hell?!" My voice is thick with sleep as I glare at Molly, who's leaning over me.

The real shocker is that she's already dressed and ready for school.

I bring my left wrist close to my eyes so I can see my watch. It doesn't help because my sight is blurry from just waking up.

I growl at Molly, "What time is it?"

"Ten past six." She sits down on the side of my bed. "I got up early, so we can talk while you get ready."

I stare at her, totally sure she's losing her freaking mind.

Climbing out of bed, I walk to the closet while saying, "You never get up early. Are you feeling okay?"

She rolls her eyes. "I'm fine." Sitting cross-legged on my unmade bed, she gives me an expectant smile.

Ugh, this early morning visit means nothing good for me.

I grab a baby-green sweater, a hoodie, and a pair of jeans.

"What's with you and all the layers?" she asks.

"I like layers," I grumble. "And it's cold outside."

"You wear layers in the summer as well. Why?"

It's way too early for this.

"Because I want to," I snap while scowling at her. "Do we really have to do this so early in the morning?"

Grinning at me, she nods. Her voice sounds almost like a purr when she asks, "Why is Ryan sitting next to you in every class?"

Ugh, really. She woke me up to ask me about Ryan?

I can't believe she got up this early just to remind me Robert and his asswipe friends are trying to play me for a fool.

Letting out a sigh, I say, "It's a prank, so just sit back and watch as Ryan completes his initiation. Then, you can laugh right along with your boyfriend and his dipshit buddies."

Her eyebrows draw together, and her features grow serious. "I would never laugh at you, and you know that. Besides, I'm sure it's a misunderstanding. Robert wouldn't be mean to you."

I raise my eyebrows at her. "You sure about that?"

"I know Robert better than you do," Molly says all defensively, quick to protect her boyfriend. She gets up from my bed. "I'm going to grab some breakfast. See you downstairs."

She's out the door in a flash, as if guilt is pushing her from the room.

When will she learn Robert is nothing but a bastard who cheats on her with Megan and bullies half the kids in school? He's trouble, but still, she ignores all the red flags and sticks with him.

I quickly go through my morning routine, and once I'm dressed, I head down to the kitchen.

Molly's almost done eating a slice of toast and pauses between bites to say, "You have a minute to grab some coffee before we leave."

"Why are you in such a hurry to get to school?" I ask.

"Robert keeps flirting with Megan, so I want to pay him back by doing the same with Ryan."

Robert does more than just flirt with Megan, but I'm happy to hear Molly's tired of looking the other way.

When there's an unhappy twinge in my chest because she's setting her sights on Ryan, I frown and shove the unwelcome emotion away.

Making myself a cup of coffee, I add extra milk so I can swallow it down quickly.

I don't have time to rinse the cup and hurry out of the

29

kitchen to catch up with Molly.

During the drive to school, we're both quiet. I really hope whatever joke Robert and his friends are trying to play on me is over and done with. I'm not in the mood for a repeat of yesterday.

Molly has one of the best parking spots in the school, situated near the entrance. When she stops the car, I notice Ryan's truck take one of the other reserved parking spaces.

Yep, he's definitely one of them.

Getting out of her car as fast as I can, I tell Molly, "See you in class."

I keep my head down as I hurry across the patch of lawn to get to the home ec building.

Hopefully, Ryan won't be in this class, as the boys have a choice to take something else instead.

"Wait up," I hear Ryan say, his voice sounding a little cautious before he falls into step beside me. "Morning."

Shoot.

I contemplate ignoring him but then give in and mutter, "Hey, Ryan."

I feel his eyes on my face as he asks, "How are you?"

Are we really going to do this?

Squaring my shoulders, I stop walking and turn to face him. "Why are you talking to me? Did the guys put you up to this? Because you can tell them I'm not falling for the prank again. Fun's over."

His eyes narrow on me as he shakes his head. "There's no prank. I'm talking to you because I want to."

When I realize he's really serious right now and even looks a bit upset, it takes the wind right out of my sails.

"Why me?" The question's out before I can stop it.

I feel my face changing color, so I do the next best thing and almost sprain my neck as I snap my head down to stare at my boots.

Ryan takes a step closer, and my eyes dart to his boots, which are scuffed and not a well-known brand like the elite of the school prefer to wear.

Am I wrong about him?

"I'm new in town and could use a friend," he says. "I was hoping you'd be that friend." I'm so stunned by what he's telling me I almost miss it when he asks, "Which guys are you talking about, and what prank?"

Once again, my eyes have a mind of their own, and I can't keep from looking at his face. He's still frowning and even looks a little pissed off.

I glance toward the home ec building, then say, "It's nothing. Just Robert and his friends." I take a step away from him. "I have to go, or I'll be late. See you around."

"I'll see you in biology," Ryan murmurs, his eyes not leaving me as I start to walk away.

When I reach the classroom, I glance back toward the main entrance and see Ryan's still staring at me. I try to act casual but then notice many of the girls are watching the interaction between him and me.

Yup, Ryan's talking to me. Eat your hearts out, girls.

CHAPTER 3

JANE / ALCHERA

I've hardly taken a seat when Molly sits down next to me. I roll my eyes, knowing what's coming. "First, you sit in front of me, and now you're sitting next to me. Big step for you, Molly. Aren't you scared of what your friends might think?"

"They'll get over it." She's almost sitting on my damn lap. "Spill it."

I shake my head and can't help but smile at her eagerness to find out what happened between Ryan and me.

"He just said hello. You're the popular one. Why don't you go talk to him yourself?"

She stares at me as if I've lost my mind. "Firstly, a girl does not approach a guy. It would make me look desperate. Out of everyone in the school, you're the only one he's given any attention to. He apparently snubbed Robert's invite to hang with them."

So it wasn't an act? Ryan really wants to be friends with me.
Holy shit.

I'm stunned by this piece of information but manage to hide my reaction from Molly.

I grin at her. "Looks like he has brains and taste."

Molly falls for my act and doesn't see how her news has thrown me for a loop.

"Ugh, you're no help," she snaps at me.

Getting up, she returns to her loyal followers, who are eagerly waiting to hear what she could find out about Ryan.

During class, I can't stop thinking about what Molly said and the fact that the hottest guy I've ever laid eyes on wants to hang out with me.

The bell rings, and when I walk to my next class, I feel all the students staring at me.

Geez, it's going to take a while before they find something new to focus on.

When I walk into biology, Ryan's sitting at our desk, drumming his fingers impatiently on the wood, but the moment he lays eyes on me, he visibly relaxes.

Now I feel like shit. Maybe he struggles to make friends like I do.

As I get close, he gets up and pulls out my chair. I stop dead in my tracks, flabbergasted by the chivalrous gesture.

Holy crap, not only is he hot, but he's also a gentleman.

Wait. Am I still asleep and dreaming?

That would suck ass.

I almost pinch myself but suppress the urge before moving to my seat while murmuring, "Thanks."

"You're welcome," he says and sits down again.

I let out a slow breath, and when I glance at Molly, it's to see her and every other girl in class staring at us in complete and utter confusion.

Yeah, me and them both.

I don't have a damn clue what's going on and why Ryan's showing an interest in me. From my experience, the good-looking guys are usually shallow and arrogant, but that doesn't seem to be the case where Ryan's concerned.

Mr. Clayton starts handing out pamphlets on dissecting frogs, which we'll be doing the next day.

Note to self: Ditch Bio tomorrow.

I feel people peeking at us throughout the lesson, and it's beginning to work on my nerves.

As we move from one class to the next, I can hear everyone whispering, and it doesn't help that Ryan sticks close to me.

When the bell rings for lunch, I let out a sigh of relief, and while I gather my stuff, Ryan asks, "Can I hang out with you during lunch?"

My gaze darts to his face, and when I see he's smiling at me, it does funny things to my insides, especially in the region of my stomach where a kaleidoscope of butterflies is fluttering like crazy.

I swallow hard before whispering, "Sure."

"After you." He moves back so I can walk first.

Which fairytale did this guy escape from?

Heading in the direction of the cafeteria, I'm overly aware of Ryan right beside me, and it's super overwhelming.

Entering the cafeteria that's already buzzing with students, I point at the food section. "I don't like the food here, but do you want to grab something to eat?"

He shakes his head. "I'm good."

I nod toward the exit. "I like sitting outside. It's not crowded out there."

Ryan follows me out the door, and when we get to my little corner, he says, "It's a nice day."

"Yeah, it's not too cold."

"Thanks for letting me hang with you," he murmurs, his deep tone doing things to my heart.

When I sit down, he takes the spot beside me instead of the seat across from me.

My heartbeat speeds up again, and I'm struggling to deal with all the exciting emotions he evokes in me.

I've never been interested in a guy before, and I have a feeling that by the end of the day, I'll be crushing hard on Ryan.

Not knowing what to say, I glance at the two willow trees, their branches bare. They usually give plenty of shade in the summer.

"I just want to be friends," he suddenly says, and it has my eyebrows drawing together.

My heart clenches in my chest.

Did I give away that I'm attracted to him?

"I didn't say I wanted to be anything more," I mutter.

Ryan's eyes lock with mine. "That's not what I meant. I'm just trying to make you feel more comfortable. You look like you're about to run for the hills."

Well, he has that part right. My whole body is tense. I'm so used to being alone that I feel entirely out of my depth.

I nod at him, then admit, "I just don't understand why you don't hang out with the cool crowd. You're going to kill your reputation if you keep sitting with me. You're hanging out with the wrong person."

The frown on his face darkens. "I don't see anything wrong with you, and I don't care what others think about me."

I stare at him with wide eyes as I mumble, "Okay."

Ryan smiles a crooked smile that turns my legs to jelly, and it unravels my nerves at the speed of light.

Dear God. Don't look at me like that. I'm going to overheat.

"I'm not good at the whole friends thing," I admit. "I'm a loner, so don't be surprised when I'm super awkward."

He gives me a piercing look as if he's trying to see inside me, and it unnerves me even more. I start to fidget with my hands, pulling at the hem of my hoodie.

Letting out an awkward chuckle, I admit, "This is all new to me. I don't even know what to talk about."

Ryan clears his throat. "We'll just get to know each other." He's silent for a moment, then he adds, "You could show me around."

Another hot grin from Ryan has my stomach stuck on the spin cycle.

"Don't get too excited," I mutter. "There's not much to see, and I'm actually quite boring."

"I'll be the judge of that," he chuckles.

Damn, he's too hot for me to handle.

"So..." I say, "Why did your family move to Steamboat Springs, of all places?"

"It's work-related," he answers vaguely.

"It must suck, though." I glance through the window into the cafeteria and see that everyone's staring at us. "You must miss your old school and friends."

Ryan just shrugs then turns his head to see what I'm looking at. "Don't mind them."

"It's hard when everyone's staring at us," I mutter.

"They don't matter."

My eyes fly to his face, a take in the serious expression tightening his features.

"You really don't care?" I ask.

"Not at all."

"Wow." I let out a burst of laughter. "I wish I had your confidence."

The bell signals the end of our break. Getting up, I let Ryan walk one step ahead of me toward our Spanish class.

One after the other, I hear the unwelcome comments from the other students.

"What's the new guy doing with the freak?"

"What does she have that I don't."

"Is he blind?"

"Dude must like his girls vanilla as fuck."

I glance at Ryan, wondering if he hears them.

He should, they aren't being very discreet about their opinions.

But he doesn't seem worried by them in the slightest.

If someone had told me yesterday that an attractive guy was going to walk up and demand to be my friend, I would've asked them whose socks they've been smoking.

Yet, here I am, walking a step behind him while everyone is talking wildly about us.

RYAN / RAIGHNE

I have to constantly tell myself not to lose my temper with the other students.

Hearing the things they're saying about Alchera makes anger bubble in my chest.

I've only been at this school for one and a half days, and I'm starting to understand why Alchera doesn't have any friends.

None of them are worthy of her.

Jane. She's called Jane here.

It's hard thinking of her as Jane because she's always been Alchera to me.

Just don't slip up around her.

When we reach the doorway of the classroom, I move to the side and gesture for Alchera to enter first. Not thinking, I place my hand on her lower back as we walk inside.

Getting to touch her again, a comforting warmth spreads up my arm and engulfs my entire body. I can feel our bond pulsing in my chest and reaching out to her, desperate to connect.

I hate when I have to pull my hand away from her so she can take a seat, and as I sit down beside her, my eyes flick over the rest of the class.

Students keep shooting us curious and confused looks, and I almost let out an agitated growl.

Turning my head to Alchera, I ask, "What are your plans for after school?"

She shrugs as she takes the required textbook from her bag. "Nothing. Why?"

"Want to show me around town?"

Please say yes.

My eyes are glued to her face as I watch her contemplate my question, then she replies, "There's not much to show you. At least, not in town." She sucks in a deep breath, then adds, "But I can take you to a waterfall just outside of town. That's if you're okay with hiking a short distance."

A smile spreads over my face. "I'm okay with hiking."

The corner of her mouth starts to lift into a smile, but then the teacher comes in, and Alchera focuses on the lesson.

Seeing as we'll leave Earth in the next three weeks, I don't pay any attention to what's being taught.

Glancing to the side, I watch as Alchera opens her sketchpad, and every now and then, she adds something to the picture.

When I first saw the sketch of the Virtutes Falls, I thought the spell Janak and Aster cast over her had worn off, and her memories had returned. But hearing she dreamed about it causes me to worry because it means her visions might've started already.

We're not close enough for me to ask her if that's the case, and if she hasn't had any visions, she'll think I'm insane.

My eyes lock on the man in the pool of the Virtutes Falls. She's drawn me to a T without the elixir's glamor that makes me look human.

38

It has to be from a vision. She's seen me coming.

Maybe I should just grab her and forcefully take her back to Vaalbara.

No. Be patient and gentle.

I'm bored out of my mind as we attend the remaining classes for the day, and by the time the final bell rings, relief fills my veins.

"Finally," Alchera sighs. "Let's get out of here."

When we get up from our seats, I take hold of her bag and shrug it over my shoulder. "I'll carry it."

She gives me an incredulous look but doesn't say anything as we step out into the aisle and head to the door.

The instant we walk into the hallway, a girl says, "Jane, do you want a ride home?"

"I'm going to hang out with Ryan," Alchera answers. "I'll see you later."

"Oh," the girl replies, looking shell-shocked. "Ahh...Okay. Have fun."

We head down the hallway, and once we're out of hearing distance from the girl, Alchera says, "That's Molly. She's my adoptive sister."

I only nod, and when we leave the building, I gesture in the direction of my truck. "I'm parked over there."

I can feel a nervous energy coming from Alchera when we reach the truck, and glancing at her, I see her features are tense with an anxious expression.

"You okay?" I ask.

"Yeah." She lets out an awkward-sounding chuckle. "It's not every day I get into a truck with a guy I barely know. Maybe we should put off going to the waterfall?"

"You told Molly you're spending time with me. If anything happens, I'm the first person they're going to suspect."

"True."

I open the passenger door and nod to the seat. "The choice is yours."

Alchera hesitates, and her eyes flit to my face before she glances over her shoulder at the other students who are watching us. The next second, she climbs into my truck, and I let out a relieved breath.

Thanks be to Awo.

I place her bag in the back of the truck before getting into the cab, and when I start the engine, I smile at her. "Thanks for not changing your mind."

"Just don't kill me, and we're good," she teases.

"You're safe with me," I promise.

There's nowhere you're safer than by my side.

"The waterfall is just off the road you took yesterday."

"When you ducked into the bushes?" I ask.

"You saw that?" she gasps, a blush forming on her neck and cheeks.

Chuckling, I nod.

"God," she groans. "Not embarrassing at all." She's quiet for a moment, then asks, "What were you doing out there?"

"Just looking for some peace and quiet."

"Then you'll love Fish Creek Falls." She smiles, and it feels like the sun is shining on me.

Before thinking it through, I comment. "You have a beautiful smile."

Instantly, she looks awkward again and glances out the window while murmuring. "Thanks."

With every mile I drive, the air grows tenser, and as I turn up the road that leads to the spot where I can park the truck, Alchera asks, "Did you mean it when you said you want to be friends?"

"Yes." I glance at her before turning my attention back to the road.

"So you're not going to try anything?"

Not sure what she means, I ask, "Try what?"

I steer the truck off the road, and finding the spot by the trees, I bring the vehicle to a standstill.

"You're not going to try..." she pauses, and when I look at her, her cheeks are flushed pink, "your luck."

It takes me a moment before I realize what she's asking, and I quickly shake my head. "No, that's not why I'm spending time with you."

"Oh good," she breathes as she pushes the door open. "Because I'd hate to kick you in the junk."

I let out a burst of laughter because I'd actually like to see her try.

After climbing out of the truck, I follow Alchera to the trail she likes to take, and we're both quiet until we reach the waterfall.

Alchera gestures at the waterfall like it's a masterpiece. "Tada. Welcome to my fortress of solitude."

When she sits down on a patch of grass, I drop down beside her. Sitting with my knees bent, I rest my forearms on them.

Even though I know the answer, I ask, "Do you come here often?"

"As often as I can," she murmurs. Her eyes leave the waterfall and settle on me. "So, Ryan Jackson, tell me about yourself."

The corner of my mouth lifts. "There's not much to tell."

"Where did you live before moving here? What was your previous school like?"

Prepared with suitable answers, I say, "I used to live in Boulder, and it was pretty much the same as this school."

"What's it like living in a city?"

"Too busy for my liking," I answer honestly.

She glances at the nature around us before muttering, "I can't wait to leave this town."

My eyes are locked on her face. "Why?"

She shrugs before meeting my gaze. "I just feel like there's more to life than just this."

There is so much more, my charge.

She sucks in a deep breath, then lets it out slowly. A nervous expression flickers over her features. "So, out of all the open seats in class, what made you pick my desk to sit at?"

Unable to lie, I answer, "You're the only one I wanted to sit next to." Staring deep into her eyes, I add, "No one else interests me."

A light frown forms between her eyebrows, and she looks skeptical, but she doesn't comment on what I just said.

You'll learn to trust me.

"How about you?" I ask. "Have you lived here all your life?"

"Kind off," she replies. "I was found at this waterfall when I was thirteen." She doesn't look at me as she continues, "No one knows what I was doing here, and I had no memory of my past. It's been almost five years, and I still don't remember anything."

Hearing the sadness in her tone, I murmur, "I'm sorry."

I should've come with you.

She shrugs as if it's nothing. "It is what it is. Mayor Calder was kind enough to take me in, so it hasn't been that bad. I'm actually lucky."

Needing to hear the answer, I ask, "Have they been good to you?"

She nods before she glances at me. "Yeah."

Thanks be to Awo.

"I'm glad to hear that."

She gives me a questioning look. "Why?"

"No reason. I'm just glad."

The corner of her mouth lifts, then she asks, "What's your family like?"

"I have two older brothers. Twins," I answer truthfully. "It's just us and my dad. My mom died when I was younger."

Alchera gives me a compassionate look. "I'm sorry to hear that."

"It's okay. It happened a long time ago."

Silence falls between us, and I struggle not to spend every second staring at her. The last thing I need is for her to think I'm a creep.

CHAPTER 4

JANE / ALCHERA

I t's twilight, where I'm standing in a park. There are no chirping birds but just a dead, chilling silence all around me.

I can feel every hair on my body rise as a strong electric current sizzles in the air.

Glancing up, I see the heavens begin to churn, dirty gray clouds massing above my head. I suck in a breath, and suddenly, there's an explosion of sound. It's so loud my ears ring.

It nearly drives me to my knees as I grab at my ears, but I'm not fast enough to block out the noise. Blood starts to trickle from my ears, seeping through my fingers.

I can hear trees screeching all around me, and I smell flesh burning.

Everything is dying!

My breaths explode over my parted lips while it feels as if my heart is being torn from my chest. The pain increases horribly, and a fear I've never felt before envelopes me entirely as I try to scream.

My vision blurs, and when it clears again, I find myself in the middle of a road where everything around me is being torn apart. There's nothing I can do. I'm standing on quaking ground, shocked to my very core, while people scream and die around me.

Oh God!

The earth shudders violently, and huge chunks of ground start to disappear, leaving deep black gaping holes.

I watch helplessly as the ground gives way beneath people's feet, and they plunge to their deaths.

My heart lurches in my chest at the horrifying sight unfolding around me. It feels as if my feet are glued to the quaking ground. Fear and panic engulf me until I'm struggling to take a breath.

"Alchera!" I hear a man calling.

He sounds familiar, and I want to turn around to see who he is, but I can't break out of the fear and panic that holds me in its grasp.

Dreadful chaos surrounds me. Trees are being uprooted, and one whips past my head, a branch missing my face by mere inches.

"Alchera, we have to move. Dammit!" Strong hands grab hold of me, yanking me tightly to a firm chest. I feel a comforting warmth flow through me.

Before I can turn to see who it is, everything mercifully darkens.

"Jane, wake up!"

Hearing Molly snap while shaking the living hell out of me has my eyes popping open.

"What?" I gasp as I shoot into a sitting position.

"Wake up so we can talk."

When my eyes focus on her smiling face, I have to suppress the urge to slap her. "Geez, woman. You could at least make me coffee if you're going to wake me up so early."

Ignoring my comment, she asks, "What time did you get home?"

I slump back on the bed and let out a groan as I snuggle into my pillow while mumbling, "Just after ten."

"So late? Were you with Ryan?"

"Yes," I mutter around a yawn.

I'm in no mood to be interrogated.

"This hot guy is into you, and I want to know why."

"We're just friends."

When I remember the nightmare I had, the sleepy feeling vanishes.

I climb out of bed and say, "I'll walk to school. You can go."

As always, I'm ignored.

"After what I saw yesterday, you expect me to believe there's nothing but a friendship going on between the two of you? What did you do after school?"

She's really starting to annoy me. From being alone most of the time to having someone buzzing around me every damn morning is one hell of an adjustment.

"We hung out and grabbed something to eat at the diner. He just wants to be friends, so drop it now. The way you're going on, you'd swear I'm sleeping with the damn guy!"

I bite my lip when I see her smile grow bigger.

"He's only been here three days. There's no way we're having sex!" I exclaim while shaking my head hard. 'Get your mind out of the gutter."

"Fine. Don't tell me everything," Molly says as she walks to the door.

The smile on her face as she walks out of my bedroom tells me the whole school is going to think I'm having sex with Ryan before classes even start.

Shit. I screwed up.

Not wanting Ryan's reputation destroyed, I hurry out of the room and catch up to Molly at the top of the stairs.

"Please don't spread any rumors," I beg. "Ryan's a nice guy, and we're really just friends. I promise."

46

She lets out a heavy sigh as she heads down the stairs. "Fine, but I'll only keep quiet if you make sure Ryan's at the party I'm throwing."

"Okay," I lie because I have no idea whether Ryan's into parties. "Do your parents know about the party?"

"Of course not," she chuckles.

"Did you tell Stephen?"

She shrugs. "You know he doesn't care about what we do as long as we don't burn down the house."

Shaking my head, I walk back to my bedroom and quickly get ready for the day. After shrugging on one of my favorite jackets, I grab my bag and head out of the house.

The moment I step onto the porch, the winter chill hits me, and I quickly wrap my arms around my middle.

Once I'm done with school I'm moving to a warmer place.

My thoughts turn to the nightmare I had, which was really unsettling after dreaming about the waterfall the past two weeks.

The disaster and danger felt so real.

I've only managed to walk to the stop sign when a familiar truck pulls up to the curb beside me.

"Morning. Need a ride?" Ryan asks, looking way too hot first thing in the morning.

Can't say no to my friend, now can I?

"Sure." Climbing into the truck, I smile at him. "Thanks."

"I didn't know you walked to school. I can pick you up and take you home after school."

It doesn't sound like he's asking me. It sounds more like he's already made up his mind.

"I usually ride with Molly, but I was late, so…yeah, you don't need to go out of your way."

As he starts to drive again, he says, "It's not out of my way."

I'll get to spend more time with him.

"Okay. Sure. That would be great."

A smile lifts the corner of his mouth, and he looks more than pleased that I agreed.

"Are you warm enough?" he asks.

"Yeah, thanks."

During the drive to school, I remember the day before and how nice it was to hang out with him. Nothing weird happened, and I can actually see us becoming good friends.

Warmth trickles into my chest at the thought of having a friend, and a happy grin spreads over my face.

After parking in his usual spot, we walk across the stretch of grass to the entrance.

Together.

Of course, everyone notices. Ryan moving to our small town and picking me as his friend will be front-page news for quite a while.

I can hear the other students' whispers and how they're laughing because they think it's insane that Ryan's showing any kind of interest in me.

They can all go to hell. If Ryan doesn't care, then I'm not wasting my time with them, either.

Ryan clears his throat next to me, ripping me out of my thoughts. When I glance up at his face, he looks deep in thought, and I wonder what he's thinking about.

Does he hear all the whispering?

Shoot. Maybe it's getting to him, and he's rethinking being friends with me.

Ugh. I hope that isn't the case. It would suck big, fat, hairy donkey balls.

I'm upset that I care. Worst of all, I actually like Ryan.

A lot.

Fine, I might be developing a slight crush on him, and I'd hate for the other students to turn him against me.

When we enter the class, it's no surprise that everyone is sneaking glances in our direction.

I try to ignore all the attention, and after taking my seat, I pull out my sketchpad. Just as I flip to the page I'm working on, my vision blurs.

"Alchera, we need to talk. We've both said things better left unsaid, and you've had a very exhausting day."

It's the same voice from my dream. It sounds so familiar, almost like Ryan's, but this voice sounds so far away and much deeper.

I glance around only to find myself lying on a bed, feeling like I've been hit by a freight train. Feelings swamp me – exhaustion, disappointment, but mostly anger.

"Raighne, just leave me alone," I sigh. "I don't have any strength left to hear more of your insults."

"Alchera, please understand."

I'm about to get up and glance back so I can see who's talking when I feel a hand take hold of mine.

I crash back to reality with a jerk. The first thing I feel is the same warmth from when Ryan touched me yesterday, spreading up my arm and quickly through the rest of my body.

Some of the blurriness in my mind clears, and I blink as I try to make sense of what just happened.

"Jane?" Ryan whispers, his tone tense with worry as he squeezes my hand.

My heart starts beating faster and faster when I realize I just zoned out in class.

What the hell just happened?

Was that a dream or something else?

Alchera. The name feels familiar.

"Jane, are you okay?" Ryan asks as he reaches his other hand to my face, his fingers taking hold of my chin.

I quickly pull away, muttering, "I'm fine."

"You don't look fine. What's going on?" Ryan keeps his voice low so the other students won't hear, which I really appreciate.

I shake my head, trying to rid myself of the groggy feeling left behind by the weird dream.

"I'm fine. Just daydreaming." I try to add a smile, but it must look like some half-ass attempt.

I'm not sure what stuns me more, the dream thingy I just had or Ryan's concern for me. Either way, embarrassment trickles into my chest.

My eyes land on where he's holding my hand, and my eyebrows fly up.

"Jane. Ryan. Attention up front!" Mrs. Woods snaps, glaring at us from over her glasses.

My face goes up in flames from being called out in front of the entire class.

"We'll talk at lunch," Ryan whispers as he moves our hands beneath the desk, resting them on his thigh.

I just nod, staring at where Ryan's fingers are wrapped around mine.

Holy shit.

Our first class goes by way too fast, and as we walk into the hallway to head to biology, Ryan doesn't let go of my hand.

It gives the impression that we are a couple, which will only add fuel to the gossip already spreading throughout the damn school.

Hold up. Biology.

There's no way I'm cutting open some poor frog. I was planning on skipping class, and somehow, I have to get Ryan to let go of my hand so I can throw a disappearing act.

I tug on Ryan's hand to get his attention as we squeeze our way through the crowded hallway.

Stopping dead in his tracks, I almost slam into his arm.

He leans down, and for a moment, I'm flustered from having him so close to me. "What's wrong?"

Strands of his silky, dark brown hair hang slightly across his forehead, and for a crazy second, I'm tempted to brush it away.

I clear my throat then decide to go with the truth. "I can't cut open a frog. I'm skipping biology."

"Okay," he says, his tone gentle.

My eyes jump to his face, but he's already turning around and tugging me toward the exit.

When we leave the building, I shiver from the cold. Ryan lets go of my hand, and placing his arm around my shoulders, he pulls me right against his side.

I'm stunned, but then his body heat starts to warm me, and I let it slide. When we reach his truck, he opens the passenger door and waits for me to get in before shutting it.

My gaze follows him as he walks around the front of the truck, and once again, I'm struck by how attractive he is.

He held my hand for thirty minutes.

Friends don't hold hands. Right?

For a few seconds, I allow myself to wonder what it would be like to date him, and I instantly blush.

When he slides in behind the steering wheel, I pull the hoodie of my jacket over my head to try and hide my reaction to the mere thought of dating him.

Ryan leans a little forward, and seeing my face, he asks, "Why are you blushing?"

Ugh. Just my luck.

"I'm not blushing," I mutter.

Ryan tugs at my hoodie, and as it falls back, I quickly glance the other way.

"You sure about that?" he teases me.

"Let it go, or I'm getting out of the truck," I warn him.

"You're cute when you blush," he says, and as I reach for the handle, he quickly adds, "I'm dropping it." He reaches for the glove compartment and pulls out a brown leather pouch. "I have something for you. Consider it an apology gift for teasing you."

A gift?

My eyes jump between the pouch and his face, then I watch as he takes out a necklace. It has a leather cord with a cluster of gems and crystals hanging from it.

He seriously got me a gift.

Why?

Feeling a little overwhelmed, I swallow hard before saying, "You hardly know me. Why would you give me something so pretty?"

"It's to celebrate you giving me a chance and not kicking me to the curb," he explains, a crooked smile on his face. "Can I help you put it on?"

"It's an amazing gift, but it wouldn't feel right taking it."

He nods but then says, "I already got it, though, and it will definitely look better on you than on me."

I let out a chuckle, and not wanting to be rude, I murmur, "Okay."

My eyes widen when he leans into me, and feeling his fingers brush lightly against my skin, tingles rush over my body. Moving my hair out of the way, I suck in a deep breath while trying to calm my suddenly racing heart.

Ryan pulls slightly back, and when our eyes lock, he says, "I want you to know I'm here if you ever need me for anything. Just call, and I'll be there in a flash."

Stunned by the intimate moment, I mutter like a dumbass, "I don't have your number."

"Let's fix that." He pulls his phone from his pocket and says, "Give me yours, and I'll call you."

I recite my number, and a few seconds later, I feel my phone vibrating in my pocket.

"Now you can call me at any time," he says, a hot grin curving his lips.

"Okay." Lifting a hand, I touch the gemstones and whisper, "Thanks for the necklace. It's beautiful." I smile at him before adding, "I actually know a bit about the magical properties of the stones."

"Yeah? What do these stones mean?"

I brush the tip of my finger over each stone as I say, "The hematite, emerald, obsidian, and lapis lazuli all carry similar properties. They're all about improving memory and mental clarity." I take a breath before continuing, "The amethyst is all about stability and strength, whereas the opal is for protection." I roll the seventh stone between my fingers. "I've never seen this one before."

Ryan leans closer again, and when his fingers brush against the stone and my skin, his touch wreaks havoc in my body as I'm engulfed with tingles.

"It is an azurite stone, also known as a stone of heaven," he explains. "Azurite was a sacred stone, and it's said that it helps awaken psychic abilities. Opal, by the way, is also known as a stone of happy dreams and changes." He hesitates for a moment before he adds, "It helps bring on visions."

Ryan's eyes flick to mine, and it feels as if he's waiting for some kind of reaction from me.

"Thanks for this." I tug at the necklace then glance at our surroundings. The parking area is quiet, and clouds are rolling in.

"How about we have that talk now?" he says as he relaxes against the seat.

"What talk?" My heart begins to beat faster in anticipation of what's coming. I was hoping he'd forgotten about my weird daydream earlier.

"What happened in class?" he asks.

I wave my hand casually in the air, brushing off the incident. "Oh, that. It was nothing. I just zoned out."

I'm feeling anxious about the direction this conversation is taking.

"It didn't look like you were just zoning out. I said your name a few times before you responded."

"I'm just tired from the late night we had," I whisper in a pathetic attempt to avoid telling him the truth.

The truth? I don't even know what that is.

How do I explain that I had a weird ass dream while being wide awake?

With a slight shake of his head, he looks away and sighs. "You can trust me, A...Jane." He clears his throat before looking at me again. "I know I'm new in your life, but I want you to know you can talk to me about anything. No matter how crazy it might sound."

For a reason I'll never be able to explain, the words leave my mouth before I can stop them. "I had a weird dream of a disaster and people I don't know dying." Shaking my head, I let out a sigh. "It felt real, though, and I can remember every little detail clearly."

I turn my head away from him, regret pouring into my chest the instant I'm done talking.

"How often do you have dreams like that?"

"Just twice. Last night and in class." I turn my head back to him. "I had a dream while wide awake. Who does that?"

Instead of looking at me like I'm weird, his face is filled with understanding. "Try not to worry about it too much."

When Ryan reaches for my hand, my heart skips a beat before setting off at a crazy pace.

He links his fingers with mine, then whispers, "Your hand is half the size of mine."

Relieved that he doesn't think I'm crazy and is changing the subject, I relax.

"Are friends supposed to hold hands?" I ask, keeping my tone playful.

A grin tugs at his lips. "Yes. Friends can definitely hold hands."

"People are going to think we're dating," I warn him.

Shaking his head, he locks eyes with me. "I've told you before. I don't care what anyone thinks."

Right.

Maybe I should start doing the same.

CHAPTER 5

JANE / ALCHERA

While I grab my bag and hurry out of the house, it hits me that Ryan and I've been friends for a week already. It's still hard to believe, but with every passing day things become more and more comfortable between us.

The rumors at school haven't died down one bit, and even though I try not to let them get to me, I can't help but feel annoyed. I wish everyone would focus more on their own lives than mine.

When I rush out of the front door, Molly yells from the top of the stairs, "Remember to tell Ryan about the party!"

"Okay." Reaching the truck, I open the passenger door and climb in. "Morning."

"Morning. How was your night?" Ryan asks as he pulls away from the curb.

"Same old. Yours?"

"Nothing exciting."

For some reason, I'll never understand, Ryan's latched onto me, and he doesn't care about befriending anyone else.

I'm not going to lie. It makes me feel real damn special.

Before I forget again, I say, "Molly is having a party this

Friday. You're invited."

His eyes flick to my face. "Will you be there?"

"Unfortunately, yes, seeing as we live in the same house," I grumble.

"Then I'll be there."

A smile starts to form on my face. "Yeah?"

"Sure. We can hang out and watch a movie or something," he says as he slows the truck down to turn into the parking area of the school.

"Now that sounds more like my kind of party," I chuckle.

He brings the truck to a stop in his regular spot, and leaning toward me, he grabs his bag that's lying by my feet. I get a whiff of his delicious cologne and try to ignore the fluttering in my stomach.

I've somehow managed to keep my growing feelings for Ryan a secret so he doesn't notice, and I plan on keeping it that way.

You can feel the change in the atmosphere when we get to school on Friday morning. Everyone's excited about the party later today.

Even I'm looking forward to it because I'll get to spend more time with Ryan.

Yep, I'm crushing hard on my friend, but just being around him is enough for me.

The day takes its sweet time, and when the final bell rings, everyone rushes out of the building to get to their cars.

"We need to hurry," I tell Ryan. "I forgot to lock my bedroom door."

I grab his hand and practically drag him toward the parking area.

"Why are we rushing?" he asks as I climb into the truck.

"I don't want some horny couple making out on my bed," I mutter.

He shuts my door, then jogs around the front of the vehicle. As always, my eyes follow him, and I drink in the sight of every hot inch of his body.

He slides behind the steering wheel and soon we're heading home.

I glance at his strong hands gripping the steering wheel and let out a dreamy sigh.

I love the way he drives.

Scratch that. I love everything he does.

Ugh, I'm so screwed.

Within minutes, he parks the truck in front of the house because the driveway is already packed with cars.

Damn, I won't be held responsible for what I'll do if I find someone in my room.

Grabbing our bags, we quickly get out and hurry into the house that's crowded with partygoers. I rush upstairs, and when I open my door and find the room empty, I let out a sigh of relief.

"Thank God."

"Now you can relax," Ryan says as he places his hands on my shoulders, rubbing them as he pushes me into the room. "Let me see what your bedroom looks like."

He steps around me and walks toward my dresser.

Crap, not the dresser!

My diary is sprawled open on the piece I wrote about how dreamy he is.

I dart forward and grab the book, squashing it against my chest.

The corner of his mouth lifts in a mischievous grin. "Hmm...what are you hiding there?"

I try to play it off as nothing. "Just a book."

"Oh." With one hand casually in his pocket, he walks closer. "Just a book? Why are you clinging to it if it's just a book?"

"It's my diary," I admit. "You're not seeing it, Ryan."

His eyes lock on mine, and I feel the intensity of his stare deep in my heart.

"So if I want to know all your secrets, then that's the book I should read."

"Read it and die," I warn him.

I shut the book, and walking to my closet, I shove it beneath my underwear before closing the door so he can't see my haphazardly packed clothes.

Ryan glances around the room while walking to the window. He stands there in silence for a good few seconds before glancing in my direction.

"You have a nice room," he murmurs. "It feels like you."

I shrug as I glance around my private space.

It might be my room, but it's never felt like home.

Suddenly, he asks, "When's your birthday?"

A frown forms on my forehead. "Huh? Why?"

"Just curious." He turns his body to face me and leans his shoulder against the wall.

"I don't know when it is, but I celebrate it on the day I was found at the waterfall."

"Next week," he says, catching me completely off guard.

"How did you know?"

His eyes widen slightly. "You told me."

I don't remember telling him, but I shrug it off. "When's your birthday?"

A hot-as-hell smile curves his lips. "December nineteenth."

"So you're only a month older than me."

He stares at me for a moment it feels like he knows something

I don't.

Maybe he doesn't like birthdays.

Changing the subject, I ask, "Want to get something to eat and drink?"

"Sure." He pushes away from the wall, and when we leave my room and head down the stairs, he throws his arm around my shoulders. "What are you feeding me today?"

"Hot dogs?"

"Sounds good."

A drunk girl staggers into our way, and we have to sidestep her.

"Damn, she didn't waste any time getting trashed," I mutter.

"Molly's parents allow alcohol at the party?" Ryan asks.

"No, but it doesn't stop people from bringing their own."

Walking into the kitchen, I quickly make the hot dogs and place them all on one plate.

I hand our food to Ryan. "Guard it with your life."

He lets out a chuckle as he picks up a hot dog and takes a big bite.

Heading outside, we find a spot on the lawn where we sit down and watch as some people swim while others dance.

The music is turned up louder as more people arrive, and I wonder how long it will take before the neighbors call the cops.

Mayor Calder will lose his shit if the cops are called on us.

I take another bite of my hotdog and watch as Molly argues with Robert about the volume of the music before she turns it down a little.

One minute, I'm swallowing my last bite of my food, and the next, everything blurs.

"A pillow? Really?" I hear someone asking, his tone sounding incredulous.

"Yep, without it, I won't get any sleep," a girl answers.

"Did I say to bring one?"

It has to be Ryan. Only he sounds older.

"No, but it counts as an essential item in my books."

"This is an essential item." I can't make out the man's face as he gestures in the opposite direction of a waterfall. *"By the way, if you need to go, head out there."*

"There's toilets?" the girl asks.

A burst of laughter escapes him, then he shakes his head. "You dig a hole."

"You're enjoying this, aren't you?"

"The expression on your face is priceless," he admits while I try hard to make out his features. *"Let's help them get the fire going."*

"Jane?" I hear Ryan's voice, worry tensing his tone.

Slowly, my sight returns, and I'm met with Ryan's concerned eyes flicking over my face.

"Are you okay?" he asks.

I suck in a deep breath before letting it out slowly. "Yeah."

Ryan climbs to his feet, and taking my hand, he pulls me up until I'm standing in front of him.

He tilts his head to catch my eyes. "You sure you're okay?"

I nod, my tongue darting out to wet my lips.

He steps closer, and lifting his hand to the back of my neck, he pulls me against his chest before wrapping his other arm around me.

Ryan's holding me.

Holy crap.

My entire body explodes with tingles while my stomach's overwhelmed with an intense fluttering sensation.

Not wasting a second of this amazing moment, I wrap my arms around his waist and hug him as tightly as I can because I don't know when I'll get the chance again.

"Was it another dream?" he asks, his tone low and serious.

I nod, my cheek rubbing against his shirt.

"Want to talk about it?"

Reluctantly, I pull back and shake my head as I mutter, "It was about a stupid pillow and didn't make any sense."

"Let's go inside," he says. "It's noisy out here."

It's a mission and a half making our way through the crowd of partygoers, but when we get back to the room, I realize we didn't bring anything to drink.

"Damn, we forgot something to drink. I'll be right back."

"Okay," Ryan says while looking at the pictures I've drawn that are stuck to my wall.

I hurry back to the kitchen and grab two sodas. While heading to the stairs, I'm deep in thought about the weird dreams I've been having lately and the amazing hug I got from Ryan.

Just as I reach the top of the stairs, I'm suddenly grabbed from behind and hauled into Molly's room.

"What the hell?" I gasp, my heart instantly beating faster from the shock.

Dropping the sodas, I try to pull away, but there's no budging as the person instantly tightens his grip around my neck.

Panic flares hot through my veins when I realize I'm alone in Molly's room with some guy.

"Let me go!" I hiss, trying to glance over my shoulder.

"Oh, come on, sweetling. How long are you going to keep up the act? After all, we're almost family."

Robert. Yuck.

I smell alcohol on his breath as it wafts into my hair and sticks to my skin. He's the last person I want to deal with right now.

Robert spins me around and shoves me forcefully against the wall. I hit the back of my head, and the pain is sharp for a second.

"Asshole!" As I lift my hand to my head, the bastard grabs my wrists and pins them to the wall.

"Dammit, Robert," I growl, in no mood to be bullied tonight. "Get your hands off me."

"What if I say no?" he sneers.

He pulls me slightly away from the wall, only to slam me back against it. It hurts even more the second time around. I'm sure there are going to be bruises.

"Come on, sweetling. Show me the goods that have Ryan eating out of your hand."

I swallow a whimper back, determined not to be weak in front of him, and I try twisting my wrists free from his brutal hold.

"I'll t-tell Molly if you d-don't let go of me."

No! Why do I have to stutter in front of him? I haven't stuttered in months.

"I'll t-t-t-tell Molly," he mimics me. "Tell Molly what, exactly?" His hot, sticky, drunken breath fills my nose, making my stomach turn.

He starts to force my hands above my head, and I fight back, trying to twist out of his grip. He's too strong for me, and he pins both my hands with one of his above my head. The plaster digs into my skin from the force he's using.

I squirm and try to yank free of his hold, but nothing helps. It only seems to excite him more.

"Stop!" I shout. His other hand moves down to my left hip, and I freeze as panic claws at my chest.

What the hell is he doing?

Then he starts feeling his way toward my chest.

"No!" I buck wildly, trying to twist my body out of his reach, but it only makes things worse. He steps closer, pinning my body to the wall with his own.

Oh, God, no!

"Robert, no!" I try kicking him, but that doesn't work either because he's standing too close.

He's like a pile of crap, clinging to me like glue.

His heavy breaths mingle with mine. It's disgusting, making me feel sick to my stomach.

Don't let my first kiss be with Robert. Please.

"Get off me, Robert!" I scream, hoping someone will hear me.

He shoves himself against me, and I feel his hard-on. My stomach protests as bile begins to rise, burning its way up to my throat. His hand grips my wrists so tightly I'm sure he's going to leave imprints on my skin.

"You know you want me," he hisses.

"You're insane! G-get...off!" I plead, close to tears.

I can't believe this is happening to me. I can't believe he's taking it this far.

He starts to laugh, clearly enjoying my fear and panic.

"Are you scared of me?" he whispers. "Imagine the fun we can have together." He takes a deep breath of me as if he's sniffing me like a dog. "I can teach you a few things that will make Ryan one happy man."

Panic slams so hard into my gut that all I can think of is Ryan still waiting in my room.

"Ryan!"

It feels as if my soul is calling out to his.

When Robert's hand fumbles to get under my shirt, I forget about being strong and start to cry.

This is too much for me to handle.

Suddenly, Ryan growls, "Get your hands off of her!"

He grabs hold of Robert's shoulder and rips him away from me before his fist connects with Robert's face.

Blood spurts like a fountain from Robert's nose, and he covers it with his hands while looking shocked.

"Jesus, man. You broke my nose," Robert whines.

Ryan grabs hold of my arm and pulls me in behind him.

My legs go numb, and as his scent envelops me, surrounding me like a mist, a sob escapes me. I grab hold of his sweater and cling to him as if he's my lifeline.

Tears keep spilling over my cheeks, and I bury my face against his back.

I'm so thankful he came to look for me.

Relief floods every inch of my trembling body.

"I didn't know she was taken, man. Sorry," Robert says in his cocky way.

"She *is* taken. Stay away from her, or I'll end you." Ryan's voice is nothing but a low growl, promising misery and pain.

I peek around Ryan's arm and see a glimmer of fear on Robert's face while he tries to wipe the blood away from his face with his shirt.

The sight fills me with some satisfaction.

"Jesus. It was nothing," Robert mutters before he walks to the doorway. "She asked for it."

The coward quickly leaves the room, and Ryan turns around to face me. When I look up into his smoldering eyes, they're so alive with anger it sends a shiver down my spine.

My frantically beating heart beats even faster, and my nerves feel frail.

A second later, I'm flooded with embarrassment because of the awful situation Ryan had to rescue me from.

He lifts his hand to my face, and his fingers brush over my cheek, wiping the tears away.

A breath shudders from deep within me.

He takes hold of my chin and nudges my face up to his, but I keep my eyes down. I can't make eye contact with him right now.

"Are you okay?" he asks, his tone still brimming with anger.

I let out a heavy sigh. "Yeah."

"I'm sorry I didn't get to you sooner."

I shake my head. "You didn't know."

I do my best to regain control over my chaotic emotions, and walking out of Molly's room, I pick up the sodas before heading to my bedroom.

As I set the bottles down on the dressing table, I hear Ryan shut the door behind us.

"Th-thanks for helping me," I say.

God, I hope this didn't bring the stuttering back. It's something that started after I was found at the waterfall, and it took four years to get rid of it. The doctors couldn't explain why it came and went like that.

A lost sob shudders through me, and I hate that I cried in front of Robert. Just thinking about it makes me want to cry again, and I wipe angrily over my eyes.

"I should've given him the beating of his life," Ryan mutters. He takes hold of my shoulder and turns me around so I'll face him.

"I'm so sorry. I d-didn't mean f-for you to get caught up in this mess."

"Don't apologize." He pulls me against his chest, his arms wrapping tightly around me.

I snuggle against him, and it feels so good to have his arms around me after what just happened.

"None of this is your fault. You did nothing wrong. He's the animal."

After the shock passes a little, I pull away and gesture at my bed. "Want to sit down?"

"Sure."

Once we're sitting on the covers, I clear my throat and dare a glance at Ryan's face. He still looks pissed as hell.

He shakes his head, and taking hold of my arm, he pulls me to his side as he lies down and presses my head to his chest.

When I feel him kiss my hair, I close my eyes and let the

warmth from his touch spread through me.

"Want to hear a story?" he asks.

I nod while closing my eyes.

"There's a place not far from Earth called Vaalbara, where a race called immortalis lives. They're waiting for one of their own to return. She's been gone for far too long and is very important to them. Once she returns, there won't be any time for celebrations. She'll have to prepare for training in combat and learn the ways of her people."

"Hold on." My head darts up, and I frown at him. "After all those years of being gone, this poor girl gets combat training for a welcome home present?" I poke at his chest. "You, my friend, suck at telling stories."

His chest shakes as he chuckles.

"Be patient," he mutters. "It gets better. After her vigorous training she becomes the best of all the trainees. Then, the whole village throws a huge celebration for her return. Happy now, you little story killer?"

"Yeah, that's much better." I smile as I snuggle against him, feeling much better after the incident with Robert.

CHAPTER 6

JANE / ALCHERA

S *tanding in a foreign city, people are screaming all around me in a language I don't understand. Everyone is panicking, running with no real direction, rushing to find a safe place.*

I can feel their hopelessness, their utter dread.

As I glance around me in total shock, I see dead faces, some burned beyond recognition, while a cloud of ash hangs thick in the air.

Intense panic spreads through me as I take in the destroyed buildings and the gaping holes in the roads. It looks like a bomb hit the area.

Is it a terrorist attack?

I suck in a breath of ash and start to cough, my lungs burning from the heat in the air.

A stench of rotten eggs fills the air, and above me, dark, threatening clouds gather – a mass of swirling blackness, where the edges are tainted dark red, blending into the brightest yellow.

The heavens seem to be on fire.

A horrifying fear floods my body when I realize I'm standing in the middle of a volcanic eruption.

Tears burn in my eyes as the ground shakes beneath my feet.

Suddenly, something slams hard into my chest. I fly backward from the force of whatever hits me, and I drop to the ground.

My chest feels as if it's being ripped open.

"Alchera! No!" I hear a man shout, and then someone falls over me. I'm just about to make out his face...

"Jane!" I'm shaken so hard by Ryan that it rips me out of the dream.

I shoot upright in bed while coughing as if I'm still inhaling ash, the ache in my chest lessening by the second.

Loud music is blaring through the house from the party, and I blink a couple of times to get rid of the haziness of the nightmare.

Ryan's face starts to come into focus, and then I register the worried expression in his eyes.

"It was only a dream," I say to put him at ease.

I rub my eyes, my head spinning from the intense nightmare that felt way too real.

"What did you dream?" he asks.

When I duck my head low, resting my forehead against his chest, his fingers brush over my cheek before slipping behind my neck.

Not wanting to talk about it, I mutter, "It was nothing."

"It wasn't nothing. You stopped breathing," he snaps, actually sounding angry because I won't tell him.

When I climb off the bed to put some space between us, another dizzy spell hits. I breathe through it and once it passes, I grab my jacket and shrug it on.

"Let's get out of the room," I say while pushing my feet into the nearest pair of sneakers. "I need some fresh air."

Ryan gets up and quickly puts on his boots.

We stay quiet as we walk out of the bedroom and through the house. A headache starts to pulse behind my eyes, and when we finally leave through the front door, I suck in a deep breath of the cold air.

The moment we're sitting in Ryan's truck, he says, "Talk to me. What did you dream about?"

"It was just a nightmare," I mutter while he starts the engine and steers the truck away from the curb.

"It's important that you tell me," he insists, and it has me frowning at him.

Important, my ass.

Shaking my head at him, I lift my hand and rub my chest where it's still aching from whatever slammed into me in the dream.

Did someone shoot me?

"Jane, talk to me," Ryan sounds impatient, his eyes flicking between the road and me. "Now."

"Dammit, can you just chill," I snap at him. "God. I just woke up from one hell of a nightmare. Give me some time to process it."

When Ryan pulls over to the side of the road, I realize we're close to the waterfall.

I don't mind. The peace and quiet out here will do me a world of good.

We get out of the truck, and as we walk toward the waterfall, I can feel tension coming off Ryan in waves.

I pull my jacket tighter around me, glad for the full moon giving us some light so we can see where we're going.

God, it's cold.

The moment we reach the waterfall, Ryan lets out a sigh and says, "What I'm about to tell you might sound crazy, but just bear with me." Lifting a hand to my face, he tucks a few strands of my hair behind my ear. "To really hear me, you need to listen with that part within you that feels like you never belonged here. Listen with that piece of your soul that tells you you're different from

70

others."

Confused as fuck, I ask, "What the hell are you talking about?"

"Vaalbara is a real place. It's our home. Your people are waiting for you to return, and I've been sent to bring you home."

The. Fuck?

With a raised eyebrow, I gawk at him for a moment, wondering if he's lost his mind.

"Did you get drunk while I was sleeping?" I finally manage to ask.

He shakes his head, a serious expression tightening his features. "I need to take you home."

He's actually starting to scare me, and it has me snapping, "Th-that's enough, Ryan. Is this some k-kind of sick joke?"

He shakes his head again, his voice remaining calm. "I'm serious. You'll need to clear your mind of everything so I can take you home."

I take a cautious step away from him, regretting that I came out here with him.

Crap, he can kill me, and no one will be around to hear my screams.

When Ryan darts toward me, he moves so fast I don't even have time to make a sound. His arms wrap tightly around me, trapping my body to his in a steel embrace.

God, he's much stronger than he looks.

Panic takes over, but before I can shove at Ryan to try and free myself, he moves so fast wind swirls around us, whipping my hair into my face.

Holy shit!

He slams us into the icy waterfall, the speed alone taking my breath away, never mind the freezing water that rushes over us, quickly soaking our clothes.

"Don't think of anything, Alchera. Clear your mind. Let me take you," Ryan says urgently, right by my ear. "Please let me take you. Let me keep you safe. You belong with me."

Intense fear fills me from how quickly Ryan went from being my friend to a dangerously insane stranger.

I didn't see any of this coming. How stupid am I?

Before another panicked thought can enter my mind, I'm overcome with a sickening feeling, and the world blurs and spins around me.

The water begins to grow warmer, and when I'm pulled away from the waterfall, bright sunlight stings my eyes.

What. The. Hell. Is. Happening?

It feels as if my head is going to explode from intense pressure, and I struggle to breathe as I'm dragged through a pool until I can feel slimy ground and pebbles beneath my feet.

Finally, I'm able to take a deep breath, and the pain lessens in my head. When I look behind us, I see a beautiful blue-green curtain of water, like the one from my dream.

Holy shit. The waterfall looks precisely like the one I've been drawing.

"It took me a few times before I got used to shifting," Ryan says, his voice much deeper than it was a few seconds ago.

My eyes snap to his face, and I'm so shocked by what I see, I shove away from him and fall backward into the water.

Splashing, I fight to regain my balance, my eyes not leaving the man in front of me.

Oh my God.

Drops of water sparkle in his dark brown hair, and he's much taller.

HolyShit.HolyShit.HolyShit.

His eyes sparkle like amethysts, and he looks older. Easily ten to fifteen years older.

My mind is completely frazzled, and I can't process what I'm seeing at all.

There's no sign of Ryan, the teenage boy I was falling in love with. Instead, I'm staring at a man that's twice my size.

One hell of a strong man by the looks of his muscled body.

Is he wearing leather?

I start to frown and shake my head because none of this makes sense, and I figure it has to be another weird dream.

Yep. That's it. You're dreaming.

You're fast asleep in your bed.

This isn't real.

Everything feels weird and out of place.

A familiar crooked smile tugs at the corner of his mouth, and it confuses me even more.

"I've changed slightly. The elixir wore off as soon as we entered Vaalbara."

"Slightly?" I whisper as I let out a chuckle that almost turns into a sob.

Dear God. What is this?

"You've changed too," he says, his tone a million times calmer than I feel. He gestures at the water. "Take a look."

My confusion only grows, and when I glance down, I almost have a heart attack.

A gasp explodes over my lips as I look at my wobbly reflection in the water.

I see sparkling emerald-green eyes wide with shock and confusion. My hair is black with silver streaks on the left side of my head.

I lift a trembling hand to my face, and my breath catches in my throat when my fingers brush over my perfect creamy skin.

"That can't be me," I whisper.

Panic grips my chest, squeezing the air from my lungs until it starts to hurt.

My heart pounds in my ears.

When my vision starts to blur again, I look at Ryan.

I want to ask him what he did to me, but my tongue is numb with pins and needles.

Ryan darts forward, and as his arms wrap around me, he says, "Breathe, Alchera."

I shake my head as my body goes limp, and my vision grows spotty.

"Everything will make sense soon," I hear him say as he lifts me into his arms bridal style.

"Peace be, Raighne," I hear another man's voice. "Is the princess okay?"

"Peace be. She's just in shock. I have to get her to Janak and Aster."

I manage to pry my eyes open and see a blur of greens and browns before I pass out.

CHAPTER 7

RAIGHNE

I tried to be as patient as possible, but with the visions happening more often and that bastard, Robert, attacking Alchera, I had to bring her home.

With my charge in my arms, I start to make my way to the training camp, where Aster should be at the infirmarius.

I glance down at Alchera's unconscious face, and seeing her without the glamor of the elixer, an intense sense of possessiveness fills my veins.

Mine.

I'm relieved to have my charge back on Vaalbara with me. Pretending to be a seventeen-year-old boy was frustrating as fuck.

I have to remind myself I'm still a stranger to Alchera. She never got to meet me before she was sent to Earth, even though we were bonded the moment she was born.

As I carry Alchera while I make the trek to the training grounds, I don't grow tired at all. I could walk with her for days on end without any rest.

I keep glancing at her, checking for signs that she's regaining her consciousness, but as the hours pass and she doesn't come to, worry fills my veins.

I focus hard, and entering her mind, I find nothing but blissful darkness. Even though it sets me at ease, I pick up my pace and start to run.

When I finally carry her through the opening of the large tent that serves as an infirmarius, one of the caretakers calls out, "Aster! Come quickly."

I head to the nearest bed and gently place Alchera on it. As I straighten up, Aster rushes into the room, and the moment she lays eyes on my charge, emotion washes over her face.

"Praise be to Awo for your safe return," she says as she begins to take Alchera's vitals.

"Will you remove the spell you cast over her?" I ask, impatient for Alchera to remember Vaalbara.

I hate how scared she was because she didn't remember her world and people, and I want her memories back as soon as possible.

"Yes." Aster nods her head, and a moment later, Janak comes rushing into the room.

I take a couple of steps backward to give them space so they can tend to Alchera.

My eyes never leave my charge as they begin to reverse the spell, the air filling with swirls of lights and sparks.

It takes too long for my liking and once they're finally done, I ask, "Will she remember?"

Janak nods. "But it might take some time for all her memories to return, and some might be lost forever. We won't know until she wakes." His eyes meet mine. "I'll send word to the King and Queen that Alchera has returned."

I suck in a deep breath as I move closer to the bed. "How long before she wakes?"

"It all depends on her," Aster says. "She's in good health,

Raighne. There's no need to worry."

Easier said than done.

I bring my hand to Alchera's face and brush strands of her hair away. Positioning my palm over her forehead, I close my eyes and focus on her so I can enter her mind where I don't find any dreams. There's only the peaceful darkness of a deep sleep.

That's good. Rest, my little dreamer.

I let out a sigh as I pull my hand away from her, and staring at my charge, I start to worry about the training. We have a lot to learn so we can communicate telepathically and strengthen our bond.

With time, it will get easier for me to feel what she feels and hear her thoughts.

ALCHERA

Coming to, I feel groggy, and whispering voices break through the fog in my mind.

My head lolls to the side as I pry my eyes open, and the first thing that registers is I'm lying on a bed in a large room of sorts.

I blink a couple of times before I notice a row of identical beds.

Turning my head, I see a stand with cotton balls, bandages, and other medical supplies in the far corner. Shelves line the walls, stocked with various brown bottles.

Am I in a hospital?

An elderly man and woman stand not too far from me, the woman holding a small bottle in her hand. It looks different from the ones on the shelves. This one is clear, with a small base.

The longer I stare at the elderly couple, the more familiar they start to look.

Wait a second.

The woman is the first to notice I'm awake. She has blonde hair and blue eyes and seems to be in her fifties.

I remember her. Aster. She's the head priestess.

It feels as if the words drift to me from afar. "Aster?" Clearing my dry throat, I try again. "Aster? Janak?"

"Welcome back, child. How do you feel?" she asks as they hurry closer to me. "Do you remember us?"

"Yes." I still feel out of it as I glance between them. "What happened?"

Janak takes my hand and squeezes it softly. "You'll feel better soon. The effects of the spell are still wearing off."

Spell?

Aster gives me a serious look. "Don't fight the memories. Let them in."

Already feeling tired again, I close my eyes, and then one memory after the other trickles into my mind.

I remember being brought to Aster on my sixteenth birthday. She gave me something to drink.

I gasp as my mind is suddenly flooded with muddled flashes of my past.

My family! Mom. Dad.

I remember my older sisters. Brenna and Thana. And my brother, Roark.

An overwhelming emotion makes tears sting my eyes.

I miss them so much.

I remember a younger and happier me. Because my brother and sisters are so much older, I used to be adored by everyone.

I was loved.

The day of my sixteenth birthday fills my mind, and remembering how I was brought to Janak and Aster makes me feel sad.

They cast a spell over me, and before I lost consciousness, I saw a man.

He held me as if I was the most precious thing to him.

When I woke up, I was alone at Fish Creek Falls.

They left me all alone in a foreign place.

For five years!

Oh my God.

My breathing speeds up, and my heart beats faster and faster as an intense feeling of abandonment forms a crack right down the middle of my soul.

Then Ryan came and pretended to be my friend, and I was once again ripped away from everything I held dear.

"Ryan," I whimper. It hurts to think of him and how he played me for a fool.

"Ryan's name is Raighne," Janak informs me. "He's your guardian."

I open my eyes and look at the two elders who played a part in deceiving me.

"Well, you're home now," Aster says. "Do you remember anything from before we sent you to Earth?"

"Not much," I whisper as anger and heartache bubble in my chest. "Why was I sent to Earth?"

Before they can answer me, my chest fills with every emotion I felt on Earth.

The fear of being a vulnerable child, alone with no memory.

The intense loneliness of not belonging anywhere.

The hatred I felt for Robert.

The rejection when I didn't fit in at school.

"We had to do it, child. You needed to live as a human in order to understand them," Janak answers my question. "It was spoken so by Awo."

"You sent me to a foreign world," I bite the words out, my anger growing by the second. "I was left alone for five years!"

Aster smiles gently at me. "You have every right to be upset, but we did what was best for you."

I shake my head at her. "Wow, that makes it all better." Then I remember my family again, and ask, "Where are my parents? My brother and sisters?"

I desperately want to see them and be with my own people.

"Your family is well. They've been waiting for the news of your return with great excitement." Janak's face falls as he looks to Aster for help.

My muscles tighten, and I worry they're going to give me bad news.

Aster looks at me with sympathy. "You can only see your parents after you've completed your destiny. It's too dangerous for them to meet with you right now as they might lead Adeth to you."

What the hell?

"What destiny? Who's Adeth?"

My anger doubles, curling around me like a thick cloud while I try to deal with the disappointment of not being able to see my parents.

"You have to learn how to be a warrior, Alchera. You need to be able to protect yourself and the chosen ten when you go to retrieve them from Earth. There's barely enough time for you to train."

The vague reply to my questions confuses me. Then it sinks in what Aster just said.

"Hold your horses," I pull myself up into a sitting position. "I have to learn how to be a warrior?"

"Yes," Janak answers. "Now that you're home, you'll regain your strength, and soon your talents will appear."

"What talents?"

"You'll have visions of the chosen ten and the future."

I almost mention the dreams but decide to keep the information to myself.

"You're no ordinary, fragile human anymore," Aster says. "You need to practice your strengths and talents so you can master them."

Just fucking perfect.

When I scowl at them, Aster clears her throat. "We have to leave you now. Thana is anxious to see you, and Raighne and his brother are also here. There are so many others waiting to welcome you home. Your life will soon be full."

"What?" I sit stunned and watch as Aster and Janak leave without another word.

What in the everloving hell?

Sitting alone in the room, I shake my head as I try to wrap my mind around everything.

I'm home.

After five long and lonely years, I'm home only to be told I have to train and get ready to fulfill my destiny. They're insane.

I was sixteen when I left, which means I'm turning twenty-one next week and not eighteen.

I've lost so much time.

My thoughts turn to the Calder family, and I wonder if I'll ever see Molly again. I didn't even get to say goodbye to her.

Holy crap. I can't believe what the elders did to me.

When the realization hits again, I'm so angry my body's trembling.

Just as I throw the covers away from me, Ryan, or should I say Raigne, comes into the room.

My eyes lock on him, and for a moment, my anger is forgotten as I stare at the hot as fuck man that's apparently my guardian.

The leather pants look downright sinful, where the fabric

clings to his muscled thighs, and the matching shirt does nothing to hide his strong arms.

Damn, the clothes look ridiculously good on him.

"Raighne," a woman calls, and he turns to face her, "Princess Alchera's quarters are ready."

"Thank you, Fleur," He replies, but I'm way too busy staring at his back as I realize I've seen him before.

"It was you," I whisper, shocked from learning I've been dreaming about Raighne coming for me.

"Alchera," he murmurs to get my attention, and it's only then I realize I zoned out for a moment.

Swinging my legs off the side of the bed, I rub a hand over my face as I mutter, "God, this is all too overwhelming."

"Your visions started earlier than we expected. I would've come sooner had we known," he says.

"Visions?" Lifting my head, I look at him. "Who are the 'we' you're referring to?"

"King Eryon, Queen Mya, my father, and Janak." He sits down beside me on the side of the bed and tilts his head to catch my eyes. "And me. Awo bonded us the day you were born."

"Bonded?" I shake my head and try to remember what it means.

The corner of his mouth lifts, and he actually looks proud as he says, "I'm your guardian, and you're my charge. You'll learn what it means during training."

I vaguely remember my sisters had guardians, but I can't remember what it entails.

"So you all decided it was a good idea to ship me off to Earth and just leave me there all alone?" I climb off the bed and take a few steps away from him. "All because of some destiny I'm not even aware of?"

I remember the past two weeks and how I thought he was my

friend.

God, I was falling in love with him.

Anger and hurt explode in my chest, and glaring at Raighne, I say, "You betrayed me. You can take our bond and shove it where the sun doesn't shine."

He rises to his feet, his features drawn tight. "I did what was best for you."

"You didn't!" I snap. "Instead of pretending to be my friend and playing me for a fool, you should've just dragged me back here and gotten it over with." I throw my arms in the air, intense disappointment filling my chest as I let out a bitter chuckle. "I really thought you wanted to be my friend."

When his lips part, I shake my head and continue, "You lied to me. Everything I thought I knew about you was a lie." I let out another bitter chuckle. "I have to admit, you're a damn good actor. You had me going there for a while."

As a tear spirals down my cheek and I angrily wipe it away, Raighne suddenly moves so fast, and for a moment, he's nothing but a blur.

When he grabs hold of my shoulders, I gasp and stagger a step backward.

Then I see the anger in his eyes, making his purple irises much darker.

"Don't you dare say that! I have never lied to you about our friendship. Everything we shared on Earth was real." His features soften a little. "I understand you're angry, but it will pass."

"You don't get it, do you?" I shake my head at him. "You're supposed to be my guardian, but you hurt me."

Once again, I realize I've lost the only friend I've ever had, and it breaks my heart.

I really cared about him.

My voice is hoarse when I say, "I don't care about bonds and destinies, and my anger won't just pass. My feelings don't come with a switch you can flip off when you feel like it." I step away from him, my whole body trembling. "You took my trust, and you threw it back in my face. So no, Ryan, or Raighne, or whatever the hell your name is, I don't accept the bond. I don't trust you and don't want you as my guardian."

"With time, you'll accept me," he says as if it's an inevitable fact I have no choice in.

Maybe it is. But right now, I'm too heartbroken and angry to care.

Lifting my hand, I rub my tired eyes. "Do you know how it feels to have your world ripped out from under you? I don't know what's real anymore." I choke on a sob as my feelings overwhelm me, and I quickly wipe the tears away, feeling embarrassed for crying in front of him.

I'm stronger than this.

"All will be well." He doesn't give me a chance to pull away as his arms wrap around me, hugging me tightly to his chest. I feel his warmth spreading through me, and I hate that I find it soothing.

As much as I want to deny it, his touch makes me feel better, and I can't fight it as my body relaxes against his.

With one hand, he gently caresses my back while his other arm stays firmly around my waist.

All I can do is close my eyes, rest my very confused head against his chest, and breathe in his familiar scent.

"You're not alone in this, Alchera. I'm here for you. I'll help you through the training. I'll be right by your side every step of the way, no matter what happens." He pulls back and frames my face with his hands. With his thumbs, he wipes away my tears. "Our bond is the most important thing to me, Alchera. I live for you, and I'll die with you, but I will never leave you."

God, then he goes and says something like that. How's a girl supposed to stick to her guns and stay angry?

Even though I just want him to hold me, I step backward and glance around the room so I don't have to look at him.

"I need time. This is all too much for me to deal with."

"Okay."

Feeling exhausted, I ask, "What happens now?"

"Your sister is outside. She'd like to see you."

My sister.

CHAPTER 8

ALCHERA

When I follow Raighne OUT of the infirmarius, the sun is so bright I have to squint my eyes until they adjust.

I notice we're in a camp of some sort, then my eyes land on a woman who doesn't look much older than Raighne. I don't immediately recognize her.

A glow hugs her petite frame, and she's the most beautiful person I've ever seen. Staring at her golden hair and eyes, I'm at a loss for words.

She moves with such grace she seems to be gliding. Lights flicker over her skin, like fireflies dancing around her with every step she takes.

"I'll give you some privacy," Raighne says, but when he turns to walk away, my hand shoots out and I grab his forearm.

Even though I've missed my family, it's clear a lot has changed since I was last here.

Right now Raighne feels most familiar after I spent the past two weeks with him.

Even though I'm angry, I whisper, "Stay."

Raighne nods and takes a step closer to me.

"My talents have grown since we last saw each other," the woman says. "I used to have blonde hair and amber eyes."

My gaze darts nervously over the woman, and when she smiles warmly, it helps ease the tension a little.

"Peace be, Alchera. I am your sister, Thana. Brenna, Roark, and I have been waiting for your arrival with great excitement."

Wow, she looks completely different from what I remember.

I suck in a deep breath before I say, "Hi, Thana…" An awkward-sounding chuckle escapes me. "I'm sorry. It's a lot to take in all at once."

I thought I would be happy to see my family, but all I feel is apprehension.

What if they don't like me?

What if I'm a disappointment to them after being gone for so long?

What if it never feels like home again?

Thana closes the distance between us and when she hugs me, she smells like a warm summer's day and blossoms in the spring.

I'm so scared I'll hurt her, so I keep my touch gentle when I return the hug.

Emotions overwhelm me as we hold each other, and I feel tears sting my eyes.

My heart hurts from getting to hold my own blood again. It makes me realize how lonely I've been over the past five years.

"Welcome home, my sister," she says. "May Awo's blessings be upon you." Thana pulls back and holds me at arm's length, taking in my appearance. "You're more beautiful than I remember and so grown up. It's such a shame we can't celebrate your birthday with you next week."

She looks at me with so much love I can barely breathe, making my tears come hot and fast. She reaches up and wipes some of my tears away, the look on her face gentle.

Her voice is hoarse as she whispers, "I missed you too, Alchera."

If all my family is like her, then I don't need to worry, right?

But I have questions, and I'm hoping she'll answer them.

"Why didn't they send you away? Why only me?"

"We're not so much a threat to Adeth as you are. Awo gave you the talents of visions and hope."

I stare blankly at her. None of what she just said makes any sense to me.

Her honey-golden eyes fill with sorrow, confusing me.

"Unfortunately, only you can perform the task at hand. We each have our destiny to fulfill in the coming days."

When a breeze picks up and blows some of my hair into my face, I quickly brush it away before asking, "What do you mean?"

"You had to go to Earth to live as a human," Thana explains. "You had to feel how they felt in order to have compassion for them."

I sure wasn't feeling any compassion toward Robert and his friends.

But the Calders. They were good to me.

"You needed to go on this journey so you'll understand the chosen ones when the time comes to retrieve them."

Thana moves away, leaving golden streaks of light trailing in her wake.

"Who are these chosen ones I have to retrieve?" I ask, just glad someone's actually answering my questions.

Thana sighs heavily, and worry tenses her features before she says, "The end of the human world is coming, Alchera. Armageddon is upon Earth, as it's been written in so many scriptures. Until you receive your visions, we won't know who the chosen ones are, but they will be the only ten humans who'll be saved and brought here."

My lips part with a gasp as shock shudders through my body.

"All living species on Earth will come to an end. All except for the chosen ones you'll bring to Vaalbara – the *new* Earth. You can only return to Vaalbara when you have all of them."

My mouth falls open as I stare at her in utter shock.

This has to be some cruel joke.

How can they expect me to only save ten people out of billions?

Fear shoots through my body. "I can't be responsible for saving the human race. That's insane!" I shake my head wildly. "You can't expect me to do that. Are you all crazy?"

My eyes dart from her face to Raighne's. He watches me with a worried look carved into his handsome features.

Realizing they're serious, horror slams into my gut, and I keep shaking my head at them.

This has to be a nightmare. It just has to. I have to wake up!

"I know it's going to be difficult, but we all have our parts to play," Thana says, her tone filled with sorrow. "You'll have Brenna and Raighne by your side throughout it all."

My face must show the horror I'm feeling as I gasp, "How can you just stand there and tell me it's the end of the world without at least trying to stop it?" I look at her in disbelief. "Surely there's something we can do."

My heart races in my chest.

Wake up!

You have to wake up.

"The human race has brought this upon themselves," Thana says, her tone suddenly harsh.

I stare at her as more shock pours into my chest, frazzling my already overwhelmed mind.

I can't believe she just said that. So many innocent people will die, and none of them deserve it.

Thana lets out a heavy sigh. "They've been warned by so many different religions and visions we've sent over the centuries, yet they refuse to change their destructive ways."

I raise my eyebrows at her as I cross my arms over my chest. My voice trembles as I snap, "It's going to take more than that shitty excuse to convince me it's okay wiping out an entire planet."

"They've ignored all the warnings, Alchera," she exclaims before her features soften again. "I feel for them and wish there was another way, but we can't stand in the way of Awo. They've destroyed their Earth and must face the consequences of their selfish actions."

She places her hand on my arm, and I watch as some of her light transfers to my jacket.

Her voice is filled with anguish as she says, "In less than three months, the worst natural disasters Earth has ever experienced will be unleashed on them. There's nothing we can do but to preserve the human race by saving the chosen ten."

Thana pulls her hand away from me and brushes her palm over her forehead, looking as tired as I feel.

"But there are so many good people," I argue. "There are certainly more than ten."

"I know, but it's not for us to question the ways of Awo."

"Why me?"

I'm not happy with taking on this responsibility.

Hell, I'm not even twenty-one yet.

"Awo has spoken it," is all she says.

I vaguely remember that Awo is the source of all life. When you die, your life's essence returns to Awo.

I suppose humans would call Awo God, but it's so much more than that.

Needing to know more, I ask, "If I have to retrieve the chosen, then what's your destiny?"

A smile wavers around her mouth. "I have the power to control water, wind, fire, and earth." She exhales a heavy breath. "It's my destiny to ensure Earth returns to dust."

God, and I thought my destiny was bad.

She has to destroy Earth? That's horrible.

My chin quivers as I stare at my sister. After long seconds I manage to whisper, "I'm so sorry."

I don't know what else to say.

"There's nothing to apologize for." She tries to give me an encouraging smile. "It is my destiny, and I'm proud to fulfill it."

Hoping she knows why, I ask, "Why can't I see our parents?"

"It's too dangerous." She gives me a compassionate smile. "Just trust that it's for the best."

Yeah, I don't think so.

Raighne takes hold of my hand and says, "That's enough information for now. It's time for Alchera to go to our camp, where she can wash up and eat something."

Thana nods. "Yes, you should rest. I'll see you again once your visions of the chosen ones start." She closes the distance between us and gives me a quick hug. "It's good to have you home, Alchera."

I nod, and when she pulls away, Raighne tugs at my hand.

"See you around," I say before I follow Raighne in the direction of a hill.

My heart feels heavy from the terrible information I just learned, so I don't free my hand from Raighne's and let his warmth flow through me.

In a matter of hours, my entire life has changed irrevocably, and I have the feeling it's only going to get worse.

As if I'm coming out of a daze, I slowly focus on my surroundings. The first things I notice are the lush fields and hills and the different colors of the wildflowers.

I've forgotten how beautiful Vaalbara is.

I suck in a deep breath of air that tastes sweet compared to the polluted air on Earth.

When we reach the top of the hill, I see a bigger camp than the one we just left. There's a forest behind all the tents and it stretches for as far as the eye can see.

I hear chirping and notice a pond nearby where birds are bathing, and when I glance to my left, I notice mountains in the distance.

As we get closer to the other camp, that's made up of numerous large tents and a building that stands to one side, people stop what they're doing to stare at me.

Oh, just great.

I swallow hard as my stomach begins to spin with nerves, and without realizing it, I move closer to Raighne. My cheek brushes against his arm, and it has him looking down at me.

"It's okay," he says, his tone firm and filled with confidence. "They're all happy to see you."

Suddenly, the crowd makes way for a beautiful woman who looks sexy as fuck. With thick auburn hair that reaches below her shoulders and eyes made of onyx stones, she looks like a force to be reckoned with.

Damn, she gives me the impression she can kick some serious butt.

"You've finally decided to grace us with your presence," she says, her tone biting.

Uhm...come again?

When she stops in front of me and crosses her arms over her chest, I get a full display of her cleavage.

Damn, it must take some powerful magic for the tiny leather top to stay on.

"Brenna," Raighne mutters. "Watch yourself. You, of all people, know Alchera had no say in any of this."

Brenna?

My eyes widen, and I stare at her. Last I saw Brenna, she was as skinny as me and wouldn't hurt a fly, whereas the woman in front of me is nothing short of a warrior.

She takes a step closer to Raighne, lifting her chin as if she's challenging him.

My eyes jump wildly between them.

"*Guardian,* you better watch your tongue, or I will sever it from your mouth," she threatens him.

From out of nowhere, I'm hit with one hell of a protective feeling toward Raighne, and before I can stop myself, I step between them.

With a look of warning, I say, "Back off."

Her eyes flick over my face before she lets out a burst of laughter. "Would you look at that? Seems you grew a spine on Earth, little sister." She looks me up and down as if I'm nothing but a piece of shit. "Sadly, I don't think it will keep you alive for long."

Jesus, what did I do to her to make her act so hostile?

"Enough!" Raighne's voice thunders over us, making me flinch.

He tugs me back to his side, and stepping forward, he levels Brenna with a glare that has fear slithering into my chest.

Raighne squares his shoulders and clenches his jaw, and I can see how much it's taking for him to stay calm.

"Alchera is my charge, and I have custody over her, which makes me more than a *mere* guardian."

His tone carries more authority than I've ever heard him speak with, and it makes me feel a little scared of him.

Another man comes up behind Brenna and places his hand on her shoulder. Her head whips around, and I almost think she's going to attack him, but then she immediately calms down at the sight of him.

"Brenna, this is a time to be happy," he whispers to her.

She frowns and shakes her head. It looks like she wants to go against him.

He slips his arm around her waist and gives me a warm smile.

"Peace be, Alchera. Welcome home." His eyes flick to Raighne, and he nods. "Brother. It's good to see you again."

Raighne's fingers tighten around mine. "Finian," he mutters. "Control your charge."

Finian is his brother and Brenna's guardian?

I'm surprised when Finian nods and Brenna actually allows him to pull her away. I watch as they whisper to each other.

"What the hell just happened?" I mutter, stunned by the altercation.

"Brenna will come around. She just needs time to adjust," Raighne says as if all that didn't just go down.

"She's been here all along." I let out a bitter chuckle. "Adjust to what?"

My sister obviously has some serious issues with me, and it makes hurt blossom in my chest.

This wasn't the family reunion I wanted.

"You'll both get past this. It's Brenna's destiny to assist you, and she feels it's beneath her. She and Finian will join us when we go to retrieve the chosen ten."

"By the looks of things, that's going to be fun," I mutter sarcastically.

Raighne leads me to a tent that's situated next to an old oak tree.

"Brenna is also responsible for training you in combat," Raighne says, dropping a bomb between us.

My eyebrows fly up, and I glance at him. "It looks more like she wants to kill instead of train me."

"She's just emotional from receiving her destiny, but she'll calm down, and hopefully, you can become friends." Even he sounds doubtful. "Concentrate on the present and leave the future for later."

I shake my head, highly doubting that will happen.

CHAPTER 9

ALCHERA

The tent is much bigger inside than it looks from the outside.

There's a room with wooden chairs situated around a coffee table. Brown and cream-colored pillows and soft-looking quilts add warmth to the otherwise bland decor.

We walk further into the tent, which opens into a smaller space with a bed.

Just seeing the covers and pillows, exhaustion washes through me.

All I want to do is sleep until this nightmare ends.

On one side of the room stands a tub and sink. There's also a cupboard beside a window, a pattern of flowers and vines carved into the wood.

"This will be your home while we train," Raighne informs me.

I glance around again and say, "Thanks."

"My living quarters is next to yours. Your clothes are in the cupboard, and your aide will be here shortly with something to eat."

Nodding, I turn to face him.

For a moment, my anger and heartache were forgotten with all the information that was dumped on me, but the emotions quickly return when I meet his eyes.

Exhausted to my core, I whisper, "I'd like to be alone."

Raighne nods, his eyes drifting over my face with worry still etched deep into his features, then he tells me, "Tomorrow will be very busy, so I suggest you get to bed early."

I stand frozen like an idiot when he leans down, his hand wrapping around the side of my neck. He presses a kiss to my forehead, then says, "I'll see you in the morning."

I hate when a fluttering explodes in my stomach, and I clench my jaw as I watch him leave.

Staring at the doorway, I shake my head.

You have to get over the unwanted feelings you have for the man.

Finally alone, I let out a heavy breath and glance around the room that will be my home for the unforeseeable future.

I still can't process everything that's happened and feel utterly overwhelmed.

Sighing, I walk to the cupboard, and when I open it, I find a few pairs of leather outfits and boots.

God, I'm going to miss jeans and sneakers.

When I take an outfit from the cupboard, I notice it's nothing but a short skirt and a leather top similar to the one Brenna wore.

Hell no. You won't get me dead in this.

On closer inspection I see the bottoms are a cross between a skirt and hot pants.

I throw the clothes back into the cupboard, and walking to the sink, I pick up the decanter and pour some water out into the bowl. Scooping water into my hands, I splash it over my face before grabbing the towel.

As I pat my skin dry, I mutter, "You're not in Steamboat

Springs anymore, that's for sure."

My eyes lock on my reflection in the mirror, and I gasp.

The sparkling emerald green eyes staring back at me and black hair with silver streaks look foreign. Never mind the fact that I'm three years older.

I barely recognize myself.

Unable to look at my reflection for a second longer, I turn around, an intense urge to scream building in my chest.

I walk closer to the bed, and sitting down on the edge, I press the towel to my mouth and scream into the fabric.

Holy fucking shit.

I can't believe what's happened.

It's insane.

They just left me at a waterfall and made me believe I was thirteen. They left me completely defenseless.

Tears of anger burn my eyes as I clench my jaw, my entire body trembling.

And five years later Raighne just swoops in and rips me away from the life I had to build on my own.

He made me believe we were friends.

My heart clenches when I think of everything I lost in the blink of an eye.

And now they're telling me Earth will be destroyed, and I have to save ten people.

God, I can barely keep myself alive. This is all too crazy.

Standing up, my fingers dig into the fabric of the towel as I start to pace up and down.

Holy shit.

What do I do?

How do I begin to process all of this?

Realizing my breathing has sped up, I inhale deeply and close my eyes.

Calm down. You need to think clearly about everything.

I take another deep breath and let it out slowly.

You've survived the past five years without them, you can survive whatever lies ahead as well.

When I open my eyes, movement by the door catches my attention. There's a pretty blonde girl, her hair tied in two pigtails. She gives me a hesitant look as if she's waiting for permission for something.

She's at least a head taller than me. Her eyes are something else, though, sparkling like soft pink gems.

"Hey," I say, tossing the towel onto the bed.

Her face instantly lights up with a friendly smile. "Peace be, Princess Alchera. I'm Fleur." She takes a step into the room. "I'll be your aide."

"Just call me Alchera," I mutter.

"I brought some food and thought we could eat together. You must be starving."

She has a beautiful, open smile, but I'd rather be alone. Instead of declining, I say, "Yeah, I can eat."

Following her out of the bedroom, I make myself comfortable on one of the chairs. When she hands me a bowl of something that looks like pot roast, I murmur, "Thanks."

I watch as she sits down, giving me a cautious smile before she takes a bite of her food.

Overcome with all the chaotic emotions and memories, I stare down at the bowl in my hand.

"Don't you want to eat?" Fleur asks.

Letting out a sigh, I scoop up some of the food into my spoon and take a bite.

It tastes much better than it looks, and realizing how hungry I am, I focus on finishing everything in the bowl.

When I place the empty bowl on the coffee table, Fleur gives me a satisfied smile, then says, "You can ask me anything. I'm here to help you while you adapt, and I'll answer any questions you might have."

Her features soften, then she adds, "I'm hoping we can be friends."

Friends. I don't think so. The last one hurt me enough, thank you very much.

When I keep quiet, she asks, "Do you have any questions?"

I've had enough information today to last me a lifetime, but there's a lot I still don't know.

I lift my eyes to hers and say, "My memory is very spotty. Can you tell me about the people on Vaalbara?"

Her smile widens again, and she seems relieved that I asked a question.

"We're called immortalis. Janak and Aster are our elders. They're also the oldest. Do you remember your parents?"

"Vaguely."

"They're our monarchs. You're a daughter of House Regales." She looks excited as she asks, "Did you know Raighne's father is King Eryon's guardian?"

A frown forms on my forehead as I search my memory, and I remember glimpses of my father and his guardian. "I don't remember much about them," I admit.

"Griffith's his name. He's our strongest guardian, and he trained Raighne, so you're in good hands."

"So Raighne's whole family guards mine?" I ask.

"Pretty much. It's their destiny."

I nod, then ask, "I had normal green eyes when I left."

"Oh, they changed because your talents are coming into effect."

"So not everyone has sparkly eyes?"

"No, not everyone." She lets out a burst of laughter. "Most

guardians have purple eyes when they initially bond with a charge. Their eyes change as their powers grow. Griffith's eye color is similar to that of the lapis lazuli stone, but it just means he can heal the King."

"Oh, that's a nice power to have," I mutter.

She nods, then continues, "Your eyes are emerald, so I think part of your talent must have to do with nature. Brenna's is onyx, as she is a warrior princess. But if you ask me, they should be ruby red and spitting fire because she has quite the temper."

Suddenly, she looks guilty for insulting my sister.

"Don't worry. After running into her earlier, I totally agree," I say with a chuckle.

Fleur's smile returns. "Thana's eyes are golden, like a spessartine stone. Everyone loves her, especially Brenna. They're very close."

Great, my sisters are close, and I've lost touch with them because I was sent away against my will.

I try to think of something else I can ask Fleur when she gets excited again. She seems to be in her element. "Griffith also has the ability to make himself unseen. Now that's a talent I wouldn't mind having."

"Do you have a talent?" I ask.

She nods. "I can create spells and elixirs. Once the chosen ten have joined us, I'll study under Aster."

"Damn, yours sound awesome. Want to swap talents with me?" I joke. "Because mine sucks ass."

She shakes her head. "Unfortunately, that's not how talents work."

"Raighne said I'm starting my training tomorrow," I mention. "Will you be there?"

"If you want me there." Fleur stands up and gathers the dirty dishes. "I'm here to help you with whatever you need, Alchera."

She glances at the doorway. "You should get some rest. I'll see you in the morning for training."

"Thanks for the food," I say as I climb to my feet.

"You're welcome."

I watch as she leaves before heading to the bedroom. Kicking off my sneakers, I think about all my belongings that I had to leave behind on Earth.

I wish Raighne had given me time to pack a bag.

Opening the cupboard, there's only a nightgown for pajamas.

Finding clean underwear, I check the tub, and when I open the faucets and water pours in, I let out a relieved sigh.

As soon as the tub is full, I quickly strip out of my dirty clothes and climb in. Lying back, I close my eyes and let the balmy water ease the tension in my muscles.

God, what a day.

I let out another sigh, wondering what's in store for me.

I never thought I'd miss Steamboat Springs and my boring life there, but damn, what I'd give to return to the sleepy town where nothing exciting happens.

I soak in the tub until the water starts to get cold then quickly wash my body and hair before getting out. After drying myself, I put on clean underwear and the nightgown.

I'm going to have to do something about pajamas because I don't like nightgowns. I'm a shorts and T-shirt kind of girl.

I brush my teeth, then take a seat on the side of the bed and use the towel to squeeze all the excess water out of my hair.

After brushing all the knots out, I get up and walk through my living quarters, turning off all the lamps. Stopping by the doorway, I glance outside and see a group of people sitting around a fire.

My eyes land on Raighne, and when I see him smile at another man, there's a mixture of emotions in my chest. My stomach still flutters at the mere sight of the man, but the crack in my heart because he betrayed me runs deep.

I really fell for his act and thought I finally made a friend I could call my own.

God, I was a dumbass.

A lump forms in my throat, and I wrap my arms around myself.

I trusted him.

For the first time in my life, I was falling in love.

Suddenly, Raighne's eyes flick in my direction, and we stare at each other for a long moment.

A tear threatens to fall, and when Raighne stands up, I shake my head and disappear into my tent.

Crawling beneath the covers, I let out a quivering breath before burying my face in the pillow.

How am I supposed to process everything?

Something slams into my chest, and I fall backward as excruciating pain tears through me.

Lying on the ground, I stare at all the debris floating in the air as I gasp through the pain.

"Alchera! No!" I hear Raighne shout before he drops to his knees beside me.

My vision blurs as I stare up at him, and I try to focus on his face that's torn with worry.

Leaning over me, he breathes, "Awo, no."

I cough, and droplets of my blood hit his neck.

It takes more strength than I have to lift my hand to his face.

My vision blurs again, and I realize I failed in fulfilling my destiny.

I failed.

There's no hope for humankind.

"You're going to be okay," Raighne says, his tone harsh and determined as he presses his hand to my chest.

I feel his warmth flood me, and my vision goes spotty before I start to drift in and out of consciousness.

As I startle awake, a tear rolls down my temple before disappearing into my hair.

Jesus. What was that?

My lips part, and I suck in a deep breath before a sob bursts from me.

Turning onto my side, I bury my face in the pillow as the hopeless emotions from the nightmare wreak havoc in my chest.

Did I just have a vision of my death?

It's the second time I had a similar nightmare, and if it's a vision, it means I won't fulfill my destiny.

Sitting up in bed, I wipe the tears from my cheeks, and as I throw my legs over the side, I can hear birds chirping outside.

Still struggling to process the nightmare, the memories of everything that happened the day before rush through my mind.

Even though I slept through the night, I feel tired as hell.

Climbing to my feet, I walk to the basin and stare at my reflection in the mirror.

The black hair with silver streaks doesn't look as weird anymore, but the sparkling green eyes will take some getting used to.

With a sigh, I pull the brush through the messy strands before brushing my teeth.

Is any of this worth it if I'm destined to die?

After patting my hands and mouth dry, I walk to the cupboard and stare at the clothes.

I hear footsteps in the living room and glance down at the nightgown I'm wearing. Hopefully, it's Fleur, and she can get me something else to wear.

I walk to the doorway, but instead of Fleur, I see Raighne, where he places a cup of coffee down on the table.

When he glances in my direction, he says, "Morning, I brought you coffee."

"Thanks," I mumble, and moving closer, my eyes drift over the leather clothes that look ridiculously hot on him.

Will I ever get used to the fluttering in my stomach just from seeing him?

God, I hope so.

I pick up the cup and sip on the much-needed caffeine before taking a seat on one of the chairs.

"After you've gotten dressed, we'll head out to the training field."

"I'm not wearing the clothes in the cupboard. They're too revealing, and I won't have my ass hanging out for the world to see." Trying my luck, I ask, "Can't we go back to Earth to get my clothes?"

Raighne sits down across from me and shakes his head. "You have to blend in with your people, and that means wearing the same clothes as them, Princess."

"Don't call me that," I snap.

And they're not my people.

"I want pants," I demand. "Similar to what you're wearing."

Raighne lifts an eyebrow and before he can shoot my request down, I say, "Let's get one thing straight, Raighne. I've been ripped from my home. Twice. Very little makes sense to me, and the least you all can do is give me decent clothes, or you're not getting shit from me." I point to the door. "Go get me long pants and a shirt that covers more than just my nipples."

I'm surprised when he nods, and without arguing, he leaves my quarters.

That was much easier than I thought.

Hey, at least I've won something.

While I drink the coffee, I stare at the open doorway. It's quiet outside, and soon, my thoughts return to the nightmare I had.

Should I tell Raighne about the dream?

I shake my head before the thought can take root.

No one needs to know until it actually happens. Maybe I can use the visions and do something to change the future.

CHAPTER 10

ALCHERA

When Raighne comes back into my quarters, he places a stack of clothes on the coffee table. "These should be more to your liking."

I get up and look through the three sets of clothes, then gathering them in my arms, I say, "Thanks."

"Fleur will be with you shortly. I have a meeting, but I'll be back in an hour so I can take you to your training session."

"Training session?" I ask.

"With Brenna."

Right.

With the dream from hell rattling me, I temporarily forgot the training.

When I don't say anything, he looks at me for a few seconds before asking, "Are you okay?"

"It doesn't matter whether I'm okay," I mutter, my tone harsh.

Raighne takes a step closer to me, a frown line appearing between his eyes. "It does."

I shrug and turning away from him, I carry the clothes to the bedroom.

From the doorway, I hear him say, "Alchera?"

I still need to get used to the name.

God, I need to adjust to everything. Is it even possible?

A burst of cynical laughter escapes me, and shaking my head, I say, "Just drop it, Ry...Raighne. I'm a big girl, and I'll get over it."

I hear him move closer and as I glance at him from over my shoulder, he says, "You can talk to me about anything."

Yeah, I don't think so.

"I have to get dressed."

So my sister can kick my ass.

Lifting an arm, he wraps his fingers around the side of my neck. "Things won't seem so foreign for long. You'll adjust."

Feeling his skin against mine makes tingles rush over my body, and just wanting to end the conversation, I nod. "I'll see you later."

He stares at me for a moment longer before nodding.

When he walks out of the room, my eyes follow him, then I turn my attention to the clothes.

I listen for any movement, and when I'm sure I'm alone, I take off the nightgown and quickly put on the pants. It's a little big but at least there's a leather belt so I can tighten it around my waist.

The top looks more like a corset, and it gives me a cleavage I never knew I had. I pull the strings as tight as possible and make a double knot so it doesn't come undone while I'm training.

Digging the boots out of the cupboard, I put them on before glancing down at my body.

I wish I had a full-length mirror.

Sucking in a deep breath of air, I decide to braid my hair so it doesn't get in the way.

Just as I finish the braid, Fleur appears in the doorway. "Morning."

"Morning," I say as I turn to face her. "How do I look?"

She glances up and down. "Good." A smile spreads over her face, then she asks, "Would you like breakfast?"

I shake my head as I walk toward her. "No. Let's just get the training over with."

"Shouldn't we wait for Raighne?" she asks.

"No, he knows where to find me once he's done with his meeting," I mutter, determined to get the training session over and done with. "Show the way to where I have to meet Brenna."

"It's just over the hill," She tells me, and as we leave my living quarters, she asks, "Did you sleep well?"

"I slept okay," I answer, trying not to think of the nightmare.

I glance around the campsite, where everyone's busy getting ready for the day.

Nothing feels familiar.

I wonder if Molly and Stephen have noticed I'm gone. Will the Calders worry?

The thought that most of the people in Steamboat Springs will die settles heavily in my heart.

We're quiet as we walk toward a hill, and once we leave the camp behind, she asks, "What are you thinking about? That's if you don't mind me asking?"

"I'm just thinking how my sister is going to kick my ass," I lie, not wanting to talk about my chaotic emotions. "Brenna doesn't seem to like me."

Fleur offers me an encouraging smile. "Don't worry. I'll be there."

"Great," I chuckle." Someone to pick up my body once she's done killing me."

When we get to the field where the training will take place, Brenna's already waiting.

"I'll wait over there," Fleur says, pointing at a tree.

As I walk closer to where Brenna is standing, her eyes settle on me with disdain, making my stomach twist nervously.

"Peace be, Brenna," I greet her, hoping today won't be too bad.

Her eyes drift over me, and without saying a word, she turns around and moves a couple of steps away while pulling a knife from the holster on her hip.

Knife? We're using weapons?

Fuck my life. I'm dead.

Without any warning, she draws her arm back and lunges forward. All I see is the silver of the blade glistening in the early morning sun, and I hear the whistling sound as it cuts through the air.

I don't even have time to flinch as the blade narrowly misses my throat by mere inches.

Holy shit.

I gasp, and as Brenna comes to a standstill, she says, "Today, you'll learn how to hold and attack with a blade."

So much for first learning the basics.

She throws the blade at my feet, and it pegs into the grass.

When I don't pick it up fast enough, she raises an eyebrow at me before glaring at the blade that looks more like a cross between a sword and a massive butcher's knife from a horror movie.

"You need to pick it up, idiot," she snaps.

My temper flares hot, and as I bend over to yank the knife out of the grass, I say, "What the fuck is your problem, Brenna?"

"You don't deserve the destiny of saving the chosen ten," she spits the words out. "You're weak, and you'll get them killed."

The nightmare flashes through my mind, and it keeps me from arguing with her.

"Let's just train," I mutter.

She holds her arms open and gives me a cocky smirk. "Attack me."

I have no idea what to do, but figuring I can at least try, I lunge forward.

Brenna moves so fast, and for a moment, she's a blur. She grabs hold of my arm and twists it behind my back, making pain explode in my shoulder and forcing me to let go of the knife.

When she moves away from me, I have to clench my jaw, so I don't show any of the pain on my face.

"Again," she spits the word at me.

My shoulder hurts something fierce as I pick up the knife, but before I can even attack, she darts forward, and with a high kick to my already aching shoulder, she sends my ass sprawling over the grass.

The bitch.

The pain engulfing my shoulder and arm is so intense I have to bite on my bottom lip to keep a cry from escaping.

Determined not to give her any satisfaction, I pick up the blade again and throw it at her face out of pure frustration.

Brenna twists her body, easily evading the knife, but there's a look of surprise on her face.

I lunge at her, not wanting to lose my element of surprise, but before I can grab hold of her, she backhands me across the cheek and sends me straight to the ground.

Shit.

Tasting blood, I spit it out before lifting my head and glaring at Brenna.

My heart is pounding loudly in my ears from all the adrenaline pulsing through my body, and my breaths are rushing fast, making my lungs burn.

Sitting back on my haunches, I lift a hand to my face, and touching my mouth, my fingers come away with blood on the tips.

Just as I begin to climb to my feet, Brenna darts toward me, and a kick to my ribs has me gagging as I fall back to the grass.

Oh God. That hurts like a motherfucker.

My eyes water from the pain, and I struggle to suck in a wheezing breath, but somehow, I manage to struggle to my feet before staggering a few steps away from her.

Brenna looks at me with a smirk plastered on her face, and it makes me wish I could punch her lights out.

Annoyed with her teaching methods, I spit more blood from my mouth before muttering, "Shouldn't you be showing me how to fight rather than kicking the crap out of me?"

She begins circling and advancing on me at the same time. "This is the way I teach. Hopefully, you won't be stupid enough to make the same mistake twice."

She lunges at me, and the next thing I know, she twists my left arm painfully behind my back. Then she presses the blade to my throat.

"Now that I have you where I want you, let me make myself clear," she snarls in my ear. "I don't want to train you. I think of you and your training as a waste of time. You're a weakling who will only stand in the way of saving the human race. I should've received your destiny."

Her words tear at my heart because I know she might be right.

Tightening her grip, Brenna presses the blade harder to my throat, and it cuts into my flesh. Panic flares hot through my body.

She wouldn't really kill me, would she?

Suddenly, the knife is ripped away from my throat, and at the same time, I fly forward and out of Brenna's hold.

When I plow into the grass, I can't stop a painful gasp from exploding over my lips.

Holy shit. What just happened?

"What's the meaning of this?" Raighne's voice thunders over the field.

Brenna lets out a chuckle. "Just teaching my *little sister* how to fight."

"The fuck you are," I mutter as I push myself up off the grass.

There's training, and then there's standing around like an idiot while allowing someone to beat the everloving shit out of you.

I don't want to meet the jackass who trained her.

Done with everything, I turn around so I can walk away, but instead, I slam into a wall of muscle.

I bounce back, hissing as pain tears through my body. "Dammit!"

"You must be Alchera," the man says.

My eyes dart to his face, and shock shudders through me.

He looks like the masculine version of me.

"Peace be, Alchera. I'm Roark, your brother. Welcome home."

When I just stare at him, he lets out a chuckle. "We last saw each other when you were twelve. I left for training shortly after and only returned once you were sent to Earth."

Feeling overemotional, I let out a trembling breath and glance away to stare at the trees in the distance.

"Why didn't you wait as you were told," Raighne snaps at me as he comes into my line of sight.

"Because I wanted to get this shit over with," I mutter.

His eyes sweep over me, and his features turn to stone as anger darkens his eyes.

"At least she didn't kill me," I say, my words dripping with sarcasm. "But hey, there's always tomorrow."

Roark's eyes lock with Brenna, and his tone is icy when he says, "We'll talk later. You can leave, Brenna." When he turns his attention back to me, his features soften. "I'll take over your training, and I'll deal with Brenna."

His eyes touch on my bloody lip and the cut on my throat. "I'm sorry. You weren't meant to get hurt."

Whatever.

"Go to the healers so they can tend to you," he says. "Meet me at the training field near my camp first thing tomorrow morning."

I'm in no state to train tomorrow, but I keep my mouth shut because I'm too upset and can't trust anything that will come out of my mouth right now.

I watch as Roark walks away, wondering what other surprises will come my way.

I smell Raighne before his fingers brush near the cut on my throat. When I turn my head to look at him, I see him wipe my blood on his shirt.

Our eyes meet, and the gutted expression on his face makes a lump form in my throat.

"You should've waited for me," he says, his tone tense with anger.

I lift my chin, wanting to look stronger than I feel. "Hey, at least I got a new trainer out of it. Hopefully, Roark won't kick my ass as badly."

I try to pass Raighne, but he brings up his arm and blocks my way. His hand curls around my right shoulder as he steps into my personal space, his chest almost touching mine.

Turning my head away, my eyes land on three people in the far distance. It looks like they're sparring.

Raighne lifts a hand to my face, and taking hold of my chin, he nudges me to look at him.

The moment my gaze locks with his, the lump in my throat grows, and I struggle to swallow it down.

"I'm sorry I took so long to get to you," he murmurs, his tone low and rough around the edges. "Once our bond strengthens, I'll get better at sensing when you're in danger."

"It's fine," I say, letting out a tired breath.

Raighne surprises me when he leans down and presses his forehead to mine.

I close my eyes, and feeling his breath on my lips, it only makes me more emotional and overwhelmed.

"The minute I felt your pain, I ran to get to you."

Wait. What?

Pulling a little back, I open my eyes to look at him. "You felt my pain?"

He tilts his head, his eyes drifting over the bruises on my face and neck.

"I feel everything you feel. That's how I know when you need me. It's something we have to work on, though. With time, the bond will get stronger."

I don't like the idea of him feeling my pain one bit.

Needing to know precisely what this bond entails, I ask, "You feel my pain and emotions?"

He nods. "It comes and goes right now, but when you experience something intensely, it gets through to me."

Noooo.

Does he know about the stupid crush I have on him?

"What else?" I ask, my tone tense.

He shakes his head. "One thing at a time. You're dealing with enough as is."

He can say that again.

Letting out a sigh, I glance around us, then ask, "Which way is the infirmarius?"

"It's north from here. On the other side of Roark's camp." He places his hand on my lower back. "Come, I'll take you."

I shake my head. "I can find it. I'm sure you have to get back to your own stuff."

Ignoring what I said, his hand nudges at my back and he gestures with a jerk of his head for me to start walking.

As we head in the direction of the infirmarius, the aches in my shoulder and chest grow, and it becomes harder to take full breaths.

You already had your ass handed to you today, so suck it up and don't show Raighne how much pain you're in.

I focus so much on trying to keep the pain from showing on my face and keeping control of my emotions that sweat starts to bead on my forehead.

God, what a shitty morning.

114

CHAPTER 11

ALCHERA

We've walked for a couple of minutes when Raighne says, "Let me carry you."

I shake my head. "I'm fine."

My legs are growing numb, and my body aches, but I'm too stubborn to admit I need help. Everyone thinks I'm weak, and the last thing I need is my guardian carrying me like I'm a damn baby.

A minute or so later, we hear someone call out, "Raighne."

He stops and turning, a smile spreads over his face, making him look way too hot.

Ugh. I don't have the strength to stand around and talk to someone.

"Peace be, River," he greets the other man, who's a little shorter and leaner built than him.

"Peace be, my friend. Roark mentioned you were home." He lifts an eyebrow as he glances at me. "You must be Princess Alchera."

I'm starting to feel downright awful and can only nod.

"Yes, this is my Alchera," Raighne replies, the word 'my' making my eyebrows fly into my hairline.

Like hell, I'm not some piece of property he can claim.

My mood sours even more, and feeling miserable, I wish I

could just go to bed.

Raighne must see something on my face because he says, "I mean it in the way a guardian would refer to his charge."

Not wanting to argue about it, I nod.

Just as I'm about to continue walking, River says, "Peace be, Princess. Welcome home."

"Don't call me that," I snap, immediately regretting my harsh tone. "Ah...I'm going to go." I don't even glance at Raighne as I add, "See you around."

"Walk with us," I hear Raighne tell River.

Just great.

I have to suppress the urge to growl as I focus on putting one foot in front of the other.

My vision starts to blur when I hear Fleur call out, "Alchera!"

I don't stop walking because I'm afraid I'll just sink to the ground and cry my heart out.

"By Awo," she gasps when she catches up to me. "When it looked like things were getting out of hand, I went to find Raighne but I see he's already found you." Her eyes are filled with worry as she glances up and down my body. "Are you okay?"

I hook my arm through hers so I can lean on her and whisper, "Just get me to the healers before I pass out."

"Of course." Wrapping her arm around my lower back, she tries her best to support me.

As she helps me walk, she smiles at Raighne and River. "Peace be."

Raighne doesn't say anything, but River returns her greeting, which makes a blush form on her cheeks.

If I weren't dying of pain, I'd be curious whether something's going on between the two of them.

I try to pick up my pace, but my aching body doesn't want to know a thing. Chills spread over my skin, and I wipe sweat from my forehead.

Suddenly, an arm wraps around my waist and another slips beneath my knees. I gasp when I'm picked up bridal style, and my face ends up inches from Raighne's.

He doesn't look at me as he mutters, "That's enough. I'll carry you the rest of the way."

The instant I feel his body heat, it somehow manages to ease the pain a little. Giving up on getting my stubborn ass to the healers on my own, I let out a sigh and rest my head against his shoulder.

"We're almost there," Raighne says, his tone comforting.

My vision blurs again, and I let out a groan before I lose consciousness.

I wake up with a start as a horrible sharp pain shoots through my shoulder and into my neck and back.

I'm unable to stop a cry from bursting over my lips, and feeling feverish, I can barely focus on anything.

"Be gentle with my charge," Raighne snaps angrily.

"I had to put her dislocated shoulder back in place," a man mutters. "It would be better if you waited outside."

"Not happening," Raighne growls.

I pry my eyes open and see a man wearing a white coat getting an injection ready.

"This will help with the pain," he says.

When he brings the needle to my arm, I turn my head, and my sight falls on Raighne, who's standing next to the bed, looking like he's a second away from killing the healer.

I become aware of Raighne's hand gripping mine tightly, and when our eyes meet, his features soften a little.

With his other hand, he brushes his palm over my forehead. "It will be over soon."

God. I hope so.

My eyes fall shut, and as I drift in and out of consciousness, terrifying flashes of torture fill my mind until it feels like I'm sucked into the pits of hell itself.

I stare at a woman and watch as her face begins to change. It's subtle at first, then thorn-like bumps form on her forehead.

Shit.

I can only stare in horror as small spikes appear on her ears and black veins run along her lips, creeping over the rest of her face.

Bile rises in my throat as I realize I have a front-row seat to the unveiling of the monster that wants to end all of humanity, and the odds are good I'm going to die now.

God.

As I begin to come to terms with the fact that I won't be getting out of this hell alive, I slip up and think of Raighne.

Warmth immediately floods my chest, and it's so comforting to feel him, I almost let out a sob.

For the first time since I was captured, I lower my head so they can't see my eyes because I don't want them to know Raighne's able to sense what's happening.

"Ares," the woman hisses, "make her understand!"

A hand closes around my throat, and I wait for him to start squeezing, expecting to be suffocated. Instead of having my air supply cut off, an awful burning sensation starts at my feet, making its way slowly up my legs.

It feels as if my flesh is being scorched from my body, and I can't keep the screams from tearing loose. I writhe in agony, the burn increasing as it crawls up my body.

By the time it reaches my thighs, it feels like I'm on fire, burning from the inside out.

"Stop!" I scream, my voice hoarse. "Please."

I'm weeping from the unbearable pain, but there are no tears left to cool my face.

The man just stares at me, his eyes dead and merciless.

When I feel Raighne stirring in me, as if he's trying to pass some of his strength into my body, I sob out loud.

I want to push him away because I don't want him feeling any of this pain. Unable to stop Raighne, he flows through my mind, and as he floods my body, his warmth battles the fire, easing some of the blistering pain.

"Raighne," *I groan internally.* "I don't want you here. Leave."

"Never." *His voice is clear in my mind.* "I'll find you. Don't give up."

My whole body slumps, and totally exhausted, I just soak in Raighne's comforting presence.

Then another voice enters my mind, sounding threatening, "Tell her, or I will be forced to kill you slowly and hand your soul to her."

I shake my head as more sobs spill over my lips.

The sadistic bitch steps closer, enjoying my pain and despair. "You may stop, for now, Ares. Let's see whether our little bird is ready to sing."

The excruciating pain stops the minute he removes his hand, and I hang limply from where a rope is tied around my wrists.

"Tell me who the chosen ones are," *she demands.*

My body jerks as I come to, and it takes a moment before I realize Raighne's carrying me somewhere.

The vision I just had shudders through me, and I'm hit with a wave of utter despair.

Raighne must think I'm reacting to the pain of the wounds Brenna inflicted on me because he presses a kiss to my forehead and murmurs, "We'll be home soon, then you can rest."

I press my face to his shoulder, and unable to stop the tears, they soak into the leather of his shirt.

The sound of voices drifts to us, and soon, we're moving through the camp.

When we enter my living quarters, I pull my face away from his shoulder.

He carries me into the bedroom and lays me down on the covers. "Try to get some sleep."

I shake my head and stare at nothing in particular as the visions I've been having replay in my mind.

Raighne sits down on the side of the bed, and leaning over me, he braces a hand beside my hip. Tilting his head, he catches my eyes and says, "Talk to me."

I stare at his face, that's so familiar but at the same time foreign, and I remember how his strength flowed through me while I was being tortured.

My entire life has been thrown into chaos and the visions are only getting worse.

His eyes soften on me, and bringing his other hand to my face, he cups my cheek. "Talk to me, Alchera."

I hate it as the words leave my lips. "I'm scared."

"Of Brenna?" he asks.

I shake my head again, then admit, "I've been having visions."

Frown lines appear on his forehead, and his thumb brushes tenderly over my skin. "Want to tell me about them?"

I lean into his palm, and closing my eyes, I say, "The one I've had twice, I'm in a foreign city, and people are running around. There are bodies, their faces burned." I suck in a deep breath, trying to fight the despair flooding me just from thinking about it.

"Go on." Raighne encourages me, keeping his tone gentle.

"It's raining ash and debris," I whisper, my tone raw. "At some point, I look up to see where the ash is coming from, and there are dark clouds. The middle is swirling, and the edges of the black clouds are dark red as if it's been dipped in blood." I try really hard to keep my voice from trembling. "The clouds look like they're on fire." I take another deep breath, and my ribs feel tender. Exhaling, I continue, "I think a volcano is erupting." I glance down at my hands. "It erupts, and I'm not concerned about my own safety. I just feel empty...like a wasteland." I swallow hard. "I feel dark inside."

When I lift my eyes, it's to see a very concerned expression etched deep into Raighne's features.

I stare at him for a moment, wishing we could go back to being Jane and Ryan, just two teenagers without a care in the world.

Even though it's only been a day since he dragged me back to this world, it feels as if an eternity has passed.

Pulling away from Raighne, I scoot off the bed and walk to the window. Looking outside, I see the old oak tree's shadows in the dark.

I hear him stand up, and I take a deep breath, or as deep as my bruised ribs will allow, before I continue, "The part that bothers me most is when I turn around, and something slams into my chest."

I turn around to face Raighne, who's standing by the side of the bed.

Maybe I shouldn't tell him.

I contemplate it for a moment but then decide against keeping it a secret.

"I think someone is going to shoot me."

Looking at his worried face, I wait for him to say something.

"Did you see the person who's going to shoot you?" he asks, his tone tense.

I shake my head. "I only remember feeling an overwhelming need to get this person away from danger." I try harder to remember, then say, "You're there."

Raighne shakes his head hard. "If I'm there, then you won't get shot. If I'm with you, no harm will ever come to you."

"Really?" I wave my hand over my body. "What do you call this?" I regret the words the moment I say them. "Sorry, I didn't mean it. I'm just saying you can't stop everything that will happen to me. Shit happens."

His muscles strain as he stares at me, his expression downright scary.

Suddenly, my body jerks forward. I let out a startled shriek as I'm yanked through the air until I collide with Raighne. Pain shudders through me from the sudden movement.

Holy shit.

My hands slam against his shoulders, and I grab hold of them.

His arms wrap around me, and I'm shocked out of my everloving mind about how I just flew through the air.

"What the hell just happened?" I whisper, feeling panic bubble up inside of me.

It's only then I remember earlier on the field when the knife was ripped away from my throat, and I flew backward.

Oh my God.

His breaths are coming fast, then just as quick as it happened, he lets go of me and puts a safe distance between us.

"I'm sorry," is all he says before he turns around and leaves the bedroom.

Shit. Raighne just moved me clear across the room without touching me.

He has the power to move things.

Shaking my head, I wonder what else he can do that I don't know about.

Exhausted, I sink down on the side of the bed and stare at the floor. I wipe my hand over my forehead and once again try to make sense of the chaotic mess my life has become.

CHAPTER 12

ALCHERA

After not getting much sleep, I wake up while it's still dark out, feeling like a truck ran me over.

Every muscle aches so badly it takes me a few minutes just to get to my feet and to slowly stretch out.

Letting out a groan, I make my way to the tub and open the faucets. I brush my teeth and untangle my hair before getting a clean set of clothes from the cupboard.

God, I'm not looking forward to today at all.

Once the tub is full, I close the faucets. I strip out of my nightgown and sink into the balmy water.

Oh yeah, this is much better.

Slowly, my muscles begin to unwind, and I let out a satisfied moan.

Soooo much better.

I soak until the water starts to cool before I wash my body with my right hand, seeing as my left shoulder is still tender. I thought it would've hurt more but whatever the healer gave me must speed up the healing process.

Thank God for small mercies.

Once I'm done, I climb out of the tub and dry myself off before putting on the clean clothes. The more I move, the better I feel, and when I walk out of my living quarters, the sun's just starting to peek over the horizon.

Leaving the camp, I climb a hill that leads to Roark's camp, and at the top, I stand and watch as the sun rises.

The pinks and purples in the sky are beautiful, and for a while my mind is clear of all worries. I let my eyes roam over the natural beauty around me, and I get glimpses of a creek that's twisting through trees and shrubs to my left.

"Please tell me you didn't sleep out here," River suddenly says from behind me.

I turn around to face him while shaking my head. "I just got up early."

"I saw you standing out here and thought you could do with some coffee before the training," he says as he hands me a cup of coffee. "How do you feel?"

"Better." I take the much-appreciated caffeine from him. "Thanks."

We stand in silence for a while, just enjoying our beverages, then River says, "It will get easier with time."

I nod, my eyes drifting over the picturesque landscape.

A moment later, he says, "Come, it is time for breakfast before training."

Even though I didn't eat yesterday, I shake my head and hold my empty cup out to him. "You go ahead. I'm not hungry. Thanks again for the coffee."

Luckily, River doesn't argue, and when he walks back in the direction of our camp, I sit down on the grass and pull my knees up to my chest. Wrapping my arms around my shins, I stare at the fields and wildflowers.

The visions I've had fill my mind, and I wonder if all the

training isn't for nothing.

Will I be able to become stronger?

Will I save the chosen ten or die long before I can even try?

When I think of the billions of people that will be killed, my heart aches and frustration pours into my chest.

God, how can any of this be fair?

I hear movement behind me, and a second later, Raighne sits down beside me, resting his forearms on his knees.

Minutes pass as I stare at the flowers, then he asks, "How do you feel?"

"Better." I turn my head and let my eyes drift over his attractive features. "What happened last night?"

A heavy breath escapes his chest before he meets my gaze. "I can move things."

I nod. "Why didn't you tell me?"

"Because yesterday was the first time it happened."

"Oh!" My eyebrows lift. "Well, congrats on getting a new power."

It's better than having visions.

"Talent," he corrects me. "We call them talents."

Giving him a curious look, I ask, "Do you have any other talents I don't know about?"

The corner of his mouth lifts, and he climbs to his feet. Reaching a hand out to me, he says, "You'll find out soon enough."

When I take his hand, his fingers wrap around mine. He pulls me to my feet and doesn't let go immediately but instead steps closer to me.

He lifts his other arm, and his fingers brush over the cut on my throat that's healing much faster than it would've on Earth.

Something electric ignites between us, and it rushes through my body.

Oh wow.

All the emotions this man has made me feel since we first met flood my chest. Once again, I stand before him with a racing heart and fluttering stomach, trying my best not to fall in love.

It feels like I'm fighting a losing battle, and unable to hold back, I close the distance between us and wrap my arms around his waist. Hugging him might be overstepping, but I really need it right now.

Luckily, he doesn't push me away but instead wraps me up in a tight embrace.

Closing my eyes, I take a deep breath of his scent.

He smells so good.

I wish I could just stay in his arms and forget about everyone and everything.

Raighne's hand brushes up and down my back, and he presses a kiss to the top of my head. It feels like something a protective father would do and not a man who's romantically interested in me.

Shoot.

Reluctantly, I pull back while trying to hide the disappointment I feel.

"I better get my butt to training," I mutter, my tone sounding awkward.

He just nods, and when we start to walk, I say, "You don't have to come with me. I can find the field on my own."

"Where you go, I go," he grumbles.

Glancing up, I see a frown on his forehead. He actually looks upset.

"Did I do something wrong?" I ask, wondering if hugging him was crossing a line.

He shakes his head but doesn't meet my eyes.

When we near the field, I see two people standing beneath a canopy of trees.

The man looks different from the others I've seen, his light brown hair cut short, whereas Raighne and River wear theirs a bit longer. His eyes are so light they remind me of ice.

The woman is a different story altogether. She doesn't look friendly at all as she practically gives me the evil eye.

She's tall and built quite muscular and can probably kick my ass like Brenna did.

"Peace be, Princess Alchera." Both voices pipe up at the same time. It sounds like a rehearsed phrase.

I try not to scowl at the princess part. "Morning, just call me Alchera."

The guy is the first to smile, while the scowl remains on the girl's face.

"I'm Storm, and this is Blair. Don't mind her, she doesn't speak much."

Just then, I hear Roark call out, "Training will begin now."

As I turn around, I see Raighne standing to the side, talking with River. Great, just what I need, spectators to watch me make a total ass of myself.

Raighne's eyes flick to me, and he stares for a moment before returning his attention to whatever River's saying.

"Alchera, Storm will show you how to hold and handle a knife while I finish yesterday's session with Blair," Roark orders, pulling me out of my thoughts.

"Sure thing," I say as I turn to face Storm.

Nerves begin to spin in my stomach because if he trains me the same way as Brenna, they're going to have to scrape my dead body up off the grass.

Here goes nothing.

Instead of jumping into action and kicking my ass, Storm gives me a patient smile. "Watch how I hold the knife. It's important so you don't cut yourself by accident."

As I watch the way his fingers wrap around the handle, a slow smile spreads across my face. He swipes the blade expertly through the air and then holds it out to me. "Your turn."

I take it carefully and hold it the way he showed me.

"Your hands are smaller. I suggest you hold the handle here for better grip." He slides my hand further up the handle, and my grip feels firmer.

Storm turns out to be a patient teacher, which I appreciate after the two days from hell I've just had.

After a three-hour session of holding and stabbing, I'm not tired at all. Unlike yesterday, where after ten minutes, it felt like I was dying.

Roark finishes up with Blair, and as he heads toward us, Storm takes the knife from me.

"Thanks for being patient with me," I say. "I really appreciate it."

The corner of Storm's mouth lifts in a genuine smile. "You're welcome. Just keep practicing, and you'll get the hang of it."

When Roark reaches me, his eyes lock with mine. "How do you feel today?"

I stare at my brother's face, that's so similar to mine, and try not to focus on the sense of loss because I never really got the chance to know him before now.

I swallow the lump of emotion in my throat and answer, "Better. Thanks."

"That's good." He places his hand on the small of my back, then says, "The first thing you do in the event of an attack is to bend your knees slightly so you can move swiftly and bounce on the balls of your feet."

I do as I'm told and get a satisfied nod from him.

God, I have a big brother.

The emotions threaten to overwhelm me as he orders, "Now

you'll practice kicking. Stand as you are, then go down to the grass as if you're doing a squat. Coming back up into your original standing position, bring your right leg up until your foot is at knee level with your left leg."

I do as I'm told and look at his face as he nods. "Yes, like that. Now, when you kick out, use only your leg muscles. Keep your upper body still."

I'm so damn happy he's pleased with what I'm doing that it quickly gets easier to perform the kick.

"Use your arms to balance yourself. Hold them out in front of your chest as if you're getting ready to punch someone." Roark adjusts my arms a little, placing my right arm a bit higher than my left.

"With your left arm, you need to block. With your right, you'll punch while kicking."

"I'm left-handed," I tell him.

"Okay, then just switch hands."

I adjust my arms and carry out the move while ignoring the pain in my shoulder. A grin spreads over my face when I get it right.

"Good," my brother praises me. "Keep practicing."

As the hours pass, I get better, and the exercise feels good.

By the time the sun starts to set, my stomach grumbles something fierce, and it has Roark saying, "Let's call it a day. You did well. Same time, same place, tomorrow morning."

Feeling like we've bonded a little today, I smile at him. "Thank you for taking the time to train me."

He nods, and lifting a hand, he gives my right shoulder a squeeze. "Go get something to eat, then rest."

"Have a good night," I say, watching as he walks toward River before they head back to the camp.

Storm and Blair also leave, and when it's just me and Raighne,

I grin at my guardian. "I actually learned something today."

"I saw," he murmurs, not returning my smile.

Damn, is he still upset from the hug I gave him?

He starts to walk back to our campsite, and I follow behind him, wondering why a hug would upset him so much. It's not like I professed my undying love to him.

Geez, he's making a big deal out of nothing.

When we reach my living quarters, Raighne just nods at me before heading to his own tent.

I'm staring at his back when I hear Fleur snap, "Where have you been? I've looked all over."

I turn my head to her. "I was training with Roark and Storm."

Her eyes widen. "Oh wow. That's such good news. They're the best, and you'll learn fast." The surprise fades from her face, and she gives me a serious look. "But next time, let me know. When I brought your breakfast and found the tent empty, I almost had a heart attack."

Frowning at her, I ask, "Why?"

She takes my hand and tugs me into my tent, looking as if she's about a share one hell of a secret with me.

She glances around, then leans in and whispers, "I thought Adeth got a hold of you."

Having heard the name before, I ask, "Who's Adeth?"

Fleur's eyes widen with shock, and her grip on my hand tightens. "You don't know about her?"

"No."

"We're not supposed to talk about her," she whispers. "She wants to end all life on Earth. She doesn't want humankind to survive." Fleur glances around the living room again, looking anxious as she continues, "I've heard she wants you so she can stop you from retrieving the chosen ones. You have to be careful. She's dark and powerful. Always be on guard and never go anywhere alone."

What the everloving hell?

"You've got to be shitting me," I mutter. "Are you telling me I have some psycho woman coming after me?"

Fleur steps closer to me. "We'll keep you safe. I just thought you should know so you don't wander off alone."

Remembering my vision from the night before, my eyes widen. I quickly pull my hand from Fleur's and turn my head away so she can't see the worry on my face.

"I'm pretty hungry," I say. "Want to go get us some food?"

"Oh yes. Of course." Luckily, she doesn't pick up on my change of mood and she quickly leaves.

Adeth.

Is that the name of the woman I saw in my vision? The one with the guy called Ares? Are they a team?

God, does the vision mean they'll get a hold of me?

I remember the agonizing burning, and wrapping my arms around my middle, my teeth worry my bottom lip.

When Fleur returns with two plates of meat, veggies, and mashed potatoes, my appetite is long gone.

I take a seat and give her a smile as she hands one of the plates to me.

Not wanting to talk about Adeth, I steer the conversation in a different direction by asking, "Is there something going on between you and River?"

Fleur almost chokes on the bite she just took and clears her throat before asking, "What makes you think that?"

"You almost choking, for one." I force a grin to my face. "You really like him a lot, don't you?"

Worry flashes over her pretty face. "By Awo, is it that obvious?"

Not wanting her to panic, I shake my head. "I just picked up on the way you look at each other." I scoop a bit of the mashed potatoes onto the fork, then add, "I think you'll make a cute couple."

"The way we look at each other?" she asks, her cheeks turning pink. "River doesn't even know I exist."

I lock eyes with her. "Trust me, girl. He knows. You're the nicest person I've met on Vaalbara, and I'm sure he sees it too."

A wide smile spreads over her face. "Do you really think so?"

"Of course. You're beautiful, and he'd be blind not to see you."

A dreamy expression fills her eyes, then she leans forward and whispers, "I've had a crush on him for years. Don't tell anyone."

"Your secret's safe with me."

We chat about random things while we enjoy our food, and when Fleur collects our empty plates, she says, "Don't run off without me tomorrow."

"Do you mind getting up early?" I ask.

"Why?"

"I'd like to watch the sunrise."

She nods, then says, "See you at the crack of dawn."

"Bring coffee," I add before she can disappear out the door.

"Will do," she chuckles.

I get up from the chair and head to the bedroom. While I go through my nightly routine, my thoughts alternate between Raighne's behavior today and the visions.

Once I'm dressed in a white nightgown, I walk to the living room and stand in the open doorway. My eyes drift over the other tents and a bonfire where a group of people are sitting on logs.

When I see Fleur sitting beside River, the corner of my mouth lifts.

I recognize Storm, then my eyes land on Raighne. He's smiling at something a woman says, and there's an unexpected burst of jealousy in my chest.

Not wanting to see anymore, I turn around and walk to one of the chairs. Taking a seat, I pull my legs up and rest my chin on my knees.

Thinking back to when Raighne pretended to be my friend and how happy I was, the crack in my heart runs deeper.

I looked forward to finding his truck parked in front of my house and our short drives to school. I miss all the times we sat by the waterfall talking about our lives.

Come to think of it, I did most of the talking.

I let out a sigh, and intense loneliness digs its claws into my heart.

Yeah, being on Vaalbara, nothing has changed. I'm just as alone here as I was on Earth.

At least I have Fleur.

I hear movement, and turning my gaze to the doorway, I see the woman from the bonfire and Raighne standing a few feet away from my tent.

She gives his arm a possessive squeeze while saying, "Get a good night's rest."

"You too," he replies.

I quickly look away when Raighne begins to turn his head in my direction.

I hear him come into my living quarters and hate that I feel excited because he's here.

He takes a seat across from me, and resting his forearms on his thighs, he links his hands. I can feel his eyes burning on me, but I refuse to meet them.

"Have you had any other visions?" he asks.

My heart sinks heavily in my chest because it's clear he doesn't have a personal interest in me. He's just here to do his job.

I clear my throat and lie, "No." Climbing to my feet, I walk to my bedroom while saying, "I'll let you know if I have another vision. Good night."

I don't hear him get up and leave as I crawl beneath the covers. Gripping the extra pillow to my chest, I listen for any sign that Raighne's still here.

Long minutes pass before I hear a chair creak, and my heart instantly starts beating faster.

I see his shadow fall in the bedroom's doorway, and I close my eyes, pretending to be asleep.

When I hear him move closer to the bed, I struggle to keep my breaths even.

He places his hand on my forehead and keeps still for a moment.

What's he doing?

Does he know I'm awake?

Probably.

"Why are you pretending to be asleep?" he asks as he sits down on the side of the bed, the mattress dipping under his weight.

He moves his hand to my shoulder, and feeling his skin on mine, tingles rush over my body.

"I'm tired," I whisper.

He's quiet for a moment, then asks, "You didn't have any other visions besides the one of being shot?"

The vision of Adeth flashes through my mind, and Raighne's grip on my shoulder tightens.

He pushes me to lie on my back, and leaning over me, his eyes burn into mine. "Tell me about the vision."

"I did," I lie.

He shakes his head, anger tightening his features. "The one of Adeth."

How did he know? I didn't tell anyone.

Acting ignorant, I ask, "Who's Adeth?"

134

Raighne stares at me for a while before he says, "You can trust me."

It has nothing to do with trust. I'm just not ready to talk about it.

He lets out a heavy sigh, then lets go of me. "Fine. We'll talk when you're ready, but don't wait too long. It's important for you to tell me what you see in your visions so I know what to expect."

As he climbs to his feet, a frown forms on my forehead. It feels like Raighne is able to anticipate what I'm thinking without me having to say anything.

Feeling unnerved, I watch as he leaves the room.

God, I miss the easy-going friendship we had on Earth.

This...whatever's between us...just sucks all kinds of ass.

CHAPTER 13

RAIGHNE

Watching Alchera move through all the actions Roark has taught her the past two months, a heaviness fills my chest.

She says she hasn't had any more visions, but whenever I touch her, I get glimpses of them.

She's seen Adeth and Ares, and it fills me with dread.

Few people know Adeth is my aunt, and Ares my cousin. They turned dark after my mother died, and nothing any of us said changed their minds about destroying Earth.

I know Alchera's visions can change, and they're not set in stone, but just the thought that it might happen makes me want to hide her somewhere no one can find her.

But I can't do that. She has a destiny to fulfill.

With my eyes glued to her, I feel frustrated that she hides her visions from me. It tells me she doesn't trust me, and I'm not going to lie, it hurts.

There was a morning, not long after she got back to Vaalbara, when I thought I felt a spark between us, but since then, there's a gaping distance I can't cross.

Alchera won't let me.

She loses her balance and falls flat on her butt, laughter exploding from her and echoing over the field.

When Storm helps her to her feet, there's a twisting sensation in my chest, and before I can stop myself, I take a couple of steps closer.

I hate seeing him touch her, a possessive feeling bursting in my chest.

She's mine.

Storm pats her on the shoulder, and I fist my hands at my sides.

She's only your charge, and it doesn't mean you have a right to claim her.

Alchera is the only one who gets to choose who she'll marry.

My brothers are lucky in that regard. Brenna and Thana have chosen them, and it's made the bond between them so much stronger.

Alchera lets out a chuckle, but when her eyes land on me, her smile fades, and she quickly looks away.

Awo, will she ever forgive me for what happened on Earth?

No matter how many times I tell her I didn't pretend to be her friend and it was all real, she refuses to believe me.

Letting out a sigh, I cross my arms over my chest and glance at the surrounding area.

Soon, we'll leave for the desert so we can work on our telepathic connection. I've put off telling Alchera about it because I know it's going to upset her when she learns she has to let me into her mind.

Another heavy sigh escapes me, and then I see River and Fleur smiling lovingly at each other.

My eyes flick back to Alchera, who's sparing with Storm while Roark gives them instructions.

Storm gets Alchera in a chokehold, and when her body strains against his, I don't think and just react. Within seconds, I use my talent to rip Alchera away from Storm, a threatening growl rumbling from my chest.

When Alchera slams into my chest, Storm's features are tense as he glances around us.

"What's wrong?" Roark asks, also checking the area for any sign of danger as River moves closer to him.

Everyone's on guard from my irrational behavior.

Fuck. I screwed up.

I let go of Alchera, who's staring at me with wide eyes and parted lips.

Not knowing how to explain myself, I shake my head and mutter, "My mistake."

Walking away, anger pours into my chest, and only when I'm out of hearing distance from the others do I snap at myself, "What the hell was that?"

I suck in a deep breath, and feeling the intense jealousy burning in my veins, I shake my head.

I have to get my shit together where Alchera's concerned.

But it's hard caring about her and keeping romantic feelings out of the picture.

Especially when she's taking everything so well and getting stronger by the day. Instead of hating us for what we did to her, she's moved on and tried her best to meet every high standard that's been thrown her way.

It's earned my respect and that of everyone else.

I turn around and watch as she gets back to training.

And by Awo, she's so fucking beautiful.

With her body becoming more toned, it's hard not to notice her curves. I'm actually relieved she refuses to wear skirts and insists on long pants.

With my heart pounding in my chest and my emotions for Alchera growing by the second, it's hard to shove it all to the back of my mind so I can focus on my job as her guardian.

ALCHERA

Things have been both good and weird.

Good, because training has been going really well, and I've grown closer to Roark. It's incredible having an older brother, and I've loved getting to know him better.

My friendship with Fleur has deepened, and for the first time in my life, I have a friend I can gossip with. Spending time with her is always fun, and I've had a front-row seat to her and River falling in love.

A smile curves my lips when I think of their blossoming relationship, but then my thoughts turn to Raighne, and my heart clenches painfully.

With every passing day, he's putting more distance between us. He's downright grumpy most of the time, and it's starting to get to me.

I have no idea what I've done to upset him.

Lost in my thoughts, I stare at the bag on my bed.

"You're not done packing?" Raighne's voice rumbles behind me. "Everyone already left for the desert."

"I'm packing," I mutter as I shove a pair of pants into the bag.

"You have ten minutes," he orders. "Bring only the essentials."

When he stalks out of the room, my heart hurts, and I let out a heavy sigh.

I do as I'm told and hurry to get everything into the backpack so I don't upset him even more.

I almost forget the most important item of all and squeeze one of my pillows into the bag.

If I'm sleeping out in the desert, I want my favorite pillow for comfort.

"Alchera, are you ready to go?" Fleur calls.

"Yeah, I've just finished packing." I shrug the strap of the bag over my shoulder and head into the living room.

"I came to give you this." She holds out a little brown vial to me.

"What is it?" I ask as I take it from her.

"I made you an elixir. It will give you clarity of mind when you're tired and discouraged, seeing as you won't have my awesomeness there to cheer you up."

"What do you know that I don't?" I mutter as I tuck the vial into my bag.

"Nothing."

"I wish you could come," I say as I pull her into a tight hug. "I'm going to miss you."

"I'm going to miss you, too." Her voice sounds sad, and it makes me hold her a few seconds longer.

"Alchera," Raighne grumbles from outside.

I let go of my friend, and when I hurry out of the tent, it's to see Raighne sitting on a massive black horse.

Crap, I've never been on a horse.

I glance around and not seeing another horse, I'm not sure what to do.

"Come," Raighne orders.

Oh, just my luck, we're sharing a horse.

I walk closer, not sure how I'm going to get on the beast.

Raighne takes my backpack and fastens it to the side of the saddle, then reaches down to me.

Reluctantly, I place my hand in this, and the next second I fly up, and my butt hits the horse's back hard. Sitting sideways on the horse, I grab hold of Raighne's shirt so I don't fall off while shooting him a glare.

"Dammit," I hiss at him. "You don't have to manhandle me."

"The others have already left, and we need to catch up," he mutters, then he digs his heels into the horse's sides.

When the beast sets off at a fast gallop, I let out a shriek and grab hold of Raighne.

Oh God, I'm going to leave an imprint of myself on his chest.

An uncomfortable silence wraps around us, and for a long while, there's only the sound of the horse's hooves slamming down on the ground.

When we see the others up ahead, Raighne slows his horse down a little, and I feel his chest expand as he sucks in a deep breath.

Loosening my hold on Raighne, I try to put an inch of space between us without falling off.

Suddenly, Raighne's voice rumbles above my head. "Once we get to the desert, we're going to work on our telepathic link."

I glance up at him. "Telepathic link?"

Being so close to him does things to my insides, and I squirm.

Raighne's eyes flick to mine, then he drops the bomb of all bombs on me. "Besides being able to feel what you feel, I can hear your thoughts, and with training, we'll be able to communicate telepathically."

Say what now?

My mouth drops open as what he just said sinks in, then I mutter, "You're kidding."

No.

God, say it ain't so.

He can hear my thoughts?

NoNoNoNoNo.

I swallow hard as an overwhelming feeling of mortification floods me.

Does this mean he's heard my every thought? Even the ones about him?

Oh God, take me now.

My voice trembles as I ask, "Have you heard everything? Even when we were on Earth?"

This is so, so very bad.

That explains a lot. No wonder he's upset with me.

My shoulders sag, and I wish the ground would just open up and swallow me whole. I've never been this embarrassed in my life.

Raighne slows the horse to a stop, then says, "I can control listening to your thoughts and only listen to them when I feel a strong emotion from you."

My feelings for him are pretty strong, so he must know about them.

Kill. Me. Now.

"I worked on controlling it before I went to retrieve you, and right now, I have to touch you in order to hear them clearly."

I scoot another inch away from him.

When he reaches for my face, I jerk my head backward. "You just said you can hear my thoughts clearly if you touch me, so I'd appreciate it if you don't touch me right now."

He lets out another sigh. "Look at me."

I shake my head, glancing at the others as the distance between us and them grows again.

"So, you know everything I've thought about?" I ask, not happy at all.

"No. I've only checked on your thoughts a few times."

Ugh.

"What did you hear?"

"That you weren't being truthful about the visions."

My head snaps to him, and I meet his eyes. "So you know what's going to happen?"

He nods, a serious expression on his face. "Why are you hiding the vision of Adeth from me?"

My shoulders slump, and I look away again. "I don't want to talk about it. It's too upsetting."

"You have to tell me about the visions so I can be prepared. Visions aren't set in stone, and the future can be altered."

My eyes fly back to his. "Really?"

He nods. "So don't keep them from me."

"Okay."

He nudges the horse to start walking again.

Needing to be sure, I ask, "So you only heard the visions and not other things I was thinking about?"

"Yes."

I relax a little. "Can you hear everyone's thoughts?"

Raighne shakes his head. "No, just yours. It is part of the guardian-charge bond. That way, we know when our charges are in trouble. You can call for me like you did when Robert attacked you. It also makes it easier for me to find you should we be separated. I can see through your eyes and sense where you are."

He goes silent for a bit, and all I can think is holy shit.

"Feeling what you feel only helps me so much, but allowing me to see where you are helps me track you down."

God, now that I know Raighne can read my mind, I have to control my thoughts.

That's if he's not lying, and he already knows about my unwelcome crush on him.

Under no circumstances do you think of your feelings for him. Shut that shit down.

CHAPTER 14

ALCHERA

Slowly, the landscape changes from the forests and lush green fields to sand, dunes, and rocks as far as the eye can see.

Raighne wasn't joking when he said we're going to the desert. My ass hurts from sitting on a horse for hours.

"How long will we be here?" I ask as we reach the area where the others have stopped for a break.

"A month."

"What?" I gasp. "Why so long?"

"It all depends on how quickly we strengthen our telepathic bond. We might be able to head back sooner."

Raighne slides from the horse and placing both his hands on my hips, he lifts me off. I grab hold of his shoulders to make sure I don't fall and try to ignore the fluttering sensation in my stomach.

When my feet touch the ground again, my legs feel weird.

"Finally," Storm calls out. "What took you so long?"

Raighne lets go of me, his features drawn tight as if he's angry.

When he starts to walk away, the words burst from me. "Why do you do that? What do I do wrong that upsets you so much?"

He just shakes his head. "Nothing, Alchera." He points toward Storm. "Don't keep your *friend* waiting."

I stand like a confused idiot and watch him stalk away.

"Everyone gather closer," Roark calls out.

Letting out a sigh, I join the group, counting ten people in total.

Seeing Brenna and Finian, my heart sinks.

There's a man and woman who look around the same age as me. But with everyone being immortal, I can't tell for sure how old they are.

Where the woman has silver hair, the man's is golden. They look like brother and sister.

When Finian walks closer to me, I'm a little surprised.

"Peace be, Alchera. I am Finian, Brenna's guardian. We didn't get to officially meet the last time."

No shit.

"Don't be rude to my brother," Raighne's voice suddenly sounds in my mind.

"What the hell?" I gasp, a wave of shock rippling over my body.

Now many things have startled the hell out of me, and there have been times I've wanted to pee my pants since arriving on Vaalbara, but hearing Raighne in my mind takes the cake.

Finian looks at me with confusion in his eyes.

"Sorry, I just heard Raighne in my mind for the first time."

Finian nods, clearly understanding my crazy talk. "You'll get used to it."

Yeah, I don't think so.

He pats me on the shoulder before walking back to where Brenna's standing.

Telepathy? Sharing of feelings and hearing my thoughts?

It's all too much.

Even with all the open space of sand and rocks around me, I start to feel claustrophobic.

"Peace be, Princess," a soft voice says behind me.

When I turn around, I get a closer look at the woman with silver hair. Her eyes are dark silver, and never in my life have I seen skin as white as hers.

"Hi," I say, forcing a smile to my lips.

"I'm Luna," She points to the guy with the golden hair. "And that's my twin brother, Lucius."

"Are you also here to train?" I ask.

She nods.

Feeling curious, I ask, "What kind of talents do you have?"

"Nothing as important as yours," she chuckles. "My talent is to control moonlight. I'm here to find out what I can do with it."

I notice her brother walking toward us.

"Lucius, come. Let me introduce you," she says, her smile growing wider.

I see the love she has for her brother as she talks to him, and it makes me relax even more.

Suddenly, one hell of an intense pain rushes through me, forcing me down. My knees hit the ground hard, and I dig my fingers into the hot sand.

Jesus.

It feels as if my body is being ripped to shreds.

"Alchera!" I hear Raighne call out, but he sounds miles away.

Images start to flash through my mind, and I'm unable to hold back the scream as it tears from me while my vision goes black.

Adeth disappears, and relief washes over me.

I can still feel her nails digging into my cheek and the blood trickling down to my jaw.

My wrists are raw, where they're tied to a rope hanging from the ceiling.

I can't take much more of this.

Ares begins to advance on me, and as he pulls his arm back, I shut my eyes tightly.

All the pain is getting the better of me. I'm sure I'm dying.

His fist slams so hard into my gut all I can do is gag for air. My body swings from the impact, but it doesn't stop him.

He grabs me by the hair, and I have no time to recover before the next blow slams into my ribs.

Excruciating pain becomes the sum of my being, and it feels as if every agonizing breath might be my last.

But, the relief of death doesn't come, only a new level of pain when a whip cracks over my already raw and bloody flesh.

Coming too, a sob escapes me, then I whimper, "It hurts."

Arms are holding me tightly, and I feel warmth flood my body, chasing away the chill and pain left behind by the vision.

Feeling sick, I push against Raighne and manage to turn to the side before I vomit whatever I had to eat earlier in the day.

My body convulses horribly, and when I slump back against him, a flask of water appears in front of my face.

"Drink some," he orders.

With trembling hands, I grip hold of the flask. I take a sip and rinse out my mouth before I drink greedy gulps of the cool water.

I hand the flask back to Raighne, and pressing a hand to my stomach, I try to breathe through the horror left behind by the vision.

I'm going to die an agonizing death.

A sob bursts over my lips, and I quickly cover my mouth with my hand.

"No, you're not," I hear Raighne's voice clearly in my mind.

He helps me to my feet, then says, "Come. Let's go to Roark." His arm wraps around my shoulders, and he holds me tightly to his side. *"You can't talk about your visions in front of everyone. Only*

Roark, Finian, and Brenna can hear the details."

Raighne helps me walk, and when we reach Roark and the others, he asks, "What did you see?"

I frown as I look up at him. "Didn't you see?"

He shakes his head. "I can't follow you when you have a vision. I can only see when you think about it after you've had the vision."

I suck in a deep breath of air while pressing a hand to my stomach again.

Raighne steps closer. "Can you think of it again? Let me see."

"No!" I shake my head wildly.

My chin starts to tremble, and I feel the tears coming. I don't want to be weak, but it was horrible.

There's no way I want to relive any of it ever again.

Brenna steps forward, her face an unreadable mask. I'm surprised when her voice doesn't hold the usual bite. "What did you see?"

"I can't," I gasp, a tear spiraling down my cheek.

I try my best to block the memory, but the image of the man flashes through my mind, his lifeless eyes burned into my memory.

I suck in a trembling breath. "I see a man, but I don't know him."

Raighne's head snaps toward the others, and his features are tense with anger. "She saw Ares."

Taking hold of my shoulder, he pulls me to his chest, and when his arms wrap around me, his warmth gives me instant relief from the hell I just experienced.

"How many visions has she had?" Brenna asks.

"A few. One that I know of has come to pass. She saw me coming to get her," Raighne says, his voice sounding downright predatory.

"What else has she seen?" Roark asks.

Pulling away from Raighne, I clear my throat and answer, "I've seen a volcano erupting, the aftermath, and then someone shooting me." I wrap my arms around myself before I add, "I've also had a vision of Adeth and Ares before. They...they..." I shake my head.

They're going to kill me.

"*No, they won't,*" Raighne growls in my mind. "*Not while I'm alive.*"

"You haven't had any visions of the chosen ones?" Brenna seems surprised as she asks the question.

"Not that I'm aware of." My head begins to pound, and my stomach feels like it's stuck on spin cycle.

I can't talk about any of this anymore. I need to be alone.

"We should let her take a break," Raighne says, his tone unyielding. "We can look into the visions later when she feels more rested."

"Let her rest and let the memories fade," Brenna snaps. "This isn't about your precious Alchera, Raighne. It's about the chosen ones."

Before any of us can reply to her outburst, she storms off, with Finian following after her.

I turn in the opposite direction and start walking, trying to focus on processing the vision so I can file it away under shit I never want to see again.

"Come." Raighne suddenly takes my hand and leads me down an incline. It gets really steep, and he wraps an arm around my waist to keep me from falling as we climb to the bottom.

He takes hold of my hand again, and we walk for quite a distance. Not that I mind. It gives me time to think about what happened.

God. It was awful.

"*I won't let anything happen to you,*" he reassures me.

I have to admit, this time, it feels soothing hearing him in my frazzled mind.

He lets go of my hand and wraps his arm around my shoulders, tugging me to his side.

Right now, I don't care about whatever issue there is between us, I just need to be close to him.

The terrain begins to change and patches of grass appear here and there, but nothing to get too excited about.

We walk around a massive boulder, and I let out a surprised gasp when I see the most beautiful sight.

"It's a waterfall," I breathe.

Raighne lets out a huff. "It's the best I can do under the circumstances."

"Oh my God," I whisper. "Thank you so much."

I quickly take off my boots, and not caring about my clothes, I walk into the pool of refreshingly cool water.

Jesus, now this is food for my soul.

I move my hands through the water as I head in deeper until the pool reaches my chest.

I hear water splashing behind me, and when I glance over my shoulder, I see Raighne making his way to me. When he reaches me, he takes hold of my waist and lifts me against his body.

My lips part on a gasp as I grab hold of his shoulders.

"Wrap your legs around me," he orders, his tone low and gravely.

I do as I'm told while he carries me deeper into the pool.

His left hand grips my thigh, his fingers skimming my butt, and my eyebrows almost pop right off my head as they fly into my hairline.

Don't think.

Don't think.

Don't think.

"What are you doing?" he mutters, actually sounding amused.

"Keeping you out of my mind," I mutter.

Glancing over my shoulder, I see he's taking us toward the curtain of the waterfall, and when he steps beneath it, all I can hear is the rushing of water.

It feels so good.

Cool water pelts my hot skin and shivers race over my body.

The weirdest thing happens, and I begin to feel the energy of nature flow through me, soaking into my soul. It feels as if I'm being recharged.

Raighne moves out from beneath the spray into a cave-like area behind the waterfall's curtain.

When I look at his face there's a smile tugging at the corner of his mouth. "Feeling nature is one of your talents."

Right. I forgot about that.

"Why haven't I felt it before?"

"You did. The peace and calm while watching the sunrise. Recharging after school at Fish Creek Falls."

"Oh yeah."

It feels as if we're in our own little cocoon, and I never want to leave.

Raighne looks deep into my eyes, and his features soften.

"I'll always take care of you. Your needs and safety come first."

I nod, and just needing to be close to him, I wrap my arms around him and press my face into the crook of his neck.

"Thank you," I send the words to him.

He presses a kiss to the side of my head. *"Feeling better?"*

"Yes."

I pull back a little, and when I realize how close Raighne's face is to mine, I freeze like a deer in oncoming traffic.

His breath skims over my skin, and as our eyes lock, there's one hell of an intense fluttering in my stomach.

The droplets running down his tanned skin make him look next-level hot, and I swallow hard on the attraction I feel for him.

Lord, have mercy on my ovaries.

The second the thought crosses my mind, I shove away from Raighne and free myself from his hold.

Ducking beneath the water, I swim in the direction of the embankment while I consider drowning myself right here, right now.

I come up for air and make my way out of the pool. Not caring that my feet are wet, I struggle to put on my boots, but before I can make a run for it, Raighne steps out of the water.

I make a huge mistake when I glance at him, and seeing the leather clinging to his muscled body like a second skin, my abdomen clenches hard.

Shit. Don't look.

"What happened?" Raighne asks, his tone tense again.

Feigning ignorance, I shake my head. "What do you mean?"

"You're blocking me from your mind."

"I am?" My head snaps up. "You can't read my mind right now?"

"No." He shakes his head, and I let out a breath of relief.

Thank you, sweet baby Jesus.

Raighne narrows his eyes on me. "Is something wrong?"

I quickly shake my head. "Not at all. I just needed privacy." His eyes search mine, and I add, "Really, besides the vision from hell, I'm fine. Thank you for bringing me to the waterfall."

He seems to be satisfied with my explanation, and once we have our boots on, he says, "Let's return to the group."

I nod, and falling into step beside him, I'm grateful when he doesn't try to make conversation, because I'm too focused on hiding my attraction from him.

CHAPTER 15

ALCHERA

When we get back to the campsite, everyone stares at me as if I'm the weirdest thing they've ever seen.

"They're not looking at you like you're weird. What you're seeing is a group of people concerned for your welfare." Raighne's voice sounds in my mind.

"Uh-huh," I mumble.

"Is she rested now?" Brenna snaps, the bite back in her tone.

"Yeah, Raighne, she sure looks concerned."

"Enough, Brenna, she's our sister," Roark's voice booms over us. "How can you vow to protect her when you can't even show her any support?"

I watch as her expression changes to respectful, then she murmurs, "I apologize."

Oh wow. At least someone can control her.

"Do you feel better, Alchera? We don't want to strain you too much so soon after your vision," Roark says.

Ugh, I really don't want to talk about the visions.

Letting out a slow breath, I nod. "I feel better. Thanks for asking."

Raighne surprises me by speaking on my behalf. "Alchera won't be able to talk about the vision. I felt her pain, and I can understand why."

Brenna steps up to us, her eyes blazing. "It's not for you to decide what she does and doesn't share, guardian. The chosen ones–"

"Quiet, Brenna," Raighne's voice is downright icy. "I'm Alchera's guardian, and it's for *me* to decide what's best for *her*. She's my charge, and I get the final say regarding her life. She won't talk about it, and don't forget the role you play in all of this. You're only here to assist her."

I'm practically gaping at Raighne by the time he's done laying into Brenna.

I know he's my guardian, but not about the part that he gets the final say in my life.

What does that mean?

His eyes snap to me. *"It means nothing in your life happens without my approval."*

"Like hell!"

"Not now, Alchera," he snaps. *"We'll talk about this later."*

Anger bubbles in my chest, and I decide to walk away before I say something I'll regret.

Heading to where Storm is standing, I take deep breaths to cool my temper.

When Storm glances in my direction, a smile tugs at his mouth. "You didn't look well earlier? Are you okay?"

"Yeah," I mutter. Stopping near him, I cross my arms over my chest. "I'll get over it."

Just like I've had to get over everything else.

Storm glances around us, and his eyes stop on Luna. When he stares for a moment too long, my eyebrow lifts, but I don't say anything.

"We're not stopping here," he mentions. "We'll camp near the waterfall."

"Oh, I've just been there. It's pretty."

He lets out a chuckle. "It's where we'll bathe."

Surprised, I gasp, "Like, all of us?"

When he nods, I start shaking my head. "I'm not bathing next to you."

A burst of laughter explodes from him. "Stop stressing. We'll take turns."

I give him a playful slap on the shoulder. "Now is not the time to joke with me."

He shrugs. "Hey, at least I made you smile."

Locking eyes with Storm, I say, "Thanks. I needed it."

Everyone starts to move to their horses, and it has him saying, "Let's move out so we can set up camp."

"See you at the waterfall," I tease him before I turn away and walk to where Raighne's adjusting the straps on the horse.

When I reach my grumpy guardian, he doesn't even bother looking at me as he mutters, "You and Storm seem to get along really well."

I shrug. "He's a good friend."

His eyes flick to me for a second. "Just a friend?"

I narrow my eyes on Raighne. "What's with the twenty questions?"

He lets out a sigh before climbing onto the horse without any effort. "Forget, I asked."

He reaches down to me, and when I place my hand in his, he pulls me up to sit in front of him. Instead of sitting sideways, I straddle the horse with my back to Raighne.

"Comfortable?" he asks as his arms wrap around me to take hold of the reins.

I glance down at his forearms and shamelessly drink in the

sight of the veins snaking beneath his tanned skin.

"Alchera," he says to get my attention. "I asked whether you're comfortable?"

My cheeks flame up, and I nod quickly.

Praying to all that's holy he didn't pick up on me drooling over him, I ask, "Did Roark train you as well?"

It's the first question I could think of.

"No." He nudges the horse to start galloping, then answers, "I was trained by my father."

Hearing the love in his voice, I say, "It sounds like you respect your father a lot. I've heard only good things about him."

"He's the greatest guardian there is." There's a moment's silence, then he adds, "He's the only one who's faced Adeth and lived to tell the tale."

Feeling Raighne's solid chest behind me and his thighs hugging my hips make it hard to focus on the conversation.

I can't stop myself from leaning back against him as I ask, "He faced off with Adeth?"

"The day before your sixteenth birthday," he murmurs near my ear, making goosebumps scatter over my body. "She tried to kill you, but she underestimated my father. Don't you remember?"

I shake my head.

"I grabbed you and took you to Janak and Aster while my father fought her. That's partially the reason why we sent you to Earth." I feel as he takes a deep breath and exhales. "It's said the ground shook from the fight."

It's so nice talking to him that I don't want to stop, so I think of another question to ask.

"Are you okay with being bonded to me?"

He answers without any hesitation, "Of course. It's an honor." I feel his breath stir strands of my hair. "Our souls became one when we were bonded. You're my other half."

God.

Raighne wraps an arm around my waist, holding me tighter, and I practically melt against him.

I'm enjoying being close to him when a worry trickles into my mind. Before I can stop the words, they burst over my lips, "What happens when you fall in love?"

"What do you mean?"

"Well, I wouldn't be happy sharing my man with another woman," I say, already regretting that I asked the question, but I push through because I'm too curious for my own good. "Surely you'll have to put your girlfriend or wife first."

He removes his arm from around me, then says, "I'll never marry."

"What?" I gasp, and when I glance over my shoulder to look at him, it puts our faces an inch apart.

His eyes lock with mine. "No one comes before you. I'll never marry. My life belongs to you."

My eyebrows draw together, and unable to be selfish and rejoice that I don't have to share him with another woman, I have to think about him.

"But that's so unfair to you," I whisper.

He shakes his head. "No, it's not. Some guardians never receive a charge, and they have no destiny to fulfill. I'm one of the lucky ones."

It's the longest conversation we've had since we returned to Vaalbara, and seeing as he's answering my questions, I dare to ask another, "So what happens if you want to be with a woman? Or are you celibate?"

I glance at the other riders and our surroundings while I hope he doesn't get offended by my intrusive questions.

When he lets out a chuckle, I'm caught by surprise.

"No, I'm not celibate."

He doesn't explain his answer further, and I don't have the guts to ask another question.

He's not celibate, which means he's probably been with his fair share of women.

Remembering the night when he laughed with the woman by the bonfire and how she touched him, I wonder if there's something more between them.

Jealousy rears in my chest, the emotion so strong I shift on the horse.

"No, I haven't been with her."

Oh God.

My entire face goes up in flames, and I mutter, "Stay out of my head."

He wraps his arm around me again and holds me tightly to his body.

Unable to stop myself, I place my hand over his forearm and close my eyes.

If moments like this are all I'll ever have, I'm going to savor them.

When we finally reach the area where we'll set up camp, I can hear the waterfall.

Raighne climbs off before he takes hold of my hips, lifting me from the horse. This time, he lets my body slide down his, and my eyes widen.

Sweet Jesus.

The crooked smile I love so much tugs at the corner of his mouth, then he surprises me by hugging me to his chest.

"I enjoyed today," he murmurs, his voice low and deep.

"Me too."

He pulls back, and lifting a hand to my face, he tucks some wild strands behind my ear.

"For the next month, we have to focus on our bond. We have

to strengthen it as much as possible."

I nod, then ask, "Is it true that your talents grow if we have a strong bond?"

He nods. "The sooner I can heal you, the better."

I let out a chuckle. "Yeah, that would be great."

As the sun sets, I glance over the area and notice a stream nearby.

At least we have plenty of water.

"Find yourselves a comfortable spot to sleep tonight," Roark calls out so everyone will hear. "We rise before dawn. You'll need all your strength and clarity of mind, so get a good night's rest."

I glance around, wondering where to sleep, but then Raighne says, "At the side of the cliff is a good spot."

He unfastens our backpacks, and I follow him to the area where the cliff offers some protection against the elements.

I watch as he opens his bag and removes a tarp and blanket.

"I don't have those," I mention.

"We're sharing."

We are?

I try to suppress the burst of excitement in my chest.

Dammit, I need to control my emotions better, or he's going to find out I have the hots for him.

I help Raighne straighten the tarp on the ground before I open my bag and pull my pillow out.

"A pillow? Really?" Raighne asks, sounding a little incredulous.

"Yep, without it, I won't get any sleep."

"Did I say to bring one?"

"No, but it counts as an essential item in my books."

When Raighne takes a roll of toilet paper from his bag, my eyebrows fly up.

"This is an essential item." He gestures in the opposite

direction of the waterfall. "By the way, if you need to go, head out there."

"There are toilets?" I ask.

A burst of laughter escapes him, then he shakes his head. It actually looks like he's amused as he says, "You dig a hole."

I dig a hole? Ugh. I'm going to hate the next month.

I scowl at Raighne. "You're enjoying this, aren't you?"

"The expression on your face is priceless," he admits with a grin. He glances at the others, then says, "Let's help them get the fire going."

Hold on. I've had a vision about this conversation.

The realization sends chills down my spine because if this one came true, then it means the others will as well.

I decide not to mention it to Raighne and follow him to where the others are gathered. Not knowing how to help, I watch as he, River, and Storm stack wood before Lucius throws a ball of light at it. Flames roar to life, and I have to admit that's one hell of a talent to have.

Blair and Brenna bring a bowl with meat threaded onto sticks, and everyone grabs one.

I watch what the others do and try not to burn the hell out of my dinner as I hold the stick over the open flame.

I listen in on random conversations and smile at Storm when he comes to stand between Luna and me.

"Have you done this before?" I ask. "Camping out in the desert."

"Yes. We do it once a year," he replies.

"I never asked, but are you a charge or a guardian?"

"Neither."

Curious, I ask, "Do you have talents."

He just nods, and before I can ask another question, he walks away.

Glancing at Luna, I ask, "Did I say something wrong?"

She shakes her head. "Storm doesn't use his talents, and he doesn't speak about them."

My eyes widen. "Why?"

She shakes her head again. "No one talks about it."

I let it go, not wanting to pry any further.

Once the meat looks cooked enough, I pull a piece off the stick, and when it tastes good enough, I eat while glancing around the fire at my companions.

Turning my attention to Luna again, I ask, "Who are you training with?"

"My brother." She gives me a smile, and glancing up at the moon, she lifts her arm and opens her hand.

My lips part with a gasp as a silver light starts to glow in her palm, and when she closes her fingers in a fist, the light snakes up her arm until it settles in her eyes, making them glow.

"Holy crap." Impressed, I grin at her. "That's cool."

"Time for bed," Raighne suddenly says from behind me.

I smile at Luna. "See you tomorrow."

"Have a good night's rest," she says before turning her attention to Lucius.

Walking to our sleeping area, nerves start to spin in my stomach, and I wait for Raighne to lie down before I put a safe distance between us.

I try to get as comfortable as possible on the ground and tuck my pillow beneath my head.

Staring up at the stars, I whisper, "I can see the Milky Way clearly."

"There's no pollution on Vaalbara," he murmurs.

We lie in silence, and my thoughts start to drift. The vision I had earlier pops into my mind, and I shake my head, trying to suppress it.

When I see Adeth's face, Raighne must pick up on it because he says, "Adeth wasn't always dark. She's my mother's sister."

I turn my head, staring at him as surprise shudders through me. "She's your aunt?"

He tucks an arm beneath his head and keeps looking at the night sky as he replies, "After my mother's death, Adeth went to the shadowlands. To this day, we don't know why he didn't kill her.

"He?"

"Void. He's everything that's dark and will drive you to insanity while sucking your soul dry until there's nothing left of you but an empty shell." Raighne takes a deep breath before he continues, "Besides Adeth and Ares, Janak is the only other person who's seen Void, and he never talks about it."

I turn onto my side, my eyes locked on Raighne's face.

He glances at me, then says, "He's one of the few things that can kill us."

My eyebrows lift. "What else can kill us?"

"Being beheaded, and Adeth has a blade forged from the ashes of the volcano in the shadowlands. I've heard rumors Ares can rip a soul from a body, but no one knows if it's true."

Horrified, I whisper, "Jesus."

"Some of us have talents that can kill." His eyes lock on mine, "But something like a bullet won't be able to kill you."

My lips part, and intense relief pours through me.

"It will hurt, though," he adds. "We'll have to be careful on Earth. The longer we're away from Vaalbara, the more vulnerable we become."

He pauses for a moment, then admits, "That's where my mother died. She loved Earth. It was her destiny to bring the animals here before she was beheaded by terrorists."

Oh my God.

Not thinking, I scoot closer to him and take hold of his hand. "I'm so sorry, Raighne."

He pulls his hand free, and wrapping his arm around me, he tucks me against his side. When I rest my head on his chest, I whisper, "You can use my pillow."

I feel his chest shake with silent laughter while he tucks my pillow beneath his head.

"Rest well, Alchera."

"You too."

I hesitate before I wrap my arm around his waist, and closing my eyes, I suck in a deep breath of his scent.

Besides the vision, today was actually a really pleasant day. I loved the time I got to spend with Raighne.

Maybe a month in the desert won't be so bad after all.

Chapter 16

Alchera

It has to be a nightmare because there's no way in hell someone is trying to wake me up ten minutes after I've fallen asleep.

"Go away," I grumble sleepily.

"Alchera, you have to get up. We only have ten minutes to get ready." It's Luna's sweet voice, whispering words of bitter reality.

"Noooo," I groan as I pry my eyes open.

There's no sign of Raighne as I sit up and rub the sleep out of my eyes.

"Come, Alchera," Roark calls from where he's standing with Blair, Storm, and Lucius.

I get up and suppress a yawn as I walk with Luna toward the others.

"You'll head into the desert as a group," Roark orders, "and you'll spend the day out there, learning to work together."

Silence meets him.

"If you have a guardian, you'll be separated so you can focus on your telepathic bonds."

A whole day out in the hot sun. Just great.

"Get some water. You have five minutes before you move

out."

I glance around and see Raighne jogging toward me with a flask in his hand. He gives it to me, then says, "I'll be with you every step of the way."

"Mentally," I mutter. "What if something happens and you can't get to me in time?"

"The others in your group can protect you."

"Come closer," Roark orders.

My eyes dart back to Raighne's. "I guess I'll see you later."

Lifting his hand, he wraps his fingers around the back of my neck, and I'm stunned when he presses a kiss to my forehead.

He doesn't say anything as he lets go of me, and with a sigh, I join the others.

"You'll take full responsibility for each other." Roark gives us a serious look. "May Awo guide you and good fortunes meet you on your way."

"Come, Alchera," Storm says to my right, and I don't hesitate to stick close to him as we head out into the darkness.

Soon, the sun starts to rise, and although it's a beautiful sight, it quickly gets hot. Sweating like crazy, I wipe my hand over my forehead as I stare at the miles and miles of sand.

"How are you doing?" Raighne's voice echoes in my mind, almost giving me a heart attack.

"Next time, knock," I joke. *"I'm doing okay. It's just hot."*

"Drink plenty of water and catch up to the others. You're lagging. You need to walk with your group, not behind them."

"Yes, sir."

I start picking up my pace, and we walk for what feels like hours when an eerie silence descends all around me. A chill creeps down my spine, and I glance around me.

"Raighne, something's wrong."

He doesn't answer me, and I stop walking, my eyes searching

for any sign of a threat.

"*Raighne?*"

A chilling voice sweeps through my mind. "*No, not Raighne.*"

I gasp, and my heart almost explodes from my chest as it starts to beat at a crazy pace.

"*Ares.*"

I break out into a run, screaming, "Storm!"

He swings around. "What?"

Panic burns hot through my lungs, and I don't even make it halfway to Storm when I'm yanked backward. I fly away from him before slamming into the scorching hot sand.

Jesus.

"Alchera!" Blair screams, and as I lift my head, I see her running toward me.

An arm comes from out of nowhere and grabs me forcefully around my neck, yanking me up into the air.

Unable to suck in a full breath, my heart is pounding wildly, my skin clammy with fear.

It's happening.

"Alchera!" Luna cries, and I watch as Lucius draws light from the sun before blasting it my way.

Ares easily deflects it with a wave of his hand, dark smoke curling around his fingers. Then he hisses, "Stop, or I'll kill her right here."

They all freeze in their tracks.

No!

Fear soaks into my bones, and with every bit of training Roark has given me over the past few months, I start to fight to free myself from Ares' brutal hold.

"Please, let her go," Luna begs, her face torn with horror.

A sickening feeling comes over me, and the group starts to blur in front of my eyes.

"Nooo!" I hear Blair scream before everything turns black.

An icy chill spreads deep into my body, and when we materialize again, we're back at camp.

I'm shivering even though we're still in the desert. Ares' grip is so tight on me that his icy, dark aura coats my skin.

"Ares, finally, you're here, and I see you've brought me a gift," My eyes snap to Adeth, and intense horror fills every inch of me. "My dear Alchera, how kind of you to join us."

My eyes dart to the others, and when they lock with Brenna's, and I see the same horror in her gaze that's gripping my heart, I just know I'm good as dead.

When I see Raighne, I whimper, "Raighne."

Raighne makes a move toward me, but then Adeth shouts, "Any closer and Ares will rip her head from her body, nephew."

Raighne stops dead in his tracks and glares in the woman's direction. "You won't get away with this," he growls.

She lets out an evil chuckle. "We'll see about that." She walks closer to me then smirks at Raighne, "I just wanted to see your face when I take her from you."

My eyes dart back to Raighne, and it sinks in there's nothing he can do to save me.

A tear escapes, trickling down my cheek.

The next second, Raighne's arm darts out, and I'm ripped from Ares' hold while a blur that can only be River shoots toward me.

As I fly through the air toward Raighne, I reach out my hands to him.

A bolt of electricity zips past me, coming from Finian, and Brenna charges toward Adeth with a warrior's cry.

They're all fighting for me, but just as I'm about to touch Raighne's hand, a frosty sensation creeps over me.

"No!" I gasp, and my fingers brush against Raighne's. Our eyes lock, and I see the worry etched deep into his face right before I'm grabbed from the side and ripped away from him.

A sickening feeling whirls in the pit of my stomach, and I know what's coming.

"Raighne," I cry as he lunges for me, his face is torn with emotion.

And then he's gone, and darkness swallows me whole.

A few seconds later, we materialize somewhere else, and I'm thrown to the floor, landing on all fours.

Terrified, I keep my head down as I suck in desperate breaths of air.

Oh God. No.

Ares slowly walks around me, like an animal stalking its prey.

"Please," I beg as I lift my head.

He flickers in and out of my sight, then grabs hold of my face, his fingers digging into my cheeks.

Leaning in close to me, his lifeless black eyes lock with mine.

"Shh! No noise. Not a sound," he hisses, his dark tone sending chills over my body.

Suddenly, he lets go of me and shakes his head hard as if he's fighting something before letting out a growl and kicking me in the stomach.

I fall to the side, gagging from the pain ripping through me. I'm battling to get air into my lungs so I can breathe some of the pain away when his foot connects with my ribs, ripping a cry from me.

I want to beg him to stop, but I can't get any words out. I try to roll away from him, but he follows me and delivers another hard kick to my stomach.

Shit.

I gasp, tears streaking down my face as I try to climb to my feet so I can defend myself, but there's no strength in my body, and

I slump back down to the floor.

Ares crouches in front of me, and reaching a hand out to my face, his thumb swipes one of my tears from my cheek, and in absolute horror, I watch as it turns to ash on his skin.

I manage to suck in a painful breath of air, but it whooshes from me when his fist connects with my cheek.

I'm sucked into darkness and mercifully lose consciousness.

RAIGHNE

The moment Ares disappears with Alchera, intense horror bleeds through my body.

My arms fall to my sides as I sink to my knees.

"Noooo!" Brenna screams, her tone hoarse with distress.

"Dear Awo," Roark breathes in absolute shock.

They have Alchera.

I've failed my charge.

Not even a minute passes when I feel intense pain tear through my mind, and the air explodes from my lungs.

"Alchera!"

There's only silence as I struggle to get through to her.

Climbing to my feet, I break out into a run in the direction of the village.

"Raighne!" Finnian calls out.

I ignore my brother, and knowing it's a full day's ride by horseback to get to Janak and my father, I push myself hard.

A full day where Ares will torture Alchera for information about the chosen ones.

I can do it in half the time. Maybe less.

"Fuck!" I growl when it feels as if my soul is being torn in half, but the pain Alchera's experiencing only forces me to push my body even harder.

The landscape blurs around me, and my focus is solely on reaching the village as soon as possible.

"Hold on, Alchera. I'm coming for you."

I pray to Awo that she can hear me as my legs eat up the miles.

ALCHERA

Waking up in a small room, the air around me has a thick, musty smell to it that would have me sneezing like crazy if I was still on Earth.

But I'm not on Earth.

Lifting my head, I let out a groan. I glance around me and notice I'm locked in some sort of a shack made of old, rotted wood.

Shit.

I start to get up but move slowly, my stomach and ribs aching something fierce.

I wrap my arm around my middle and glance everywhere to see if there's anything I can use as a weapon.

When I see a pair of leather pants ripped to shreds on the floor, I slowly glance down as horror bleeds through me. Realizing I'm only wearing my underwear and bra, my body shudders, and I let out a panicked whimper.

This is really bad.

A wave of fear shudders through me, but then it's chased by a warm sensation, and not even a second later, I feel Raighne's strength.

"Alchera, please answer me." Raighne sounds torn up, his tone hoarse with worry.

Our connection isn't clear, but at least I can feel him.

"Raighne." Just thinking his name pushes tears to my eyes. I suck in a breath of air, and closing my eyes, I focus as hard as I can. *"I'm here."*

"Are you okay?" His voice cracks in my mind. *"Can you see where you are?"*

I can't hold back my tears anymore, not when he sounds so broken.

I glance around me again. *"I'm in some kind of shack."* Moving as quickly as I can to the door, I try to push it open, but it won't budge. *"I can't get out."*

"I'll find you," he vows, his voice growing stronger in my mind. *"You hear me? I'll find you."*

I shake my head, and I can't keep the fear from trembling in my tone as I say, *"This is what I saw in my vision. We can't stop it. They're going to kill me."*

"So glad to hear the visions have started," Adeth's voice suddenly echoes around me, followed by a slow clapping of hands.

I move to the nearest wall and press my back to it, assuming the fighting stance Roark has taught me.

"Alchera, what's happening?"

"She's here."

I can't see her anywhere. There's only the echo of her voice and applause sounding through the room.

"I don't know if I should be upset because of this little conversation going on between the two of you or if I should welcome it," she mutters, her tone bored.

Silence follows her words, in which I can only hear my own rapid breaths. I glance wildly around, waiting for her to attack, my heart hammering in my chest.

"I think I'll welcome it for a while so your guardian can feel your pain."

No. I forgot he can feel what I feel. I have to block him to spare him from what's coming.

"Don't you dare, Alchera!" Raighne shouts, making me flinch.

"I have to." I close my eyes and focus. *"I'm sorry."*

When I feel his warmth fade away, my pain increases drastically, and I suppress the sob building in my chest.

Suddenly, a blow comes out of nowhere, slamming into my stomach, and I double over as I gag.

Just as I manage to suck in a painful breath of air, I'm grabbed by the hair and thrown across the floor.

Scrambling to my feet, I assume a fighting stance again while screaming, "Show yourself, you fucking coward!"

Ares appears a few feet away from me, and I get my first good look at him.

He's the same height as Raighne and has the same dark hair. He locks his dead blue eyes to mine, then hisses, "I will give the orders here."

He disappears, and I feel the frosty bite of his aura right before his entire body slams into mine. He knocks me hard into the wall, causing unbearable pain to vibrate through every inch of me.

I clench my jaw to keep a cry from tearing free.

When he steps back, I slide down to the floor, and I barely have enough strength to lift my head, never mind climbing to my feet.

Ares grabs me by my hair again, and when he starts to drag me to the middle of the room, I grip hold of his wrists.

When he lets go of me, I look up, and seeing he's tying a rope to a hook hanging from the ceiling, I try to scramble away from him.

I'm grabbed by the back of my neck and hauled into the air.

"Stop! Please," I sob.

I don't want to, but I can't help looking at him, meeting his eyes. I can't find any sign of emotion, and it scares me more than anything has scared me before. They're completely empty and devoid of life.

"Why?" I whimper as he forces my arms up.

I try to fight, kicking and yanking against his hold, but he's so much stronger than me, and I only manage to knee him in his side.

Ares throws me back down to the floor and wraps his hand around my neck. He squeezes hard, cutting off my air supply. I try to take a breath, but nothing gets past his grip on me.

I hit his arm, then try to rip his hand away, but I'm not strong enough.

"*Alchera!*" Raighne's voice slips through because I'm too busy fighting for my life to block him. I feel his familiar warmth flood me.

Ares narrows his eyes on me and shakes his head. "*Get out of her!*" he hisses inside my mind.

A chill sweeps through me, and I force myself to stop fighting so I can focus on blocking Raighne.

Ares yanks me up, and when he ties the rope tightly around my wrists, I can't stop the whimper from escaping my lips.

"No. Questions. No. Nothing!" Ares spits the words through clenched teeth.

He gives the rope around my wrists one last look before he vanishes right before my eyes.

I'm hanging inches above the floor, my body shaking violently, when I feel Raighne's warmth again.

"*I wish I could trade places with you.*" Raighne's voice is raw with emotion.

I glance around me, taking in my surroundings.

Jesus, I'm royally screwed.

I have to break total contact with Raighne otherwise, he'll

keep slipping through.

"I won't allow you to do that, Alchera!" He sounds desperate. *"We live together. We die together."*

"No," I sob, shaking my head. *"I won't let you die with me."*

I have to protect Raighne.

It takes more willpower than I posses to think the words. *"I don't want you anymore. I can't handle you in my head. I only have enough strength to face them. I can't do this with you as well."*

"You don't mean that." I can hear the hurt in his voice.

"This is hard enough for me, Raighne. Your aunt and cousin are trying to kill me. Stay out of my mind."

I know he's going to worry about me, but desperate times call for desperate measures.

I do my best to switch off, not to think or feel.

Somehow, I have to survive so I can fulfill my destiny. The survival of humankind depends on it.

"Only the chosen ten matter now."

"Don't do it," Raighne groans. *"I beg you."*

Praying to all that's holy that it will work, I think, *"I reject our bond."*

As I think the coldhearted words, a sob forces its way up my throat.

The next moment, Ares appears, and his fist slams into my ribs with brutal force, making my body sway as an agonizing scream is ripped from my soul.

CHAPTER 17

ALCHERA

When the air starts to crackle around me, a sure sign that something bad is coming, I snap out of the trance I've managed to fall into after the last beating Ares gave me.

My head whips up as I hear Adeth's voice purr, "Hello, my dear Alchera. Why do you have to be so difficult?"

She makes her appearance, and the sarcastic comment I wanted to sling her way flies out of my mind when my eyes focus on her.

Adeth is beautiful, but still, every nerve ending in my body prickles, and my muscles tense more than I thought was possible.

She slowly glides across the floor, and lifting her hand to my face, she gently takes hold of my chin.

She's face-to-face with me, even though I'm hanging from a rope.

I've never felt so small in my life.

Her jet-black hair hangs in light curls down to the middle of her back. Her skin is pale white, giving it almost a translucent glow. It's as if she's never been out in the sun.

All she needs is blood-red lips, and she could pass for *Snow White*'s evil twin.

"Alchera...tsk, tsk, tsk. How dare you send Raighne away? I made it clear that I want him to suffer. I don't look kindly upon people who go against my wishes."

"I don't care what you think," I spit at her.

Her forefinger slides up and down my cheek.

I yank my face away, but she only laughs at me.

She grabs hold of my chin again, and there's a sharp prick before a burning pain spreads beneath my skin.

My breaths speed up as she slices my cheek open with her sharp nail. The first drop of blood forms, and I feel it follow an uncertain trail to my chin. My body trembles uncontrollably as fear for this woman engulfs me.

I swallow hard and force myself to keep looking at her. No matter how scared I am, I won't give in.

"Ahh, Alchera, I have you at last. It's been too long." She gives me the impression that she's talking to herself. "Mmm, it's really unfortunate you should find yourself in this little predicament."

Inspecting my face, she admires her handiwork. Her black eyes are shining with the delight of having me in her grasp, and I swear I can see shadows moving in her irises.

I scowl, totally disgusted by her.

"How rude of me. I haven't introduced myself." There's a deceivingly friendly smile on her face that gives me the creeps. "I'm Adeth."

I press my lips together and continue to scowl at her.

She lets out a sigh and shakes her head. "You should know I don't tolerate lies."

Anger bubbles in my chest, and I hiss, "I don't give a shit."

She ignores what I say and continues, "My name carries the meaning of death, so how can I not live by it? Even though Awo insists I'm damning myself by doing so." She stares blindly at me, her eyes glazing over.

Oh boy, she's definitely missing a few vital ingredients to make up a healthy brain cell.

"Those who lie to me will meet an untimely and unfortunate end." She moves closer to me and takes a deep breath as if she's trying to inhale me. "Tell me, Alchera, do you know why I've brought you here?" She dips her head slightly and glares at me from beneath long, full lashes.

"No." I lie.

"It's actually quite simple. I ask you a question, and you give me the answer I want. I feel it's quite unnecessary to make things. .." she looks at my tied wrists, and a small smile plays around her lips, "...overly dramatic."

Turning, she glides around the room, trailing her fingers along the wall. My eyes widen when healthy green vines sprout from the rotten wood. Out of the vines blossom the most beautiful velvet-kissed Hibiscus flowers, only they're black. The vines themselves change from healthy green to red, like veins pulsing with blood.

Jesus.

Ares appears out of thin air, and when he comes to stand beside me, I cringe.

"Don't you think they're beautiful?" Adeth asks, pleased with what she's created.

"Sure," I mutter. "In a creepy as fuck way."

I'm still trying to process everything because it's not an everyday occurrence to see flowers and people intent on killing me appear out of thin air.

"I have a few questions to ask," she continues. "Should your answers be satisfactory, you'll be free to go. However, there will be consequences to face for every unacceptable answer you give."

The corner of her mouth lifts in a smile. "I think I've made myself very clear, and we can start."

Adeth has to be anyone's worst nightmare, and here I'm lucky enough to get her full and undivided attention.

God help me.

A chill ripples down my spine as I remember the question she kept asking in my vision.

She glides back to me, and instantly, the air tenses. I suck in a desperate breath of air, my stomach coiling and my nerves frail.

My eyes dart from Ares to Adeth, and fear makes me tremble as I wait for the questions to start.

"I heard you talking to Raighne," Adeth says. "Have your premonitions begun?"

"What premonitions?" I ask, pretending not to understand.

I feel a wave of dizziness wash over me and try to remember the last time I ate or drank something.

God, how long I've been here?

A day? Longer?

"Prophecies! Have they started, child?" She raises an annoyed eyebrow.

"I don't understand what you're asking me," I snap.

"Stupidity does not become you, child. Have you had dreams of the future?" She bites the words out, clearly losing her patience with me. "Who are the chosen ten?"

I swallow hard, then answer, "I've only seen disasters, and I can hardly remember them."

I close my eyes, hoping the consequences won't be bad. I'm determined not to give her too much information in case something I say might lead her to a chosen one.

"You can hardly remember them?" she asks, her tone deceptively soft.

"Yes."

"There have been no visions concerning the chosen ones?" she asks.

I suck in a fortifying breath, and opening my eyes, I answer, "No."

Adeth looks furious, and I know it means nothing good for me.

This is it! I'm a goner. Oh God!

"Then why have a guardian?" She shrugs as humorless laughter spills over her lips. "You're useless and of no worth to me. Your parents managed to hide you for the last five years, and it was all for nothing?" She glances at Ares and my eyes dart to him.

Before I can register any movement from him, a dreadful pain spreads across my face. His fist slams hard into my jaw, knocking my head back.

A copper taste fills my mouth, and I force myself to swallow the blood.

The next punch is more brutal, splitting my lip. I don't bother swallowing the blood this time. Instead, I spit it at Adeth's feet.

"You and your son can go fuck yourselves," I slur.

Ares walks behind me, and I try to keep an eye on him, but I can't.

When I lose sight of him, my fear intensifies. I hear something fall to the floor, and my stomach coils into a hard knot. My whole body is wound so tightly that I'm shivering uncontrollably.

I hear something drag across the floor, then it hisses through the air.

A whip cracks, and I cringe, trying to make myself smaller. When the leather lashes at my back, white-hot pain licks at my skin, ripping a scream from me as I try to arch my body away from the whip.

But it cracks through the air again, hissing toward me a

second time. As it strikes, the pain sears itself into my flesh.

Ares doesn't stop, and with each strike, I grow weaker until my head hangs limply. I stare at the blood dripping from my feet to the dusty floor, forming a pool beneath me.

When the torture finally stops, I can only hear a ringing in my ears, and my body's on fire with pain.

God. I'm not going to last much longer.

"If you *are* Alchera, you should be having visions," Adeth snarls. "You should be seeing your precious chosen ones."

"If you don't believe me," I let out a miserable-sounding chuckle, "...that's your damn problem."

"You're a brave one to speak to me in this manner," she says, her eyes narrowing on me. "Hmm...either you're brave or very foolish."

For a long moment, Adeth's angry gaze holds mine captive, then she says, "You're strong to keep me out of your mind, dear Alchera." She shakes her head. "Poor Raighne. He must be out of his mind with fear for your safety." She slithers closer like the damn snake she is. "Let me into your mind, and I'll set you free so you can run home to comfort your guardian. How can you let the man you love suffer so much?"

Shit. How does she know about my feelings for Raighne?

I keep quiet, just staring at her.

"Tell me what you remember of your visions, or I'll let Ares take you apart, piece by little piece, before sending your lifeless body back to Raighne."

No. What will something like that do to him?

"Why do you want to know about the chosen ones?" I ask, trying to buy some time.

"You want to save these humans of yours. As if they deserve it," she spits the words out with disgust. "They don't deserve anything! It is time for the human race to come to their end and I intend to see to it personally."

I shake my head. "You're not answering my question."

"You lived among them. Surely you've seen how depraved and selfish they are? Why do you still want to save them?" She sucks in a breath, her eyes burning on me. "Tell me about your visions!"

"I can't remember the details," I snap. "They start out as nightmares. Only after returning to Vaalbara was I told they were actual visions, and by then, I'd forgotten them."

I give her as little information as possible, hoping it's enough to convince her I'm being sincere.

"Do not patronize me, Alchera!"

Okay, so much for convincing her of anything.

"I didn't mean to patronize you. I'm sorry," I say quickly, hoping to calm her down.

Of course, it doesn't work, and the air starts to crackle with some sort of electric current.

Adeth's face begins to change. It's subtle at first, then thorn-like bumps form on her forehead.

Shit.

I can only stare in horror as small spikes form on her ears and black veins appear along her lips, spreading out over the rest of her face.

Bile rises in my throat as I realize I have a front-row seat to the unveiling of the monster that wants to end all of humanity, and the odds are good I'm going to die now.

Oh God. This is the part I've seen in a vision, and I know what's coming next.

I won't be getting out of this hell alive, and just like in the vision, I slip up and think of Raighne.

Warmth immediately floods my chest, and I'm shocked that he's able to restore our bond. Either that, or I didn't manage to sever it like I thought.

But it's so comforting to feel him, I let out a sob.

I lower my head so they can't see my eyes because I don't want them to know Raighne's able to sense what's happening.

"Ares," the woman hisses, "make her understand!"

His hand closes around my throat, and I squeeze my eyes shut. *ShitShitShit.*

An awful burning sensation starts at my feet, slowly making its way up my legs.

When it feels as if my flesh is being burned from my body, I can't keep the screams from tearing loose.

I writhe in agony as the burn increases, clawing its way up my body.

By the time it reaches my thighs, I'm on fire, burning from the inside out.

"Stop!" I scream, my voice hoarse. "Please."

I'm weeping from the unbearable pain, but there are no tears left to cool my face.

Ares just stares at me, his eyes dead and merciless, as always.

Raighne's warmth stirs in me, and it feels as if he's trying to pass some of his strength into my body.

I want to push him away because I don't want him feeling any of this pain.

Unable to stop Raighne, he flows through my mind, and as he floods my entire being, his soothing warmth battles the fire, easing some of the blistering pain.

"*Raighne,*" I groan internally. "*I don't want you here. Leave.*"

"*Never.*" His voice is crystal clear in my mind and filled with so much confidence it makes hope trickle into my chest. "*I'll find you. Don't give up.*"

My whole body slumps, and totally exhausted, I just soak in Raighne's comforting presence.

Then Ares' voice enters my mind, sounding threatening as hell, *"Tell her, or I will be forced to kill you slowly and hand your soul to her."*

I shake my head as more sobs spill over my lips.

Adeth steps closer to me, finding delight in my pain and despair. "Ares, you may stop for now. Let's see whether our little bird is ready to sing."

The excruciating pain eases the instant he removes his hand.

"Tell me who the chosen ones are," she demands once again.

I keep quiet because there's no use trying to talk to her.

Adeth reaches out to me and when her hand settles over my stomach, there's a weird tugging sensation.

Before I can take another breath, it turns into gut-wrenching agony, tearing a scream from me. It feels as if she's twisting my insides, trying to rip them through my skin.

I start to gag, making it so much worse as my body convulses.

The pain becomes all-consuming until it's all I can think of, while sweat beads on my skin as every muscle in my body strains.

Suddenly, she stops and grabs hold of my face. Her nails dig into my cheek until they tear through my skin, and I'm too weak to try to yank away.

"I'll return, and you *will* tell me everything. This, I promise you, Alchera."

She disappears, and I feel relief wash over me, but it's only for a split second.

I can still feel her nails cutting into my cheek as Ares begins to advance on me. He draws his arm back, and I close my eyes.

I can't deal with this anymore.

All the pain is getting the better of me, and I'm sure I'm dying.

Raighne was wrong. There are more ways to kill an immortalis.

Ares' fist slams hard into my gut until it hurts too much to breathe. My body swings from the impact, but it doesn't stop him. He grabs my hair, and I have no time to recover before the next blow comes.

Excruciating pain becomes the sum of my being, and it feels as if every agonizing breath might be my last.

But, the relief of death doesn't come, only a new level of pain when the whip cracks over my already raw and bloody flesh.

When Raighne whispers inside me, I sob out loud. I want to thank Awo that it will be Raighne's voice I hear one last time before I die.

"Alchera, hold on for me. Please don't give up. We're coming for you. I will find you!"

I know I should keep him away, but hearing his voice feels like heaven calling to me in the middle of hell.

"I can't." The words slip through because I'm too weak.

Adeth immediately reappears and grabs me by the neck. "You tell that guardian of yours that if he comes near you, Ares will rip your soul from your body. Tell him!" She spits the words at me as her eyes change to a bitter, angry orange color. "Now!"

"I heard her. Just hold on for me."

"He heard you," I gasp, my voice hoarse from all the screaming.

I don't understand how it's possible I'm still conscious, let alone alive.

Adeth steps back and takes a good, long look at me, then a glass of water appears in her hand.

I'm thirsty and will do almost anything for water, but when she holds the glass to my mouth, I let my head roll to the side.

Exhausted, I mutter, "I'd rather die of thirst."

"You need to drink," Adeth murmurs, almost sounding motherly. "You'll be of no use to me dead."

When she presses the glass to my mouth, a few drops spill

onto my feverish lips. Sadly, it's all the encouragement I need. I get two greedy gulps down before she snatches it away.

"Ah-ah-ah, not too fast. You can have more in a minute." The glass disappears, and I feel a sudden pang of loss. "You don't look too good. Maybe you'll speak now. We don't want any more misunderstandings, do we?"

Shit.

"Who are the chosen ones?"

Consumed by pain, I whisper, "I don't know."

She lets out a bark of laughter. "Foolish girl. You will tell me."

Little black and red spots begin to spark in front of my eyes.

"Go to hell!" I spit at her.

I try to smile just before the darkness I've been praying for comes.

CHAPTER 18

RAIGHNE

I'm losing my mind.

The longer I'm away from Alchera, the more I feel our bond weakening. After she tried to sever it, it took everything I had to break through the barrier she put up between us.

I've worked my ass off to sense where she's being held, and now we're wasting time arguing about who's going to free her.

"I'll go," my father says, and it has everyone looking at him.

"You're the King's guardian," Janak argues.

"She's my charge," the words rumble from me.

"I'm the only one who has faced Adeth and survived," Dad mutters. "This time, Ares will be there as well."

He's right.

"Then we both go," I say because there's no way I'm staying behind.

"Who will guard the King?" Janak asks, his tone tense with worry.

We look at him, and Dad says, "You." He steps closer to our elder. "I only trust you."

Janak sucks in a deep breath, then nods. "Fine." He looks to where the rest of our group is gathering and waves a hand in the air. "Luna, Lucius, come."

The twins are exhausted after traveling non-stop to get to the village.

When they join us, he orders, "You'll stay by King Eryon's side at all times."

My father looks at the twins. "Assist Janak and protect my charge with your lives."

They nod, looking nervous as hell.

Done with this conversation, I turn away from them and begin to stalk in the direction of the forest.

"Son," Father calls as he jogs to catch up with me. "Let me take the lead."

I nod, and when he picks up his pace, I run beside my father and head into the dense forest.

"I'm on my way, Alchera. Just hold on for a few more hours."

There's only silence, and a fist of fear grips my heart.

As long as my heart still beats, I know she's alive. It's all that matters.

ALCHERA

I'm unsure how long I've been out, but I wake up on the floor with every part of my body engulfed in agonizing pain. I can't even bring myself to move a muscle.

"I thought you were never going to wake up. Welcome back." Just hearing Adeth's voice has me wishing I'd never opened my eyes. "Come, you must eat and drink something before you faint again."

A bowl with something mushy is shoved near my face. Ares

also sets down half a glass of water in front of me.

I'm holding onto the faint hope of being saved, and it's the only reason I force my body up. Leaning heavily against the wall, it hurts like hell when I reach for the glass. I drink every drop before I take a couple of bites of the tasteless porridge.

"I have decided that I believe you," Adeth states.

Oh wow. Aren't I the lucky one.

"You'll remain here until your visions of the chosen ones begin, which should be very soon. Then you'll tell me what I need to know, and we can put all this nasty business behind us."

I stare at Adeth, and it's actually bloodcurdling how insane she is.

If the visions start, I'll just have to hide them from her. Raighne will eventually come for me, and he'll kill her. I'll just keep telling myself that, and hopefully, I'll start believing it soon.

Without another word, they disappear, and my head rolls to the side.

Every passing hour feels like the worst day of my life. I think my wounds are infected, and I have a raging headache.

I'm struggling to keep my eyes open.

I'm sure most of my ribs are broken, and my left arm has been wrecked from trying to protect myself. My back is flayed raw, and I smell like death.

Desperation passed a while ago, and I feel numb inside. I prefer it this way. It's easier to cope with all the shit that's happening to me.

I stare at the dirty floor I'm sitting on when my vision blurs once again, and I'm thrown into a different time and space.

Birds are chirping all around me. Beautiful cages line the sides of a passage, filled with colorful birds of every shape and size.

I can hear a man talking in another language. The weird thing is I understand what he's saying.

I try to focus on everything around me. The man is talking to someone about where he's going to put each of the birds and how to make the cages even better for them.

As I walk closer, I realize he's actually talking to the birds. I see where he's busy changing their water at the end of the passageway.

The birds flutter around as I pass them, and it amazes me that they can sense me.

The man glances in my direction, and I stop for a moment.

When it's clear he doesn't see me, I walk closer until I'm right next to him. He has light brown hair with dark brown eyes, and he's a head taller than me.

There's so much love surrounding him while he talks to his birds, I want so badly to be a part of it.

His words and quiet actions make me wish that I could bottle some of that love for myself.

Turning his head, he looks straight into my eyes. I know he can't see me, though I have a feeling he can sense me.

"Jason," I whisper.

His name comes easily to me as I stare at my first chosen one.

I return to my private hell with lingering feelings of Jason's love.

Shit. That was a vision.

I pry my eyes open as panic flares in my chest, and not even seconds later, Ares appears in the middle of the shack.

No!

My body automatically convulses at the sight of him. I quickly duck my head, scared he might see something regarding the vision in my eyes.

Don't think about anything. Clear your mind.

When I'm not able to stop thinking, I picture random words, places, and people.

Waterfalls. Horses. LA. Molly. Fleur. Canada. Robert.

My mind latches onto Robert, and I replay the night when he attacked me in my mind in case Ares is able to hear my thoughts.

I'd rather sacrifice Robert than one of my chosen ones.

I can feel Ares stare at me for a long moment until my skin begins to crawl, then his low and deadly voice fills the air as he says, "I have something special for you. With love from Adeth, of course."

Before today, Ares has hardly spoken a word to me. My eyes dart to him, and I see a bottle and knife in his hands.

Oh shit.

He stalks closer, and when he grabs hold of my hair, my right arm darts up, and I grip his wrist.

He starts to drag my broken body across the floor, and I'm unable to suppress a cry.

The moment he lets go of me, I try to stand up, but I have zero strength and can only lie in a pathetic heap.

When Ares grabs hold of my ankle, I'm confused, but then he drags me into the air, and realizing what he plans to do, I try to kick at him.

"No," I growl, a hopeless feeling gripping my chest tightly because, in the end, there's nothing I can do to protect myself from this monster.

Blood rushes to my head, and I feel nauseous from the slight swinging motion, as he hangs me in the air by my feet, tying the rope tightly around my ankles.

"You're a coward," I spit through clenched teeth, trembles racking through my body. "Fucking asshole."

Ares comes to crouch in front of me and holds the bottle and knife in front of my face. "Which one should I use first?"

I don't know what's in the bottle. It's plain white.

Locking eyes with him, I use every ounce of meager strength I have to say, "Fuck. You."

He raises to his full height, and when he moves in behind me, my heart beats wildly in my chest. My body bucks as I try to see what he's doing.

Suddenly, the blade of the knife stabs into the back of my thigh, and the sharp pain has me screaming.

Once I'm able to breathe through the pain, I yell, "Mother fucking son of a bitch!"

He yanks the knife out of me, the pain threatening to rob me of my sanity.

I feel something cold drip on my back, and I instinctively try to swing away, but a second later, fire starts to lick at the raw lashes.

It's not as bad as the time Ares choked me. Whatever is in the bottle smells like vinegar. He turns the whole bottle on me, and I take my words back.

It feels like he lit a match to my torn-up back, and I can only sob and whimper as I writhe in pure agony.

I have no idea how much time passes, and when my body goes limp, I can't even make a sound.

Ares unfastens the rope around my ankles, and somewhere between all the pain, it sinks in that he's being gentle with me as he lays me down on the floor.

Prying my eyes open, I'm shocked to see a hint of emotion flash briefly in his eyes.

Was it sadness? Guilt?

That's not possible.

For a moment, he just stares at me, then his arm moves, and I try to brace myself for the punch, but instead, he brushes my tangled hair away from my cheek.

The tender touch makes me feel sick to my stomach. I would've preferred a punch.

"Forgive me, Alchera," he whispers. His features tense, and

his eyes begin to change from black to light gray. The dark aura always surrounding him fades, and for a second, he doesn't look as threatening.

I lose my ability to breathe as I watch him transform from monster to man.

"Ares?" I whisper, stunned by what's happening, but before I can say anything else, he disappears from the shack again.

I have no idea whether I've been here a couple of days, a week, or a month.

It rained earlier and the sound of the drops pelting the shack's roof sounded so beautiful I almost cried.

I haven't seen Ares since he asked my forgiveness, which is something I'll never give.

I'm listening to the leaves rustling outside the door, welcoming any noise to break the silence hanging heavy around me.

Jason. I have to survive so I can save Jason.

I pry my eyes open and let out a groan.

I hear twigs snap and lift my head off the floor. Ares never uses the door.

I see a shadow pass by the inch-sized space beneath the door, and a moment later, it returns.

It stills for a breathless moment, and then I hear the wood rattle as someone tries to open it.

Oh my God.

"Hello?" I croak, the word barely audible.

Suddenly, the door shudders open with a bang, leaving it hanging on one hinge, and a man I've never seen before stands tall in the doorway.

"Help," I whimper, not sure whether I should get my hopes up or not.

"Son, she's here," he says.

The second Raighne appears behind the man, I can't hold the sobs back, and they rack through my chest. *"You found me."*

"Fuck," he whispers, shock tightening his features when he sees the horrible state I'm in.

He darts forward and falls beside me on his knees. His hand trembles as he reaches for my face, and when his palm brushes over my hair, I try to move so I can get closer to him.

"I'm so fucking sorry," he groans in my mind.

"Get me out of here before they come back," I beg. *"Please!"*

Raighne carefully pushes his arms beneath me, and picking me up bridal style, he cradles me to his solid chest.

When his warmth starts to seep into my body, I feel feverish, and my head slumps against his shoulder.

He walks out the door with me in his arms, and every step he takes makes excruciating pain shudder through me.

"I'm sorry. It's going to hurt," his voice fills my mind.

I try to nod. *"Just get me away from here."*

As soon as we're outside, Raighne starts to run unbelievably fast, the other man following close behind us.

The movements jar my body, and I clench my jaw and ball my fists against my chest, trying to be strong. Tears slip from my eyes and spill silently over my cheeks.

Raighne runs at an incredible pace and doesn't stop until it's well into the night.

I'll take the pain if it means he's getting me away from Adeth and Ares. The more distance between me and that hellhole, the better.

When he slows down to a stop, I can't keep a groan from rippling over my dry lips. I shiver in his hold as he kneels on the ground, gently pulling his arm from beneath my knees.

A moment later, he holds a flask to my lips, and I drink greedy gulps before he helps himself to some water.

When my eyes drift to the other man, he says, "I'm Griffith, Raighne's father. We'll be home shortly."

Raighne's eyes flick over my face and body, then he asks, "Ready?"

I have zero strength and can only whisper mentally to him. *"Yes."*

He climbs to his feet again, and the movement sends shockwaves of pain through me, causing a whimper to slip through my lips. I regret it immediately.

I have to be strong. Weakness has no place in this world.

I soon lose track of time and how long he's been running, but I'm relieved when we finally reach a camp.

A voice that sounds vaguely familiar cries, "Alchera! What have they done to her?"

Gentle arms take me from Raighne's, pulling me close against a comforting chest.

I open my eyes and look into the same green eyes as my own, only they're older and filled with horror.

The love and intensity that fills me is overwhelming as I realize I'm looking at my father.

Memories of happy moments in my childhood flash through my mind.

"Alchera. Oh, my Alchera," he weeps. He falls to his knees, holding me as tenderly as he possibly can.

For a moment, he cries into my hair, and silent tears of my own join his.

When he lifts his head, he orders with the power of a King brimming in his voice, "Hunt down that woman! We leave at dawn. Adeth will *die* for this!"

He buries his face in my bloody, knotted hair, and all I can do is whimper, "Dad?"

"Please, forgive me," he groans. "I've failed you."

"My King, we need to tend to her," Aster says softly behind us, but I have no intention of letting go of my father. Not after all these years.

He gets up without loosening his hold on me and walks into a tent, and I can feel Raighne close by.

Taking a seat, my father places me on his lap while cradling me in his arms like a baby.

God, even though it hurts like hell, it feels so good to be held by him.

"You may tend to her in my arms," Dad orders before pressing a soft kiss to my forehead.

Many different fragrances fill the air in a matter of seconds. Someone begins to wash my arms, and another starts on my legs. I keep my eyes locked on my father, trying to brace for a world of pain.

After long minutes of them cleaning me, Aster murmurs, "I'm afraid we'll have to cut her hair."

I have no say in the matter as my father mutters, "Do what you must." He brushes his hand over my cheek, and his tone is loving when he whispers, "It will grow back, my sweet girl."

My sweet girl.

The term of endearment makes tears leak from my eyes, and I squeeze them shut.

I feel as they cut my hair, and once they're done, Aster says, "You need to place her on the bed, Your Highness. We need to tend to her back."

Reluctantly, my father climbs to his feet and carefully helps me to sit on the side of a bed.

Aster starts to pull a curtain around the bed, then glances at my father. "We need to remove her underwear."

He presses a kiss to my forehead, then tells me, "I'm right outside."

I nod and watch as he leaves. When Raighne doesn't budge a muscle, Aster gives him a questioning look.

He shakes his head hard, "I'm not leaving her side."

"She needs privacy," Aster argues.

He moves in behind me, then says, "Tend to her wounds, Aster. I'm not leaving my charge."

"Stubborn boy," she chastises him before turning her attention back to me.

I cross my right arm over my chest while my broken one lies limply at my side.

At first, I feel nothing as they get to work. There's only a weird tugging sensation as they pry the bra straps loose from the scabbed-over welts.

When I sway forward and almost fall off the bed, Raighne moves fast, and within a second, he's in front of me. He wraps his hand around the back of my head and allows me to rest my cheek against his abdomen.

"Better?"

"Yeah."

"This is going to hurt, Alchera. I wish there was another way, but I have to clean the wounds." Aster's voice cracks over the words.

I move my right arm and grip hold of Raighne's side. His fingers tighten in my filthy hair, that's much shorter now that it's been cut.

I feel his warmth move through me as Aster starts to soak the raw lashes with a wet sponge.

The wounds itch and sting, but as she continues her slow assault on my raw flesh, a fire starts to burn in my wounds.

"Raighne," I gasp, my back arching to try and get away from

the pain.

His other hand grips me behind my neck, and when the burning becomes too much and a cry escapes me, Raighne crouches down until he's at eye level with me.

"Focus on me," he orders.

"I can't. It hurts too much."

Our eyes lock, and more of his warmth pours into me.

"I've got you, my little dreamer," his voice cools the fever in my mind. *"Just keep looking at me."*

Somehow, the pain lessens until all I feel is Raighne. I don't dare break eye contact, scared of what will happen if I do.

"That's it." His palms cradle my face, and he leans forward until I feel his breaths on my lips. *"Let me take all your pain."*

I watch as his eyes darken and his features tense, and I hate that he's in pain, but I have no strength to fight him.

As his breaths speed up, my tears fall faster, and in this moment, our bond has never been stronger as my guardian takes every lick of agonizing pain from me.

Slowly, the color of his eyes starts to change from purple to dark blue until I swear I can see the night sky staring back at me. Silver flecks sparkle like stars, and I gasp as I realize taking my pain is a new talent Raighne's developed out of pure desperation to make me feel better.

"Thank you," I whisper as I lift my right hand to his face. He leans his jaw into my palm, the brustles scratchy against my skin.

"I'll do anything for you."

My eyes stare deep into his as I think, *"I'm sorry I said I rejected our bond. I wanted to spare you."*

"I know." He closes the small distance between us, and his lips press against the corner of my mouth. *"But never do it again. It's my destiny to be your guardian, not the other way around."*

I let out a burst of laughter, and pain flashes over his features, then he orders, *"Keep still. If you move, the pain intensifies."*

I don't dare move a muscle and just keep my eyes locked with his.

"I wish I wasn't weak so you didn't have to take my pain."

His palms brush over my cheeks and hair, his eyes softening on me. *"You're so fucking strong. Thank you for not giving up."*

When Raighne rests his forehead against mine, and his breaths become labored, I close my eyes and focus so the pain returns to me.

It knocks the air from my lungs, and I cover my mouth with my hand to keep cries from escaping.

"No! Look at me," he orders.

I shake my head. *"Take a break. I can handle it."*

Jesus, I can't. It feels as if they're peeling the skin from my back.

"Open your fucking eyes!" Raighne's voice thunders in my mind.

Before I can shake my head, the pain becomes so unbearable it sucks me into a world of darkness as I lose consciousness.

CHAPTER 19

ALCHERA

When I wake up, I don't feel Raighne's warmth, and for a moment, blinding panic and fear shoot through me. My eyes pop open, and it takes a second for my vision to focus on my father's face.

My body feels as if it's been shredded to pieces, but I don't reek like death anymore. The aroma of herbs and oils fills the air.

Every wound throbs as if each one has a heartbeat of its very own.

My father glances at my face, and seeing I'm awake, he murmurs, "My precious daughter has woken up. How do you feel?"

Once again, I'm struck by the similarities between us as I try to smile, but the cuts on my cheeks from Adeth's nails quickly have me stopping.

Letting out a groan, I say, "I'm still trying to catch the license plate of that bus that ran me over."

"I beg your pardon?" He frowns.

"Sorry, it's an expression that's used on Earth. I meant to say, it feels like my body has seen better days."

I'm not going to tell him how much pain I'm really in.

"It will get better. And you're safe now." His eyes caress lovingly over my face that must look like I ran straight into a wall.

"I'm going to have to leave you with Raighne and Aster."

I clear my throat, then ask, "Where are you going?"

"We're going to go hunt down Adeth." Shock from his words ripples through me. "She has to account for what she's done to you. We can't risk her attacking you again."

Shaking my head, I try to sit up and quickly grab hold of the blanket wrapped around me so it won't fall off.

"No! You can't," I protest. "She's dangerous."

I have to think of a way to keep him here. I don't want my dad anywhere near Adeth.

"You don't even know where she is. Please, don't go!" I'm talking as fast as I can, but when he stands up and starts to carry me over to the bed, I panic. "I'll go with you!"

I know I'll just be in the way, but how am I supposed to let him go? I just got him back!

"You need to rest in order to heal, my sweet girl. She could've killed you. I won't risk your life again." He takes my face gently in his two large hands and looks lovingly at me. "You are the strongest soul I know. I'm so very proud of you. I love you deeply, my daughter. I have been and will always be with you." He kisses me on the forehead and turns to leave.

"No! You can't leave," I call after him. "Please, don't go. I just got you back."

I feel the sobs building in my throat as I almost fall off the bed to go after him. Pain tears through every muscle, and my body fights me with every step I try to take. I sink to my knees and have to drag myself to the door.

My eyes are nailed to my dad's back as he walks with the pride of a King toward his horse, where a group of men are already waiting.

"Daddy, no!" I cry, my voice hoarse and raw.

Using the door, I drag myself up so I can see him better.

He mounts his horse and gives me one last warm smile before he nods at the men behind him. In horror, I watch my dad leave me.

My legs buckle under my weight, and I slump down to the ground. "Come back," I gasp through the heartache. "Come back. She's going to kill you," I sob as I lie down right where I am, crying into the dirt.

"Alchera!" Raighne shouts.

Lifting my head, I barely make out Raighne running toward me. Everything is a blur.

A blur of pain. A blur of tears. A blur of heartache.

My life has become a blur of shadows, and I can't handle it anymore.

Raighne crouches, and his strong arms slip beneath me. He lifts me to his chest, and I bury my face against his leather shirt as I cry, "It's so unfair. He left me again."

Setting me down on the side of the bed, he stands in front of me and leans down until we're face-to-face. The moment our eyes lock, the heartache lessens, and a calmness washes over me.

"*Your father will return,*" he says, and the words calm me even more.

I nod and glance away from him. Gripping the blanket tighter, I ask, "Are there any clothes here? This blanket is getting very uncomfortable to hold up all the time."

"I don't see any clothes," he replies. "Let me call someone to bring you something to wear." Slowly, he pulls away from me and walks to the door.

I duck my head, letting my hair fall forward to cover my face, but instead of long curls, there are only uneven strands brushing over my shoulders.

My throat aches from fighting the tears as I tug at the butchered leftovers of my hair.

I hear Raighne talking in hushed tones with someone and duck my head lower.

Because of everything I've been forced to endure, it feels as if a darkness is growing deep in my soul.

I feel lonely and broken.

"You should lie down," Raighne murmurs near me.

When I feel his fingers weaving through the hack job on my head, I jerk away.

"Shh. Your hair will grow back. Why don't you try to get some rest?"

Anger bubbles up in my chest, as hot as the flames licking at my back.

Before I can stop myself, my head whips up, and I hiss, "I can't! Don't you think I would if I could?" I let the blanket fall away from me, exposing my bare chest that's riddled with bruises and wounds, then I snap, "On which side do you suggest I lie?"

Raighne's features tighten, and instead of losing his patience with me, he moves as close to me as possible and grabs hold of the blanket. Fisting the fabric, he covers my front before pulling me to lean against his abdomen.

I can feel his body trembling, and his breaths warm the top of my head.

"I will spend the rest of my life making up to you for the horror you were forced to endure. I promise, Alchera. I know there's not much I can do to make it better, and there's nothing I can say to regain your trust, but I swear to Awo I will prove my worth to you."

Tears sting my eyes, and I regret my outburst. Sucking in a deep breath, I try to control the chaotic dark emotions swirling in my chest.

"You didn't do this to me."

Pulling back, Raighne lifts his hand to my face, and his fingers carefully brush over the cuts on my cheek.

I wiggle uncomfortably, not wanting him to pay any attention to my wounds. It reminds me of how awful I look.

He leans even closer and tries to capture my eyes. His breath warms my lips, and his voice is soft in my mind. *"Let me in."*

His lips move to the corner of my mouth, and an intense fluttering erupts in my stomach.

"Please stop closing yourself off from me," he begs.

He presses a soft kiss to my cheek where the cuts are.

"No," I choke the words out. I try to pull my face away from him, but he just grips hold of my chin to keep me in place.

"Let me in, Alchera," he orders, his tone harsher.

I don't want him to see the mess in my head and the shredded pieces of my soul.

I take hold of his hand and tug it away from my face. "No, Raighne. I need time."

Hurt darkens his eyes, and it's worse than when I had to cut him off because, this time, I see the pain I'm causing him.

Aster comes in with a bundle of clothes before I can try to explain myself further. "Give us some privacy, Raighne."

He goes to stand in the doorway, turning his back to us and crossing his arms over his broad chest.

"Should you so much as peek, I will cast you with blindness," Aster teases him while winking at me. "Do you feel better?"

I just nod because I think it will take a long while before I feel any better.

When she holds a white nightgown out to me, I take it and whisper, "Thank you."

"Let me help you," she says.

"I'm good."

She hesitates for a moment before nodding. "Careful with your left arm."

I wait for her to leave before I let go of the blanket, and as carefully as possible, I pull the nightgown over my shoulders and fasten all the buttons.

"Are you dressed?" Raighne asks from the doorway.

I adjust the fabric around my thighs as I glance over my shoulder. "Yeah." When he walks back to me, I say, "I'm sorry about earlier."

He shakes his head as he comes to stand in front of me. "Don't apologize. You've been through hell."

Hell. It's the understatement of the century.

God, I hope things get better, or I'm going to lose my mind.

It's getting late, and the sun is starting to set. I'm still sitting on the bed while Raighne is standing in front of me, absentmindedly brushing his fingers over my broken arm.

The silence is heavy in the room. I know he wants to talk about what happened, but I'm not ready, and I can't let him into my mind until I am.

All I can think about right now is my father out there with Adeth and Ares. That, and sitting on the side of the bed, is starting to hurt like crazy.

I wish I could lie down.

My muscles are cramping up, and my back and ribs are aching something fierce.

I need painkillers, and I'm not just talking about one. A whole bottle will do right about now.

"Are you comfortable sitting like this?" Raighne asks, obviously not missing a thing.

He tilts his head to try and catch my eyes, and I duck my head lower.

"Don't hide from me."

I let out a sigh then say, "I can't lie down."

Raighne knows about my back, the broken arm, and cuts on my cheeks but not about my broken ribs and the cut at the back of my thigh. And I don't plan to tell him about those.

He takes hold of my chin and lifts my face to his. After all I've been through, he still makes my heart beat faster with just the slightest touch.

"Let me help."

I'm too tired to fight and nod.

He carefully slips his arms beneath me and carries me to a nearby armchair. After taking a seat, he says, "Straddle me."

A blush creeps up my neck and face as I do as I'm told.

I might be in a lot of pain, but I still have a healthy pair of ovaries.

I shift on his lap, and not knowing what to do with my right arm, I just sit on his thighs and stare down at where the fabric of my nightgown has bunched up. Then, my eyes touch on the bulge between his legs.

Yeah, I'm not going to get any sleep.

Raighne wraps his hand around the back of my neck and tugs me closer until I'm leaning against his chest.

"Relax."

"Easier said than done."

He pulls slightly back, then gives me a questioning look. "What's wrong?"

Unable to say the words out loud, I think them. *"This is just a really intimate position."*

"Is it a problem?"

I narrow my eyes on him. *"I'm so not having this conversation with you."*

His features tighten, and gripping hold of my hips, he tugs me right against him.

"Relax," he orders, his tone not leaving any space for arguments.

Letting out a sigh, I do my best to relax while trying not to think of what's beneath the leather I'm sitting on.

His hand brushes over my left arm, and slowly, my muscles begin to loosen a bit.

"Much better," he sighs in my mind.

I feel myself melt into his body and tuck my face into the crook of his neck, letting out a breath of relief because I think I can actually sleep in this position.

His hand keeps brushing up and down my left arm, and I swear the pain is lessening. I glance down at where he's touching me, and when I see a faint blue glowing light between his palm and my skin, my lips part with a gasp.

"Raighne!"

When he doesn't answer me, I pull back so I can see his face. It looks like he's in a trance as he stares at my arm, and by the time he snaps out of it, sweat beads on his forehead.

Slowly, I move my arm, and when there's no pain at all, and it feels completely healed, my eyes jump back to Raighne's.

"Oh my God, Raighne," I say, my tone filled with disbelief. "You just healed my arm."

A second later, shock flashes over his face, and his eyes lock on mine. "I wasn't aware I was doing it."

When I start to smile, I quickly have to stop because the movement makes the cuts pull. It draws his attention to my face, and he lifts his hands, framing my cheeks.

"Let me in."

I hesitate for a moment before I nod, praying I don't give

away any of my feelings for him.

His warmth pours through me, and the longer I stare at Raighne, the more I start to imagine that I see hunger in his eyes.

That's impossible.

Before I can process what's happening, his mouth crashes against mine, and I'm engulfed in everything that's Raighne. His hands move to my hair, and he fists the short strands. I can't hold back a sob when I feel him enter my mind.

I try to break the kiss, but he just tightens his hold on me. *"I don't want you to see inside my mind.'*

"You are mine," his growl echoes through me. *"Every part of you, Alchera. The only way I can heal you is if you let me in."*

His delicious scent and taste envelop me, and my abdomen clenches hard as my walls come crashing down.

Raighne groans as his tongue brushes over my lips before entering my mouth, and the primal sound sends tingles rushing over my body.

"Oh God," I moan because I didn't know this is what a kiss feels like.

"You haven't been kissed before?" his voice rumbles inside me.

"No."

My reply unleashes a storm in him, and Raighne washes through me like a tsunami, his intensity stealing the breath from my lungs.

I press closer to him, wanting as much of him as I can get. I know it's wrong because he's only trying to heal me.

He doesn't want me the same way I want him.

But I can't stop.

My heart is racing, and I'm consumed with passion for this man. It feels so good to have his mouth on mine, even if it's for the wrong reasons.

His hands move down my body before settling on the sides of

my thighs, and the nightgown bunches around his arms as he moves his hands beneath the fabric and up to my back.

I brace for pain, but there's none.

I can only feel Raighne, his lips nipping and biting mine, his tongue lashing and tasting.

He consumes me entirely until there's only him, and I have no idea how long we kiss for.

Raighne starts to slow down his assault on me, and when I regain control of my mind, I'm a breathless mess on his lap.

His hands brush up and down my back once more before he pulls them out from under the fabric, and when he breaks the kiss, he trails his fingers over my cheeks.

I swear the man took me to the heavens and beyond, and coming down, I begin to feel self-conscious.

My eyes focus on him, and seeing the serious expression on his face, I squirm and glance away.

"Look at me."

I shake my head, and it has him gripping hold of my chin and forcing me to look at him.

When our eyes lock, he asks, "How do you feel?"

I suck in a deep breath of air and focus on my back while I lift a hand to my face. The pain in my back is much more manageable, and the scabs on my cheeks are practically gone.

Slowly, a smile tugs at my mouth. "It worked," I whisper, the awkwardness forgotten as relief fills me.

"Good."

I lower my eyes from his, then ask, "So you have to kiss me in order to heal me?"

He lets out a chuckle as he shakes his head. "No, but the kiss got you to focus on me so I could do my job."

The words sting like hell, and I quickly glance away so he won't see the disappointment in my eyes while I mutter, "Right."

I begin to move so I can get off his lap, but he grips hold of my hips and frowns at me. "What's wrong?"

I shake my head, refusing to make eye contact with him. "I'm just exhausted."

When I move again, he doesn't stop me. The cut at the back of my leg is tender as fuck from the position I sat in, and the stitches pull, but I suppress the pain so Raighne won't pick up on it, because I can't handle another kiss right now.

"Thank you for healing me," I say as I walk to the bed. "At least I'll be able to sleep now."

Raighne doesn't get up and just stares at me.

"Why are you withdrawing from me?"

"I'm not," I lie. *"I'm just tired. You should get some rest as well."*

Still, he doesn't budge from the chair.

I climb beneath the covers and pull them up to my chin as I gingerly lie down, careful not to agitate my broken ribs.

Squeezing my eyes shut, I will sleep to come quickly, but instead of my wish coming true, I lie awake, highly conscious of Raighne.

"Did I make a mistake by kissing you?"

Avoiding the truth, I answer, *"It helped with the healing."*

"But?"

"No buts."

"Alchera." His tone is much harsher this time around.

"Just leave it," I snap out loud.

I hear the chair creak, and a moment later, the bed dips beneath Raighne's weight as he sits down beside me.

"Don't shut me out."

I pull the covers up higher to hide the blush on my face as I admit, *"It was my first kiss. I thought it would be more special than just being used for healing purposes."*

Raighne is quiet for a moment, and then he climbs to his feet and walks out of the room.

"*Raighne?*"

"*Rest well, Alchera.*" His tone is cold and clearly unhappy with me.

Was I wrong to admit that to him?

Confused as hell, I lie for close to an hour thinking about what happened tonight, but by the time I drift off to sleep, I'm no closer to an answer.

CHAPTER 20

RAIGHNE

It feels like every time I make progress with Alchera, she pushes me away and the distance between us grows.

Standing outside her living quarters with my arms crossed over my chest, everyone gives me a wide berth.

The past week has been hell. Feeling the pain Adeth and Ares were subjecting her to and worrying about not getting to her in time almost killed me.

Scratch that. The past week was the worst I've ever experienced.

I glance at the doorway, feeling frustrated and hurt that Alchera minimized our kiss like that.

I thought she felt the passion, but I was wrong.

Maybe it's just one-sided?

Fuck. I'm doomed to love my charge while she doesn't feel the same.

There was a moment when I believed the attraction was mutual. Alchera kissed me back.

Maybe she was just caught up in the moment.

I let out a heavy sigh, not happy at all.

My growing love for her is not the only problem I have.

Alchera keeps fighting me, never fully letting me in. Which means she's either hiding something from me or she doesn't trust me.

Both are bad because it will keep our bond from deepening.

What the hell am I going to do to get through to her?

Letting out a sigh, I stare up at the night sky as I try to find answers to the problems.

By the time I feel Alchera drift off to sleep, the camp is quiet.

Heading back into her living quarters, my eyes fall on her sleeping face as I walk closer to the bed.

Why won't you fully connect with me, my little dreamer?

She makes an illegible sound before snuggling her face deeper into the pillow, and I wish that damned pillow was my chest.

She should be in my arms where she belongs.

Careful not to make a noise, I move the chair much closer to the bed and sit down. My eyes lock on my charge's face, and my heart fills with the love I feel for her.

I almost lost you.

Never again.

And come hell or high water, I will find a way to get past your defenses.

Before she was taken, I fought my feelings for her, knowing I had no right. But after this fucked up week, I don't care anymore.

I love Alchera, and over my dead body will I share her with another man.

I'll find a way to make her love me.

I just have to.

Alchera moves in her sleep, and I reach out to take her hand but pause a mere inch from touching her.

She curls into a fetal position, and I'm surprised when her hand finds mine. "Raighne," she mumbles, and her fingers wrap around mine.

"*Shh...I'm here, my little dreamer.*"

She lets out a sigh of relief and seems to settle into a deeper sleep.

ALCHERA

A feeling of love and peace wraps around me, and I hear someone call out, "Hello, Jason. Hello, Jason."

Looking around, I find myself in the middle of a kitchen. Jason's standing in front of me, facing a large cage. The door is open, and hanging upside down from the open doorway is a beautiful red-tailed, grayish bird.

It's letting Jason lovingly ruffle its feathers.

"Pappa, Pappa." A voice calls again.

I search through the kitchen until I notice another bird, looking exactly like the one hanging in the cage, its feet slapping on the tiles as it eagerly tries to get to Jason.

I watch with wonder as the bird climbs up Jason's pant leg.

"Hey, my boy. You want some love as well?" Jason coos as he scratches the bird's head. "You're a jealous one, aren't you?"

He loves them as if they're his children.

Tears well in my eyes because I've never encountered a man who loves animals so much. I've never seen birds display such emotion, nestling their heads against his, closing their eyes, and clearly showing how much they love him in return.

I wake up with a start, the vision still fresh in my mind.

I have to get to Jason.

A moment later, I become aware that I'm clinging to someone's hand, and my eyes dart to the side of the bed.

Seeing Raighne sitting in an armchair, I relax and let out a sigh before asking, "Did you sleep here last night?"

Staring at me, he just nods.

Great. He's probably still angry with me.

"What did you see?" he asks calmly.

Pulling my hand from his, I carefully sit up. My body doesn't ache as badly as yesterday, but my broken ribs and the cut on my leg are super tender. Whatever Aster gave me for the pain must still be working, for which I'm grateful as hell.

I clear my throat and rub a hand over my face. "I saw a chosen one."

"What stood out about him?" Raighne asks.

"Never in all of my life have I felt so much love before." I let out a resentful chuckle. "He gives his animals more love than I've ever had."

When Raighne frowns at me, I add, "I mean, the love Jason feels for those birds is so humbling. And the birds love him back."

"He'll probably be the one to take care of the animals." Raighne climbs to his feet. "We'll leave as soon as you're strong enough. I'll get everything ready."

"There's just one problem." I pause, not knowing how to word this right.

"What?"

"Jason isn't going to leave willingly. I saw into his soul, and he won't leave his animals behind. Not when they're going to die while he lives."

I look at Raighne in desperation.

"He'll have to come, Alchera. Even if we have to take him by force."

My jaw drops, and shaking my head, I ask, "How can you say that?" I throw my legs over the side of the bed and climb to my feet. "I won't allow any of these humans to suffer the heartache I have. You're not just going to throw them through a damn waterfall. Besides, we're bringing animals anyway. Why not bring over his as well?"

There's an overwhelming need in my soul to fight for the chosen ten who will lose everything, just like I lost everything.

"The list has been made," Raighne says. "It is not for us to decide."

"Who decides?" I snap.

"The orders came down from Awo himself."

Letting out a frustrated sigh, I say, "I want my chosen ones to have a smooth shift from Earth to Vaalbara. I'll fight for them, and I don't care if I have to go against Awo to make it happen."

Raighne shakes his head at me and is just about to say something back when the air starts to vibrate around us.

In a flash, Raighne grabs hold of me, and his arms form steel bands around my body.

"What's happening?" I gasp.

"Awo," Raighne breathes, sounding shocked out of his everloving mind.

"I've given the orders," a voice thunders through the room, making me flinch closer to Raighne.

Oh shit.

It feels like a force is trying to make me submit, but somehow, I manage to turn around and face Awo.

I haven't survived Adeth and Ares only to back down now.

All I see is a bright light, with thousands of glimmering orbs making up a whole. They seem to be multiplying and lessening by the second.

"Ask the question burning inside of you, for this chance will only come once," the being orders.

I stand stunned for a moment, not able to find any train of thought. His voice is so beautifully thunderous, leaving me in a state of astonishment.

I have to dig deep, looking for the courage I know is inside my soul.

My tongue darts out to wet my lips, then my voice quivers as I say, "Please, bring Jason's animals to Vaalbara. He loves those animals more than his own life. He's coming to a foreign world, and he needs them. We can't just rip the chosen ten away from everything they love."

My words dry up, and I don't know what else to say.

For a few tense seconds, I can only feel the vibrations in the air, then Awo says, "You get one request. Only one. And you use it to plead for a human's earthly animals? You're in so much pain and have a quest ahead of you that will require all the strength you can gather, yet you think of another. You have no past and are in doubt of your future. Your father faces certain death, but still, you think of another."

His words hit hard and rip the very air from my lungs.

I grab at my stomach to keep myself standing.

Dad!

Awo moves closer to me until I can feel his presence surge through my soul.

"Your soul is true, Alchera. I'll bring the animals. All you need to focus on is bringing my chosen ten home. Beginning at dawn, you have only ten days to complete your destiny."

With the timeline given, I watch as the light fades and the air settles around us.

As Raighne lets go of me, I stare at the spot where Awo was a moment ago, his words echoing through me.

'Your father faces certain death.'

That means my father's going to die, doesn't it?

I could've saved him with one question, but instead, I asked for Jason's animals to be spared.

No. That can't be.

Just as I suck in a shaky breath, still trying to process what just happened, Thana comes rushing into the room with Brenna right behind her. Finian and a man who looks a lot like him also join us.

I assume he's Finian's twin and Thana's guardian, and my assumption is proven right because he moves in behind Thana and places his hand on her shoulder.

"How are you feeling?" Thana asks, her features drawn tight with worry.

"Fine," I say to avoid answering the truth because I don't think I'll ever feel fine again.

Thana glances at all of us, then announces, "I've been called to leave so I can fulfill my destiny."

Brenna sucks in a trembling breath, and her eyes start to shine with unshed tears.

Confused by her strong reaction, my gaze darts back to Thana. "What does that mean?"

Too much is happening too soon.

"It's my destiny to destroy Earth," she says.

I stare at Thana, my heart clenching because she has to kill billions of people.

"Isn't there another way?" I ask. "Maybe if we warn the humans, they will change their ways."

Thana shakes her head. "I've given them many warnings, Alchera." She lifts her chin as she looks at me. "They've had thousands of years, but all they've done is destroy the Earth given to them. Instead of caring for the animals, they've slaughtered them to the point of extinction. Their greed and selfishness are all that matters to them." Her tone grows harsh as she continues, "Forests are gone. Wetlands are destroyed. The oceans are polluted, and the sea creatures butchered." She sucks in a deep breath and shakes her head. "Countries are at war while others look the other way. That's what the world has come to – pure selfishness and hatred. This is for the best. Things cannot keep spiraling out of control."

As hard as it is for me to accept, I have to admit everything she's said is the truth. I can't worry about billions. I need to focus on my chosen ten.

Lifting my chin, I say, "I want to know what I'll be up against while I'm on Earth gathering my chosen ones."

"There will be great disasters, ripping the world apart. Please tell me you've had a vision?" She asks as she takes hold of my hand.

"Yes. I saw my first chosen one. He–"

Thana tightens her grip on my hand. "No, don't tell me. Just retrieve the chosen ones and bring them back. You have to gather all ten before you're allowed to return to Vaalbara. Not a moment before." Her voice is filled with sudden urgency.

Before I can ask anything else, her guardian walks toward us, and he removes her hand from mine. I watch as they leave the room then glance at Raighne as the bitter reality of what's to come sinks in like a heavy stone.

"I'm scared."

He closes the distance between us, and wrapping his arm around my shoulders, he hugs me to his side.

"We'll face everything together. You're not alone."

"So, when do we leave?" Brenna asks.

"At first daylight," Raighne answers. "We have to remember to get elixirs from Aster so we'll blend in on Earth."

"I'll take care of it," Brenna offers, all her aggression nowhere to be seen.

Suddenly, we hear a commotion outside, and we quickly walk out of my living quarters to see what's going on.

Raighne's hand finds mine, and he links our fingers as we move closer to where a group is gathering around two men who are climbing off their horses.

Only then do I see the two bodies draped over another horse. *God.*

"What's going on?" Finian calls out.

One of the men shakes his head, his face ashen in color. "Adeth ambushed us in the forest. It's the King."

Brenna and I dart forward, but she's the first to ask, "What about the King?"

The man shakes his head again. "Griffith is bringing him. We...we..."

No!

I swing around, and breaking out into a run, I head for the forest.

"Alchera!" Raighne shouts behind me.

My body protests, and I don't even make it to the line of trees when I'm yanked backward. A cry is ripped from me as I fly through the air, my ribs aching something fierce from the force Raighne's using to draw me back to him.

I want my dad. I need my dad.

When I slam into Raighne's chest, and his arms lock around me, air explodes from my lungs, my ribs aching horribly.

Before I can let Raighne have it, movement by the trees catches my attention, and I notice Janak first.

Then Griffith appears, looking like he lost a fight against a bear.

When I see my father's body hanging limply over the back of a horse, my chest implodes with unbearable heartache.

"Nooooo!" I scream, the air trembling around me from the excruciating emotions ripping me to shreds.

"Father!" Brenna cries, and Finian moves fast to restrain her.

Griffith looks like death as he carries our father to us, and when he lays him gently on the ground, he kneels by his fallen charge.

"He severed our bond," Griffith groans. "He severed our bond right before she killed him to spare my life."

"NoNoNo!" I cry as I fight against Raighne's hold.

"Let go of me!"

His arms only tighten even more around me.

"Please. I need to be with my father," I sob.

Raighne lets go, and I dart forward, falling to my knees next to my dad. Brenna sinks down beside me, and we stare at our father's lifeless face. His chest is charred black as if something has burned right through him.

"I'm so sorry," I whimper. "I let you die. This is all my fault." I scoot closer and lift his head onto my lap while Brenna grabs hold of his hand.

"Awo. Why did this happen?" she groans.

Because I asked Awo the wrong question.

I begin to rock my father as agonizing pain flays my soul, and I whimper, "I've failed you... all for a bunch of strangers."

My throat strains painfully as I caress his hair.

"I had no time with you," I sob.

Brenna moves closer to me and wraps her arm around my shoulders as Raighne's warmth moves through me.

"It's my fault," I tell her, my voice hoarse.

She shakes her head, sobbing, "No, it's not."

Awo said I could've asked for anything! But I didn't think of my own father.

What kind of daughter does that?

I hold my dad tightly to my chest and let out a broken cry, "This isn't fair! If I had known my father would die, I wouldn't have asked for Jason's animals. You fooled me. I want my father back." Sobs tear from my very soul, and I feel Raighne's warmth battle the darkness growing in my heart.

"Give him back to me," I beg. "This isn't fair."

"You need to calm down, child," Janak says, sounding worried.

It feels as if something snaps in me. Ice spreads through my veins as all the emotions fade until only my rage remains.

Numbly, I sink back until I'm sitting flat on my butt, and my father slips from my arms.

"*Alchera!*" Raighne's voice echoes somewhere in the back of my mind.

It feels like the last piece of my soul, of the person I used to be, splinters into nothing.

"Alchera?" Raighne crouches beside me, his hand settling on my shoulder.

Not even he matters at this moment.

Nothing matters anymore.

I feel dead inside.

Dead and dark.

My voice sounds cold and lifeless as I whisper, "Awo let my dad die. He just...let him die."

Somehow, I manage to climb to my feet while Brenna sobs beside our dead father.

I look down at my dad one last time and turn my back on all of them.

I feel Raighne right behind me as I walk into the forest, silent tears rolling down my cheeks and washing away what feels like the last of my humanity.

I'll save the chosen ten, and after that, I'll wash my hands clean of Vaalbara.

CHAPTER 21

Dreams and Visions.
A world is torn apart,
while another is said to start.
So many people are gone, now dead.
The sun has turned to its infamous red.
Only ten to be taken,
while the rest will be forsaken.

ALCHERA

I think someone once said you can die from heartache.
They're wrong.

Standing on the top of a hill, I watch as everyone gathers around Janak and my father's body that's lying on top of a stone altar of some sort.

Some are crying, while others are staring blankly ahead of them as Janak says something I can't hear.

He places his hand on my father's chest, and a moment later, a twinkling light begins to appear as my father's soul drifts up into the sky to be with Awo before his body vanishes.

A woman falls to her knees, and my eyes lock on her.

For a second, I feel a flicker of interest as she claws at her chest, but Thana and Brenna help her back to her feet, then remain standing on either side of her.

Is she the elusive mother I can barely remember?

"Alchera."

I forcefully block Raighne for the umpteenth time.

The damn man is persistent. He's been trying non-stop to get through to me since our last talk, which, by the way, didn't go down too well.

I regret what I said to Raighne yesterday, but it's done now, and I can't turn back time.

Once again, the conversation replays in my mind as I watch them honor my father.

"Alchera! Wait, please. We need to talk."

I swing around to face Raighne, and when he sees my expression, shock flickers in his eyes.

"You are grief-stricken over losing your father," he states the obvious.

"You're wrong," I hiss as I shake my head. "I'm more than just grief-stricken. I'm pissed!" When his lips part, I hold up my hand to stop him from talking. "It's the last straw. I can handle everybody messing with me, but taking out my dad, killing him off like he's some worthless being? No! He is my dad. He is your King!" My voice rises, and I have to pause to catch my breath.

Raighne wants to say something, but I silence him with a look of warning. "You don't get to speak now," I snap. "You don't get to say anything."

I walk right up to him so he can see every ounce of my rage as I say, "Don't follow me. Go back to your people and tell them I'm done. I'll save the chosen ones, but I want no part in anything to do with Vaalbara. I'm done with you and your kind. You took everything from me." I suck in a quivering breath. "I have nothing more to give."

Without giving him a chance to say anything, I turn around and walk away while forcefully blocking him from my mind.

I've also been thinking about my time on Vaalbara and how it's changed me.

Even though it's made me stronger, it's also turned me into a hard, bitter person.

I suppose it's what they wanted.

I sneak into my living quarters like a damned escaped convict while everyone's mourning my father.

Now's the only chance I have to wash up. I hurry, constantly listening for any movement outside, and when I'm finally wearing clean clothes, I let out a breath of relief.

I search through all the drawers, and finding a pair of scissors, I do my best to cut my hair into a less shitty style.

I'm wasting time, but when I'm done, my hair's cut short against my scalp and standing every which way.

Fuck. That doesn't look much better.

I let out a sigh as a pang of loss threatens to bloom in my chest, but I smother it. I don't have time to waste on stupid feelings.

With no time to spare, I rush out of my living quarters and break out into a run toward the forest.

I use the trees for cover, and finding the stream, I follow it as I make my way in the direction of the Virtutes Waterfall.

Today, I'm getting my ass off this damned planet.

I don't take in any of the lush green shrubs and beautiful sights around me and only focus as I dart over the uneven terrain.

My chest begins to ache something fierce, but I ignore the pain and push my body harder.

It takes way too long, and only when the sun is starting to set do I break through the trees.

When I reach the pool, a cool breeze feels good on my clammy skin and my breaths are wheezing over my parted lips.

Remembering the pool isn't as deep as it looks, I step into the cool water.

As I approach the curtain, I see movement up on a ledge, and shock shudders through me as a guard steps out from behind the waterfall.

Shit.

"Peace be, Princess Alchera," he says. He bows slightly but still keeps his eyes on me.

Dammit! This is the last thing I need.

"Peace be," I mutter, glancing around me for any sign of trouble. "I need to go back to Earth, and I'd appreciate your assistance in doing so."

An older guard joins the younger one and asks, "Peace be, Princess. Should you not be at your father's funeral?"

My eyes dart back to them, and I shove away the stab of grief in my chest.

There's no time to mourn.

"I was there," I answer. "I've paid my respects. Now, if you're finished questioning me, I'd like to pass through. I'd appreciate your help." There's tension in my voice, as clear as a freaking bell.

"Why do you need to shift to Earth, and where's your guardian?" the older man asks.

"My business is my own, and I'm in a hurry," I snap, anger tightening my tone.

The younger guard bows his head and heads back to his spot behind the curtain of rushing water.

"If it's your wish." The older guard turns and indicates for me to step through the curtain. "You'll need to clear your mind of everything but your destination. If you think of anything else, things could go terribly wrong. Please ensure you focus solely on your destination before you pass into the fall's curtain." He starts to move back behind the waterfall. "May Awo guide you on your travels."

"That's all I have to do?" I check with him.

"Yes," he nods, then goes back to his place on the ledge.

I wade through the water, and when I'm standing right in front of the curtain, droplets of water pelting me, I concentrate on clearing my mind.

My breathing slows, and I feel myself relaxing. I picture Fish Creek Falls in my mind's eye, but as I take the step into the curtain, a vision robs me of my ability to think.

I see Jason kneeling by a pond. He's crying, tears running down his cheeks. He punches at the water while shouting.

I feel his pain rip through me.

And then... I see nothing.

There's darkness all around me, and my stomach lurches. I try to suck in a breath of air but only manage to inhale water. It burns into my lungs, suffocating me.

I panic, and my arms flail to the side. I hit something rough, coated with a layer of slime. Pushing myself away from it, I immediately bob to the surface, and I cough before desperately gasping for air.

Jesus, the water tastes like shit.

I cough again and spit the disgusting taste from my mouth while I glance around me.

Where the hell am I?

Standing in a pond in someone's backyard, it takes a moment before I realize this is Jason's property.

Holy shit.

To my left is an artificial waterfall with a large aviary located behind it.

I must've come through the waterfall when I had the vision of Jason.

I quickly look around again but don't see Jason anywhere. After I drag my slimy butt out of the pond, I check the large aviary, but there's nothing in it, not even one tiny little bird.

I walk out onto the other side of the yard and spot more cages. Their doors stand wide open, and four dog kennels lay empty to my right. All the animals are gone.

I jog around the side of the house, and finding an open sliding door, I slip inside.

My heart is pounding in my throat, and I can hear mumbling from somewhere inside the house.

I sneak through a living room, and when I near the kitchen, I notice Jason kneeling by the large cage where I last saw the two beautiful gray birds in my visions.

He's leaning his forehead against the steel bars of the cage while his whole body convulses with sobs.

I can feel his heart breaking.

"Where are you?" he cries. "How can you all just be gone?"

As I reach out to comfort him, he startles and swings around.

"Who are you? What do you want?" Surprisingly I understand everything he says even though I've never spoken his language.

Understanding different languages must be one of my talents so I can communicate with all my chosen ones.

I drop my hand to my side, not having a clue how to handle the situation.

"I'm Raighne, and this is Alchera," Raighne suddenly says in English from behind me, giving me a damn near heart attack. "We need to talk."

I don't glance at Raighne and keep my eyes locked on one-hell-of-a-shocked-looking Jason.

"You just walk into my house uninvited and demand you want to talk to me?" Jason snaps, his accent not too thick. He doesn't take his red-rimmed eyes off us.

I can't blame the man. I sure wouldn't trust the situation if I were in his shoes.

"We mean you no harm," I say. "We're here to help."

Jason inches away from us, giving both of us apprehensive looks.

"May she use the restroom?" Raighne shoves a bag at me.

Jason throws his arms in the air, shaking his head. "Why even ask? I mean, I only live here. Normally, people ask before they trespass on private property. But, hey, who am I to say anything? Help yourself." He lets out an incredulous burst of laughter, then adds, "Down the hall, first door on the right."

"Take the elixir," Raighne mutters.

Shit. My eyes and clothes.

I hurry away, and entering the restroom, I quickly shut the door behind me.

When I catch sight of myself in the mirror, I cringe a little. It's a damn miracle Jason isn't screaming his head off.

I open the bag to discover regular human clothes.

I strip out of the wet leather and put on a pair of jeans, a T-shirt, and a hoodie. When I find sneakers in the bag, a smile curves my lips for the first time in days.

Seeing the small, brown vial, I take the top off and quickly drink the bitter elixir.

Jesus. Yuck.

Seconds tick by, and I still feel the same.

Damn, I kind of hoped the elixir would've taken away my pain as well.

The thought makes me peek in the bathroom cabinet, and

228

seeing a box with the word painkiller printed on the side, I glance at the shut bathroom door before I take the medicine.

Opening the box, I'm confused as I stare at a bunch of patches.

Who the hell uses patches as painkillers?

Well, beggars can't be choosers.

I take one and carefully stick it over my ribs before straightening out my shirt and hoodie.

The box seems to be full, so I take out another three, hoping Jason won't notice they're missing.

Hold up. Jason's leaving with us, so why not just take the whole box, right?

I stand for a moment, feeling guilty about stealing it, before shoving the whole box of painkiller patches into my bag.

I glance at my reflection in the mirror to see if the elixir has worked and notice only my eyes have changed. Instead of sparkling like emeralds, they're just plain green now.

I suck in a deep breath, and when my ribs don't ache as much, a smile tugs at my lips.

I leave the bathroom, and when I finally make my appearance, both men just stare at me.

I notice Raighne's eyes are light blue, but otherwise he also looks the same, and not like the younger version when he was pretending to be Ryan.

Seeing him wearing jeans and a T-shirt is weird, though.

Hot weird.

Jason is the first to speak. "What do you want?" His voice falls like icicles around us.

"Jason, I know this is strange and–"

"How do you know my name?" He takes a step toward me, which makes Raighne take a step forward as well.

"It's kind of hard to explain without sounding crazy." I try to give him a smile to put him at ease.

"Well, why don't we take a seat in the living room, and then you explain it to me." He shoves past me, and we have no choice but to follow him.

When I take a seat across from Jason, Raighne sits down beside me.

All the chaotic emotions I've felt the past week threaten to overwhelm me, but this isn't the place or the time to think about it, and I forcefully shove it back.

"You better start talking," Jason snaps, pulling me from my thoughts.

I look at him and take a deep breath before I say, "I'm going to tell you something that will freak you out, but try to stay calm."

He just stares me down, not giving me anything to work with.

Well, here goes nothing.

Letting out a sigh, I continue, "I know your name because I've had a vision about you."

What else am I going to say? The truth is all I have.

"I know it sounds crazy." I give him a pleading look. "In my first vision, you were standing in the passageway of the aviary at the back of your house, talking to your birds. At some point, you looked right at me as if you sensed I was there."

His eyes are glued to me, telling me I definitely have his attention now.

"In the second vision, you were in your kitchen. You had two beautiful gray birds with you. The love I felt in the visions was overwhelming, Jason. It's what makes you so special."

When he lowers his head and lets out a shaky breath, my heart squeezes for him.

I get up, and crossing the living room, I take a seat beside Jason. Needing to comfort him, I place my hand on his back.

He clears his throat, and with a thick voice, he says, "When I

230

woke up this morning, they were all gone. The birds and fish. My dogs...they're gone. Even poor Siege, who's dying of cancer. Who would take a sick, old dog?"

He covers his face, and his body shudders as he cries for his animals.

I scoot closer to him, feeling an echo of his sadness in my chest.

This is the heartache I didn't want any of my chosen ones to experience.

"They're my life," he mutters. "I just want them back."

He pulls away from me and drops his face into his hands, a heartbreaking sob shuddering through his body.

"Your animals are waiting for you safely on Vaalbara," Raighne says.

Jason's head snaps up, and my eyes dart to Raighne as I say, "You couldn't have told us this sooner? The man is in pain, Raighne. Your timing sucks."

"Vaal...what?" Jason mutters next to me. He looks from Raighne to me like we're crazy.

"I'm here to take you to Vaalbara. It's a new Earth." I pause for a moment, then break the news to him as best I can. "All hell is about to break loose. It's the end of this world, and you have been chosen to be saved. There's a new Earth waiting for you, and your animals have already been taken there."

I watch him cautiously, waiting for a response.

I'd lose my shit if someone dropped such a crazy bomb on my ass.

"It's the end of the world?" he asks, his face masked with disbelief.

"Yeah, pretty much." I nod, folding my hands on my lap. I look down and start to fidget, not knowing what else to do.

"There's a new Earth?" Jason asks, scooting to the edge of the couch.

"Yes." I really hope he's starting to understand. I don't know what else to tell him.

"My animals are there?" His voice pitches.

"Yeah, they're safely there," I assure him.

His tone is deceptively calm when he says, "You took my animals."

"Ye–"

Suddenly, Jason lunges at me, and his fingers wrap brutally around my neck. I'm shoved back onto the couch, unable to gasp as he chokes the living hell out of me.

"You took my animals?! You dare touch my children and then break into my house! I'm going to fucking kill you," he hisses in my face.

I gasp for a breath of air and grab his arms.

When I try to focus on Jason, all I see is Ares, and the horror I suffered at his hands bleeds through my soul.

I start hitting him as hard as I can while bucking my body wildly.

The next moment, I'm hitting the air as Raighne yanks Jason off me.

I grab at my throat and scramble away from them until my back hits the wall. I keep sucking in huge gulps of air, trying to ease the burn in my lungs while my ribs are aching something fierce.

I can breathe. I'm safe. There's no Adeth. No Ares. Raighne's here.

Jason drops to his knees with Raighne standing next to him, ready to restrain him if he has to.

"I'm so sorry. I've never laid hands on a woman before. I just want them back. Give by animals back," Jason begs.

I turn my face away from them, and I feel the same anger pulse through me that I felt the day my dad died. Before I can stop the words, they burn over my lips. "I chose your animals over my father." I suck in a desperate breath, and a sob sputters from me as I shout, "My father died so your animals could live."

Jason glances up at me." What?"

"I was told I could have one request, and I used it to save your precious animals," I spit at him. "I didn't save my father and let him die. I didn't know any better. I didn't understand. I begged for your damned animals. Obviously, my wish was granted." I glare at him. "It was my dad's funeral today, yet I'm standing here trying to save your life, so I fucking suggest you get your ass up and pull yourself together. I have nine other people to save before I can take you all to Vaalbara, and we're running out of time."

The air is thick with tension as Jason climbs to his feet. His eyes lock with mine, and we stare at each other.

I have no idea what I'll do if Jason keeps losing his shit. We'll have to forcefully drag him to wherever the next chosen one is.

Jesus, what if they all reject me? I can't control ten people who want to beat my ass.

Letting out a tired sigh, I say, "I know you want to see your animals again. You have one of two choices. Either you come with us willingly, or we take you by force. It's your choice how this plays out."

God, I don't want to take Jason by force.

"I'll see my animals if I go with you?" he asks, his tone still unsure.

"Yes."

"Where are we going?" he demands.

"I don't know yet. I'm waiting for the next vision, but you should pack a bag because we could leave at any moment."

His eyes stay on me for a few seconds before he nods and walks out of the living room.

I rush forward and watch as he heads to a bedroom at the end of the hallway.

"Let me look at your neck," Raighne mutters as his fingers brush over my throat.

"I'm okay, it's nothing," I mutter as I pull away.

Before I can put more distance between us, he grabs hold of my arm, and I'm yanked flush with his solid chest.

His features are carved from stone with anger, but he says nothing as he wraps his fingers around my neck.

When his warmth trickles beneath my skin, I close my eyes and focus hard to keep my walls up so he won't see into my mind.

"So stubborn," he grumbles before letting go of me.

I quickly turn away from him, and exhausted because of everything that's happened to me these past three months, I struggle to fight back the tears.

Swallowing hard, I lift my chin and force myself to suck it up.

Unfortunately, my voice is shaky when I say, "Thanks for the clothes."

"Brenna chose them," he murmurs in a much gentler tone.

"They're here?" I ask with my back still turned to him.

"Yes. They're waiting outside."

Jason returns to the living room, looking like he's ready to go to war.

He's changed his clothes and has a huge duffle bag in his hand. Taking one look at him, you'd think he's ready to conquer Mount Everest.

"Don't look at me like that," he says, giving me half a smile. "I'm not the weird one around here. I don't know where you two are taking me or what I'm in for. I want to be prepared."

"I didn't say anything," I mutter, too relieved he's coming with us and we don't have to use force.

Suddenly, a sharp pain shoots through my head, driving me straight to my knees. Just as I hit the floor, Raighne's arms wrap around me.

CHAPTER 22

ALCHERA

I'm blinded for a few seconds, and all I can do is hold my head. I can't make a sound, my jaw's clenched so tightly from the acute pain.

"Sarah, open your mouth for me, honey. Just a little more," I hear a man with an Irish accent say, worry and love coating his words.

"That's it, sis. Just a little more. You're doing so great. Here's some water. Swallow for me. That's it, down the hatch they go."

I can feel someone holding my head back so the water and pills can go down my throat. I swallow as best I can.

He holds me for a few minutes while wiping beads of sweat from my face with a cool cloth.

"You're so strong, Sarah. You'll beat this ugly thing yet. We'll beat it together."

It takes all my strength to pry my eyes open as he wipes blood from my nose.

Before my vision can focus on his face, everything goes black.

I open my eyes and feel Raighne's familiar arms around me.

"Alchera?" His face is a mask of worry as he wipes something from my face, his fingertips coming away bloody.

Shit.

I shake my head lightly and begin to sit up while saying, "The pain isn't mine."

When I try to climb to my feet, Raighne pulls me back against his chest. "No, not yet. Your nose is bleeding."

Jason comes in with some paper towels, asking, "What happened? Is she okay?"

There's remorse on his face as if he blames himself for what happened.

"I had another vision." I take a paper towel from Jason and wipe the last of the blood from my nose. "She's in a lot of pain. Her name is-"

"Don't tell us about her. We don't know how far behind us Adeth may be," Raighne warns me.

My eyes snap to his face. "Adeth is here?"

"We don't know where she is," he says. "We just have to be cautious."

This time, he lets me climb to my feet.

There's movement by the sliding door, then Brenna and Finian enter the room, giving us questioning looks. It's weird seeing them in regular clothes, and I don't know what to say to Brenna. In spite of everything, she must be heartbroken from losing our father.

"Thanks for the clothes," I mutter.

"Don't mention it." Her voice is softer, and she gives me a worried look. "Are you okay?"

Feeling awkward, I just nod.

Brenna surprises the hell out of me when she closes the distance between us and pulls me into a hug. Her voice is strained as she whispers, "We missed you at the funeral."

"I was there."

I'm still stunned that she's hugging me.

Maybe they threw something in her elixir so she would be

nicer to me.

"Where do we need to go next?" Raighne asks, and I pull away from Brenna.

"I'm not sure. The man sounded Irish, but they could be anywhere in the world. I couldn't see anything except for the guy."

I'm so frustrated with my visions, or should I say, the lack of details in them.

"Where are we now?" I think to ask.

Jason gives me an incredulous look, but answers, "Maastricht. In the Netherlands."

"We need to leave this house," Finian says. "We can be traced via the waterfall."

"You're right," Raighne agrees. "We have to find a place far from here where we can stay tonight and take it from there."

I glance at Jason. "Do you know of a motel where we can go to?"

"How far away are we talking?" he asks.

"At the very least, an hour," Raighne answers.

Jason nods. "We can take my station wagon." He looks at us. "It will be a tight fit, though."

"We'll make it work." I start to feel nauseated and place a hand over my stomach. "Can I have some water?"

"Sure. We should probably pack something to drink and eat for the road."

I follow Jason to the kitchen and take a bottle of water from him. After drinking some, I say, "Thank you for understanding. It will all be worth it in the end."

I hope I'm right and not lying to him.

He packs some snacks, sodas, and bottles of water into a bag, then nods at the door. "Let's go."

When we join the others, I try to avoid getting too close to Raighne as we leave the house.

Reaching the station wagon, I say, "I'll sit in the back with Brenna and Finian."

There's a frown on Raighne's face as he gets into the front passenger seat, and I make sure I sit behind him so he can't see me if he looks over his shoulder.

"How did you all find me?" I ask when Brenna scoots into the backseat, sitting between Finian and me.

"When you shift, you leave a trace behind. We just followed it," she says.

Jason starts the engine, and I rest my exhausted head against the window, but then my eyes catch Raighne's in the side mirror.

He looks concerned, and the moment I feel his warmth, I shake my head and close my eyes.

I don't know for how long we drive, and I have no desire to glance around the foreign country.

A dull headache begins to throb behind my eyes, and I feel restless and agitated. The patch must be wearing off because my ribs start to ache with every breath I take.

"Can we please stop somewhere?" Brenna asks.

"Do we need to?" Raighne questions as he glances at her. "We've only been on the road for thirty minutes."

"Yes. My bladder is only so big, you know," she mutters.

"We'll stop at the next gas station," Jason replies.

We drive for another thirty minutes or so, and by the time Jason pulls over at a gas station, I need to use to restroom as well.

We all pile out of the station wagon, and Raighne says, "We leave in ten minutes."

"The place where we'll stop for the night is only another ten minutes or so away," I hear Jason tell Raighne.

"Is that the map?" Raighne asks.

I glance over my shoulder and see Raighne looking at the cell phone in Jason's hand.

Damn, I forgot about cell phones and all the luxuries here on Earth. I didn't even miss any of it.

I follow Brenna into the restroom and pick the nearest open stall. I quickly relieve my bladder before digging another painkiller patch out of my bag. Peeling the old one off, I toss it in the bin. I stick the fresh one onto my thigh, hoping it will start working soon.

When I step out of the stall, Brenna's washing her hands. She glances at me and asks, "How are you feeling? I mean…after the thing with Adeth."

Her question and concern catch me totally by surprise. Who would've thought she, of all people, would care about me?

"I'm fine," I answer. "What doesn't kill us makes us stronger, right?"

"Yeah."

She looks at me for a moment before leaving the restroom.

While I wash my hands, my eyes latch onto my reflection in the mirror, and I notice dark circles forming under my eyes.

I swear I hear music playing somewhere, then my eyes turn from green to gray, and everything blurs.

Soft voices are harmonizing perfectly together. The melody is hauntingly beautiful, and I just stand and listen as they sing.

When the song comes to an end, I see a man and woman sitting on a small stage in a bar.

I recognize the man from the vision I had earlier.

They look so much alike, sharing the same blonde hair and gray eyes.

"You were great, Sarah. How're you feeling?" he asks as they step off the stage, heading to a room at the back.

I follow them inside and notice how he looks at her as if she's his entire world.

"Doug, stop your worrying. You'd swear I'm going to drop dead any second now."

239

I see the fear registering on Doug's face, his eyes filled with sadness. "Don't say that," he grits the words out between clenched teeth.

"I'm not leaving you anytime soon. You're my big brother, and I love you way too much. Be a darlin' and get me some water."

The world blurs again, and I hear them laughing.

Trees rush by, and they're driving down a narrow road. The air coming through the open window is chilly.

They drive past a sign that reads 'James Street' and something else that's a bit of a blur.

They laugh again as Doug takes a right and turns into a parking area. He finds a parking spot, and they start walking toward a huge building.

I glance around and realize they're at a hospital.

"Ready for chemo, sis?" Doug asks. I can hear tension in his voice.

My heartbeat speeds up, and my eyes dart to Sarah. She smiles up at Doug and hooks her arm into his. "I have to be. It's this or nothing."

"They could be wrong, you know." he tries to encourage her while hugging her tightly to him.

Sarah turns her face into Doug's shoulder, and I catch the heartache she's trying to hide from him.

"What if the chemo doesn't work? They said I only have a couple of months left. I might not make it, and I don't want to leave you."

Her panic is raw and real, and I desperately want to take it from her.

"You've been doing so great," Doug says as his palms frame her face. "You're a fighter. You're going to beat this." He pulls her into another hug, and it looks like he's trying to give all his strength to her.

God, I want to help this brother and sister, who love each other unconditionally, with all my heart.

I have to find them.

I look at the name of the hospital, then everything blurs again.

"Alchera?"

I blink, clearing the haziness still lingering around the edges of my sight.

Raighne is standing behind me. He reaches for my arm, but before he can touch me, I spin around.

"They're in Ireland. We have to move fast. Sarah, the woman, is dying. We have to go now."

Panic swells in my chest. I just want to find Sarah.

"She's what?" Raighne stares at me in disbelief.

I walk to the doorway, saying, "She has some kind of cancer and only has months to live. Maybe less than that. She needs me."

Raighne's hand shoots out, and he grabs my arm. "Hold up. We need to talk."

"Now?" I take a deep breath before glancing at him. "We don't have time to talk. We need to find Sarah and Doug."

I yank my arm free and walk straight to the station wagon. Without looking back, I get into the vehicle.

The last thing I want is to talk about my feelings while my chosen ones need me.

By the time we finally reach the motel, I don't care that it looks rat-invested.

Jason and Finian arrange three rooms, and I have no choice but to follow Raighne to ours.

"Go shower," he mutters as soon as he shuts the door behind us.

Letting out a sigh, I head to the bathroom, and when I'm finally alone, I close my eyes and fight to keep my chaotic emotions from exploding all over the place.

Everything's becoming too much for me to handle.

First, I'm yanked off Earth and shoved into Vaalbara. I'm forced to train for months before a sadistic bitch and her offspring kidnaps and tortures the hell out of me. Then I lose my father, and now I'm going after ten people who don't understand what's happening.

Jesus, my life sucks ass.

Inhaling a fortifying breath, I shove the self-pity aside and walk to the shower. I turn on the faucets, and while the water warms up, I strip out of my clothes.

When I step beneath the spray, and the warm drops pelt my skin, I let out a groan.

I wish I could sleep for weeks.

I wash my body, ignoring the ugly bruises on my ribs and torso. I can't see the cut on the back of my leg all that well, so I don't know if the wound is healing.

I'll deal with that problem later.

Climbing out of the shower, I grab a towel to dry my body, but a knock on the bathroom door has me freezing.

"Um … yeah?"

"It's Raighne. We need to do a healing session."

Shit.

My eyebrows dart into my hairline. I stare at the door as if it will bite me and then frantically scan the bathroom for my bag with the clean clothes.

"Crap."

"What?"

"Nothing," I call out.

I only have the towel, which I quickly wrap around my body.

I sigh heavily before I say, "Uhm…Raighne, my bag is in the car. Will you bring it?"

I wait a couple of minutes before the door opens, and Raighne comes in with my bag in his hand. His eyes flick over me while he sets it down on the counter.

Feeling super self-conscious, I mutter, "Thanks."

When he leaves, I quickly open the bag but only find a few sets of underwear and a jacket.

Shit. Did Brenna only pack one set of clothes for me?

My head whips around to where the jeans and T-shirt are lying in a puddle of water from the spray that fell outside of the shower.

Ugh. What am I going to do?

I dig the underwear out of the bag then shake my head. "Oh, come on. Seriously, Brenna!"

I stare at the matching pink lace set, then glance at the shut door.

I place the towel on the counter and put on the revealing underwear before grabbing the towel again and wrapping it around me.

This will just have to do.

I quickly pick up my wet clothes and lay them over the towel railing so they can dry during the night.

Reluctantly, I say, "I'm done."

The door opens and when Raighne sees me gripping the towel, he frowns at me. "You'll need to drop the towel so I can get to your back."

"I'm only wearing underwear," I mutter.

He raises an eyebrow at me. "So?"

You've got to be kidding me.

Scowling at the man, it's on the tip of my tongue to tell him to go to hell, but then I grow too brave for my own good.

Fine. If he wants me to drop the towel, we can both be uncomfortable with me standing in nothing but pink lace.

Keeping my eyes locked with his, I take the towel off and set it down on the counter.

Instead of looking uncomfortable, Raighne's eyes flick over my body, and the expression on his face darkens.

"What the fuck, Alchera?" he grumbles.

I glance down, and seeing the myriad of bruises on my torso and ribs, regret pours hot through my chest.

Thank God he can't see the back of my leg.

He stalks toward me, anger pouring off him in waves. Grabbing hold of my arm, he turns me to see my leg, and I let out a groan.

"I knew you were keeping secrets from me," he snaps. "Why the hell did you hide your wounds from me?"

I move backward, but it doesn't help because he quickly closes the gap between us.

"I'm fine," I argue. "You can't heal every wound I get."

I try to shove past him, but he grips me by my shoulders and shakes me.

"Enough!" His voice thunders in the small bathroom.

I cringe from his anger directed at me, and it has him taking a step away from me.

Shaking his head, he asks, "Why do you keep fighting our bond? You've become good at blocking me, but not that good. I can still get through when you're tired."

A confrontation with Raighne is the last thing I need right now. I'm already feeling nauseous and lightheaded, and the headache is making it hard to think.

I lower my gaze from his and stare at the tiles beneath my bare feet.

When I keep quiet, Raighne lets out a heavy breath and steps closer to me again.

He lifts his hands to my sides, and I feel his warmth spread through my ribs and torso.

Slowly, it becomes easier to breathe, and after a good ten minutes or so, he mutters, "Lean against me so I can check your back."

"You need to take a break," I argue.

"Lean against me, Alchera," he snaps.

Letting out a sigh, I press my body to his and close my eyes. When his hands move over my back, removing the last of the whip lashes, I have to suppress the urge to sob in his arms.

I just want him to hold me until everything is better.

I wrap my arms around his waist and bury my face against his chest.

I start to feel even more sick, and convinced I have the flu, I wonder if Raighne can heal more than just wounds.

He pulls free from my hold and crouches in front of me. I glance away because he's dangerously close to being at eye level with my lace panties.

When his hand brushes over the patch on my thigh, he asks, "What's this?"

I step backward, instantly uncomfortable under his scrutinizing gaze. "It's just something for the pain."

Darting around him, I walk into the room, and climbing onto the bed, I crawl beneath the covers.

"Where did you get it?" he demands as he follows me into the bedroom.

Shit. One bed.

My eyes widen when I realize I'm sharing a bed with Raighne.

When I don't answer him quickly enough, he snaps, "Where did you get it, Alchera?"

"At Jason's house," I reply as I lie down. "Thanks for the healing session, Raighne, but if you don't mind, I'm going to sleep because I think I'm coming down with the flu."

It feels as if a truck's parked on my chest, and I'm burning up with a fever.

Raighne leans over me, placing his hand on my forehead.

"Let me in."

I'm too sick and tired to care about keeping him out.

I feel his warmth enter my mind, and it's so soothing I start to drift in and out of consciousness.

"Get Jason," I hear Raighne snap. Time warps, then I hear Jason ask, "How many... it's for my dog...cancer."

The room grows quiet, and I feel Raighne hold me tightly, his warmth chasing away the fever and nausea.

"I can't believe you did this," he growls. "You'd rather die of pain than come to me."

As the minutes pass, I start to feel better from Raighne healing me, and I drift off to sleep.

CHAPTER 23

ALCHERA

When I come to, it feels late at night and everything's quiet.

It doesn't take long before I realize there's no pain anywhere in my body, and I feel good as new.

When I begin to sit up, Raighne gets up off the bed and snaps, "Stay where you are."

His features are drawn tight, a dark frown on his brow.

God, I've never seen him so angry.

I watch as he digs something out of his bag. It looks like a first aid kit. He takes a pair of small scissors from it and coming back to the bed, he glares at me.

My tongue darts out to wet my lips. "I'm sorry."

"Lie on your stomach," he orders, his tone promising nothing good for me.

I do as I'm told, and a moment later, I feel how Raighne removes the stitches from my leg.

"Do you realize what you've done?" he growls at me. Not waiting for an answer, he lays into me. "You took painkillers meant for dogs that have cancer. Dog medicine, Alchera!"

Done with removing the stitches, he tosses the scissors back into the first aid kit then pins me with a dark look. "Why do you keep rejecting our bond?"

"I'm not," I argue as I turn around and sit on the bed. I pull the covers over me as I explain, "I just don't want you in my head twenty-four-seven."

Because then he'd see how I feel about him, and I'd just die.

"That's how a bond works," he snaps. "I have to see what's going on inside you so I can make the right decisions."

"No!" I snap back at him as I climb off the bed.

I don't care that I'm standing in pink lace underwear, because clearly the man doesn't see me as a woman.

"To you, I'm just your charge, and there are things I don't want you to know about me." I press my hand to my chest. "I need my privacy."

"Just a charge?" he scoffs while shaking his head. His tone is much lower when he says, "I told you I live and die for you, Alchera. What more can I say to make you understand how important you are."

My heart hurts because I want to be important to Raighne for who I am, not for the bond we share and the destiny I have to fulfill.

Unable to stop myself, a sob escapes my lips, and I turn my back to him so he can't see my tears.

"I know you have a lot to deal with," he says, his tone softer. "But you're not alone. Let me in, so I can help you."

I shake my head as I cover my mouth with my hand to keep another sob from escaping.

"By Awo, Alchera," he groans, and I hear him move closer to me. He takes hold of my shoulders and turns me around to face him. He looks at me with pure desperation as he says, "You are the only being that matters to me. I will sacrifice everything I am for

248

you."

I stare at Raighne, wishing it was enough. But it's not. All I want is to be loved by him. It would make everything so much more bearable.

But I can't have what I want.

When I try to pull away, his hands frame my face and he forces me to keep eye contact with him.

"You're fucking killing me." He presses his forehead to mine. "Please. I'm begging you. Let me in."

I feel his breath on my mouth, and his lips brush against mine.

"Let me in."

Right now, I can't handle a kiss just so we can connect and yank away from him.

I close my eyes and place my hand over my stomach as my shoulders shudder.

"I can't kiss you and not feel anything," I admit one small truth as I struggle not to break down.

In a flash, Raighne grabs hold of me, pinning me to his body with one arm while his other hand grips my jaw. His mouth crashes against mine, and he proceeds to kiss the everloving shit out of me.

"Let. Me. In!" His voice strikes like a lightning bolt in my mind, and I don't stand a chance against his power as he invades every inch of me.

RAIGHNE

I'm not giving Alchera a choice anymore. I'm done playing the patient game.

Forcing her lips open, my tongue lashes at hers as I pour everything I am into her.

"This ends now," I demand.

She whimpers against my mouth before her arms wrap around my neck, and she begins to kiss me back.

My lips take hers roughly, demanding she accepts me once and for all.

Because without her, I'm nothing.

Alchera kisses me with the same passion, and when her walls come crashing down, I enter her mind before she can try to shut me out again.

God, he's going to find out how I feel about him.

Shit.

Her panicked thoughts rush around me, like prey trying to escape a predator.

I dig deeper, desperate to know her true feelings.

Shut down. Shit. Shut down.

God, he tastes so good, but I can't risk him finding out. I can't kiss him and want him when he doesn't want me in the same way.

She tries to break the kiss, but I only intensify my assault, and when there are no more barriers between us and I hear all her thoughts, I'm shocked by what I find.

I see myself through Alchera's eyes – how she admires me and thinks I'm the hottest man she's ever laid eyes on.

Holy fuck.

I feel every emotion she feels for me, how her love has grown from being infatuated with me to loving me so much it brings her heartache.

"You love me?" I ask, stunned by the discovery.

She rips free from my hold, and gasping, her features crumble as she stares at me as if I betrayed her.

"How could you?" she cries. "You weren't supposed to find

out."

Alchera loves me. How did I not see it?

Just as she turns around to escape to the bathroom, I grab hold of her arm and pull her back to me.

"No!" She slams her fist against my chest. "I'm done with this."

Feeling her panic and embarrassment, I frame her face with my hands and forcefully keep her in place as I capture her eyes and hold them imprisoned.

"Why did you hide your true feelings from me?"

"Was I supposed to run after you like a lovesick puppy?" she exclaims. I feel her temper flare, then she fights to get free from my hold. "Let go of me, Raighne!"

"Never," I growl. I close the distance between us until there's barely an inch separating our faces. *"I will never let you go."*

Tears spill from her eyes, and I feel the wave of embarrassment and frustration hit her again.

"Why are you embarrassed?" I demand.

Her gaze narrows on me. *"Seriously? How do you expect me to react when you just force your way into my mind and steal my secrets?"*

"Why keep it a secret?"

She shakes her head and stops trying to get free from my hold. Closing her eyes, she admits, "Because I don't want to be the stupid woman who fell in love with her guardian when he only sees her as his charge."

What the actual fuck?

Frowning at her, I order, "Look at me."

She lets out a defeated sigh before opening her eyes again.

"You're not just my charge, Alchera. More than once, I've told you there's no one more important."

"Yeah, because of our bond and my destiny," she mutters. "I get it."

"I'm not talking about your destiny right now," I snap, my

tone way too harsh. "This is about us. Just you and me. Man to woman."

Confusion flutters over her face, and it has me spelling out the words to her. "I love you, Alchera. Why do you think I got upset whenever you spent time with Storm? Fuck, I wanted to rip the man's head off when you smiled at him."

Her lips part in shock, and I watch as she struggles to accept what I'm telling her.

"I love you," I repeat the words, my tone a little gentler. "When I say there's no one more important to me, I mean in every aspect of my life. Only you matter to me."

A solid minute passes where she can only stare at me, utterly stunned, before she whispers, "I didn't know."

I can feel she's holding back, too scared she might be misunderstanding what I'm saying.

Closing the distance between us again, I press my mouth to hers. *"I'm not kissing you to heal you. I'm kissing you because I want to taste you."* My tongue dives into her mouth. *"Because I desperately need to claim you as mine so no other man can steal you from me."*

Happiness trickles into her heart, and it makes the corner of my mouth curve up before I begin to devour her.

Holy shit. Raighne loves me.

I can't believe it.

As I hear her thoughts clearly, I feel all her emotions and what it's like for her to kiss me. With nothing standing between us any longer, I can see through her eyes, experience everything she experiences, and hear everything she thinks.

Oh God, he tastes so good. Please don't let this be a dream.

"It's real, my little dreamer, and you better brace yourself because I'm claiming all of you tonight," I tell her mentally.

"All of me?"

I lower my hand to her thigh and brush my fingers over her

skin until I touch the scrap of lace that's been testing my limits the entire fucking night.

"*All. Of. You.*"

Nervous anticipation pours through her, then her panicked thoughts sound up one after the other.

I've never been with a man.

What do I do?

Shit, what if I'm not good at it?

Oh my God. It's really happening.

Calm down. Be cool. Just follow his lead.

Holy fucking shit, am I really about to have sex with Raighne?

I chuckle into her mouth, finding her thoughts endearing.

Pulling slightly away, I rub my finger over the lace as I say, "Deep breaths, my little dreamer. Don't worry. Let me handle everything."

She nods, the nervous expression not easing from her face.

I brush my mouth against hers and inhale the quivering breath escaping her lips.

Looking deep into her eyes, I say, "I love you so fucking much. Don't ever block me from your mind again."

Alchera nods, and when my finger strokes over her slit, she lets out a sharp gasp.

I grow impossibly hard, but I ignore my cock as I focus on her.

Able to feel every sensation she's experiencing, the corner of my mouth lifts when her abdomen tightens with need.

God, I love that smile. He looks so hot right now. And the way he touches me. I'm going to melt into a puddle of drool.

Wrapping my other hand around the back of her neck, I lean down and nip at her mouth while I push the lace out of the way. When my fingers brush over her hot pussy, I groan into her mouth before I proceed to fucking devour her.

Oh. My. God. So good. She chants in her mind. *So, so, so good.*

I massage her clit, and all her thoughts cease. A second later, I feel the pleasure she's experiencing, and it makes my cock want to tear through my jeans to get to her.

Spinning her around, I throw her onto the bed, and as surprise rockets through her, I crawl over her body.

"Are you ready for me, Alchera?" I growl as I grip hold of the lace panties.

She only nods, her eyes wide and her breaths bursting over her parted lips.

"Answer me with words," I demand.

"Yes." It's a mere gasp, but it's good enough for me.

I drag the lace down her legs and toss it to the side. When I finally see her pussy, a million men can't stop me as I push her thighs apart and lick her from opening to clit.

"Oh God," she whimpers, her back arching off the bed and her hips bucking.

I grip hold of her sides and forcefully keep her in place as I start to suck and lick her clit like the starving man I am.

"Raighne," she cries, intense waves of pleasure seizing her body with every swipe of my tongue and scrape of my teeth.

Knowing she can handle more, I push a finger inside her wet heat, and it has lights exploding in her mind as she's overcome with paralyzing ecstasy.

"That's right, my little dreamer. Come hard for me," I growl mentally while I continue to devour her virgin pussy.

"All mine." I suck and bite at her clit as I finger her, making sure to stretch her opening so she'll be able to take me. *"I can't wait to sink deep inside you."*

"Raighne," she sobs as her pleasure increases, and it makes me feel delirious.

I'm on a fucking high from her ecstasy alone, never mind my

own emotions and the satisfaction filling my heart from finally getting to love and fuck my woman.

When her body convulses for a second time, I free her clit from my mouth and kiss my way up her abdomen until I reach her breasts. I unclip her bra and pull the lace away from her breasts so I can suck her left nipple into my mouth.

Her body keeps quivering beneath me, and she's trying to focus on slowing her breaths as she comes down from her high.

I want her to be fully aware of what's happening when I fuck her, so I feast on her breasts while I give her time to recover.

"Holy shit," she breathes. "That was...It was..."

I let out a chuckle as my teeth tug at her hard nipple.

"It was out of this world," she finally manages to get the words out.

I free her nipple from my teeth and brace myself over her. "It's only going to get better."

Her eyes flick down, then her cheeks flush as she thinks, *Dammit, I'm the only one naked.*

I grip hold of the back of my shirt, and with one swift movement, I rip the fabric over my head.

Oh wow. That's so hot.

There's no way I'm telling her I can hear every thought she thinks because I know she'll try to block me again.

I move to my knees, and when I begin to unbuckle my belt, Alchera's eyes lock on my hands.

Damn, those veins snaking beneath his skin. Sigh. The man is way too attractive for me to handle, and I'm about to see him naked.

Her thoughts make every stressful moment I've suffered because of her stubbornness melt away, and knowing how she truly feels about me has my power growing.

I can feel it expand in my soul as I pull my zipper down.

I move off the bed, and when I shove the jeans down my legs, her eyes widen and her lips part.

Mother of God. It's going to hurt.

I wonder if his skin is as soft as it looks. Like velvet wrapped over steel.

Sigh, what a sight to behold.

I almost tell her it won't hurt, because I'll take her pain, but then she'd know I'm listening in on her thoughts.

Climbing back onto the bed, I take her hand and guide her to wrap her fingers around my desperate cock.

"All of me belongs to you," I say so she won't hesitate to touch me. "Only to you."

With a look of wonder on her face, she strokes her fingers up and down my cock, and it weeps for more of her attention.

"Your touch feels so good," I groan. "But I need to be inside you. Open your legs wide for me."

Alchera does as I ask, and when I move over her, her hands brush up and down my chest and abs, pure satisfaction flowing through her from getting to touch me.

Jesus, he's all hard muscle and tanned skin. I can get drunk just from touching him.

I brace my forearm beside her head as I lie down on top of her. When our skin touches, from neck to pelvis, I almost lose my fucking mind from how good it feels to have nothing between us.

I love feeling his weight pushing me into the bed, my woman moans mentally, and I give her more of my weight as my mouth claims hers.

I get high on the taste of her and have no idea how long we kiss, but when I lift my head and see her swollen lips, I can't resist sinking my teeth into her bottom one before easing the sting with my tongue.

Keeping myself braced on my right forearm, I push my left hand down between us and position my desperate cock at her entrance.

Alchera's nervousness returns tenfold, but she also waits with anticipation for my next move.

I grip her thigh and pull her leg over my hip, opening her more before I start to rock slowly into her, forcing her tight virgin pussy to take the head of my cock.

It feels fucking incredible, but I have to focus on her as I push a little deeper.

The instant she feels a sharp, burning pain, I take it from her. I make sure she doesn't experience any discomfort as I keep driving deeper into her.

She's fucking tight, and her walls fight me. With me taking all her pain, I forcefully thrust hard until I'm buried to the hilt deep inside her.

Fuck.

I'm bombarded with the pain of taking her virginity and the pleasure I feel from finally being inside her.

Fuck.Fuck.Fuck.

I push my hand between us, and pressing my palm to her abdomen, I focus on healing the tears inside her. The pain lessens, and when it's completely gone, I suck in a deep breath of air.

"Are you okay?" I ask.

"I should be asking you that question." She lifts her head and presses a tender kiss to my jaw. "Did it hurt a lot?"

"Nothing I can't handle," I reply, my voice growing hoarse from having to keep still so she'll adjust to my size.

I become aware of how full Alchera feels and that she's emotional from having me inside her.

Kissing her deeply, I move my hand up to cup her breast, which is a perfect fit in my palm. *"We're one."*

Her hands settle on my shoulders. *"Thank you for taking my pain."*

"Anything for you."

I pull out slowly, making sure none of the discomfort trickles through to her, and when I sink back inside her, the ache is not as sharp as with the first thrust.

I grind my pelvis against her clit, and her abdomen tightens with pleasure.

I draw out until only the head of my cock remains in Alchera, and locking eyes with her, I watch and feel her pleasure when I drive back into her.

Her hands move down my back until they reach my ass, and as I begin to set a steady pace, her nails dig into my skin.

God, I love the way he moves on top of me. It's so fucking hot. And his huge cock is stroking me in all the right places.

If I knew sex felt this amazing, I would've done it much sooner.

The corner of my mouth lifts. Her pleasure mixing with my own creates a deliriously intoxicating cocktail that overwhelms the living hell out of me.

"So fucking tight," I groan in her mind. *"So perfect for me."*

I lock eyes with her as I thrust faster and faster until I can't control my pace, and a primal need to fuck her senseless takes over.

A light begins to glow between us, and Alchera gasps, her eyes widening. *"I can feel what you feel. I can hear your thoughts."*

We bond at such a high level that the impossible happens, and while we're connected as man and woman, Alchera gets to experience exactly what I'm experiencing.

"Feel how much I love you?"

Our eyes remain locked as I thrust harder and harder into her.

"Yes," she breathes in mind. *"God, Raighne. I wish you'd told me sooner."*

The ecstacy we're creating is fucking glorious, casting a spell around us. While the world is going to shit, we find a moment where it's only her and me.

There's no guardian and charge.

We're just two people who love each other with our whole beings.

Our souls fuse as one, our hearts beat the same wild rhythm, and our bodies move, creating an inferno that will burn forever.

"By Awo, I get to love you for all of eternity."

She nods as her hips lift to meet mine with every powerful thrust.

"For all of eternity," she whispers, her tone filled with the love she feels for me.

Alchera arches her back as her core clenches around me, and the moment her orgasm rips through her, I groan, "You come so fucking beautifully for me, my little dreamer. Let me feel your pussy squeeze my cock."

Another wave of pleasure hits her, and she holds tightly onto me as her body convulses beneath mine.

I fuck her harder, the sounds of our bodies colliding, filling the air.

"Raighne," she sobs mentally. *"God...Raighne."*

I ride her high with her, and only when she starts to come down do I focus on myself and how fucking incredible her slick heat feels around my cock.

Her inner walls fist me as she grows sensitive, only making me hammer into her as I search for my own release.

"Jesus," she gasps.

Pleasure spirals down my spine and up my balls, and my body jerks violently against hers as my orgasm strikes.

"I didn't think you could grow bigger, but mother of God, it feels good. You fill all of me."

Her words increase my pleasure a hundredfold, and I almost black out from the intensity.

My muscles strain as I spill every last drop I have to offer inside Alchera before I lose all my strength and slump down on top of her.

She wraps her legs around my hips and clings to me with all her might.

For minutes, there's only the sound of our racing breaths and pounding hearts.

When I finally have enough strength, I lift my head and press my mouth to hers.

"Mine," I say with finality.

"Yours," she agrees.

I kiss the woman I love more than anything while relishing in the fact that we'll forever be one. No one can come between us.

There are no more misunderstandings, and we've bonded so deeply it can never be severed.

I brush my hand up and down Alchera's side before covering her breast and squeezing her silky soft flesh.

"I'll never get enough of you," I groan. *"Now that I've had a taste of you, I'm addicted."*

She smiles against my lips, and I break the kiss so I can see her happiness. And what a fucking smile it is, lighting up her face and making her look damn-near angelic.

"That was…wow," she chuckles. "For lack of a better word."

"Everything you hoped your first time would be?" I ask, the arrogant bastard in me needing to hear the words.

Alchera nods, her fingers trailing up and down my back. "So much more than I could've hoped for."

I stay buried deep inside her, relishing her tight heat wrapped around me.

Bringing my hand up, I brush my fingers through her short hair, loving the disheveled look on her.

With her pinned beneath my body, I say, "No more hiding

things from me."

She nods, emotion tightening her features, and I feel some of the pressure she's been forced to deal with trickle back into her heart.

"You're mine to protect and love, Alchera. Don't ever try to shut me out again."

Her head bobs up and down, and her eyes begin to glisten with unshed tears.

With our gazes locked, I demand, "So let me feel all of your pain."

She begins to shake her head but stops and sucks in a deep breath.

As a tear escapes her eye and spirals over her temple, she lets all her emotions surface for me to see.

Disappointment, because we sent her to Earth with no memories of her past, only to rip her away from that life before thrusting her into a world of chaos.

Anger and loneliness, which take one hell of a swing at my heart.

Fear and despair for what she was forced to endure at Adeth and Ares' hands.

Sorrow for losing her father before even having the chance to get to know him.

And regret. So much fucking regret it flays my soul raw.

"By Awo, Alchera," I whisper, hating that she's suffered for so long under the severe pressure Vaalbara has forced on her.

I shift slightly and press my hand over her heart. I've never heard of a guardian healing emotional or mental wounds before, but out of pure desperation, I focus with all that I am on my charge.

The blue light starts to glow between us, and when Alchera's face crumbles and sobs escape her, frustration pours into my heart.

"You can take away those emotions?" her words fill my mind.

"Is it working?" I ask, desperate to hear her answer.

I feel her entire being sigh with relief, and she practically becomes boneless beneath me.

Every horrible thing she's been forced to suffer lessens inside her until it all becomes bearable – and pours into my soul.

I'm hit hard with a tsunami of anger, loneliness, fear, and grief, but I take it all if it means she'll feel better.

Fuck. I did it.

Shock ripples through me, and I'm speechless for a while.

Alchera lifts her head and presses her trembling lips to mine. *"Thank you."*

"Better?" I manage to ask through clenched teeth as I work to compartmentalize the destructive emotions.

She pulls back, then her eyes widen as they dart over my face. "No," she gasps. "You took my emotions like you do my pain?" When I nod, she wraps her arms tightly around my neck and holds me to her. "God, Raighne. I didn't want that."

"I can handle it," I say so she won't worry.

I push my arms beneath her and squash her to my body while pressing a kiss to her temple.

"I can handle anything that comes my way as long as I have you," I murmur.

"I love you so much," she whispers, her tone strained, and hearing the words soothes the chaos in my heart.

"Say it again," I demand.

"I love you, Raighne."

A feeling of peace soothes my heart and soul, and still buried inside my woman, I start to drift off to sleep from the exhaustion of healing her.

262

CHAPTER 24

ALCHERA

When I wake up and feel Raighne's naked body lying partially on top of mine, a sleepy smile spreads over my lips.

I glance down at where his head is resting on my chest, and careful not to disturb him, I brush my fingers through his longish dark brown hair.

I struggle to process everything that's happened between us, still finding it hard to believe he loves me.

My eyes drift over his muscled back, and there's an intense fluttering in my stomach.

This over-the-top attractive and strong-as-fuck man loves me.

My thoughts turn to last night and how it felt to make love to him. Safe to say, my mind's officially blown.

When I got to feel his emotions and how much he loves me, it was the highlight of my entire life because I've never been loved so intensely before.

I've finally found a place where I belong, where I can be myself, and it's with the man of my dreams.

God. Thank you.

Raighne stirs, and a moment later, his eyes open. He lifts his head and stares at me for a few seconds before the corner of his mouth lifts.

"I'm surprised your body isn't numb from me lying on top of you all night," he mutters sleepily.

I shake my head, my fingers trailing over the stubble on his jaw. I love the feel of the scratchy bristles.

He pulls himself up and presses a kiss to my lips before he moves off the bed. When he sees the tinge of blood on the sheets, his eyes flick to mine.

"No pain?"

I shake my head, but when I move, I feel tender between my legs. As soon as I feel the ache, it disappears, and my eyes snap to Raighne.

"You don't have to take all my pain."

He doesn't comment but instead says, "Let's shower so we can get back on the road."

"Shower?" I ask as I scoot off the bed. "Together?"

"Yes." He gives me a cocky grin before walking into the bathroom and opening the faucets in the shower.

Things feel completely different between us, and I love it. I don't have to be on guard anymore, and it's refreshing.

I join Raighne in the shower, and when he starts to wash my body, I can only stand and grin at him because I adore having his attention and hands on me.

"I love it too," he murmurs.

I tilt my head and narrow my eyes on him. "Can you hear all my thoughts?"

He pauses for a moment before saying, "Don't freak out, but yes. Now that you're not fighting the bond any longer, I hear and feel everything where you're concerned."

I start to feel mortified, but he quickly lifts a hand to my cheek and locks eyes with me. "There's nothing to be embarrassed about, Alchera. Remember when you got to look inside my mind and how amazing it felt?"

I nod, hating that it's not permanent and only something that happened because we were making love.

"That's how it feels for me, and it's important I know everything. I can protect you better that way."

"It's going to take some getting used to," I mutter. My eyes narrow on him again. "And don't you dare use my thoughts against me. They tend to be intrusive."

The corner of his mouth lifts. "I'll never do anything that's not in your best interest."

When we're done showering, I dry myself. Finding my clothes have dried during the night, I'm relieved and quickly get dressed.

Walking into the bedroom, I'm just in time to see Raighne fasten his belt, and my abdomen flutters at the sight.

A crooked smile forms on his face, telling me he knows what I'm thinking about.

"Get used to it," I mutter, figuring there's no use fighting our bond. "You're hot, and I can't help how I feel."

He lets out a chuckle. Then closing the distance between us, he wraps his hand around the side of my neck and leans down to press a tender kiss to my mouth, sending a wave of tingles through me.

"I feel the same way about you," he admits. "Especially when you're wearing nothing but pink lace."

My cheeks warm a little, but I'm too happy to feel awkward.

His eyes capture mine, and a serious expression tightens his features. "The next nine days are going to be rough, but I'll be there every step of the way. Lean on me, and don't bottle things up again. Okay?"

I nod but say, "I'm used to weathering storms alone, but I'll try."

The intense look in his eyes softens a little. "You'll never be alone again. It's you and me forever."

"Forever's a really long time," I chuckle.

He shakes his head. "And still not long enough with you."

My heart.

Once again I'm hit with amazement that Raighne feels the same way about me.

I wrap my arms around his waist and press my face to his chest, then whisper, "Thank you for loving me."

Raighne engulfs me against his body, and I feel his breath in my hair as he presses a kiss to the top of my head. "I'm the one who should thank you. I was worried out of my fucking mind that I'd have to watch you build a life with another man."

I shake my head and admit, "Since you walked into that classroom and sat down beside me, it's been only you." I tilt my head back so I can look up at him. We stare at each other for a few seconds before I say, "This feels surreal. Like a dream."

He shakes his head. "It's not, my little dreamer."

A knock at our door pops the intimate moment between us, and Raighne pulls away from me. He straightens the covers over the bed so whoever's here won't see the tinge of blood on the sheets before he opens the door.

Brenna, Finian, and Jason look at us from where they're standing in the corridor, then Finian asks, "Ready?"

"Yes," Raighne answers.

I grab my bag and glance over the room to make sure I'm not forgetting anything.

Sucking in a deep breath, I brace myself for whatever might happen today, then I walk out of the room that will always hold a special place in my heart.

As the men go to the reception to settle the bill, Brenna's eyes flit over me.

"You look much better," she mentions. "Did you get a good night's rest?"

I nod, struggling from grinning like an idiot. "Yeah. I feel good as new."

The corner of her mouth lifts. "You accepted your bond with Raighne, didn't you?"

My eyes widen. "Is it that obvious?"

She nods. "You look healthy, which can only mean he's healed you completely."

"Yep," I murmur. "No more aches and pains."

The men join us again, and we all pile into the station wagon. This time, Finian takes the front passenger seat, and I sit at the back between Raighne and Brenna.

When Raighne places his arm around my shoulders and tucks me close against his side, I don't bother feeling uncomfortable with the public display of affection and lean against him.

"Where are we going?" Jason asks as he connects his phone to the car's GPS.

"I think we need to go to Ireland. Can you Google a street name and a hospital?"

"Yeah. Give me the names," he replies.

He checks the details, then nods. "It's in Ireland. Dublin, to be exact."

Not knowing how we're going to get there, I mutter, "Well, that's where we have to go."

"Where is the nearest waterfall, Jason?" Finian asks.

Jason just stares at him, and it makes Brenna chuckle.

"We can't travel by waterfall," I mention. "I originally planned to go to Fish Creek Falls, but I had a vision just as I shifted and ended up in Jason's pond."

"What?" Worry instantly tightens Raighne's features as he stares at me. "You could've been killed."

Yeah, I didn't think about that. It would've sucked ass if I had a vision of anything that didn't have a body of water.

"Raighne's right," Brenna agrees. "She could've died if that vision was any different."

"I have a pilot's license," Jason mentions. "We can find an airfield and hire a plane."

It's our turn to stare at him.

"What? I'm a man of many talents," he mutters. "Alchera didn't just dream me up for no reason, you know."

A smile forms on my face, then I ask, "Are you a professional pilot?"

He shakes his head. "No, I'm a veterinarian, but sometimes I need to fly out to farms to check on livestock."

"Makes sense," I say. "Let's go to the nearest airfield."

Jason checks on Google Maps, searching for one that has planes for hire, before he starts the engine and drives away from the motel.

It's early in the morning, and the roads are practically empty as we drive to our destination.

"We're going to have a problem if we can't use a waterfall," Finian mentions. "Flying all over the world will take time we don't have."

"Why are waterfalls important?" Jason asks.

"We travel through them," Finian replies.

The car swerves before Jason regains control, and he shoots a you-must-be-crazy look at Finian. "You're shitting me, right?"

"Nope," I say from the backseat. "It's all going to take some getting used to, but we travel through waterfalls, and if your mind's not blown enough, some of the people on Vaalbara have powers."

"Like superhero stuff?" Jason asks, the expression on his face telling us he doesn't believe a word we're saying.

He pulls the station wagon over to the side of the road then glances at us. "Powers? Show me."

Finian opens his hand, and a second later, a white light starts to glow. He squashes it quickly, then explains, "I have the ability to stun someone with a streak of electricity."

"My brother, Raighne," he tips his head to the back seat, "can move objects, and my twin can levitate almost anything."

"Holy fuck," Jason mutters, shaking his head in disbelief. "This is all a little too much to process, so I'm just going to pretend you're all normal."

He steers the car back onto the road, and silence fills the cab as we continue to drive.

"It's for your safety," Brenna says. "We're all here to get you to Vaalbara in one piece, so you don't have to be afraid of us."

"Ah-hah..." Jason mumbles before switching on the radio just in time to catch the tail end of a news broadcast.

'... uncontrollable fire is destroying parts of the Amazon forest. Everything is being done to stop it from spreading. And in other news just in, more than twenty whales have beached on the shores of Norway, causing chaos as rescue teams try to move them back into the ocean. Japan's Fukushima Daiichi nuclear power station is unstable after another earthquake struck off the coast of Iwaki."

"Jesus," Jason mutters before turning off the radio. "Usually, I'd care about world news, but right now, I'm a little too stressed."

I glance at Brenna and whisper, "Has it started?"

She nods, worry tightening her features.

Twenty minutes later when we reach the airfield, we wait near a hangar while Jason makes the arrangements to hire a plane.

I'm glancing around at the area when Jason comes into the

hangar, an anxious expression on his face. "Let's go."

He leads us to a medium-sized plane, and just looking at it makes my stomach turn with nerves.

"I need someone up front to help me fly this baby. Who's the fastest learner?" Jason eyes Finian and Raighne.

It's literally the last thing I want to hear before boarding a plane for the first time in my life.

"I will," Finian says. "I want to know what's going on at all times."

When we board the small eight-seater, everyone's too damn calm. Am I the *only* one nervous about flying?

"We'll be okay," Raighne tells me mentally as he makes sure my safety belt is strapped on tight.

"Uh-huh," I mutter.

It takes a few minutes before we taxi down the short runway, and when the plane leaves the ground, I shut my eyes while my stomach rolls with queasy waves.

I open my eyes again, and a wave of confusion washes over me. I'm looking up at enormous buildings. Skyscrapers made of crystal-clear glass shimmer in the sunlight as they rise to great heights.

People are going about their business when the ground starts to shake forcefully beneath my feet. I try to find my balance, but the ground is shuddering so severely that I fall backward, landing on my butt.

I hear glass shatter, splintering, and jingling high above me as the giant buildings start to crumble. They come down on us in a horrible rain of glass, concrete, and steel.

I only realize it's one hell of an intense earthquake when the ground starts to tear open on the other side of the road.

At first, the crack is small, but as it rips jaggedly through the concrete, it grows bigger until gaping holes appear.

Debilitating fear and panic fill me, and I scramble to my feet, wildly looking around me.

God, I want this vision to stop.

The glass raining down on the mass of people pierces them. There are injured people everywhere, the gaping holes swallowing cars, buildings...everything in its path.

Wake up, Alchera! Wake up.

Horror soaks into my bones as I anxiously search for a way out of this disaster.

One after the other, the tremors grow stronger and they come faster by the second until it becomes near impossible to stay on my feet.

I hope with everything I have in me that one of my chosen ones isn't here.

A sign crashes down next to me, barely missing me, and I let out a shocked scream as I scurry away from it while reading the words printed in bold.

SAN FRANCISCO BUSINESS DISTRICT

ShitShitShit. Doesn't San Francisco have the worst earthquakes?

I scramble away and start running as fast as I can. When the ground shudders horribly beneath me, I grab hold of the nearest lamp pole and hang on for dear life while letting out a terrified sob.

A huge gorge opens up not even a hundred feet from me, making horror bleed into my soul.

The ground slants upward in such a way that everyone and everything around me is sliding into the gorge, and I cling with all my strength to the pole.

Horrified out of my everloving mind, I can only gasp for air as I watch people plummet to their deaths.

I want to cover my ears. I can't bear to hear their cries and terrified screams, but I'm forced to listen as I hold on to the pole.

Sobs tear from my chest, and I keep shaking my head, the devastation around me too much to handle.

"Raighne!" I cry, despair soaked into my voice. "Get me out of here."

The piece of ground that tears loose is so big I can't see how far it stretches, but I know it's about to cause devastating destruction.

It's as if the whole Bay Area is being torn loose from the mainland, becoming its own fiery island of death. I look up at the sky, wanting to scream for help, but my breath gets ripped from my lungs.

Thana is hovering far above us, a light as bright as the sun shining from her.

No.

My sister is the one responsible for all this destruction and death.

While I suffer the experience of this nightmare, she has to suffer the reality of knowing she's killing so many people.

My mind reels at the thought that this is what Awo wants. The horrible death of millions.

A sob tears through me, and my heart aches for my sister and all these people.

The suffering around me is devastating, and I'm unable to breathe past the sorrow suffocating me.

A crying baby rips my attention back to the chaos happening around me.

People are being crushed, while others simply drop to their deaths. It's a gruesome sight that changes me forever.

The tremors below me keep coming. It's like a roaring beast has awakened from its long hibernation and now demands blood.

My arms are tired from the vibrations, but I hold on with all my might.

Suddenly, a woman grabs hold of the same pole I'm hanging onto in an attempt to save herself.

I try to take hold of her, but my hand goes through her.

"God...oh God," she hyperventilates with terror etched deep into her face. "I don't want to die!"

Seeing her struggle to keep hold and knowing I can't do anything to help her, I start to cry violently as an unspeakable heartache crushes my chest.

"No!" Her fingers grow white as she tries to cling to the pole. She screams, and it's a raw sound filled with absolute dread.

I have to close my eyes when she finally slips away.

Then the unthinkable happens. I begin to feel the racing heartbeats of many and how they're snuffed one by one.

A strong wind begins to tug and blow as the ground finally tears loose from the mainland.

A thunderous boom echoes through the air, vibrating every particle in the air. Deafening screeches slam against my ears as if a billion fingernails are being scraped across a hellish blackboard.

A strong wind surrounds me, and I struggle to breathe. Wrapping my legs around the metal pole, I try desperately not to be blown away.

Panic and terror stain everything around me as the cries and prayers for mercy of the dying fill my soul.

CHAPTER 25

ALCHERA

The first thing I hear is the panic in Raighne's voice.

"I fear for her, Brenna. She called to me." Raighne holds me tightly to him. Through the haze, I can hear his heart beating fast in his chest. "She stopped breathing at one point. Something horrific must be happening in her vision."

My arms and legs are wrapped tightly around him as if he's the pole I was clinging to.

I'm bombarded by flashes of the vision I had. The terrible earthquakes and the chaos that followed. All those people. All the suffering and death.

My body starts to shudder from shock and tears roll down my cheeks. My heart is heavy with despair, and I'm swamped with a rollercoaster of emotions.

I choke on the cries that finally make their way out of me.

"Alchera?" Raighne grabs my tear-streaked face and holds it up to his.

The moment our eyes lock, I feel him explode inside of me, his warmth rushing through my mind.

My fingers curl into his shirt as his eyes darken with sadness, and he presses me back against his chest while he eases the aftermath of horror from my mind.

"Shhh, all will be well. You're safe. I'm here," he murmurs softly while focusing on taking the devastating emotions from me. "I'm so sorry you had to experience that."

My body slumps against his, and I suck in desperate breaths of air while the horror slowly lessens in my mind.

"It was dreadful," I whimper. "They're all going to die. Millions. I could feel their terror and how their hearts stopped beating."

"I wish you didn't have to see it," he says, his love finally breaking through the darkness in my mind.

I let out a relieved sigh. All I want to do is to hide in his arms from the hell that's about to break loose on this planet.

"We're here," Finian says, just as the plane shudders when it touches down on the runway.

"Here?" I ask as I pull away from Raighne.

"Ireland," Brenna reminds me.

There are so many images flashing through my mind, most of them pictures of disaster and pain. I remember getting Jason, and then…

When I'm finally able to focus on the present, I'm filled with an urgent need to get to my chosen ones.

"Sarah. Doug," I say, desperation coating my words. "We have to get to them as soon as possible."

Raighne walks to the door and helps me out of the plane as Jason says, "We landed without permission, so we're going to have to make a run for it."

Like a bunch of criminals, we run across the tarmac and past a hanger. The place seems to be deserted, and when we reach a road, we stop to catch our breaths.

"What now?" Jason asks.

I glance at him. "Your phone. Can you get us a cab?"

"Good thinking," he mutters.

He signs into an app, and after he arranges for a car to pick us up, I find a spot on the grass at the side of the road where I can sit down.

"How are you feeling?" Brenna asks as she crouches beside me.

"Better. Raighne took most of the emotions."

"What?" she gasps, her eyes darting between Raighne and me. "He can take your emotions?"

"It's a talent I gained last night," Raighne explains.

"I've never heard of that happening before," Finian says, sounding surprised.

"Yeah, I'm never going to get used to the things you people talk about," Jason mutters. He checks his phone. "Our ride will be here in ten minutes."

Suddenly, the ground starts to tremble beneath us, and I jump to my feet, but it stops as quickly as it started.

"God," I groan. "Thana said we have ten days. That means she'll hold off on destroying everything until we get the chosen ones off Earth. Right?"

Brenna shakes her head. "No, it means we have ten days before the Earth is obliterated." She places her hand on my shoulder. "You have to get the chosen ones while the disasters are happening."

"Disasters?" Jason asks.

"Earthquakes, tsunamis, hurricanes, and everything else that classifies as a disaster," Brenna mutters. "That's why we have to hurry."

Jesus.

As panic tightens my muscles, Raighne takes hold of my hand, immediately calming me again.

An SUV comes down the road, and when it stops, we pile into it. I have to sit on Raighne's lap to make space for Brenna and Finian in the back while Jason takes the passenger side.

"We're going to need a bigger car for all the other chosen ones," I tell Raighne mentally so I don't freak out the cab driver.

"I don't think we'll be able to use human transport for much longer. We'll have to risk waterfalls."

My eyes lock with his. *"What if I have a vision while shifting through a waterfall?"*

"I'll keep hold of you and stop you from going somewhere you're not meant to go."

"You can do that?"

"Together, we can do anything."

Not thinking about the others, I kiss his jaw before tucking my face into the crook of his neck.

I'm just about to relax when the whirring of the wheels on the concrete starts to sound like a gale-force wind roaring in my ears.

I wrap my arms around Raighne's neck, mentally crying, *"It's happening again. Don't let go of me."*

"I've got you," I hear him in my thoughts before everything blurs.

I slowly peek around me, scared to death of what I'll see this time.

It looks like in a forest, the wind bending the trees while leaves and debris fly everywhere.

I'm hardly able to breathe from the strong winds ripping at me.

My eyes lock on a young Asian girl, and I watch as she falls near a pool of water. With fear etched onto her face, she looks up at the heavens.

Her black hair whips wildly around her, then she turns her head and looks right at me.

Relief makes her face go slack, then she surprises the hell out of me when she says, "My name is Sky. I'm waiting for you, Alchera. I'm at the Kegan Falls in Japan."

I see the tears sparkling in her eyes.

"*You don't have long, Alchera. It's coming!*"

I come to with a jolt.

"*What is it?*" Raighne asks, worried.

I realize we're still driving, and I suck in a shuddering breath before I reply, "*After getting Sarah and Doug, we have to find a waterfall and shift to the Kegan Falls in Japan. My fourth chosen one is there, and she knows I'm coming.*"

Soon, the cab turns onto St. James Street, and I immediately recognize the area.

"God, I hope they're here," I mutter.

"They should be," Brenna says, keeping her tone low. "Otherwise, you wouldn't have seen them here."

We soon find ourselves in the familiar parking area, and the moment the cab comes to a stop, Raighne pushes the door open. We climb out, and I glance around, wondering where to go next.

As the cab drives away, I wave around us. "I have no idea what to do now. This is all the vision showed me of this place. What use am I if I can't even sense them?" I feel so hopeless, and it scares the hell out of me. "They're all going to die, and it's going to be my fault."

"You're doing fine," Raighne says, "Don't think like that."

My eyes search the parking lot for any sign of Doug and Sarah, but there are none.

Panic grips my heart as I think of Sky waiting for me to save her from whatever's heading her way.

I start to feel frustrated, but it's weird, and I realize it's not my emotion. A headache begins to pulse behind my eyes, and I automatically start walking to the other side of the parking area.

With every step, the headache gets worse, then I hear a familiar voice say, "Sit down, Sarah. Catch your breath."

When I come around the back of a van, I see Sarah sitting on the passenger seat with her legs out of the vehicle while Doug crouches in front of her. There's a wheelchair beside them.

"Take deep breaths," he murmurs to her. "I'm going to move you to the wheelchair. Okay?"

I've found them. Thank God.

"Hi," I say just as Raighne comes to stand behind me and the rest of our group catches up to us.

"Can I help you?" Doug asks as he rises to his full height.

"Yeah." I nod and move a step closer. "My name's Alchera, and these are my friends. I know it's going to sound crazy, but I'm here to help you."

Doug shakes his head, giving us a suspicious look. "We don't need any help."

Thinking of Sky, who's waiting for me, I know I don't have time to break the news gently to them, so I say, "I really hope you'll believe me because we're running out of time. I've come for you and Sarah."

Doug takes a threatening step toward me, demanding, "How do you know my sister's name?"

"Doug." I give him a pleading look. "I've seen you in a vision, and you're two of ten chosen people to be saved."

"Fuck the hell off," he hisses, giving me a look of warning.

"I know you're dying of cancer," I say as I look at Sarah. "But if you come with me, I can help you."

I glance at Doug. "You're amazing, the way you care for her. I know you don't want to lose Sarah." His jaw clenches, and it looks like he's a second away from attacking me.

"Please, Doug," I beg. "Come with me and let me save her. I know it's a leap of faith, but it's all you have. This planet is about to be destroyed."

As if by command, the ground beneath us starts to tremble, and a deep, low moan shudders through the earth.

It sounds all too familiar, sending a wave of fear through me.

When the tremors increase, my whole body goes cold and adrenaline starts to pump through me, sending me into overdrive.

"Get into their van," I shout at the others.

"What?" Doug snaps.

I lock eyes with him and say, "If you want to survive the disasters that are about to be unleashed on this world, you'll come with us."

The quaking intensifies, and Sarah cries, "Let's go with them, Doug."

"I'll drive," Jason says while Finian grabs hold of Doug, shoving him into the back of the van.

Brenna, Raighne, and I quickly get in, and seconds later, Jason steers the van out of the parking area.

Finian is restraining Doug while I try to reassure him by telling him, "You're safe with us."

"Jason, we need to go to the nearest waterfall," Raighne orders.

"Got it," Jason replies, then he grins at Sarah. "Don't worry. I'm a good driver."

She just stares at him with wide eyes, then whispers, "There's a waterfall at Iveagh Gardens. It's the closest."

Jason hands his phone to her. "Pull up a map and tell me where to go."

I glance at Doug, and seeing the panic and fear on his face, I give him a compassionate look. "We won't hurt you. We're here to protect you."

"I swear, if you hurt my sister, I'll kill you," he threatens, his features drawn tight.

"I want to save her," I say, not knowing how I'll get through to him.

When Jason brings the van to a screeching stop right outside the gardens, Sarah points at an entrance. "Through there."

"Let's go," I say as I pull the door open.

We all pile out, then Sarah says, "I'll wait here. We left my wheelchair at the hospital, and I can't walk too far."

"I'll carry you," Jason tells her, and not waiting for anyone to argue, he opens the passenger door and picks up Sarah as if she weighs nothing.

That solves one problem.

"I'll take my sister," Doug snaps, but Jason starts to walk, and Finian keeps hold of Doug's arm to control him.

"Wait for us by the waterfall," I order before I start to jog toward the entrance.

The ground shakes again, making me break out into a flat-out sprint in the direction of the waterfall.

Seeing boulders around the pool, that doesn't look too deep, I leap over them and splash into the water. I swallow some before I rush to the curtain.

Raighne grabs hold of my hand, and I clear my mind, only thinking of Sky as we step into the waterfall.

When we come out on the other side, a gale-force wind rips at us, and I stagger backward, but Raighne pulls me through the rough waters toward the embankment that seems to be in a cove of rocks.

It's dark as hell, and I can't see much with the storm raging around us.

"Sky!" I scream.

"Alchera!" Her voice is faint, being carried away by the strong winds.

I hope she's close by, but it's too dark to rely on my sight.

"Sky! I'm here. Keep calling out. I'll follow your voice," I shout, but I can hardly hear my own voice above the roar of the storm.

The trees around us are bending severely, taking heavy strain from the wind. Pieces of debris slam hard into my body.

"Where are you?" I cry.

"By the waterfall!" she shouts, sounding closer.

My eyes finally begin to adjust to the darkness, and I catch sight of movement to my right. "I see something and really hope it's you. Can you see me?"

"Yes! Yes, I see you!" She cries with relief drenching her words.

"Thank God!" Using every bit of power I have, I push myself up off the grass.

I don't know where the strength comes from, but I need to get to Sky. She is all that matters now.

When she sees me, she starts to cry, her small frame trembling violently. "You came for me. You didn't forget me," she cries and grabs hold of me so tightly I almost lose my balance. "You really came for me."

"I've got her," Raighne says as he turns so she can climb onto his back. "Let's get out of here."

"Don't let go of Raighne," I tell her before I fight my way back into the pool.

I swallow some of the muddy water as I fight to keep my head above it. The wind is making the water's surface turbulent, and I'm quickly growing tired.

We're almost to the curtain when I hear a deafening roar.

"Jesus, what's that?" I ask.

"Tsunami," Sky screams. "Faster. It's coming!"

Ice ripples through my body, and fear settles hard in the pit of my stomach. I glance over my shoulder, and my eyes jump from Sky's terrified face to the colossal wall of water rushing toward us like a dark shadow, crushing trees and everything else in its path.

Oh. My. God.

"Move, Raighne!" I shout, waiting for them to get in front of me.

He powers through the water and reaches the curtain first.

"Go," I gasp. "I'm right behind you."

With a mass of pure destruction coming directly at us, my heart beats wildly in my chest as I fight my way through the pool.

Just as Raighne shifts through the curtain, the water around me starts to rise.

Shit!

A smaller wave hits me, carrying me forward, and I quickly think of the waterfall in Ireland as I slam into the curtain.

Water propels me forward, hurling me into the air before I crash painfully hard into a boulder. The air is knocked from my lungs as I roll off the boulder and slam into the footpath around the pool of the waterfall. I skid over the rough surface for a few more feet before coming to a groaning standstill. It feels as if my right arm has been torn off.

I lie still while gasping for air as I stare up at the clear sky.

Holy shit.

"Alchera," I hear Brenna call out, but I don't have the strength to lift my head.

"What the fuck?" Doug gasps. "Make this make sense."

I hear Jason talk to Doug, but I can't focus on what they're saying because the pain increases tenfold in my body.

"I'm here." Raighne drops to his knees beside me, and when his hands fold around my arm, a cry rips free from me. Shivering uncontrollably, I glance down only to see a bone protruding from my arm, and almost pass out at the sight.

Brenna frames my face with her hands and forces me to focus on her so I don't look at Raighne as he works to heal my broken limb.

"Just look at me," she says as she brushes her palm over my

283

wet hair. "You did well. I'm proud of you."

"Yeah?" I gasp. "So I have to almost die to get you to like me?"

She shakes her head. "I've always loved you. I was just angry and shouldn't have taken it out on you."

I hear the bone snap back into place, and Raighne lets out a painful grunt, "Fuck."

I pull my face free from Brenna's hold and turn my head so I can look at him. His features are drawn tight with pain, but he keeps working on my arm.

"Stop," I mutter as I try to sit up, but Brenna pins me down to the ground by my shoulders.

"Keep still," Raighne growls. "It hurts more when you move."

"Stop!" I snap at him. "I can handle the pain."

He just shakes his head at me, and it breaks my heart to see him taking all of my pain.

I glare at Brenna. "Let go of me."

"Just stay still," she says, her tone brisk. "He's almost done."

When strength returns to my body, Raighne's still working to close the deep gash from where the bone ripped through my skin, but I manage to shove Brenna away from me and climb to my feet.

"Will you fucking stop," Raighne snaps, raising his voice at me.

"Enough," I hiss. "I'm not going to let you take all my pain."

He moves so fast I have no time to evade him. One of his hands clamps around my throat while the other closes over the gash on my arm. I'm yanked right against him as our eyes lock.

"*Stop!*" he demands, pouring all his power into the single word.

With my breaths racing over my lips, I'm unable to move a muscle while he finishes healing me. Only once he's done does he break eye contact, and the force that's keeping me in place disappears, freeing me.

Before I can say anything else, I hear the wind stirring through the leaves of the trees, and I shiver. *"The wind, Raighne."*

"There's no wind," he replies, his eyes flicking over my face.

"Raighne," I whimper, and his arms engulf me as my vision begins to blur and the sound of the wind gets stronger.

"I've got you." I hear his words as if he's speaking from the end of a tunnel, and I feel my body float into the air as he picks me up.

CHAPTER 26

ALCHERA

"*There's no time to rest! If we don't keep moving, we might as well kill ourselves,*" *a man says, his tone commanding.*

Glancing around me, I'm standing on a rocky hill and looking down at a lake.

It's beautiful.

The wind blows, sending shivers down my spine, and when I glance over my shoulder, I see a waterfall.

Thank God.

"*I'm not as fit as you. I'll only hold you back. Go on ahead. I'll catch up with you,*" *another man says.*

"*Don't give me that shit. Give me your bag,*" *the first voice snaps.*

Finally, I see two men making their way to the waterfall. A tall guy looms over a shorter one, and everything about him screams military. He's well-built, his brown hair cut into a crew-cut style. The shorter man has an intelligent light shining from his eyes.

"*Come on, Matt. We have to move faster,*" *the military one snaps again.* "*We need to get to the cave.*"

"*I'm trying my best,*" Matt *says, but he struggles to keep up.* "*Will we really be safe in the cave?*"

"It has water and shelter. It's all we need."

"What about food?"

"I'll hunt," the military guy mutters.

I see the mountain rising behind the waterfall.

"I'm tired, Dylan," Matt gasps.

"Fine. We can rest here for ten minutes. We were lucky to get away from the city. Half of the country is gone. The radio said that tsunamis have struck all over the world. We're going to take cover as high above sea level as possible and wait this thing out."

"Okay," Matt groans as he sits down on a small boulder. "I can't believe all the disasters. It's terrifying. What if hiding in a cave doesn't help?"

"It has to," Dylan mutters, his eyes roving over their surroundings as if he's watching for threats.

The ground beneath them begins to tremble, and Matt immediately jumps up and moves to Dylan's side.

As the vision fades from my mind, my head hurts so badly I can only let out a soft groan.

Raighne's fingers brush over my temple, easing the ache, then he asks, "What did you see?"

"Two men somewhere in the US."

I lift my head from his thigh and push myself off the ground, climbing to my feet.

When I move toward the waterfall again, Raighne orders, "Slow down. Tell us what we're walking into."

I glance at my group, then letting out a sigh, I say, "Finian and Brenna, please stay with the group." I turn my attention to Raighne. "Two men. Dylan and Matt. I think they're brothers. Dylan gave me the impression he's had military training, and Matt gives me a professor vibe. They're in a national park of some sort and near a waterfall, so we have to move fast."

Raighne nods, and placing his hand on my lower back, he

walks with me into the pool. We wade through the water to the curtain, and I take hold of his hand before I bring up the image of the waterfall we need to shift to.

"Ready?" I ask.

"Yes. I can see the waterfall clearly. Let's go."

Stepping into the curtain, I feel dizzy. Everything is taking one hell of a physical toll on me, and I don't know how much longer I'm going to last.

When I come out on the other side, I suck in a few deep breaths and wait for my head to stop spinning.

After wiping the water from my eyes, I scan the area. It looks the same as in my vision.

"We need to move," I hear Dylan say.

"What if we go into the cave, and another earthquake hits, and we're buried alive," Matt rambles, clearly scared of everything that's been happening.

Thank God. At least they're still nearby.

I wade through the water toward the embankment, and Raighne helps me out. When we're both standing on a grassy patch, I point at the boulders where Dylan and Matt are resting.

"I'll let you handle it, but if one of them gets aggressive, I'm taking over."

I glance up at Raighne. *"Just don't hurt them."*

I'm sure I look like some crazy swamp woman, and I hope it doesn't freak the two men out too much.

When we move closer and make our way around a boulder, Dylan's head snaps in our direction, and he quickly moves closer to Matt.

"Hey," he mutters, giving us a cautious look.

"Hi," I respond, keeping my tone non-threatening. Noticing Dylan is armed, I hope to God he doesn't shoot me.

Here goes nothing.

"My name is Alchera, and this is Raighne. I'm sure you've noticed all the disasters around the world."

"Yeah," Dylan replies, his eyes flicking between Raighne and me. "That's why we're out here. You?"

"Please, don't freak out," I cringe, already knowing this isn't going to go well, "but I'm here to save you and Matt. You need to come with us."

Dylan's eyebrow lifts, and the next second, he reaches for the weapon at his hip.

When Raighne moves slightly in front of me, Dylan yells, "That's close enough." He points the gun right at us. "I suggest you leave the way you came."

"Go back to the curtain. I'm going to move Matt your way. Grab him and shift back to Ireland. I'll follow with Dylan." Raighne's voice sounds in my mind.

"You sure? He has a gun."

"Which can't kill us. Go, Alchera."

I move cautiously back to the pool, holding my hands in front of me so Dylan can see them at all times. "We're going," I tell him, hoping to set him at ease.

"You too," he growls at Raighne.

"I'll move as soon as she's safe."

When I climb into the pool, Dylan frowns at me, and shaking his head, he yells, "What the fuck are you doing?"

I quickly wade to the curtain. *"Now!"*

Raighne doesn't move a muscle, but suddenly Matt flies through the air with a terrified cry ripping from him.

"What the fuck!" Dylan shouts.

The moment Matt plows into me, I think of the waterfall in Ireland, and as I drag him into the curtain, I glance at Raighne and Dylan. I see how the weapon is ripped from Dylan's hand before Raighne slams him into the pool.

Jesus.

I shift with a terrified Matt and the moment we appear in Ireland, I help him to stay on his feet.

He glances wildly around us while he gags, probably feeling sick from shifting for the first time.

"You're okay," I say, keeping my arms wrapped around him as I pull him to the walkway around the waterfall. "The nausea will pass."

Finian and Brenna come to help me, and once we have a dazed Matt sitting on one of the boulders by the walkway, I say, "Take deep breaths."

"Dylan?" he gasps.

Just then, Raighne comes through the waterfall, forcing a struggling Dylan to move.

Finian runs into the pool to help Raighne control Dylan.

"Calm down," Raighne snaps at Dylan. "We're doing this to help you."

"What the fuck?" Dylan keeps muttering while shaking his head to rid himself of the dizzy spell caused by shifting.

"Now I've seen everything," I hear Doug mutter.

Dylan's eyes lock on Matt, and he yanks free from Raighne. When he reaches his brother, he pulls him to a standing position and holds him as he glances at the group.

"Who are you people?" Dylan asks, sounding stunned out of his everloving mind.

"I'm Alchera," I say again, thinking there's no way he'll remember my name from when I introduced myself before we shifted.

"That's Raighne and Finian, and this is my sister, Brenna." I point to the other humans. "Doug, Sarah, Sky, and Jason. They're chosen ones, just like you and Matt. This planet is going to be destroyed in a matter of a week, and we're here to take you to a new Earth called Vaalbara." When Dylan's lips part, I hold up my hand. "I know it sounds crazy as hell, but there's no other way to explain it. I still have to get four other people before we can return to our world, where you'll start a new life."

"The fuck?" Dylan mutters, struggling to deal with the shock.

"I think we should all go to our house. It's not far from here," Sarah says, sounding weaker than earlier. "I need to take my meds and get some rest."

"Sarah's right," Doug agrees. "We could all use a break where everything can be explained to us."

I look at Dylan. "Will you come?"

"Do we have a fucking choice?"

"Yes," Raighne mutters as he walks toward me. "Either you come willingly, or I'll force you."

"Not much of a fucking choice," Dylan growls.

"Dylan," I say to get his attention. "Please let me save you. Save Matt."

He lets out a disgruntled sigh but doesn't argue as he gestures for us to walk.

While Finian takes the lead, Raighne waits for everyone to start moving before he brings up the rear.

"Thank you for helping," I tell Raighne mentally.

"That's what I'm here for."

"You look angry."

"I'm fine. Let's get out of here."

We all pile into the van, and I worry about how we're going to get around if we get more chosen ones because it's already a tight fit.

The moment Raighne sits down beside me, he pulls me onto his lap to make more space for the others. With one arm wrapped tightly around me, he uses his other hand to take hold of my jaw. Nudging my face so I'll look at him, we lock eyes.

"How are you holding up?"

"I'm just tired."

I feel his warmth pour into me, and I know he's searching for any signs that I'm not coping.

"How are you doing?" I ask.

"I'm built for this. Never worry about me."

"Easier said than done," I grumble.

He lets out a chuckle as he nudges me to rest my head against his shoulder and presses a kiss on my forehead. More of his warmth fills me, I can't stop myself from drifting off to sleep.

Ares crouches in front of me and gestures to our left, where my father and Jason are hanging. "Who should I kill first?"

Locking eyes with him, I hiss, "Fuck you. I won't choose."

He raises to his full height, and when he moves toward them, my heart beats wildly in my chest.

"No!" I start to strain against the rope tied around my body and fall to my side. Air explodes over my lips as I watch with horrified eyes when Ares moves closer to my father.

"Your father or your chosen one?" Ares asks again before chuckling. The sound is pure evil.

A knife appears in his hand. The blade looks like it's made of black obsidian.

"Let them go and kill me," I cry. "I choose me."

Ares chuckles again as he shakes his head. "No. It will never be you." He moves in behind my father, and pressing the blade to his neck, he slices Dad's throat open and blood pours from him like a waterfall.

"No!" I scream, ugly sobs tearing from me.

"Wake up, Alchera." I hear Raighne's voice as his warmth battles the darkness in me.

My eyes flit wildly between my father, who's bleeding out, and Jason as Ares moves in behind him.

"Please!" I beg. "Kill me."

Ares chuckles again as he slits Jason's throat, and a wail of grief echoes around the room.

"Alchera!" Raighne's voice thunders in my mind, but the intense sorrow and guilt I feel drown him out.

Ares moves closer to me, and unfastening the ropes keeping me imprisoned, his touch turns gentle as he brushes his palm over my temple and hair.

"I've got you," he says, his tone sounding loving. "I'll always have you."

I try to shake my head as he leans closer to me, and when I feel his breath on my face, agonizing terror grips my soul.

Black smoke creeps past his lips and forces its way into my nose and mouth.

"You're just like me, Alchera," Ares whispers. "We're both doomed."

Suddenly, a bright light chases the darkness back to the farthest corners of my mind, and Raighne's warmth is so intense it rips me out of the nightmare.

My eyes snap open and it takes me a second to focus on Raighne's face that's tense with worry.

My heart is pounding in my throat, and my breaths come fast and hard.

Ares's voice is still echoing through my mind as Raighne squashes me to his chest.

My torturer is out there somewhere, and I can feel him coming for me.

"I won't let him near you," Raighne's voice drifts like a cool breeze through my feverish mind. *"Just focus on me. You're safe."*

My mind feels like a piece of chewed gum. The visions and nightmares are starting to take their toll on me.

I let Raighne hold me until my heartbeat and breaths return to normal, then say, "I desperately need to take a shower."

"Okay." He helps me off the bed while his eyes search my face for any signs of distress.

I let a smile form on my face and say, "I'm fine."

"I'll get you something to eat while you wash up." He gestures to a dresser. "Sarah left clean clothes for you to wear."

I nod and watch as he leaves the room before I glance around me.

There's only a dresser and two single beds in the otherwise empty room. I grab the clothes, which consist of a pair of sweatpants, a sweater, and socks. Walking out of the room, I find a bathroom to my right.

I'm thankful when I see bottles of shampoo, conditioner, and body wash and quickly switch on the faucets in the shower.

I better enjoy this shower because God only knows when I'll get to have one again with the world going to shit around us.

I strip out of my damp clothes, feeling grimy from the day I've had.

When I step beneath the warm spray, I let out a moan.

So good.

I take my time washing every part of my body, and when I feel much better, I switch off the faucets and dry myself. Finding body lotion, I rub some into my skin before getting dressed in the clean clothes. The sweatpants are a little long, so I roll the fabric up around my ankles.

I use my finger to brush my teeth and rinse my mouth twice with minty mouthwash. Looking at my reflection in the mirror, I tug my fingers through the short strands to tame the wild mess.

Once I'm done, I stare at myself, wondering how I'm going to survive the days to come.

How long will Ireland stay intact? If this country is devastated by a disaster, we might not have the waterfall to shift through anymore.

Will we be able to find a plane again so we can travel to where the remaining chosen ones are? How long will it take to get to them?

"Don't think about any of that," Raighne mutters in my mind. *"We'll deal with everything as it happens. Come eat."*

Leaving the bathroom, I walk down a short hallway until I find a kitchen on my left.

Not seeing Raighne, I ask, *"Where are you?"*

"Living room."

I walk past the kitchen, finding everyone huddled in a smallish living room.

There's a round table with four chairs in the corner with sandwiches stacked on a plate.

Raighne comes to me and hands me a ham and cheese sandwich.

"Eat it all."

I nod as I take it from him, then glance at my chosen ones, who are all staring at me.

"How are you all holding up?" I ask while giving Dylan and Doug cautious looks.

"I've decided to just go with the flow because there's no way I can explain everything I've seen today," Doug mutters.

Dylan is leaning against a wall, his arms crossed over his broad chest. For a moment, he stares at me, then he says, "If everything y'all said is true, then I guess we should count ourselves lucky. It's just hard to wrap our minds around it."

I let out a chuckle. "I know. I felt the same way."

Dylan frowns. "The same? You're not one of them?"

"Oh, I am, but I was sent to Earth at sixteen and lived here for five years as one of you. I recently found out everything, and it was one hell of a shock to the system." I smile at him. "So I understand how you feel."

He nods at me then says, "You should eat."

Right.

I take a bite of my sandwich and give Jason a grateful smile when he brings me a bottle of water.

"How are you holding up?" Jason murmurs, keeping his tone low.

"Better."

His eyes meet mine. "Just let me know if there's anything I can do to help."

I glance at the other chosen ones, then turn my attention back to him again. "Just help me keep an eye on all of them, please."

He nods, his gaze drifting to Sarah. "I will."

"Especially her," I whisper, hoping she'll survive what's to come.

As if Sarah can sense we're talking about her, she looks our way then asks, "Are the clothes okay?"

"Yes. Thank you so much. How do you feel?"

"Better after I got my meds and some rest."

My eyes drift over her pale face. "Just hold out a week. Okay? Once we're back on Vaalbara, they'll heal you."

There's no excitement or hope in her eyes that we'll actually be able to heal her, and it chips away at my heart.

Honestly, I'm not even sure Aster and Janak can heal Sarah. But I seriously doubt Awo would choose her only to let her die on Vaalbara. It just doesn't make sense, so I'm holding onto hope there's a way they can cure Sarah.

"I'll put your other clothes in the washing machine so they're clean for tomorrow," Brenna says.

"Thank you. I left them in the bathroom." I give my sister a grateful smile before sinking my teeth into the sandwich again.

Doug picks up the remote control then says, "Let's see what's happening in the world."

We all turn our attention to the TV screen, and I continue to eat as an announcer sits behind a desk with disasters flashing on a screen behind her.

"The west coast of the United States has been declared a dead zone. With millions fleeing to the borders of Canada, the Canadian government is doing its best to assist the survivors."

I only manage to eat half the sandwich because when more images of disasters and dead bodies fill the screen behind the announcer, my appetite vanishes.

"Chile, Hawaii, Japan, New Zealand, Indonesia, Malaysia, and the coast of India have all been struck by monster tsunamis caused by the San Andreas fault line earthquake, and the death toll is well into the hundreds of thousands if not millions."

"God," Sarah whimpers.

We all stare horrified at the TV.

Sky covers her mouth with her hands as a sob breaks free. "My family."

Matt quickly wraps his arm around her shoulders. "I'm sorry. We lost people, too."

"All communications with those countries have been lost," the announcer continues, "and there's no possibility of sea rescue due to the ocean's unstable manner."

I feel grief pouring from my chosen ones. Flashes from the visions I had of the disasters bombard my mind, and the plate slips from my hand.

I hear the terrified screams.

I feel their heartbeats stopping one after the other.

I see the blood, the maimed body parts, and the horrific destruction.

"Switch it off," Raighne orders before he frames my face, forcing me to look at him. "Focus on me."

My lips part, and I inhale a shuddering breath while it feels like shadowy fingers creep over my mind, threatening to rob me of my sanity.

Raighne leans closer, and his warmth pours into me. "Just focus on me."

I stare into his eyes as his presence soothes the darkness, calming the chaos that the visions and nightmares are causing in the deepest parts of my soul.

"Is she okay?" Jason asks.

I suck in deep breaths then nod. "I'm good."

"Panic attack?" Matt asks. "I get those too."

Sky pats Matt's hand while giving me a worried look.

"Really, I'm fine," I say to reassure everyone.

Just as Raighne crouches to pick up the plate and half-eaten sandwich I dropped, the air vibrates around us.

"What the fuck?" Dylan snaps.

"Raighne!" Finian hollers, and the next second, Ares appears with a woman's hand gripping his throat.

Then the rest of Adeth materializes with Griffith and Roark trying to restrain her.

Ares lands on his back, and as he skids into one of the couches, I'm filled with horror.

No!

Ares slams his hand into Adeth's chest, and it sends her flying through the air before she hits a wall while Roark and Griffith fall to the side.

"Help us," Roark orders as he darts back to his feet.

Raighne instantly throws his arm out in Ares' direction, using his power to keep him from moving.

"Ares is with us," Griffith shouts.

What. The. Actual. Fuck?

I stand rooted to the spot as Raighne's other arm reaches toward Adeth, and he forcefully keeps her pinned to the wall.

Light shoots from Finian, stunning her, and before Finian

can stun Ares, Griffith again snaps, "Ares is with us. Free him, Raighne."

Oh my God.

My eyes flick wildly over my chosen ones before I shout, "Dylan, Jason! Get the chosen ones out of the room. Now! She wants to kill you."

Doug picks Sarah up, and they're the first to rush past me. Jason herds Matt and Sky away from the danger while Dylan pulls out his gun and trains it on Adeth.

"Get out of here, Dylan. You can't kill her with a bullet."

He gives me an unsure look and moves closer to me. "I'm not leaving y'all to fight alone."

Before I can say another word, shadows fill my mind, and I hear Adeth.

"Have you missed me?"

My eyes flick to her. *"No."*

"They won't dare kill their precious dreamer." An evil smile tugs at her mouth as she keeps her gaze locked with mine. *"Let me in."*

CHAPTER 27

RAIGHNE

The moment I can't feel Alchera, my eyes flick to her. There's a lifeless expression on her face as she slowly takes a step toward Dylan.

"Alchera," I snap, at first thinking she's blocking me from her mind.

Her eyes remain glued on Dylan as she keeps moving closer.

"Are you okay?" Dylan asks her, an unsure expression on his face.

Adeth lets out a maniacal burst of laughter, and a knife appears in Alchera's hand.

"What the fuck!" Dylan exclaims, turning his weapon on Alchera.

"Awo. No!" I whisper when I see the blade of death in Alchera's hand.

Roark and my father dart toward Alchera, and I can feel Ares trying to use his power to shimmer so it will free him from my hold. I have to focus harder on keeping him and his evil mother in place.

"Alchera!" Roark shouts as he closes in on her.

Ares breathes heavily as he tries to move. "She's under Adeth's control." He fights my power and manages to climb to his feet, strain showing on his face. His eyes lock with mine. "Kill. Adeth."

Needing to focus on the woman I love more than anything, I free Adeth and Ares.

Roark gets to his sister first, with my father right behind him. As I focus all my power on Alchera, she darts forward.

Ares shimmers, disappearing before reappearing right behind Alchera. He takes my focus off Alchera, and as I use my power to rip him away from her, Roark darts between Alchera and Dylan, and she buries the blade of the knife in his side.

"No!" Brenna shouts as she grabs hold of Dylan, yanking him away from the danger. Finian grabs hold of her before she can get near Alchera.

It all transpires so fucking fast it takes a moment to realize what just happened.

Adeth's laughter fills the room, then Ares disappears again. This time, when he reappears, he's right by Alchera, and ripping the bloody knife from her hand, he throws it at his mother.

The blade slams into her throat, and a second later, she makes a gargling sound as shock tightens her features.

Roark drops to his knees, and Dad catches him.

Adeth slides to the floor, and she manages to pull the knife from her neck, her eyes locked on Ares.

"Thank you," she whispers, a peaceful expression making her look like the aunt I used to know before she turned dark. She keeps staring at her son, and her words are so soft, I have to read her lips as she says, "I'm sorry."

Ares nods, his expression filled with a mixture of relief and heartache as he watches his mother struggle through her last breath.

Alchera snaps out of whatever control Adeth had over her, and letting out a cry, she falls to her knees. Her eyes fill with horror as she stares at her dying brother.

"What have I done?" she gasps, her face torn with agony.

It takes one hell of a swing at my heart to see her like this.

When Ares takes a step toward her, I use my power to throw him to the other side of the room as I quickly close the distance between Alchera and me.

I wrap my arms around her, but then she starts to struggle against my hold. When I let go of her, she crawls to Roark, heartbreaking sobs tearing from her chest.

"I'm sorry," she whimpers. "I'm so sorry."

With the last of his strength, Roark tries to shake his head, then his final breath ghosts over his lips.

Brenna yanks free from Finian and falls down beside Alchera, too horror-struck to make a sound.

"NoNoNo!" Alchera cries. She grabs hold of her brother and holds his head to her chest. She chokes on sobs, and with my eyes locked on her, I force my way into her broken mind and start to take the pain from her.

Her head whips in my direction. "Don't you dare!" Her eyes are dark with grief and anger, and the next moment, I'm shoved out of her mind.

As Brenna and Alchera weep over Roark's body, it sinks in that we just lost our next king.

Fuck. All the men of House Regales have been wiped out.

I suck in a shocked breath as my eyes flick over the chaos in the living room.

My eyes fall on Adeth's body.

We've feared her for the longest time, and she's finally gone.

I see the shocked expressions on the chosen ones' faces as they huddle together, and I realize we'll have to sacrifice everything to keep them safe.

This is only the beginning because we still have to deal with Ares. There's Void as well, and it's impossible to kill him.

I look at Roark again, then think to ask, "Where's River? Why wasn't he with Roark?"

When my father shakes my head, my heart squeezes painfully. As I lower my head, he says, "Adeth killed River right before Ares brought us here."

My head snaps up. "What?" My eyes flick to Ares, who's standing to the side, and as I throw my arm out and slam his body against the nearest wall, I shout at my father, "Why the hell did you come here? Bringing the enemy right to the chosen ones!"

Dad climbs to his feet, his eyes darting between Ares and me.

"Adeth forced Ares to bring us here." Dad holds his arms up in a gesture meant to pacify me, but it doesn't do shit to calm the rage burning in my chest.

"You should've killed them on Vaalbara," I growl as I increase my power on Ares, making the plaster on the wall crack around his body.

"Raighne!" Dad shouts. "Wait. You don't want to kill him."

With Alchera weeping at my feet, I bite the words out through clenched teeth, "I will liquefy his insides. He doesn't deserve to live."

"Ares is your cousin. Let him go, Raighne," Dad says, moving cautiously closer to me. "He's your family. Our family."

Alchera climbs to her feet, and slowly shaking her head as if she's caught in a daze, she glances between Ares and my father. When she turns around and locks eyes with me, I swear I can see shadows creeping into her green irises.

"Kill him," she demands, her tone hoarse from the trauma she's battling.

With my eyes on the woman I love, I begin to close my

fingers into a fist, and it has Ares letting out a pain-filled groan.

Dad grabs hold of my arm. "Stop, Raighne!" He steps closer to me as he tries to explain, "Ares was under Adeth's control. Just like Alchera was. He had no choice. He's as much a victim as she is."

I stare at my father in disbelief. "You saw what he did to Alchera. You were there when we found her. How can you forgive him?"

Dad moves between Ares and me, and I can't believe he's protecting him.

"Let them kill me," Ares groans, his tone filled with exhaustion. "They'll be doing me a favor."

Everyone looks at Ares, where he's leaning against the wall, bits of plaster lying by his feet.

"There's been enough death," my father snaps. "We need all the help we can get right now." He sucks in a breath before exhaling slowly. "We need to return Roark and Adeth to Vaalbara. Let's all remain level-headed while we deal with the loss we've suffered."

My father keeps an eye on me while he orders, "Come, Ares. Shimmer us back to Vaalbara."

When Ares moves, Alchera darts to my side, and I quickly grab hold of her hand.

The silence is tense as we all watch my father and Ares take hold of Roark and Adeth. The moment they disappear, Alchera pulls her hand from mine and rushes out the sliding door that leads to the backyard.

Brenna goes after her, and as the sisters step outside, I glance at Finian.

My brother looks as shocked as I feel but says, "Father knows what he's doing."

"Does he?" I mutter.

"Are we safe?" Dylan asks. "Shouldn't we hightail it out of here?"

I let out a sigh as I shake my head. "We'll leave as soon as Alchera has a vision of the next chosen one."

"So we're staying?" Jason asks. "No one else is going to appear out of thin air to kill us?"

I still believe Ares is a huge problem, and knowing he's moving freely around keeps me from answering Jason.

"Let's clean up," Sky says. "And I think everyone can do with a cup of coffee."

"Fuck coffee," Dylan mutters. "Is there anything stronger in this place?"

"I'll get the whiskey," Doug says, his features tense with worry.

I stand frozen as the chosen ones get to work, picking up the scattered sandwiches and putting the furniture back in its place.

Finian comes to place his hand on my shoulder, then he murmurs, "If what Father said is true, then we need to give Ares a chance."

"The shadowlands will cease to exist before I do that," I mutter.

ALCHERA

My butt hits the steps outside the sliding doors, and I wrap my arms around my shins.

Still feeling Adeth's darkness creeping in my mind like shadowy tentacles, I can't process the devastation of what just happened.

When Brenna sits down beside me, I can't bring myself to

talk.

Roark's dead.

I killed him.

My chest implodes with devastating guilt and grief, but I can't cry.

When I close my eyes and suck in a shuddering breath, Brenna wraps her arms around me and pulls me against her chest. She brushes her hand over my hair.

"It wasn't your fault. Adeth killed him," she whispers, her tone raw with heartache.

I can't even shake my head to argue.

It feels as if all light has been drained from me, and only Adeth's darkness has remained.

I have no idea what happened. One moment, I was hearing Adeth in my thoughts, and the next, I watched as Roark slumped to the floor.

The time between is filled with a shadowy haze.

Brenna lets out a sob, and I barely have enough strength to wrap my arms around her.

We lean heavily against each other as we try to process the loss we suffered.

Try to process? God, I haven't even processed all the other shit that's happened. It feels like every time I try to rise to my feet, something knocks me down.

I'm not strong enough for all of this, and Raighne can't keep taking it all from me. I won't let him suffer in my stead.

Jason comes out of the house, and when he crouches in front of us, I notice he's holding two cups of coffee.

I shake my head, and Brenna says, "Thanks, but I don't think either of us can stomach anything right now."

He sets the mugs down and places his hand on my shoulder. "Is there anything I can do?"

"Just keep an eye on the others," I whisper, my voice filled with the shadows growing in me.

"I will." He gives my shoulder a squeeze. "I'm sorry for your loss."

I turn my face into Brenna's hair and hold her tighter, which makes her cling to me.

When Jason leaves, I say, "You should go back to Vaalbara."

Brenna pulls away, giving me a what-the-hell look.

"Father and Roark died because of me. I don't want you near me, Brenna. It's not safe."

"I'm here to help you," she argues.

My features tighten as desperation and grief flay me to the bone, and my voice is thick as I say, "I don't want to lose you as well."

She lifts her hands to my face, and framing my cheeks, she says, "If I die on this mission, it's not because of you. We all have our part to play, Alchera. You're not responsible for our father and brother's deaths. It was Adeth. Do you understand?"

We'll never agree, and knowing this, I just nod so we can stop talking about it.

I pull Brenna's hands away from my face, and needing to be alone, I say, "Will you check on the others?"

Brenna climbs to her feet, and after she heads back into the house, I let out a heavy breath.

I'm hit with a wave of destructive emotions that shudders through my body.

Not even a minute later, Raighne comes out and sits down beside me. I feel his warmth skirt around the edges of my mind, and unable to stop it, a sob rips from me as I throw myself at him.

His strong arms engulf me, and I'm pulled onto his lap as his essence floods every inch of me. The relief I feel when he starts to take the hellish grief and guilt from me is so intense I just slump against his chest as silent tears spiral down my cheeks.

When I start to feel better, and I'm able to think clearly, I ask, *"How do you cope with everything you take from me?"*

"Knowing you don't have to feel any of it makes it bearable."

I let out an exhausted sigh. *"You're so much stronger than me, but you can't keep taking it all from me."*

"I can." He presses a kiss to the top of my head. *"It's one of my talents as your guardian."*

With my mind clearer, I think about the loss we've suffered. *"I can't believe Roark's gone."*

"River, too."

God. Poor Fleur. My mother.

"Why do so many of us have to die?" I ask.

"There's no limit to what we have to sacrifice so the human race can continue."

A new fear bleeds into my heart, but before I can put it into words, Raighne says, *"If I die, I'll become a part of you. You'll always feel me because we share the same soul."*

"I don't want you to die." A sob bursts over my lips, and wrapping my arms around him, I cling to him for all my life is worth.

"None of us know how much time we have," he murmurs above my head. "It doesn't help to live in fear, my little dreamer. We just have to make every second count."

I hold onto the man who's the only thing keeping me standing through all the hell I've had to face.

I have no idea how much time passes before I say, "I'm so glad you're mine. I don't know what I'd do without you."

The air displaces around us, and the next second, I'm pulled to my feet by Raighne, who immediately takes a defensive stance.

A few feet from us, Ares appears with Griffith right beside him.

Even though there's a glamor making Ares look human, my body shudders with revulsion at the sight of the monster who tortured me.

He must've taken an elixir before coming back because his eyes are the same light blue as Raighne's.

Griffith holds his hands up. "Let's talk before anyone overreacts."

"Overreacts?" Raighne growls. "How can you stand beside such evil, Father?"

Griffith shakes his head, giving Raighne a pleading look. "Son, Ares never meant to hurt Alchera. He was under Adeth's control, the same way Alchera was earlier. You can't hold him accountable for what happened."

I struggle to accept what Griffith is saying. I'll never forgive myself for the parts I played in the deaths of my father and brother.

I'll never forgive Ares.

If we were stronger, Adeth wouldn't have been able to control us.

Raighne's eyes snap to my face, then back to Ares, and I see the moment he starts to believe what Griffith is saying.

Pulling away from him, I shake my head.

"I know I'm the last person you want to see, Alchera," Ares says. His eyes are filled with the same guilt I feel. "And I know nothing I say will change anything, but I'm sorry. I didn't want to hurt you."

I shake my head wildly, moving a couple of steps backward while hissing, "Don't talk to me."

"I can't erase what happened between us, but please allow me to help. Let me try to make up for what I've done to you. I can help you fulfill your destiny by transporting you wherever you need to go."

Just the sound of his voice makes me feel sick to my stomach, and darting away from them, I only make it to a tree before my body convulses as I vomit.

A second later a hand rubs over my lower back, and Raighne's healing touch quickly settles my upset stomach.

"Enough!" Raighne snaps at his father and Ares. "There's no way we're working with Ares. You can both leave."

"We can't," Griffith replies, his tone firm. "Awo has given a destiny to Ares. He has to help Alchera by transporting her to the chosen ones. Awo heard her concerns and answered them by sending Ares."

"What the hell?" Raighne gasps.

I'm starting to think Awo hates me.

I shake my head as I walk to the house to get away from them, my body trembling like a leaf in the shitstorm my life has become.

"Alchera," Griffith calls. "Don't walk away. We need to settle this matter."

Ignoring him, I head into the house, and I don't stop until I shut the bathroom door behind me. I take a minute to brush my teeth before washing my face and hands.

When my eyes meet my reflection in the mirror and I see the shadows growing in my irises, I sink down to the floor, sitting flat on my butt.

I'm no better than Ares. Where he just tortured me, I killed Roark.

I killed my own brother.

I'm worse than Ares.

"*No!*" Raighne's voice thunders through my mind right before the bathroom door opens and he comes inside.

When Raighne picks me up, I rest my head against his shoulder. He carries me to a bedroom and gently places me on the covers before he lies down beside me. I snuggle against his chest as his body engulfs mine.

"What do we do?" I ask.

"We'll deal with everything once you've had some rest."

I take deep breaths of Raighne's scent, and the next second, I drift off to sleep.

CHAPTER 28

ALCHERA

A res is standing over me with his whip, ready to begin another day's torture.

"I don't want to hurt you, Alchera. Please forgive me," he begs as tears roll down his face.

I don't understand why he's crying.

"Ares?" I look into his light blue eyes, alive with pain. He lifts his arm to hit me, and I reach out to him. "You can fight her. Please don't," I beg.

My plea doesn't stop him from bringing the whip down over my broken skin.

"No," I sob. "Please stop."

The words echo around me, and I realize it's not my voice, but Ares who's begging.

I find myself in some sort of cave, and I can hear water dripping, the stench of rotten eggs filling the air.

I glance wildly around, and when I see a weak and beaten younger version of Ares lying on the floor, I gasp in horror.

Adeth raises her arm high and brings the whip down hard on his back.

When she raises her arm again, I race forward and throw myself over Ares. I cover him with my body and brace myself for the impact, but the whip goes through me.

Ares grinds his teeth, and when I look into his eyes, I know that he sees me.

"Ares!" I wake up crying his name.

I'm slumped over Raighne, my face pressed against his stomach. His hand brushes over my hair, and I wrap my arms tightly around his waist, pressing my whole body as close to him as possible.

Tears spill from my eyes. I can't believe Adeth did that to Ares, and then she made him torture me. How could she be so sick? How could she do that to her own son?

"Alchera?"

"Yeah," I whisper, trying to hide the conflicting emotions I'm feeling.

"What did you see?"

"It's just a nightmare," I lie.

"Then I should've been able to see it."

Shit. Right.

I let out a heavy breath. *"Don't worry about it."*

His hands take hold of my shoulders, and he pushes me onto my back. He places one hand next to my head and moves his body until he's leaning half over me. I focus on how good it feels to have his hard body pressing against mine.

His eyes search mine. "Let me see."

I shake my head, and wanting to distract him, I lift my head and press my mouth to his. *"I don't want to think about it. Just make me forget."*

Raighne tilts his head, his tongue brushing over my lips before slipping into my mouth.

I wrap my arms around his neck and try to pull him down so

313

he'll lie on top of me, but he resists.

"We're not alone in the room. Sarah and Sky are sleeping on the other bed, and Doug and Jason are on the floor."

We stop kissing, and I glance to my left, where the women are fast asleep.

Knowing I won't be able to sleep more tonight, I look at Raighne. *"I'm going outside for fresh air."*

"I'll come with."

I shake my head. *"Sleep. You don't have to babysit me."*

"I'm not letting you out of my sight," he mutters as he climbs off the bed. *"Ares is here."*

Right.

I crouch by Jason and shake his shoulder gently. When his eyes snap open, I whisper, "Sleep on the bed."

He nods and slaps Doug's back. When he groans, Jason mutters, "Let's move to the bed."

"I'm not sharing a single bed with you," Doug grumbles. "You take it."

Jason doesn't argue, and as he climbs onto the bed, I leave the room with Raighne.

We make our way to the sliding doors, careful not to wake the others, and once we're outside, Raighne says, "You didn't get much sleep. Only three hours."

"I'm okay." I give him a smile so he won't worry.

I sit down on the steps and stare at the small garden as the sun starts to rise.

"You know what would be nice?"

"What?"

I grin at Raighne. "Coffee." I can see he's about to tell me he's not leaving me alone, which has me saying, "I'll be fine. Besides, everyone's sleeping."

He hesitates then climbs to his feet. "Stay right here."

I nod and watch as he walks into the house before I let out a deep sigh.

Keeping my walls up so Raighne won't hear my thoughts, I think about the vision I had of Ares. It had to be a vision. Otherwise, Raighne would've been able to see it.

Still, it's the first time I've had a vision of the past, though. Is Awo trying to tell me something?

Sympathy trickles into my heart, and I can't stop it from taking root. How long did Ares suffer at the hands of his mother?

Thinking of our time together in the shack, I remember the moments when it seemed like he was fighting something.

He was trying to fight Adeth so he didn't have to hurt me, but he wasn't strong enough.

Just like I wasn't when I killed Roark.

"Alchera."

At the sound of Ares' voice, my head snaps up and I see him standing a few feet away.

"Don't panic," he says quickly. "I won't hurt you."

Unable to think of what I should do, I can only stare at the man who made me pray for death.

We're both doomed.

He shakes his head. "No, you're not. I've seen how strong you are. You can fight it."

Shock shudders through me, and I climb to my feet. "You can hear my thoughts?"

"I can hear everyone's thoughts. It's a talent." He shrugs. "Or curse, depending on how you choose to look at it."

I'm torn between hating him for what he's done to me and feeling compassion because he suffered at the hands of his mother.

"I had a vision of you," I admit. "I saw some of what Adeth did to you."

He shakes his head, his eyes resting on me with so much guilt it finds an echo in my chest.

Not commenting on what I just said, he asks, "Will you let me help?"

"It's not up to me." I sigh, and sounding a little bitter, I mutter, "Awo made the decision, and we just have to abide by it."

"I know you don't want to hear it, but I'm so fucking sorry for what I did to you. I tried to fight Void and my mother."

I'm just about to turn around so I can head into the house to join Raighne when an intense wave of panic and desperation hits me hard.

"Move!" a policeman shouts, his tone urgent as he gestures for crowds of people to keep running while ash and rocks rain down on them. "Don't stop. Just keep going."

"We have to leave, Riccardo," another policeman yells while the ground rumbles and quakes beneath their feet.

"Christ," Riccardo breathes as he looks over his shoulder. "We're not going to make it."

"Come!" the other policeman shouts as he starts to run away from whatever danger they're facing.

Riccardo follows the other policeman, constantly glancing over his shoulder. Suddenly, I hear something that sounds like a crack of thunder, and Riccardo ducks down for cover. He reaches for his weapon while he twists his body to land on his back.

Absolute horror tightens his features as he gasps, "Mother of God."

I hear the sound of a gunshot, and an intense pain spreads through my chest.

When my vision starts to blur, I shout, "Riccardo!"

"Alchera, please!" Ares' voice sounds panic-stricken in my mind.

I feel him pressing his hands hard repeatedly against my chest, then I feel his mouth on mine as he blows air into my lungs. He presses hard against my chest again.

"*Don't die. Please. You need to give me a chance to show how sorry I am. Please,*" Ares worried words bombard me.

Panic fills me. Firstly, because Ares is giving me mouth-to-mouth, and I can't tell him to stop, and secondly, because I can't move a muscle.

"What did you do to her?" I hear Raighne shout, accompanied by the sound of cups crashing on the ground.

Ares' hands disappear from my chest, and a moment later, I hear him fall somewhere with a grunt.

"She fainted, and her heart stopped. I'm trying to help her."

"Stay away from my charge," Raighne growls, sounding so aggressive it makes goosebumps erupt over my skin.

I feel Raighne's hands and warmth, but it doesn't do anything to lessen the pain in my chest.

I want to tell him I'm fine, but I can't move.

"*Alchera?*"

"*I'm here,*" I gasp.

"*Look at me,*" he orders.

"*I can't.*" I try to move again but still find myself frozen in place with the heavy pain paralyzing my heart.

"*I can't take the pain from you,*" Raighne says, his tone drenched in fear.

"*The pain isn't real. At least not yet. I think my next chosen one is going to shoot me.*"

Raighne scoops me into his arms and brushes his palm over my cheek. "*It won't happen. Not with me by your side.*"

It takes a few more seconds, and then the paralyzing pain eases enough for me to suck in a desperate breath of air.

I force my eyes open and stare at Raighne's worried face.

"Is she okay?" Ares asks, concerned for my well-being tightening his words.

I don't think I'll ever get used to Ares sounding normal and not like the monster I came face-to-face with in that shack.

Raighne's head snaps to Ares. "You better disappear from my sight before I end you."

Ares hesitates for a moment, then shimmers away.

Raighne turns his attention back to me when I move into a sitting position.

"Riccardo," I say. "The next chosen one is in Nepal, Italy. Near Mount Vesuvius. I think it's the volcano I saw erupting in the first visions I had."

"Just take a moment to catch your breath." Raighne lets out a sigh as he presses a kiss to my forehead. "I dropped the coffee. Come with me so I can make you another cup."

"We need to wake the others," I argue. "We don't have time for coffee."

He gives me a stern look. "We have five minutes for you to eat and drink something."

Knowing I won't win, I just shake my head as I follow Raighne back into the house.

My eyes drift over his broad shoulders and muscled back, the fabric of the black T-shirt stretched tightly over his torso.

"You look good from behind."

"Don't try to distract me," he grumbles as we walk into the small kitchen. "What happened with Ares?"

"Nothing," I mumble.

While Raighne makes me a slice of toast, I prepare two cups of coffee, avoiding making eye contact with him.

"You're lying to me," Raighne says, not sounding happy at all.

"Nothing happened," I mutter. "He said he's sorry, and when I began to walk away, I had the vision."

Once I'm done making the coffee, I push a mug closer to Raighne before sipping on my own.

I watch as he spreads cream cheese on the toast, and even

though I'm not hungry, I take it from him and eat.

"Good girl," Raighne murmurs, the corner of his mouth lifting.

My eyebrow flies up while my abdomen clenches hard. "Now look who's the distraction."

He lets out a chuckle and shakes his head while leaning back against the counter.

I watch as he drinks some of the coffee, then ask, "How old was Ares when he and Adeth turned dark?"

"It happened after my mother's death," Raighne answers. "Give or take forty years ago."

I blink at Raighne as I try to comprehend what he's saying. "Forty years? How old is Ares?"

"One hundred and ninety-eight."

"What?" I gasp, my eyebrows flying into my hairline. Then, another thought pops into my mind. "How old are you?"

Raighne chuckles again, the sound hot. "Do you really want to know?"

My head bobs up and down, my coffee and toast totally forgotten in my hands.

"Two hundred and four."

"Holy shit," I gasp. "But you don't look older than thirty."

"As immortals, we age differently. Janak is over five thousand years old."

"It's way too fucking early to hear this shit," Dylan mutters as he comes into the kitchen.

Still processing what Raighne told me, I just smile at Dylan as he fixes himself a cup of black coffee.

"You okay?" Raighne asks.

"Yep. Just processing the fact that you're a hundred and eighty-three years older than me."

He walks closer to me, and, taking hold of my chin, he forces me to make eye contact with him. With a serious expression that only makes him look even more attractive, he asks, *"Is it a problem?"*

Shaking my head, I murmur, *"No."*

"Good," he sighs before pressing a kiss to my forehead. *"Finish your coffee and toast."*

After everyone's awake and has had a chance to freshen up, we meet in the living room.

I glance at my chosen ones, then ask, "Why can't we send them to Vaalbara before collecting the last four?"

"Awo has commanded it," Brenna answers. "I think it's so they'll get to know each other through the worst of times and form a bond."

"Lucky us," Jason mutters from where he's standing beside Sarah.

"Where are we going next?" Griffith asks.

"Nepal," I say. "Somewhere near Mount Vesuvius." I suck in a deep breath before I break the bad news to the group. "The volcano is erupting, so we're heading into a disaster zone." Concerned for the chosen one's safety, I say, "Maybe you can all wait here while Raighne and I go with Ares."

"It's too risky," Griffith replies. "It's better if we don't separate from each other."

I sigh, not liking the idea one bit of taking the chosen ones into a disaster area. Looking at Sarah, I say, "If we have to run, Finian and Brenna will help you so you don't fall behind."

Sarah nods. "I'm sorry I'm not stronger."

I quickly shake my head. "Don't apologize."

"Is everyone ready?" Griffith asks.

"Sarah needs to take her medicine," Doug says, and then he heads to the kitchen, followed by Jason and Sarah.

"Everyone has five minutes before we leave," Griffith

announces.

I walk over to Sky to get away from Griffith's gaze that's constantly examining me. Never mind the fact that I'm trying to ignore Ares. I might understand him a little better, but I'm far from ready to be friends with him.

"How are you doing?" I ask Sky, who's standing with Dylan and Matt.

"I'm okay. Matt's been very supportive since we met," she smiles timidly and glances at Matt.

"Oh, he has?" I grin at them, then ask, "How did you know I was coming for you before I did?"

"I kind of have psychic abilities. Sometimes, I have dreams about the future. I read tarot cards as a part-time job, but my true love is learning everything about different cultures."

"That sounds cool," I say, giving her a friendly smile.

"Can you shimmer twelve of us at once?" I hear Raighne ask Ares in a harsh tone, drawing my attention to them.

Ares nods, and glaring back at Raighne, he answers in the same brisk tone, "It will be tiring, but I can do it." He lifts his chin an inch as if he's accepting a challenge.

My eyes dart from Raighne to Ares as Griffith mutters, "Everyone is ready."

"Form a circle," Ares orders as his eyes flick over the group.

I take Raighne's hand, and when Ares moves closer to me, I inch right against Raighne's side.

Ares' eyes lock with mine, then he says, "I need to touch you to see where we're going."

Shit.

I swallow hard, and a cold sweat breaks out over my body.

"Touch her and die," Raighne growls.

Ares gives Raighne an impatient look. "How do you expect me to see where we're going?"

"I'll show you," Raighne replies, a threatening wave of anger coming off him.

"Fine." Ares moves to stand next to Raighne, and giving him a derisive look, he takes hold of Raighne's wrist. "Show me where to go, Alchera."

I suck in a deep breath then bring up the area I saw in my vision.

"Got it," Raighne murmurs to me.

"Everyone take hands and don't let go of the person next to you. If you break the link, you'll break my concentration," Ares instructs.

I take hold of Sky's hand and wait for Ares to shimmer us to Italy.

God, I hope this works.

I try to brace for the sickening sensations I felt the first time Ares shimmered me to the shack, but instead, a cool breeze rustles through me right before the living room starts to blur.

CHAPTER 29

ALCHERA

As my vision comes into focus again, I quickly glance around us but don't see Riccardo.

Shit.

Ares sinks to his knees, and sitting back on his haunches, he sucks in desperate breaths of air.

There's a glimmer of worry in my chest, and I instinctively move closer, but Raighne grabs hold of my arm, pulling me back with a stern shake of his head.

Jason darts forward and crouches in front of Ares, saying, "Your nose is bleeding. Tilt your head back."

I watch with a weird sense of worry as Jason hands Ares a tissue to wipe up the blood before checking his vitals.

Staring at the man who tortured me, I struggle with the conflicting emotions in my chest. The hatred and fear I have for him buckle beneath the compassion that has no business being in my heart.

"He's just exhausted," Jason says. "The shimmer thing he did took a blow at him."

"There's no time to rest," Finian mutters.

"Matt's puking his guts out," Dylan mentions, his tone strained and looking a little pale himself. "We could all use a minute or two to recover."

I glance at where Sky is crouching near Matt with a water bottle, which makes me think back to what Brenna said about them forming bonds with one another.

It seems more like some are forming romantic relationships.

Turning my attention back to Ares, I watch as he climbs to his feet, muttering, "I'm good to go."

I let out a relieved breath, then take in the area around us.

We're standing in a park that's surrounded by old buildings. The few people who are out on the streets this early in the morning don't even notice us, because they're too busy rushing to their destinations.

The air feels tense, and it makes a shiver ghost down my spine.

Needing a moment to try and focus on sensing where Riccardo is, I pull away from Raighne and walk toward a tree that offers some shade.

"You okay?" Raighne asks.

"Yes. Just need a minute. Check on Matt and Sarah for me, please."

"Alchera." Hearing Ares' voice in my mind has me looking over my shoulder at him.

"Stay out of her fucking mind," Raighne growls.

"It's okay," I tell Raighne. *"I have to talk to Ares at some point."*

"No," Raighne refuses, the brutal expression on his face spelling nothing good for Ares.

"Raighne." I give him a pleading look. *"I'll be okay. Give me privacy."*

He shakes his head at me before giving Ares a look of warning. *"One wrong move, and you're dead."*

"Got it," Ares bites out before turning his attention back to

me.

I'm relieved when Ares doesn't attempt to move closer to me, but when his expression softens, it fills me with a weird sense of confusion like it did when he asked me to forgive him in the shack.

Wrapping my arms around my middle, I hold his gaze. *"When we were in the shack, and you asked me for forgiveness, did Adeth's control on you slip?"*

"Don't." He shakes his head, *"Please."*

"Don't what? Talk about it?" I lift my chin. *"You taught me something, you know. Thanks to you, I can now handle a shitload of pain."* I glance at his right hand, the hand I know so well, and remember when it felt like he was burning the skin from my body.

Ares clenches his jaw, and a tear slips down his cheek, but he doesn't stop me from talking.

"I remember our last time together in the shack. Right before you left, I saw something, and I want to know if I imagined it or if it was real."

I can't believe how calmly I'm talking to him. I have to be insane.

"I couldn't control what I did, but I...Alchera," he pauses and gives me a pleading look. *"I tried so hard to fight Adeth. She was just too strong, but I never wanted to hurt you. What I did to you..."* he shakes his head, tortured by the guilt that's clearly eating him alive, *"it killed me."*

His eyes beg me to understand. To forgive him.

Now that he's no longer a threat, it's hard to ignore that he looks a lot like Raighne and Finian. Just like them, he's good-looking, but the hell he's lived with gives him a dark and tortured look the other two men don't have.

It makes it so much harder not to feel pity for him.

I glance away from Ares and take in my surroundings. The wind is constantly blowing, never letting up. The sun has a sinister red tinge to it, giving the impression it's twilight and not early in the day.

It feels like the shadows that are moving inside me are a moment away from engulfing this world in darkness.

Not looking at Ares, I whisper, *"I'm not ready to forgive and forget."* I suck in a quivering breath. *"My memories are different than yours. They're not filled with guilt but with unbearable pain."* I start walking to where Raighne is standing with his arms crossed over his chest, watching Ares like a hawk.

"It's funny, you know." I shrug before giving Ares a last glance. *"Here you are, changing into this good person and asking for forgiveness, while I'm..."* I wrap my arms tighter around myself. *"I feel cold and dark, like I'm becoming this malicious thing. It's like we're swapping places."*

"Alchera, no!" Ares snaps as he stalks toward me.

Raighne's arm flies up, and it looks like Ares walks into an invisible barrier that keeps him from taking another step.

I move to Raighne's side and say, *"This talk ..."* I wave my hand between Ares and myself, *"whatever this is. It's finished. I've had enough."* I take hold of Raighne's hand so he'll release Ares. *"Next time, I won't stop Raighne. Stay away from me."*

While the others gather in a group, Raighne pulls me to the side, muttering, "You're not becoming a malicious thing."

Unable to make eye contact with him, I glance down the street. "We both know it's bound to happen. There's no stopping the shadows from growing in me. I'll do my best to get the chosen ones to Vaalbara, but there's no way I'm getting through this without turning into the same thing as Adeth."

Raighne lifts a hand, and taking hold of my chin, he forces me to look at him. "You're not turning into Adeth. I won't allow

Michelle Heard

it."

I try to smile but fail, and before I can say another word, I notice the clouds gathering above us. It looks like they're churning.

No.

Pressure hits me full-on, and turning to the others, I shout, "Cover your ears!"

We're hit with one hell of a blast of energy, knocking us off our feet. Raighne falls over me, his body covering mine just as another wave hits us.

When I manage to lift my head, blood trickles warm down my neck. Then I hear and feel everything - trees screech, birds drop dead, people cry, and one after the other, heartbeats stop.

A cloud of ash blocks the sun as it fills the air.

"Raighne!"

I let out a sob as Raighne helps me into a sitting position, and when his hands cover my ears, I feel him work overtime to still the chaos in me.

There's a deep rumbling coming from the ground before it starts to quake beneath us.

Crouching in front of me and holding my head to his chest, he shouts at the others, "We have to move! Get everyone up."

With the ground shuddering uncontrollably, Raighne helps me to stand, and I shake my head to rid myself of the dizziness left over from the blast.

I think the volcano just erupted.

Shit.

I groan as a gale-force wind whips through the park, making the hell around us worse. I hear people screaming not too far away, and worried for my chosen ones, I glance wildly around me.

Massive gaping holes appear as chunks of earth fall away

327

beneath people's feet. I watch in horror as they plunge to their deaths.

This time, it isn't just a vision. It's the real thing, and it makes horror bleed into the darkness growing inside me.

"Alchera!" I hear Raighne shout above the wind.

A tree whips past us, one of its branches missing my face by mere inches as he yanks me out of the way.

"We have to move." Raighne holds my arm tightly as he pulls me toward our group, that's clearly rattled by the hell being unleashed on us.

Jason picks up Sarah, and she buries her face against his neck as sobs wrack her weak body.

"I've got you. We'll get through this," Jason tells her, his worried eyes meeting mine.

Doug is watching the disaster unfolding around us with dread tightening his features.

Get your shit together, Alchera. Your chosen ones need you.

Matt holds Sky tightly while Dylan glances around us, his military voice booming over the sound of the wind, "Let's move, people. If I say stop, you stop. If I say run, you run. We leave no one behind."

"I can just shimmer us to a safer place," Ares says.

"This is where my vision of Riccardo brought us to," I snap at him as I follow Dylan, who's making his way to the side of the town that looks less affected by the disaster. "I'm not leaving without him."

With Dylan guiding us and Brenna, Finian, and Griffith protecting us from behind, we make our way through the rubble and scores of frightened people.

Shit, where is Riccardo?

The ground rips open behind us, and Griffith shouts, "Run!"

We all rush away from the immediate danger while I try to

figure out where we should go.

God, how do we survive this?

I keep glancing around for any sign of Riccardo, desperation filling every panicked heartbeat in my chest.

A car crashes ahead of us as we near a collapsed building, and the ground shudders again, slabs of the road cracking open in front of us.

We all cower close together, and Sky lets out a terrified scream, which has Matt engulfing her with his body to offer her some kind of protection.

I feel a hand on my shoulder, then Brenna says, "We can't stay here, Alchera."

A hopeless feeling settles in my gut as I look at everyone.

Dammit!

Glancing at Ares, I say, "Can you take the group to a saver place, then come back to Raighne and me?"

"We're not splitting up!" Griffith growls. "It's too dangerous."

I let out a sigh, but then the shaking suddenly stops, and everyone manages to climb to their feet.

"Let's push forward," Dylan says before looking at me. "Any idea which direction we should head in?"

No.

Thinking back to my vision, I bring up Riccardo. I give Ares a cautious look before I step closer to him.

It takes more strength than I have right now to take hold of his arm. "Can you find Riccardo?"

His eyes focus on my face, then he nods. "Give me five minutes."

I quickly pull my hand back, and the next second, he disappears right before my eyes.

"Can we keep moving, or do we have to wait?" Dylan asks.

"We can keep moving. Ares will find us through Alchera,"

Griffith replies, worriedly glancing around us.

Pushing forward, our progress is slow. We have to climb over rubble and avoid cracks in the road.

The ground shudders hard, and people scream as everyone's panic flares up again. There's a thunderous eruption and rumbling in the distance, and I glance up at the sky that's growing darker, the clouds black, red, and yellow as if it's on fire.

As a cloud of ash begins to rain down on us, I'm hit with a wave of fear and hopelessness that forces me a step back.

I can feel as everything around me dies.

The air displaces, and as I turn to see if Ares found Riccardo, they appear. Ares has Riccardo in a headlock, and with panic etched deep into Riccardo's features, his arm wildly flies up.

"Gun! He has a gun," Dylan shouts, darting forward to help Ares control a fighting Riccardo.

There's a loud bang, and the next second, it feels as if my chest is being torn open.

In shock, I stare at Ares and Dylan, who are forcing Riccardo to the ground and prying the weapon from his hand.

"Alchera!" Raighne shouts, and his arms wrap around me as my legs give way.

Shit.

Kneeling beside me, he holds me close to him. I gasp for air, but droplets of my blood splatter against his neck.

Only then does it register Riccardo shot me.

"I've got you!" Raighne says, his voice rough with worry as he presses his hand to my chest.

Ash floats around us, and my eyes are just about to focus on Raighne's face when everything blurs.

When I blink, confusion pours through me. I'm lying on ash, the area around me made of millions of moving shadows.

"Alchera," Ares' voice sounds as if it's a thousand miles away,

"focus on my voice. Let me bring you back."

I can feel Ares' like a cool breeze but not Raighne's warmth.

I hear other voices around me, and they're filled with urgency and panic.

"I need scissors, Isobel! Now!"

I stare up at an African woman dressed in casual clothes and a white lab coat.

"Can you save her, Lydia?" someone asks the doctor standing over me.

"Yes," she answers, her voice filled with confidence.

"Alchera!" Raighne's voice thunders through my mind, yanking me away from the woman.

I pry my eyes open, my lids feeling heavy.

My vision manages to focus on Raighne, but then my head lolls to the side, and I see Ares beside me.

"Stay with us," Ares says. *"Don't go to the shadowlands."*

It's weird. It feels like I'm stuck in the Twilight Zone.

My sight blurs, and when it focuses again, I see the woman who's trying to say something to me.

"...you just hold on for me, sweetheart. Have you given her the sedative, Isobel?"

"Lydia!" A man says, drawing the doctor's attention away from me.

"I'm busy. Talk fast!" Lydia snaps.

"How's the mother doing?" the man asks.

"She's hanging in there. How are the children?"

"Only one made it. The father's dead, too," the man answers.

"Shit!" Lydia hisses before focusing all her attention on me again. *"You're not going to die. Just hang in there for me."*

The pain in my chest feels like it's trying to tear my beating heart right from me.

I try to breathe, but instead of inhaling air, my lungs are filled with ashes.

"Scalpel!" Lydia orders, then I feel something slicing into my skin. The pain tears a scream from me, but I don't hear it.

I feel hands digging inside of me, ripping my heart out.

I force my eyes open again, and past Raighne and all the destruction around us, I see a shadow move toward me.

Where Awo was all light, this creature is made of millions of shadows constantly swirling and creeping over each other.

"What's that?" I ask, panic lacing my thoughts.

I can't feel or hear Raighne and Ares, and as the shadowy figure comes closer, my entire body chills until it feels like ice fills my veins.

"No. Stay away from me!" I scream, but no one hears me.

The shadowy figure moves over me, and as it hovers above me, I stare at the absolute darkness where its face should be.

It moves a hand to my chest, black veins snaking beneath translucent skin, and the most agonizingly lonely feeling coats my very soul.

"No," I gasp. *"I'm not done fulfilling my destiny. I can't die yet."*

I start to shiver fiercely as I stare into the dark abyss. "Who are you?" I breathe the words as if they are my last.

"Void." His voice is eerily soft, and it has a pull to it, drawing me away from the light. *"Join me, Alchera."*

Everything stills inside me, and unable to move, I can only stare into the dark abyss that's pulling me away from everything I hold dear.

"No," Ares' voice strikes like a lightning bolt, the light so sharp in my mind it makes Void creep back to the edge of my sanity. *"I won't let you take her."*

"Ahhh...Ares," Void hisses sinisterly. *"I'll see you soon, son."*

The icy cold disappears, and my body starts to shiver as Void disappears.

"The bullet is out," I hear Raighne say.

"Void is gone," Ares tells him. "Can you get into her mind again?"

"Let me try," Raighne mutters.

Hearing them work together to save me has my eyes stinging with unshed tears right before I'm engulfed in Raighne's warmth as he floods me.

"Is she going to be okay?" I hear Jason ask.

I'm pulled tightly against Raighne's chest, and he peppers my face with kisses as sob after sob begins to burst from me.

"I've got you. You're safe," he murmurs, his tone strained with emotion.

Finally able to move, I lift my arms and cling to Raighne's shirt as I gasp through the empty feeling left behind by the weird shit I just experienced.

"What was that?" I ask.

"Nothing for you to worry about," Ares answers as he climbs to his feet. "I'll deal with it."

"Is Alchera okay?" Dylan asks, his tone tense with worry.

"Yes," Raighne replies. Pulling back, he locks eyes with me. "Are you good to go? We need to move."

Having no choice, I nod, but Raighne has to help me to my feet.

My legs feel unsteady, and I lean heavily against him as I look at Riccardo, who's still on his knees, his face pale with shock.

Dumbfounded, he stares at all the blood on my shirt as he shakes his head, then whispers, "How? What? Christ."

"I know it's a little overwhelming, but you're safe with us," Jason tells Riccardo. "These people are here to save us, so just go with the flow."

"I shot her," Riccardo gasps. "How?"

"I'm Raighne, and as Alchera's guardian, I can heal her,"

Raighne explains. "Also, you can't kill one of us with a bullet, so don't bother trying again."

It felt like I was dying, though.

"You were just weakened, which allowed Void to get into your mind," Ares tells me mentally.

My eyes snap to his face. *"Void?"*

"My step-father for intents and purposes. He rules over the shadowlands. He's the one who turned my mother dark."

"Enough," Raighne mutters. "We need to get out of here."

It's only then that I glance around us, and seeing all the destruction and breathing in ash, panic pours through my chest.

"I had a vision of another chosen one, but I don't know where she is," I admit, my voice hoarse from the poor air quality.

"Dammit," Brenna mutters.

"Can't we go back to Vaalbara until we know where to go next?" I ask.

"No." Griffith shakes his head, an impatient expression on his face.

"We can go back to our house," Doug says. "Last time we were there, Ireland wasn't as affected as this place."

"We don't have much of a choice," Jason agrees.

"Everyone gather close," Griffith orders while pulling Riccardo to his feet. "You hold my hand and don't let go. You hear me?"

Riccardo just nods, still shell-shocked.

We all hold hands, and the next instant, Ares shimmers us back to Doug and Sarah's living room.

When the place looks the same as when we left it, I let out a breath of relief.

Coming to stand beside me, Brenna asks, "How are you feeling, Alchera?"

I just nod because I don't have words to express how I feel.

"She needs to get some rest. Maybe then she'll have another vision," Raighne says, and taking hold of my hand, he pulls me closer to the couch. "Sit." He looks at Brenna again. "Can you bring her some water?"

"Sure."

Raighne sits down beside me and wraps his arm tightly around my shoulders, nudging me to lean into his side. I feel his mouth against my hair and close my eyes.

Lydia. Where are you?

CHAPTER 30

ALCHERA

"*Shut up! Face down!*" *Lydia is lying on the floor, her eyes wildly flitting between the men who are dressed in camouflage gear, giving me the impression they're rebels.*

"Where's the medicine?" One of the men demands in broken English, the whites of his eyes yellow and bulging with hatred.

"In that cabinet...over there," a man answers, pointing somewhere behind them. "But it's all we have. Please don't..."

One of the rebels lifts his rifle and smashes the back of it against the man's head. He repeatedly beats the poor man until he sinks down to his knees, begging for mercy.

"Stop," Lydia cries. "We're just doctors."

"Shut up! I will string you up and gut you like pigs," the rebel spits the words at them, pointing the rifle at the beaten man's head.

Another rebel, who's standing by the doorway, moves closer with a savage expression on his face.

I stand frozen in pure horror. I can't believe what I'm seeing.

"We'll listen. We don't want any trouble," the beaten-up doctor tries to appease him. Blood seeps from the deep gashes on his face and head. He tries to move backward as he looks at them with terror.

"You think you can look at me? You think you're better than me?"
The rebel lifts his rifle, and the next moment, he fires several shots at the
doctor.

My hands fly up to cover my mouth as horror fills my pounding
heart. I wish Ares was here to shimmer Lydia away from this dangerous
situation.

Lydia lets out a cry, her face pale and tense from shock.

"You are his woman?" the African man grabs Lydia by the arm and
yanks her to her feet.

"Bring all the medicine!" another rebel orders from the entrance to
the makeshift medical facility. "If you kill them all, we won't get
medicine next time."

The one holding Lydia's arm shoves her hard, and she falls to the
floor.

I come to with a jolt, and just reacting, I pull away from
Raighne and rush to Ares. Grabbing hold of his arm, I say, "Take
me to her."

"Wait," I hear Raighne snap, but it's too late as Ares
immediately shimmers us away.

We appear right in the middle of the chaos left behind where
Lydia's checking the other doctor's vitals. Her head snaps to us,
and seeing the fear on her face makes me want to hug her so badly.

"It's okay," I say as I cautiously move closer to her. "I'm here to
help you."

Considering that we just appeared out of thin air, it doesn't
exactly make Lydia trust us. She darts toward a medical cart and
grabs hold of a scalpel, even more scared of us than she was of the
rebels who just attacked them.

Ares moves fast, surprising even me, and he grabs hold of
Lydia. She shrieks and drops the scalpel, taking desperate and
terrified gulps of air.

"Ares, let's get out of here," I say, my words rushed. "She's terrified, and this isn't making the situation any better."

I take hold of his arm, and the next second, he shimmers us back to Doug and Sarah's house.

When we appear, Lydia sinks to her knees and wraps an arm around her stomach. "Oh God."

Dylan and Jason hurry to her side, and I leave them to explain everything to Lydia once she recovers from Ares shimmering us from Africa to Ireland.

Another one down. Two to go.

Raighne grabs hold of my arm, and I'm yanked down the hallway. Practically shoving me into one of the bedrooms, he slams the door shut behind us.

When he turns to face me, and I see the anger etched deep into his features, I exhale an exhausted breath.

"I don't have the energy to fight with you right now," I mutter as I move away from him.

When I sit down on the side of the bed, he growls, "Never fucking do that again. You go nowhere alone with Ares."

My shoulders sag, and glancing down, I see the blood covering my shirt.

Memories of what happened after I got shot flit through my mind until the image of Void hovering over me makes me freeze.

Raighne stalks toward me, and wrapping his arms around me, he presses a kiss to the top of my head. "Don't think about him."

I tilt my head back so I can look at Raighne's face, his anger from a second ago now gone.

"Who is he?" I ask.

"Where Awo is light, Void is darkness. He rules over the shadowlands on Vaalbara." Raighne brushes a hand over my messy hair. "Thinking about him gives him access to your mind. Just block him."

Easier said than done.

Letting out a sigh, I lean into Raighne and close my eyes. "Two more to go."

"You can do it, my little dreamer," he murmurs as his hands frame my cheeks and tip my head back. His eyes drift over my face, then he leans down and presses a tender kiss to my lips. *"You're so fucking strong it amazes me."*

"I don't feel strong," I admit as I grip hold of his forearms. My face crumbles, and I'm unable to stop the tears.

Raighne deepens the kiss, his warmth engulfing me, and I'm hit by a tsunami of relief.

He consumes me in a way that forces me to focus only on him. In this moment, there's no destruction, no horror, no death. There's only the incredible love he feels for me.

"Oh. Sorry," Sarah interrupts us, and when Raighne pulls away, the shadows pour so fast back into my mind I sway like a zombie for a moment.

"I just wanted to give Alchera some clean clothes," Sarah says. "Doug and Jason are making something to eat."

"Thank you," Raighne replies as he takes the clothes from her.

"Dylan's given one of his clean shirts for you to wear. Hopefully it will fit," she tells Raighne while I sit frozen on the side of the bed as my destructive emotions bombard me.

"Thanks," Raighne grumbles while wrapping his fingers around the back of my neck. His touch is instantly soothing, and my eyes drift shut for a few seconds.

"I thought you'd like to know Lydia is doing okay under the circumstances," she informs us.

"That's good to hear," Raighne replies, his thumb skimming over my skin.

"Is Alchera okay?" Sarah asks.

"She just needs rest," he murmurs.

Sarah nods, giving me a worried look before she leaves.

With the clean clothes in one hand, Raighne slips his arm around me and pulls me from the bed. "Come. Let's get cleaned up."

I let him steer me to the bathroom, and completely drained I just stand and watch as he sets the clothes down on the counter. He opens the faucets, and while the water warms up, he comes to stand in front of me. When he takes hold of my shirt, I lift my arms so he can tug the blood-stained fabric over my head.

As Raighne undresses me, I glance down and take in all the scars on my body. The gunshot wound has closed up, the swollen skin red with a blue tinge around it.

Steam starts to fill the bathroom while Raighne quickly strips out of his clothes. My eyes drift over his chest, and I watch as the strength ripples beneath his skin with every movement.

I would've been dead by now if it weren't for Raighne.

He shakes his head as he moves closer until our bodies touch. Cupping the back of my head with one of his hands, he locks eyes with me. *"No, you'd still be alive. In a fuck-ton of pain, but alive. You're so much stronger than you give yourself credit for."*

Slowly, I shake my head. *"You're my strength. I don't know what I'd do without you."*

His eyes soften on me. *"You'll never have to find out. I live and die for you."* He closes the distance between us, and when his mouth takes mine in a tender kiss, his voice is a soothing balm in my mind, *"Only you."*

As his lips nip and massage mine, sending tingles through my mind and body, he moves us into the shower.

The warm spray falling over us feels amazing, and standing on my toes, I wrap my arms around Raighne's neck. The kiss deepens, and with Raighne filling every inch of my worn-out mind, a relieved sob escapes me.

He increases the intensity of his assault on the shadows inside me, and lifting me up against his body, he pushes me back against the tiles.

I wrap my legs around his waist, desperately needing to be as close to him as possible.

I feel him position his cock at my entrance, and when he slowly pushes into me, his hands grip my butt, and his body squashes mine against the tiles.

Caged in by Raighne and with him filling my mind and soul, all I can do is feel as his cock pushes inch by inch deeper into me.

The sensation is so intense I stop breathing and cling to him with all my strength.

By the time he's buried all the way inside me, our breaths are already rushing over our lips. He pulls slightly back so he can meet my eyes, and seeing the look of absolute love and devotion on his face, I can't keep the tears from falling.

The moment between us is so intense that I'm completely overwhelmed by the good emotions I desperately need.

My tone is hoarse as I whisper, "I love you so much."

"You're my entire being, Alchera."

As Raighne's mouth finds mine in a kiss that touches the deepest parts of my soul, his hard length pulls out of me before slowly pushing back inside.

It feels as if he's savoring every second, every movement, every touch of our skin.

I lose myself in Raighne, where there's only love, hope, serenity, and pleasure. It's intoxicating, and as the world around us goes to shit, I moan against his mouth, begging for more.

With a low growl rumbling from his chest, he increases his pace, his thrusts becoming a dominating force that strips my soul bare.

One with him, I moan, *"Raighne."*

With every powerful thrust, his cock strokes my inner walls, making my abdomen clench more and more until I explode, and Raighne's the only thing keeping me together.

He becomes my beginning and end, and I know with dead certainty that without Raighne, I'm nothing but a million broken pieces.

I whimper and moan into his mouth as pleasure seizes my body, holding onto the man I love more than anything with all my might.

"I love you. I love you. I love you," I chant as I'm taken to heights where nothing can touch me.

I'm caught in a daze of warmth, love, and pleasure, and I have no idea how much time passes before I drift down to reality.

The first thing I become aware of is Raighne's body jerking against mine as he finds his own release.

Then I feel the heat of the water as it washes us clean.

I suck in a deep breath, my lungs expanding and my body deliciously numb from the pleasure Raighne wrung from it.

I blink a few times, and as Raighne's face comes into focus, he fills me one last time before keeping still and staring deep into my eyes.

"I thank Awo that I exist to be loved by you." His words are like a soothing balm, dulling the sharp edges inside me. *"You are my everything."*

Our pleasure fades, and returning to the present, I hate when Raighne pulls out of me.

"Once we're home, I plan on staying buried inside you for as long as possible."

I let out a breathless chuckle. *"Who needs food and sleep?"*

Raighne squirts some body wash into his palm, then brushes his hands over my skin, cleaning the day's hell from me.

"I can feed you and you can sleep with my cock buried deep inside

you."

My cheeks warm from the provocative words, but I love hearing them.

I squeeze body wash into my hand, and silence falls between us as we wash each other's bodies. Once we're done, I feel a hundred times better than before the shower.

"Now for food," Raighne mutters while we get dressed. "And then you can sleep for a few hours."

"That's if I don't have another vision," I say as I put on my sneakers.

Sarah's jeans are a little too long, and I take a moment to roll the fabric up to my ankles.

Just as I straighten up, Raighne comes to stand in front of me, and I can't help but grin when he pulls his fingers through my hair to tame the strands.

"It's not the most flattering hairstyle I've ever had," I mention.

"It's sexy as fuck," he grumbles. His fingers brush over the side of my neck. "You look beautiful, my little dreamer."

His compliment boosts my self-esteem and standing on my toes, I press a quick kiss to his mouth before we leave the bathroom.

Raighne places his hand on my lower back as we walk to the kitchen, where the delicious aroma of beef stew hangs in the air. My stomach grumbles loudly, drawing a chuckle from him.

Doug glances up when we enter the kitchen, and he points at two bowls filled to the brim. "I already dished up for you. We used what we had to make stew, and there's some bread as well."

"Thank you," I say, giving him a smile.

"How are you holding up?" he asks, genuinely sounding like he cares.

"I'm much better after the shower," I reply as I take the spoon and bowl Raighne holds out to me.

"That's good to hear."

We stand by the counter and eat like starved wolves, and when I can't take another bite, I say, "You can have the rest of mine."

Raighne's eyes inspect my face as he stirs inside me. Happy with whatever he finds, he continues to eat while I help myself to a glass of water.

Clean and full, I struggle to suppress a yawn as I glance out of the window by the sink.

Everything looks calm outside, but I know it's just a façade. It's only a matter of time until Ireland's destroyed as well.

Raighne comes to place our bowls in the sink, and his hand wraps around my hip. "Time for you to get some sleep."

I glance at him. "I just want to check on the others."

I can see he wants to argue, but instead of forcing me straight to bed, he walks with me to the living room.

Brenna's the first to notice us. "You look much better."

"I feel better," I chuckle.

I glance over the group until my eyes land on Lydia, who doesn't seem as terrified anymore where she's sitting beside Sarah.

"Did they explain everything to you?" I ask Lydia.

She nods, then lets out a nervous chuckle. "I'm still wrapping my mind around everything. It's all a little overwhelming, and if I didn't see you appear out of thin air, I wouldn't believe any of it."

My attention is pulled away from Lydia when Riccardo steps closer to me. With remorse tightening his features, he says, "I didn't mean to shoot you. I'm so sorry."

I shrug and offer him a smile. "I'm okay. How are you holding up?"

"Confused as fuck, but I'm hanging in there," he answers honestly with a thick Italian accent.

I glance at the group again, then say, "I just need to get two more chosen ones then we can return to Vaalbara."

"I was thinking everyone can stay here while you collect the last two instead of me shimmering everyone all over the world. I'll be able to move faster, and it won't tire me out as much," Ares says from where he's sitting on the floor near the sliding doors with his forearms resting on his knees.

"I don't like the idea of the group separating," Griffith mutters.

"It might be better for everyone to stay here instead of taking them into a disaster scene," Finian says, surprising me because he's been quiet since his father joined us.

I look at my late father's guardian. "Griffith, you, Brenna, and Finian can guard the chosen ones and get to Vaalbara via the waterfall if all hell breaks loose while Ares, Raighne, and I search for the final two."

"As much as I hate the idea of splitting the group, Alchera's right," Raighne says from beside me. "But we can talk about this after she's had some sleep."

He takes hold of my hand, and considering the conversation done with, he pulls me down the hallway and into the bedroom.

I wait for Raighne to lie down before I make myself comfortable, lying half on top of him. Burying my face in the crook of his neck, I take a deep breath of his scent while my eyes drift shut.

He brushes his hand up and down my back, and within minutes, a deep breath escapes me as I drift off to sleep.

CHAPTER 31

ALCHERA

I t feels like I've barely closed my eyes when I startle awake, my body jerking.

It's only for a split second, then my vision blurs.

A thick smoke engulfs me, and I instantly start coughing. My eyes sting as I glance around me, taking in the burning trees and orange light glowing around me.

Jesus, have I stepped into an inferno?

I cover my mouth with my hands and blink like crazy, tears streaking down my cheeks while I struggle to make sense of where I am.

I hear people shout, and my head snaps in their direction. I watch as a group hurries to push boats into a wide river.

"Silvana, come!" a woman shouts.

"I'm not leaving my research behind."

I look at the woman called Silvana, who's rushing between a desk and a cabinet in a large tent.

It feels as if I glide toward Silvana, where she's shoving a laptop and hard drives into a bag.

"Your research is worth nothing if you die out here," the other woman screams. "We have to go."

"*I'm right behind you,*" *Silvana shouts, but then there's a loud crack, and a burning tree falls at the entrance of the tent, setting the fabric on fire.*

I snap out of it, and before I know what I'm doing, I dart off the bed and yank the door open.

"Ares!" I call out as I run down the hallway.

Before I can make it past the bathroom, I slam into a wall of muscle as Ares appears out of thin air and catches me by my shoulders. "What's wrong?"

A second later, Raighne's arm wraps around my middle, and I'm tugged back against his chest.

"I had a vision. She's in danger," I say, grabbing hold of Ares' forearm. "Take me to her."

His eyes lock with mine, and I feel his breeze sweep through my mind before we shimmer away in the blink of an eye.

When we appear in the tent, Silvana is lying on the ground with smoke billowing all around us and flames devouring the fabric of the tent and furniture.

I pull free from Raighne, and crouching beside my chosen one, I lift her head to my chest while trying to see if she's still breathing.

I can barely take a breath myself, the heat quickly making my clothes stick to my skin.

"We don't have time," Raighne says while coughing as he places a hand on my shoulder.

Ares moves closer, and with a hand on Raighne and me, he shimmers us back to Ireland.

When we appear in the living room, some of the chosen ones startle. I struggle to get a breath of fresh air past the burning in my throat and croak, "Lydia, check...on Silvana. I don't know...if she's breathing."

When I start to cough, Raighne places his hand on my back,

and while the burning eases in my windpipe, he struggles to suck in a breath of air. I quickly pull away and shake my head at him.

Raighne practically tackles me to the ground, and with an angry glare directed at me, he presses his hand to my chest and eases the last of the discomfort from my lungs.

When he sinks back to sit down, Jason quickly brings him a glass of water, but it takes way too long before Raighne's able to breathe normally again.

"I was fine," I bite out, not happy at all. "You can't take all the pain."

"I can," he mutters with clenched teeth. "And I will."

I climb to my feet and look at Lydia. "Will Silvana be okay?"

"What happened?" she asks.

"There was a fire. She was unconscious when we got to her," I explain. "I think she was in the Amazon forest."

"I can't run any tests, but she's breathing, and her pulse is steady," Lydia says. "Let's hope there's no damage to her lungs."

"They'll be able to heal her on Vaalbara," Brenna mentions.

"You should all get ready," I say. "I only have one more chosen one to retrieve, and then we're heading back to Vaalbara."

Turning around, I walk to the sliding doors and step outside, where I keep taking deep breaths of the fresh air.

That was too close. I almost lost Silvana, and it makes me worry about my last chosen one and what kind of situation the person will be stuck in.

"Don't fight me when I have to heal you," Raighne snaps as he comes up behind me.

I turn around to face him and level him with a dark scowl. "I don't want you healing me left, right, and center. I can take some of the pain."

"It's my duty, Alchera," he argues.

"Put yourself in my shoes," I say with a sigh. "I refuse to use you as a pain reliever. You mean so much more to me than that."

He closes the distance between us and takes hold of my shoulders, and with our eyes locked, he says, "I'm stronger than you, and I can handle it. This is not up for discussion, Alchera. I will not have you suffer if I can take pain or torment from you. Don't fight me on this, and let me protect you."

From the determined look in his eyes, I know I'm not going to win this argument. I let out an unhappy huff before I mutter, "It doesn't mean I have to approve of it."

When he realizes he's won this battle, the corner of his mouth lifts in a hot grin. "Thank you for caring about me, though."

"Hmm..." I grumble, which earns me an amused chuckle from him before he presses a kiss to my forehead. His arms wrap around me, and I'm squashed against his chest. "My stubborn little dreamer."

He holds me for a while before he pulls back and asks, "We're good?"

A smile curves my lips. "Yeah, we're good."

Raighne's eyes soften on my face, then he says, "You don't smile enough."

"It's hard with all the shit going down around us," I reply as I glance at the sliding doors where Ares is standing.

He's leaning with his shoulder against the doorjamb and his arms crossed over his chest.

"I'm just sticking close by in case you get another vision so we can leave immediately," Ares' voice drifts through my mind, which has Raighne turning to face him.

"If you have something to say to her, speak out loud. Don't enter her mind unless you need to see where we have to go," Raighne growls at him.

Ares' eyes narrow on Raighne as he bites out, "Got it, cousin."

"Silvana's awake," Jason calls, distracting us from the tension between Raighne and Ares.

I head back into the house, and find my newest chosen one drinking a glass of water.

"How do you feel?" I ask as I move closer to her.

She clears her throat and whispers, "Like death, and after what everyone told me, I'm starting to think I did die."

"You didn't," I say, and stopping beside her, I take in her disheveled look. "I'm just relieved I got to you in time."

Her eyes flick from one person to the next, then she says, "I just need a moment to process everything."

"Take your time," I murmur, patting her shoulder before I walk to the kitchen to get some water for myself.

Raighne follows me with Ares right behind him, and I let out a sigh because their testosterone is a bit much to deal with today.

I pour water into a glass and take a couple of sips while I stare out the window. "Can the two of you chill until we're done with the mission," I say before taking another sip.

"Sure," Ares mutters.

"Hmf..." is all I get from Raighne.

The tension doesn't ease at all, and instead, it feels like it gets worse.

When I hear voices shouting from afar, a frown forms on my forehead, and I whisper, "It's happening."

As the glass slips from my hand, Raighne's arms wrap around me from behind, and the next second, I find myself in the middle of chaos.

"Amandla!" a large crowd of protestors chant, and others respond by shouting, "Ngawethu!"

I'm shoved and jostled by one person after the other, and for a precious few minutes, I'm swept up by the aggressive crowd as they run through the streets.

Gunshots sound up, and where some take cover, others run toward the police force who's trying to regain control.

Windows are being smashed, and looters are raiding every store while vehicles try to maneuver their way through the chaos.

My heart is hammering in my chest, and I'm breathless as I fight my way to the sidewalk. I run to a side street where things are quieter, and as I try to catch my breath, I wildly glance around me.

Who's the chosen one?

Shit, trying to make my way through the angry mob will be insane.

I keep searching through the hundreds of people, and seeing a woman who's trying to drag an unconscious man toward the sidewalk, something about her catches my attention.

Maybe it's the fact that she's risking her life, trying to help someone in all the chaos. Two men grab hold of her, and they force her toward me while three more follow them.

No!

They drag her past me, and my eyes lock with her terrified ones.

"Pearl," I whisper in horror as one of the men starts to beat her.

I come to, my breaths racing over my lips. I'm clinging to Raighne, where we're sitting on the floor by the sink. Lifting my head, I look at Ares.

"We have to go. Right now."

He darts forward, and placing his hands on our shoulders, he shimmers us away in a split second.

When we appear precisely where I was standing in the side street, the crowd's aggressive chanting, sirens, and shouts fill the air.

My head whips to my right, and I scream, "Pearl!"

Before I can take a step in her direction, where the men are beating and tearing at her clothes, Raighne waves a hand, sending the men flying in all directions.

Ares shimmers to her side, grabs hold of her, then shimmers back to us before getting us out of the terrible chaos.

When we appear in the living room, Pearl starts to gag. I quickly wrap an arm around her and say, "It's okay. You're safe." I rub my hand up and down her back.

Letting out a sob, her body caves into mine, and as I sit down on the floor with her, I hold her tightly while she breaks down.

"I won't let anyone hurt you again," I whisper, my tone hoarse with the intense emotions I feel coming from her. "Shh...you're going to be okay."

"Let me look at her," Lydia says, her tone gentle. I pull away so Lydia can take over and climb to my feet.

"That's all ten," Griffith says. "We need to go back to Vaalbara."

My eyes flick to him and my tone is biting as I snap, "We'll leave once Lydia is done checking Pearl."

"Do you have a first aid kit?" Lydia asks, which has Doug rushing out of the living room.

A minute later he comes back with the kit and hands it to Lydia while asking, "Do you need anything else?"

"Some sugar water for the shock. It will help her calm down," Lydia answers.

As Doug goes to get the water, I crouch by the two women and place my hand on Pearl's back. She's shaking like a leaf caught in a shitstorm while Lydia wipes some of the blood from her face.

I know what it feels like to be beaten to a pulp and fearing for your life, and I hate that Pearl had to experience such a horrible situation.

Lydia's gentle with Pearl as she tends to her busted lip and the cuts on her cheeks and temple.

Slowly, Pearl's breathing returns to normal, and she keeps staring at the floor. Her voice is shaky when she asks, "Where am

I? Who are you people?"

"I'm a doctor," Lydia says. "I work with Doctors without Borders. Have you seen what's happening around the world?"

Pearl nods, wrapping her arms around her middle.

"These people came to save us. The world is dying, and they're taking us to a new one. I know it sounds crazy, but so far, they've protected us from the disasters and violence."

"I'm a doctor, too," Pearl whispers. "A pediatrician."

"We have something in common," Lydia murmurs, a smile tugging at her mouth. "It doesn't look like you need stitches."

Pearl nods before tentatively glancing at me. Her chin quivers then she asks, "You helped me?"

I nod. "With the help of Raighne and Ares." I rub my hand over her back again. "We need to get out of here before everything goes to hell. Think you can handle that?"

She glances at the group then nods.

"Is this it?" Dylan asks. "Are we leaving for good?"

"Oh Jesus," Sarah whispers. "I don't know if I'm ready. What's going to happen?"

A nervous energy fills the air, and it has me climbing to my feet.

"I'm not going to lie," I say. "It's going to be overwhelming at first. Just stick together."

"What's it like on Vaalbara?" Jason asks. "And are you sure my animals are there?"

"Yes, your animals are there," Griffith answers. "There are no big cities, and we're not as advanced as you are. Things are peaceful, and we help each other. All that matters is you'll be safe to begin a new life."

"Easier said than done," Dylan mutters.

"We've kept you safe thus far. Trust us," I say. "We only have your best interests at heart."

Dylan nods, and thankfully, it seems to set the others at ease.

"Everyone form a circle and hold hands," Ares orders. "Just like before, don't let go until we're on Vaalbara."

We all form a circle, and as Raighne comes to stand on my right, Ares takes the spot on my left.

I look down at his hand, and after the past couple of days, it doesn't fill me with hate and revulsion as I place my palm in his. His fingers wrap tightly around mine.

"Thank you," he whispers, and I only nod before glancing at the group to make sure everyone's ready.

This is it.

"Wait," I gasp as I turn my head and look out the living room's window.

I might have only lived here for five years, but it's the only home I've known. Realizing this is the last time I'll be on Earth, my heart squeezes painfully in my chest.

I only get to take these ten people. The rest will all die.

I close my eyes, and I feel the millions of hearts beating and the living force of nature.

I wish I could save it all.

I'm overcome with intense grief, and as I struggle to hold back the tears, I whisper mentally to Ares, *"Let's go."*

The air shifts around us, and everything spins for a moment before a cool breeze trickles over my skin.

"Oh my God," Sky gasps. "It's beautiful."

I open my eyes and see we're standing on a hill on the outskirts of a village that lies between a mountain and an ocean.

I can't remember ever being here, and when I glance behind me, I see the beginning of a forest.

"Jesus, your eyes," Jason says, sounding stunned.

I look at Griffith, Brenna, and Finian, and seeing their glamor is gone, my eyes dart up to Raighne's face.

Wow.

His eyes have changed to gold encircled in red, and holy shit, it looks badass.

Griffith takes hold of Raighne's shoulder, and with pride on his face, he says, "You've reached a level of guardianship none of us have ever witnessed before. Janak will want to speak with you."

Raighne just nods, his fingers tightening around mine.

Griffith turns back to the overwhelmed chosen ones and calls out, "Follow me. Let's get you all settled."

"Alchera mentioned you can heal Sarah?" Doug asks.

"Yes, our healer will look at her once we're in the village," Griffith replies as he glances at each of the chosen ones, then he adds, "They'll probably want to inspect everyone to make sure you're all healthy."

When the chosen ones follow Griffith down the hill, I remain standing between Raighne and Ares while Brenna and Finian walk a few feet away from us.

Unable to recall the village, I ask, "Is this home?"

"Yes," Raighne answers. He points to the area near the foot of the mountain. "My house is over there."

I wonder where I'll live.

"With me," Raighne answers my thought.

I feel Ares move and when I glance at him, it's to see he's walking toward the forest.

Seeing him back in his original state, without the glamor, makes an uneasy feeling slither down my spine.

"Where are you going?" I ask.

Ares pauses, and not looking at us, he mutters, "The village isn't my home."

"Where do you live?"

Ares shakes his head and without answering my question, he keeps walking toward the forest.

When he disappears behind the trees, I whisper, "Thank you for helping me."

"It's the least I could do," his voice ghosts through my mind.

I feel a twinge of sadness, then I turn my attention back to the village.

"Ready?" Raighne asks, still holding my hand.

I shake my head. "I need a moment." I pull my hand free from his, then say, "You go ahead." When it looks like he's going to argue, I add, "I just need some time alone. I'll be okay."

"You and Finian can go," Brenna says. "I'll stay with Alchera."

I watch as the men leave and see Finian slapping Raighne on the back while grinning at him. I can't hear what they're saying but seeing them act like brothers is actually weird.

Everything feels weird.

Wrapping my arms around my middle, I ask, "In which direction is the Virtutes Waterfall?"

"Come. I'll show you," Brenna says.

As we walk over the hills and planes of wild grass and flowers, we don't speak.

I take in this new world that will be my home, but I can't appreciate its beauty right now, not while I know another world is dying.

CHAPTER 32

ALCHERA

When we reach the Virtutes Waterfall, I sit down and stare at the rushing water.

"Want to talk about what's on your mind?" Brenna asks as she takes a seat beside me.

"So many people are dying right now," I whisper, my tone somber. I focus for a moment, but I can't feel the heartbeats and nature on Earth anymore. "It's such a waste of life."

"Try not to think about it," Brenna says. She nudges my shoulder with hers. "I'm proud of you. You were pretty badass."

The corner of my mouth lifts. "Yeah?"

"Yeah, but I'll still beat you in a fight," she chuckles.

Everything that's happened since I laid eyes on Raighne in that classroom flashes through my mind and unable to control my emotions, they spiral.

I suck in a shuddering breath, and when a sob escapes me, Brenna wraps her arm around my shoulders.

"It's over," she says. "Try not to think of the past."

"It's hard not to," I whimper.

"Do you need me?" Raighne's voice fills my mind.

"No, I'm okay."

"You sure?"

"Yes."

I suck in another deep breath and push the emotions down while I lean into Brenna's side.

"I remember the day you were born like it was yesterday," Brenna murmurs. "Everyone was so happy. Mom and Dad fussed over you day and night."

I sit up straighter and glance at my sister.

A soft smile plays around her lips as she stares at the beautiful sight of the waterfall. "When you were old enough, I took you horseback riding. You loved going fast and feeling the wind in your hair. Thana would spend hours combing the knots out of your hair while cursing me a blue streak."

I must've been too young because I don't remember it.

"Thana also taught you how to braid your hair."

I nibble on the inside of my cheek as I try hard to recall the memories.

"Once, you followed Roark to the training camps without anyone noticing. We spent the whole day searching everywhere for you and found you sitting on a hill, watching as Roark trained to take over as king."

Roark. God, it feels like a year has passed since his death.

"We were happy before you were sent away, and we'll be happy again," Brenna says.

I shake my head. "Dad and Roark are dead, and God only knows where Thana is."

"We'll be happy again," Brenna insists, and taking my hand, she gives it a squeeze. "It might take some time, but we'll find a new normal."

She climbs to her feet and pulls me up. "Come. There's someone who's dying to see you."

"Who?" I ask as we begin to walk back in the direction of the village.

"Mom."

With everything that's happened, I forgot about her.

Instantly, an anxious feeling fills my chest.

I search my mind for the few memories I have of her. The last time I saw her, she had blonde hair like Thana. I couldn't get a good look at her at Dad's funeral.

A memory of Mom tucking me into bed flits through my mind, and I remember feeling loved and safe.

An eternity has passed since, and I'm not so sure I'll be able to pick up where we left off five years ago.

As we near the village, people are all gathered around the chosen ones, giving them a warm welcome. There's no sign of Sarah and Pearl, and I assume they're with Aster in the infirmarius.

Brenna takes my hand and pulls me down a path that cuts between two houses that are built with some kind of rock and with roofs made of wood. Some houses have ivy climbing up the walls, whereas others have vines with pretty white and purple flowers.

Even though we're in the village, there are so many flowers and plants, it still feels like it's a part of nature.

"We'll sneak around the back so we don't get bombarded by the villagers," Brenna explains. "You can face them at the celebration they'll have for you returning with the chosen ones."

"Yes, please," I mutter as I follow her down a narrow cobblestone path, then I add, "I'm not so sure about the celebration, though."

"It's something you can't avoid," she says, giving me a teasing grin.

It's a good twenty-minute walk before we reach a large building that looks like a castle. I vaguely remember the place.

Home?

We enter via a side door, and when we walk down a corridor that's lit up with oil lamps, I feel a sense of familiarity.

As we round the bend, a woman shuts a door up ahead, then her eyes fall on us and she freezes. The blood drains from her face, and the next second, she starts to run.

"My baby!"

It takes a moment before I recognize her, and then she plows into me. Her arms grip me tightly and sobs burst over her lips.

Mom.

I stand frozen for far too long before I manage to lift my arms and wrap them around her.

"Thank Awo," she gasps. "I've missed you so much."

My throat strains and my eyes burn, then her familiar scent drifts to me, and my body jerks.

The moment is too intense, and my lips part with a silent cry as I break down in her embrace. Instantly, I feel Raighne's warmth flow through me, letting me know he's close by should I need him.

Mom's hand cups the back of my head, and she rains kisses down on the side of my face while I cry my heart out.

"Oh, to hold Eryon's baby in my arms again," she sobs. "Awo has blessed me." She keeps peppering me with kisses until the intense feelings settle into an awkwardness that tenses the air.

Mom pulls slightly back, and as her gaze drifts over my face, a happy smile spreads around her mouth. "You look just like your father."

My chin trembles, and my voice is hoarse with guilt as I whisper, "I'm sorry Dad and Roark died because of me."

She shakes her head, her features tightening with sorrow. "It's not your fault, sweetheart. They died honorable deaths."

She hugs me to her chest again and sucks in a quivering breath. "You and Brenna have returned safely to me. I'm thankful for that."

When she lets go of me again, she reaches a hand out to

Brenna and gives her arm a squeeze. "You've both made me so proud." She glances down the corridor, then says, "Come. You must be exhausted."

"We are," Brenna mutters. "I'm going to clean up. I'll see you at dinner."

When Brenna walks to the stairs and takes them up to another floor, Mom keeps staring at me.

She lifts a hand to my hair and brushes her fingers through the short strands.

"I had to cut it," I whisper.

"It will grow back." She gives me a trembling smile. "I missed you so much, Alchera."

When the urge to cry swells in my chest, I swallow hard.

"Do you remember me?" Mom asks, her voice hoarse.

I nod, then suck in a deep breath, trying to calm the overwhelming emotions.

"We'll make new memories," she says as she brushes her hand over my cheek. "But first, you need to rest."

She takes my hand and leads me up the stairs. When we near a doorway, Mom says, "We didn't change anything in your room. It's exactly as you left it."

My room.

I stop in the doorway, and my eyes flick wildly over the single bed with warm pelts. There are stars made of paper hanging from the ceiling, a wooden dressing table, and a three-legged stool.

On the dressing table, there's a hairbrush and dried flowers standing in a clay vase.

I take a step inside, then my eyes land on the doll that's made of fabric with wool for hair. I move closer, and when I pick up the doll, Mom says, "You never went anywhere without her."

I look at the brown freckles on her face and whisper, "Freckle."

"You remember her?" Mom asks, her tone hopeful.

"I think so."

I set her down on the pillow and turn to face my mother. Looking at the pale blue dress she's wearing with a leather corset, I have to admit she's more beautiful than I remember.

The awkwardness gets worse, and feeling out of place, I glance around the room again.

"I'll leave you to freshen up and get some rest. When you're ready, I'll be in the sitting room."

I nod, giving her a nervous smile. "Thanks."

"Dinner is at sundown in the dining room," she mentions as she walks into the corridor. "You can tell me all about your adventures."

Adventures.

I watch as she disappears down the corridor then shake my head.

None of what I went through was an adventure.

I sit down on the side of the bed, and covering my face with my hands, I let out a shuddering sigh.

Even though I used to live here until my sixteenth birthday, it doesn't feel like home.

I climb to my feet and hurry out of the room, heading down the corridor toward the side door. With every step I take, my emotions spiral into a chaotic mess.

"Raighne. I need you."

"On my way," he instantly replies.

I run up the narrow cobblestone path in the direction of the forest as if Adeth herself is behind me. The shadows close in on me, chilling my skin until I can't feel the heat from the sun any longer.

"Raighne!" I scream, desperation coating the word.

Suddenly, strong arms wrap around me, and I'm lifted off my feet as Raighne catches me. I'm hauled against his chest, his warmth engulfing my entire being.

"I've got you. I'm here," he says as he lifts me bridal style.

I wrap my arms around him and bury my face in the crook of his neck.

Not strong enough to face my past and my uncertain future, nor the shadows Adeth left behind in my mind, I focus only on Raighne's warmth as he carries me away from the village.

Only when I hear the rushing of water do I lift my head to glance around us. Seeing he brought me back to the Virtutes Waterfall, I let out a sigh of relief.

"I'm sorry," I whisper when he sets me down on my feet.

"For what?" His eyes drift over my face.

"Losing my shit," I mutter as I glance at the inviting pool of water.

"You've been through a hell of a lot, Alchera. I think you're entitled to lose your shit."

My eyes jump back to his face, and I tug my bottom lip between my teeth before admitting, "It didn't feel like home."

Raighne lifts a hand to the side of my neck and brushes his thumb over my skin. "That's because it's not." A frown forms on my forehead, which has him saying, "I'm your home. Your place is with me."

"My mother didn't seem to think so," I mention.

"Let me handle it." He pulls me to his chest and holds me tightly, making me sigh with relief.

Everything settles inside me, and I soak up his strength like a dry sponge while listening to the rushing of the waterfall and chirping birds in the trees.

After a long while, Raighne pulls back then asks, "Want to see your new home?"

"Your house?" I ask as I glance in the direction of the village.

"Our house," he corrects me.

When he starts to walk, I fall in beside him. "Are you sure

about having me stay with you?"

He lets out a snort and gives me a don't-ask-me-a-stupid-question look.

"Just checking," I mutter.

"I have to warn you, the place isn't big. It's a simple three-bedroom," he mentions, looking a little nervous.

I take hold of his hand and weave our fingers together, then say, "I don't care." My eyes meet his. "As long as I'm with you, nothing else matters."

The nervousness fades from his face, and we walk in silence for a while before I admit, "It's weird. It's only been four or five months since you came to get me, yet it feels like years have passed."

"A lot has happened," he replies before gesturing at a house situated next to a huge, very old looking tree. "That's home."

There's a knee-high wall around the yard that someone has been tending to since there are flowers and it's not overgrown with weeds.

Feeling nervous, I wipe my palms on my hips while my eyes dart over Raighne's home.

There's no key, and he just pushes the front door open.

"You didn't lock up while you were away?" I ask, my tone filled with surprise.

"We don't have to lock our doors on Vaalbara. Crime isn't a problem here," he replies as he waits for me to step inside.

"Right," I whisper as I enter.

I glance around the living room, which has chairs like the ones that were in my tent. There's a coffee table with fresh flowers in a vase.

"Someone expected you home," I mention as I move closer to the kitchen, where an oven stands near a back door. There's also a big oak table with six chairs that have patterns carved into them.

"We take care of each other's homes while someone's away,"

Raighne explains.

"It's nice that you're all neighborly," I whisper as I peek into a bedroom where a large bed fills half the space.

"This is your home now, Alchera. Don't feel uncomfortable."

My eyes dart to his face, and seeing the love he has for me shining in his gaze, I relax a little.

"Everything's just new," I explain.

He takes a deep breath then says, "I'm going to give you some alone time and head up to the palace to tell your mother you're with me so she won't worry."

I nod. "Thanks. I appreciate it."

When Raighne leaves, I take a seat on one of the chairs and stare at a painting of a forest that's up on the wall.

Knowing I'm in Raighne's house, I start to relax, and I pull my legs under me as I curl into the seat.

My thoughts don't return to the past, but instead, I begin to wonder about a future with Raighne. Now that my destiny has been fulfilled, do I dare dream of living a peaceful life with him?

Will the chosen ones be able to adapt to their new lives?

Will I?

Only time will tell.

Just as I start to dose off, I feel the air warm around me while the wind rips at my clothes.

"I always thought she was the most beautiful sister until I saw you."

I follow Ares' gaze to where he's looking up at Thana.

She's hovering high in the sky, her arms lifted toward the heavens above that are churning with eery-looking clouds. They paint the sky in so many different colors I can't begin to describe them all. But it feels deadly.

My lips part with shock as I watch an asteroid begin to enter the atmosphere. It turns the clouds into a blazing inferno, looking like a storm from hell is about to be unleashed on us.

"We need to get out of here," Ares says, his tone strained, then I hear Thana's voice sounding drained of all life, "You have to get them to safety, Alchera. I can't hold out much longer."

I quickly glance around me and see a house in the distance. The sound of a baby crying is carried to me in the wind.

"Save them," Thana sobs.

I fall off the chair and land on my hands and knees. Shaking my head, my mouth is dry, and my heart thunders against my ribs.

"What happened?" I hear Raighne's voice.

"Just a dream." I climb to my feet, and hurrying out of the house, I pray to all that's holy he'll hear me as I think, "Ares, I need you."

"Alchera!" Raighne's voice thunders through my mind, and I start to run. "Don't you fucking dare."

A moment later, Ares appears near me, and he holds out his hand. As I grab hold of him, I think of the area where Thana is, and the next second, we shimmer away from Vaalbara.

"Alchera!" Raighne shouts when we appear on Earth.

"I'm sorry. I'll be back soon."

"Come back right now," he demands, his tone tense with worry and anger.

Ignoring him, I glance around us. The area is pretty much deserted except for a few houses in the distance and a man kneeling in the dirt, give or take a thirty yards from us.

"I always thought she was the most beautiful sister until I saw you," Ares says, drawing my attention away from the kneeling man.

I look at where Thana hovers in the sky, and hoping she can hear me, I think, "I'm here. I'll save them."

"Please," she begs. "I can hear them crying. They're so scared."

Ares must've been listening in on our thoughts because he asks, "Who are we saving?"

I point to the house that's familiar from my vision. "They're over there."

When I hear the kneeling man groaning, "Thana," my head snaps to him.

Realizing it's Phoenix, I run to his side, but what I find shocks the living hell out of me. His skin is gray and riddled with cracks where it looks like lava is moving beneath the surface. His eyes are glazed over white as he stares up at Thana.

"Oh my God," I gasp, but before I can touch him, Ares grabs my hand and stops me.

"*Fuck,*" Raighne's groan echoes through me, telling me he can see what I see.

With a shake of his head, Ares says, "We can't help him. Thana's burning through him."

"No," I whisper as I look up at where my sister is hovering, her light so bright it stings my eyes.

"We can't save them, Alchera," Ares says, his tone urgent. "We have to leave."

"*Listen to Ares,*" Raighne begs. "*Get out of there. Now!*"

"No," I shake my head. "I'm not leaving without the children," I say as I tighten my grip on Ares' hand. "Take me to the house."

He instantly shimmers us closer to the house, the area around it looking like a farm with corn stalks reaching above my head. The moment we appear I hear a baby crying, and not thinking of my safety, I shove the front door open and hurry inside.

I find a boy who can't be older than fourteen, huddling in the living room with three toddlers and a baby. His eyes are wide with fear as he stares at us.

Shit, there's no glamor to make us look human.

"We're here to help," I say as I move closer to them. "You have to come with us."

"It's not safe," the boy argues, his terrified gaze darting between Ares and me. "Our parents left to get help and never came back."

"Are these your brothers and sisters?" I ask.

He shakes his head, looking like he's about to cry. "I'm just babysitting them."

"We'll take you to a safe place," I say, keeping my tone as gentle as I can.

"You can't, Alchera," Raighne begs. *"They're not chosen."*

"I don't care," I mutter to him. *"I have to do this."*

CHAPTER 33

ALCHERA

Moving forward, I say, "Form a circle. My friend is going to take you to a safe place."

The boy gives us a worried look, but he helps get the toddlers to hold hands.

I crouch in front of them. "Don't let go of each other. Okay?"

They just nod, their cheeks covered with tear tracks.

I rise to my full height and look at the boy. "Give me the baby."

He hesitates for a moment before handing her to me. I turn to Ares and hold her out to him. "Don't let go of her."

Even though he shakes his head, he takes the baby.

I grab the boy's arm and force him to stand beside Ares. "Place your hand on him and hold one of the toddler's hands."

When they're all linked, a thunderous noise fills the air, then Awo's voice rumbles in the air. *"A life for theirs."*

He's not saying we can't save them.

Not thinking twice about what this means for me, my eyes lock with Ares. "Go!"

"Alchera! Don't you fucking dare," Raighne shouts, his tone desperate and filled with fear. *"Don't do this to us."*

Ares shakes his head again, giving me a pained look. *"This isn't right, Alchera. I would follow you to the darkest pits of the shadowlands, but what you're asking of me..."*

With a pleading expression, I place my hand on his arm. *"I forgive you, Ares. Do this for me. Take them to safety."*

He closes his eyes, intense heartache tightening his features. *"You showed me how to be strong. You saved me."*

My throat closes up with emotion as I stare at Ares. "Go."

"Please," Raighne begs. *"Ares, just grab her and come home."*

Ares shakes his head, the veins in his throat straining, then he opens his eyes and looks at me. He begins to fade, and I feel his cool breeze whisper through me as he tries to take me with them.

Then they're gone.

Standing alone in the house while the thunderous noise around me grows, I let out a heavy sigh.

An explosion rocks the world, and I'm forced to my knees. The walls of the house shudder and crumble, and the ground quakes.

"Alchera," Raighne groans, all his warmth pouring into me and giving me the strength I need to climb to my feet.

"I'm sorry," I sob as I stagger out of the collapsing house.

The area to my left is engulfed in fire and black smoke, and above me, the sky is a dark inferno as the asteroid barrels toward the ground.

I run as fast as I can to get to Phoenix, and when I reach him, he slumps to his side. I fall to my knees and catch him in time to watch as he gasps for air, his eyes turning completely black.

"It's okay," I whisper. "You're not alone."

His eyes flutter closed, and I choke on a sob as I look up to where Thana is on fire.

A cry rips from me, and Raighne's warmth engulfs me until my skin starts to shine as if a light is trying to break free from me.

"I love you," Raighne whispers, his tone hoarse with heartache.

"I love you so much," I sob. *"I'm sorry, but I couldn't let them die."*

"I understand."

"I wish...I wish..." I'm crying too hard to form a coherent thought.

"I'll be with you until the end. I'm here. I love you, my little dreamer."

Hearing his words makes me realize Raighne will die with me, and it fills me with unthinkable fear.

"No!" My eyes widen, and Phoenix's body slips out of my arms.

I climb to my feet, and lifting my head, I stare up at the destruction bearing down on me. With every ounce of strength I have, I try to force Raighne out of my mind.

"I reject our bond."

"Don't, Alchera!" he shouts and I swear I hear his words echo in the wind around me.

"You're the best thing that's ever happened to me. Be happy, Raighne."

I close my eyes, and it takes everything I am as I let out a scream while trying to sever our bond.

I can feel Raighne fighting me, and desperate because I'm out of time, I cry, "Awo, spare him. Please!"

When I open my eyes, the asteroid's shadow is all I can see as the sand and rocks lift from the ground and pressure squeezes the air from my lungs.

It will disintegrate Earth on impact. There will be nothing left of this world I once called home.

Sobs shudder through my body as I beg one last time, "Awo, save Raighne."

Heat scorches my skin, and unable to suck in another breath,

I feel a weird calmness settle over me.

This is where I belong.

Just as everything explodes around me and the Earth shudders and roars, everything lights up so bright I have to shut my eyes.

"Alchera," I hear Raighne groan, sounding a million miles away from me.

And as I face my end, I whisper, "I love you, Raighne."

RAIGHNE

On my knees in the middle of the castle's foyer, I focus everything I am to hold onto Alchera.

Brenna's holding their mother, who's sobbing as they stare at me, and Finian stands beside them, his face pale.

"Raighne," Brenna whispers, her tone drenched in heartache while she stares at me in horror.

I glance down and see the essence of my soul shining through the cracks in my skin.

Alchera is dying.

No.

Closing my eyes, I use all my strength to hold onto her and groan, *"Alchera."*

"I love you, Raighne." Her words are faint, barely a whisper that trickles to me from afar.

Then the unspeakable happens, and I feel our bond snap with an intensity that slams me backward, sending me skidding across the floor.

"No!" I roar, despair ripping through me.

"Dear Awo," Brenna gasps before uncontrollable sobs

overwhelm her.

"No," Queen Mya weeps. "Not Alchera as well."

Lying on my back, I have zero strength to move as I stare at the ceiling. A horrible emptiness fills the hole left by the half of my soul that's been ripped away, and I'm barely able to breathe.

Finian crouches beside me, his expression torn with worry. "Brother?"

"She's gone," I gasp, my heart cracking wide open until it feels as if my very soul is hemorrhaging.

Finian grabs my shoulders and holds me as tight as he can. "I'm so fucking sorry."

I grab his arm as my body shudders through the devastation hitting me with merciless blows.

Alchera is dead. I failed her.

No!

The emptiness grows, threatening to drag me to the shadowlands where all hope and love are lost. Darkness creeps around the corners of my vision as I struggle to take a breath.

Suddenly a bright light fills the entrance hall, blinding us all, and then Awo's voice echoes around us. "There's no need to weep. A selfless act will not be punished with death."

Stunned out of my mind, I somehow manage to push Finian away and struggle to my feet, but the moment Alchera starts to appear in the middle of the light, strength returns to my body, and I shoot forward.

When my arms wrap around her, new life is breathed into my soul, and I feel our bond tie us together once again.

My body shudders from the intense relief flooding me, and I can't stop myself from gripping her as tight as possible.

"Alchera's destiny isn't over," Awo informs us. "She's been given the talent of visions and dreams. With her new destiny comes the responsibility for everyone's dreams. At night, she will bring peace to those who sleep."

Alchera stands frozen in my arms, and when I take hold of her chin, to look at her face, I see her eyes are shut as if she's caught in a deep sleep.

"Be blessed," Awo says before his light fades, and the moment he's gone, Alchera gasps as she sucks in a desperate breath of air, her eyes snapping open.

Her irises are no longer emerald green but the softest shade of blue, almost like the blue lace agate stone that brings tranquillity and calm.

And there are no signs of the shadows that tormented her the past week.

She stares at me for a moment before she throws her arms around my neck, relief and happiness bursting in her chest.

I lift her from her feet, squashing the living fuck out of her. "Don't ever do that to me again," I growl, my entire being so fucking thankful I didn't lose her. "I can't exist without you."

"I'm sorry," she whispers by my ear. "Did Ares save the children?"

"You just came back from death, and that's your first thought?" I ask, letting out an incredulous chuckle because it amazes me how selfless the woman I love is.

"They're safe," Ares' voice sounds up as he suddenly appears before it's followed by the sound of a baby crying.

I ease my hold on Alchera, and we glance at Ares, who's surrounded by a teenager, three children, and a baby.

"Dear Awo," Brenna gasps before she and Queen Mya rush to the children.

Ares quickly hands the baby over to Queen Mya, then he glances at Alchera.

"Next time you pull a stunt like that, I'm staying behind with you," I hear him tell her.

"Thank you for everything, Ares," she replies, her tone soft and grateful.

He nods before disappearing again.

I feel a twinge of pity in my chest for my cousin because I'm not sure he'll ever be able to find his way back to the light.

Queen Mya comes to place her hand on Alchera's shoulder, then says, "Go with Raighne, sweetheart. We'll talk once you've had time to get settled."

Alchera nods, her features tightening, and I feel as everything she's experienced today overwhelms her.

Wrapping my arm around Alchera's shoulders, I guide her out of the castle, and every time one of the villagers notices her, I shake my head at them so they won't approach us.

She needs time to recover before I'll allow her to interact with anyone, and after almost losing her, I also need to be alone with her because the echo of despair still clings to me.

I wish I could shimmer like Ares.

Walking is taking too long for my liking, and I stop to sweep her up into my arms. The moment she holds onto me, I begin to run, and not even a minute later, I storm through our front door and kick it shut behind us.

Sinking to my knees, I engulf Alchera with my body that's shuddering from the hell I experienced when she severed our bond and died.

"I'm so sorry," she cries as she clings to me. "I couldn't let you die."

Unable to speak, I enter her mind and force my way through her until I find her soul.

I engulf her entire being until there's nothing between us and let out a groan from how good it feels to be one with her again.

Blindly, my mouth finds hers, and the kiss is filled with overpowering love and need.

"Never again," I growl as I climb to my feet and carry her to the bedroom.

She nods as she desperately kisses me back, and once we're in the bedroom, I let her stand on her feet so I can hurriedly strip her of her clothes.

We move with desperation, and when we fall onto the bed, the need to be inside her has my cock entering her with a single hard thrust.

The moment I feel her discomfort, I take it from her, and my body starts to move, the pace feverish and rough.

A light begins to shine between us, and I can sense the moment Alchera's able to hear my thoughts and feel what I feel.

The kiss is out of control and wild, my hips moving fast and hard.

Completely connected, our souls and bodies fused as one, I say, *"Without you, there's no me."*

"I'll never risk us again," she promises, her nails digging into my back as I keep hammering into her. *"Us. Forever."*

I rest my forearms on either side of her, framing her face with my hands as I continue to make love to her with an intense need only she can satisfy.

My mouth devours hers, and I get drunk on the taste of my woman, the pleasure too powerful to fully process as it seizes our bodies.

Even though my pace slows down as our orgasms tear through us, I can't stop thrusting inside her.

Our kisses turn from wild to deep and soulful, and as day turns to night, I can't bring myself to stop loving her for a single second.

I have no idea how much time has passed when Alchera breaks the kiss to breathlessly say, "We need to get up."

"No," I mutter, pressing kisses to her jaw and down her

throat.

"I'm thirsty," she complains before chuckling.

Letting out a playful growl, I pull out of her before I climb off the bed.

While I walk to the kitchen, I hear the water start to run in the shower, and it feels so damn good to hear Alchera moving around in my house.

I quickly fill a glass of water for Alchera and find her where she's holding her hand beneath the spray in the shower, checking the temperature.

"Here you go," I say, handing the glass to her.

While she downs the cool liquid, I step into the shower and grab the soap. I work it until my hands are covered in suds, and once Alchera joins me, I begin to wash her body.

She also rubs the soap in her hands before her palms brush over my shoulders.

When our eyes lock, I say, "If we're ever faced with a life-threatening situation again, don't break our bond. Promise me that we'll live and die together. The pain of losing you is too unbearable and the worst torture I can be subjected to."

She presses a kiss to my left peck, then nods. "I promise."

I wrap my arms around her, holding her tightly to my chest where the echo of loss still ghosts through my heart. I don't think it will ever completely fade.

The blow I was dealt left a scar on my soul, and it will always serve as a reminder of how important Alchera is to me.

CHAPTER 34

ALCHERA

I'm sitting on a chair with a blanket wrapped around me while watching Raighne work in the kitchen. He has sweet potatoes on the coals and is busy frying strips of steaks, carrots, and zucchini.

A delicious aroma fills the air, and as my stomach grumbles, I say, "I never learned how to cook."

"I'll teach you," he murmurs while checking on the sweet potatoes.

I glance out the window next to the front door, but it's dark, and I can't see much.

The memory of what happened before the asteroid hit Earth shudders through me, and I whisper, "Thana and Phoenix are dead."

"I saw," he says, his tone tight with sorrow. "Thank you for being there for my brother in his last moment."

I swallow hard, and silence falls between us as I struggle to keep the memories of the past few months at bay.

The five years I spent on Earth make up most of my childhood memories.

Molly's gone.

The Calders. Everyone at school. The whole town.

I suck in a quivering breath, then feel Raighne's warmth as he eases the heartache before it can bleed through my chest.

Earth was all I knew, and now that it's gone, I don't know if I'll be able to adapt to this new life.

"You will," Raighne replies to my thoughts. *"It will just take some time."*

I turn my attention back to him and watch as he plates our food.

"Come eat," he orders while he sets the plates down on the table.

I move to the seat beside him, a smile tugging at my mouth as I look at the delicious food. "Thank you."

"You're welcome." He keeps staring at me until I spear a strip of steak and pop it into my mouth.

The flavor bursts over my tongue, and able to feel how much I'm enjoying the bite, a satisfied expression settles on his face.

We eat in silence for a few minutes before I murmur, "I'm sorry you lost River and Phoenix."

"We all lost a lot," he says.

He picks up his glass and takes a sip of water before continuing to eat.

"Can we hold a remembrance service of sorts? Something where we can honor the sacrifice they all made."

Raighne's eyes flick to mine. "That's a good idea. It will help give everyone closure. I'll speak to Janak and Aster so they can arrange it."

I nod and take a bite of the sweet potato, and once I've swallowed, I say, "The food is delicious. Thank you."

The corner of his mouth lifts as he watches me eat. *"I love taking care of you."*

My eyes drift over his face, and I can't begin to describe how thankful I am to have Raighne as my guardian.

The slight smile on his face morphs into a hot grin, and wanting to know, I ask, "Could you hear my thoughts when we met at school?"

He nods but quickly explains, "I've been trained to give you privacy. Back then, I only checked in when you were upset."

I relax a little as I ask, "Did you know every girl was drooling over you?"

He takes a bite of his steak, his eyes not leaving mine. *"Only one mattered."*

As I cut my carrot in half, I realize this is the first time in a long while we're having dinner without having to worry about all hell breaking loose around us.

There's no one left to save.

There's nowhere to rush off to.

"You can finally rest," Raighne murmurs. "Just rest, my little dreamer."

I nod, the feeling of having fulfilled my destiny weirdly empty.

Raighne tilts his head. "Didn't you hear what Awo said when he brought you back?"

Confused, I glance at him. "What did he say?"

"You have a new destiny."

"Oh God," I mutter, dropping my knife and fork. "What now?"

Letting out a chuckle, he places his hand over mine, giving it a squeeze. "You're responsible for everyone's dreams."

More confusion pours into me. "How?"

"We'll learn more about it from Janak. Don't worry now."

"Easier said than done," I mumble as I pick up a slice of zucchini with my fingers and pop the vegetable into my mouth.

Once we're done eating, Raighne rises to his feet, and leaning over me, he picks me up from my chair.

I wrap my arms and legs around him while asking, "What about the dirty dishes?"

"Tomorrow's another day," he mutters as he carries me back to bed.

We lie down, and I snuggle close to his chest, pressing my face in the crook of his neck while he practically engulfs me with his body.

"Good night, my little dreamer," he sighs, his tone filled with satisfaction.

I press a kiss to his skin before whispering, "Night."

Closing my eyes, I get lost in Raighne's scent, his warmth, and the feel of his body.

I relax more and more until I'm carried away into a dreamless sleep.

No matter how determined Raighne is to keep me at home, I say, "I just want to check on Fleur then we can come right back."

"Give it a few days, Alchera," he argues, not at all happy with me. "You need to rest."

"She's my friend. I promise it won't take more than an hour." I inch closer to him, and placing my hands on his chest, I give him the cutest pleading look I can conjure to my face.

"You're not playing fair," he mutters as he scowls down at me.

"Please," I murmur, standing on my toes and pressing a kiss to his jaw.

"Only an hour," he says, finally giving in.

A smile splits over my face, and turning around, I walk to the front door. "Where does she live?"

"It's midday. Fleur's probably at the sanitorium."

I glance up at Raighne as he pulls the front door shut behind us. "What's that?"

"It's where they learn to make elixirs and cast spells."

Right. I forgot what the place was called.

When we step into the road at the front of the house, it's only to see Fleur standing two houses away, looking down at the ground and kicking a rock.

"Fleur," I call out, and breaking into a run, a smile spreads over my face when her head snaps up.

Reaching her, our arms wrap around each other, and I hold her tightly to me.

"I wasn't sure if it was okay coming by to say hello," she says. "I missed you."

"I missed you too." I squeeze my eyes shut, happy to be reunited with my friend.

Suddenly, a sob bursts from her, and it makes me tighten my arms around her.

"I'm so sorry about River," I whisper.

She just nods as she clings to me. "I was worried I'd lose you too."

"Let's go back into the house where you can have privacy," Raighne says.

I keep an arm wrapped around her lower back as we follow Raighne into the house, then I say, "Sit down. Can I get you some tea?"

She shakes her head and hugs me again. "I'm so glad you're back."

I hold my friend for as long as she needs, and only when she pulls away from me, do I take a seat on one of the chairs.

She sits down near me, lets out a sigh, and looks at Raighne. "They say River didn't suffer."

Raighne crosses his arms over his chest. "Have they had his sepulturae?"

She nods. "Two days ago at sunrise. Roark and River ascended side by side."

My heart squeezes at hearing Roark's name.

Fleur glances at me. "I'm sorry for your loss as well. It feels like all we've done is hold sepulturaes the past week."

Has it only been a week since I left to retrieve the chosen ones?

I try to think back, but there are only memories of destruction and death, and I quickly shake my head to rid my mind of the thoughts.

"Alchera thinks we should have a ceremony to honor their lives and deaths," Raighne mentions. "I'm going to ask Janak and Aster to arrange it."

"That will be nice," Fleur murmurs, then she looks at me again. "Just a heads up, but the whole village is arranging a celebration for your return and to welcome the chosen ones."

I let out a groan. "It's the last thing I have strength for right now."

"It will be the perfect time to meet everyone and get it over with," Raighne mutters.

"And there will be drinking, dancing, food, and games," Fleur adds. "It looks like you can do with some fun."

Knowing it's not something I can avoid, I say, "Let me know when and where." Changing the subject, I ask, "What have you been doing since you no longer have to tend to my needs."

She lets out a chuckle. "I've learned how to make an elixir that cures a cold."

Lifting an eyebrow, I ask, "Do you have an elixir for making hair grow faster?"

A burst of laughter escapes her as she replies, "Yes, but we'll have to ask Aster for it. They don't like handing out elixirs if they're not needed."

I point at my short hair. "Girl, it's needed."

"I'll check with Aster and let you know," she says, but then her expression turns serious as she asks, "How was it...on Earth?"

I glance down at my hands, and seeing how long my nails have gotten, I start to pick at them as I shrug.

"It's not something we're ready to talk about," Raighne replies.

"I'm sorry. I shouldn't have asked," Fleur says before rising to her feet. "I just wanted to check on you, but I'll let you get some rest."

I get up, and we hug quickly as I tell her, "Thank you. I'll be up for a longer visit next week."

"The celebration is Saturday night," she warns me.

I nod and watch as she leaves the house, then sit down again.

"I really don't want to go to a celebration," I mutter to Raighne.

He walks to the kitchen and starts to boil water while getting things ready to make a cup of tea. "The whole village will be disappointed if you don't make an appearance." He glances at me. "Besides, it's usually fun, and I think you're long overdue for some of that."

"What happens at the celebrations?" I ask, folding my legs beneath me as I get more comfortable on the chair.

"Like Fleur mentioned, there's dancing and drinking." Raighne carries two cups back to the living room and hands me one.

He takes a seat before he continues, "Sometimes there's a fireworks show, and there are all kinds of snacks."

"Snacks?" I sit up a little straighter, suddenly very interested. "Like what?"

"Like candyfloss, candied apples, roasted nuts, crispy potatoes, and pastries."

"Okay," I say, my tone dead serious, "You've convinced me to go."

Raighne lets out a burst of laughter, and I stare at him because I can't remember if I've ever heard him laugh like that.

The sound fades away until he's giving me an affectionate look. "We'll laugh a lot more in the future."

"I hope so," I whisper.

It's not even midday yet when I hear bustling and joyful music in the street outside.

When I woke up, I could already hear the villagers moving around to get everything ready for today's celebration.

I've stayed hidden in the house for the past four days, and I'm not sure I'm ready to leave the walls that have become my sanctuary.

"It will be fun," Raighne says once again as he holds his hand out to me.

I suck in a deep breath before I place my palm in his, and linking our fingers, he tugs me toward the front door.

The moment we step out of the house, my eyes dart up and down the busy street. There are stalls lining the sidewalks, and I swear I smell fries.

When we approach the gate in the knee-high wall around the house, a man I've never met before notices us, and he instantly throws his hand in the air, shouting, "Alchera's here."

Silence falls over the street, making me feel awkward as hell.

When we step onto the cobblestones, applause starts to fill the air as everyone moves closer, forming a tunnel of sorts for me to walk through.

"Nope," I mutter to Raighne. "You said it would be fun."

"Let them welcome you home," he whispers. "You deserve this."

My muscles tense up, and not having much of a choice without looking like an ungrateful asshole, I walk down the street, doing my best to force a smile on my face.

"Welcome home, Princess," a lady calls out.

"You were missed," another shouts.

Soon, the air fills with people telling me how loved I am, and it makes it near impossible for me not to cry. I swallow hard, keeping my chin raised, but then I see my chosen ones, and the battle is lost.

Letting go of Raighne's hand, I hurry to them, and when Jason opens his arms, I plow into his chest.

He gives me a bear hug, then says, "It felt weird not getting to see you the past few days."

When he lets go of me, the others take turns giving me hugs, and when it's Sarah's turn, she sobs, "Thank you for saving us."

She looks so much better, and I assume Aster managed to heal her.

"Yes," Dylan agrees. "And sorry for the hard time some of us gave you."

I let out a chuckle as I pull free from Sarah, and looking at each of them, I'm relieved to see they seem to be okay. "How are you all holding up?"

"It's an adjustment," Jason mutters, "But it's not bad. The leather clothes are weird as fuck, though. I miss jeans and T-shirts." He gives me a happy grin. "And I'm glad to be reunited with my animals. Thank you for saving them, Alchera."

A lump forms in my throat as I nod.

Before I get too emotional, Matt says, "They said as soon as we're settled, Sky and I can work at the seminarium. I have to learn everything about Vaalbara, and I'm looking forward to it."

I glance at Lydia and Pearl. "Will you work at the infirmarius?"

They nod, and Lydia mentions, "But apparently, we need to learn about stuff called elixirs before we can start working."

"I'm glad you're all finding your place," I say.

"What about you?" Dylan asks. "Do you get some time off now that you're done saving our assess?"

"Yeah."

"It's weird seeing you with blue sparkly eyes," Jason says. "But it looks badass."

"Yeah?" I chuckle, feeling much better now that I've seen with my own eyes they're all okay.

"Alchera," Raighne says, pulling my attention away from my chosen ones. "There are more people to speak to."

"I'll catch up later with you all."

When I turn around, it's to see Janak, Aster, and my mother waiting.

"Peace be, Alchera," Janak says loud enough for everyone to hear. "We're overcome with joy to have you home."

"Peace be is the way we greet each other," Raighne reminds me mentally.

"Peace be," I reply before fidgeting with my hands because it's awkward as hell to have all this attention directed at me.

"You have made us so proud," Janak continues. "This celebration is in your honor."

My voice is strained as I say, "Thank you."

With a gesture from Janak, the music fills the air again, and the celebration begins.

Janak walks to me, and in a softer tone, he says, "You must meet with me next week so I can explain your new destiny to you."

Needing to know, I ask, "Is it bad?"

He shakes his head. "Not at all. It's nothing to worry about."

Feeling a little better, my mouth curves up. "That's a relief to hear."

"Raighne mentioned your idea of having a ceremony to honor the fallen," he says. "We'll arrange it for next Sunday."

"Thank you."

He reaches for my arm and gives it a squeeze. "Enjoy your day, Alchera."

I nod, and when he walks away to speak to someone else, Mom comes closer. Her eyes drift over my face, then she asks, "How are you doing, sweetheart?"

"Better."

When she hesitates to hug me, I move forward and wrap my arms around her.

I feel her body shudder, and I whisper, "You don't have to be careful around me. I'm okay."

She presses a kiss to the side of my head before pulling back. "The color in your face looks better. Did you get plenty of rest?"

I nod. "All I've done the past few days is eat and sleep." Not seeing Brenna and Finian, I ask, "Where's Brenna?"

"She's with the children. She refuses to leave them for a second," Mom says, letting out a sigh. "Of all my daughters, I never thought she'd be the motherly one."

"Is she okay, though?" I ask.

"Oh yes, she's fine. It's poor Finian I'm worried about because the man isn't getting much sleep."

Raighne lets out a chuckle but doesn't say anything.

"I'll let you enjoy the celebration, but if you have some time next week, I'd like to have you over for tea and sweet cakes."

"I definitely have time. I can come over tomorrow because I'd love to see Brenna being a mother hen."

"Good." She gives me another hug. "You can come over any time."

I nod as she pulls away, and when she walks to where Aster is talking to two young women, I glance at Raighne.

"Snacks." I grin at him. "You promised me snacks."

With a smile tugging at the corner of his mouth, he leads me to the nearest stall. The second I see the little paper bags filled with squares of crispy potatoes, I almost let out a happy shriek.

"Oh, you'll love these, Princess," the woman standing behind the table says.

"Just call me Alchera," I tell her as I take a packet from her. "Thank you. It smells so good."

She gives me a curious look, her eyes flicking between the snack and my face, and realizing she's waiting for me to try one, I quickly pop a crispy potato into my mouth.

On the first crunch, my eyes drift shut, and I moan, "So good. Oh my God. This is food for my soul."

"Don't moan like that in front of everyone," Raighne growls in my mind. *"Only I get to hear you make that sound."*

I almost choke, and when I cough, he pats me on the back, a mischievous grin plastered on his face.

Turning my attention back to the woman, I say, "I'll definitely be back later for another packet. Thank you."

"You're welcome," she says, looking proud of herself because I liked the snack she prepared.

By the time I get to the fifth stall, I'm so full I'm going to burst, but I don't have the heart to decline the colorful cotton candy spun around a stick and accept it with a smile.

"Enough eating," Raighne says, leading me to where people are sitting on logs around a group that's dancing.

Once we're comfortable on one of the logs, Raighne takes the cotton candy from me and hands it to three teenagers. "Enjoy."

"Thank you," one of the girls replies while they all stare at me like I'm some kind of miracle.

"It's because you are." Raighne takes my hand and links our fingers. *"You've come a long way from the Jane I found in Steamboat Springs. Everyone is proud of you."*

Jane. Wow. I haven't thought about that name in a long while.

"The shy girl turned into a selfless warrior," Raighne murmurs, his tone filled with pride.

I have to admit I've grown a lot from the socially awkward girl I used to be.

His eyes meet mine. *"I had to live Two hundred and four years without you by my side."*

My mouth lifts into an affectionate smile. *"Old man."*

He lets out a burst of laughter before his expression turns serious again. *"Will you let me love you forever?"*

"That's a solid yes. You're stuck with me."

His fingers tighten around mine. *"Does that mean you'll become my wife?"*

My eyes widen, and before I can even think of a reply, someone says, "Gosh, you've been so busy I didn't think I'd get a moment to speak with you."

I glance up, and seeing Luna, I climb to my feet. "Hi. How have you been?"

"Better than you," she says. "Just training. I'm glad you're back."

"Thanks," I murmur.

"Luna, bring her to dance with us," Lucius calls out to his sister.

She gestures with a jab of her thumb over her shoulder, then asks, "Want to dance?"

I glance at Raighne, who waves a hand at the dancing group. "Go have fun."

I take hold of Luna's hand, and as we walk to the middle of the group, she says, "I should warn you, I suck at dancing."

"We can suck together," I chuckle as I start to bounce and move to the joyful tune.

Fleur joins us, and soon, our laughter fills the air. I'm taught how to do some kind of sidestep dance, which feels more like a workout than anything else.

Night begins to fall around us and cosy fires are lit for everyone to sit around.

When I'm completely out of breath, I walk back to where Raighne is sitting with a smile on his face. Not once has he taken his eyes off me.

I hold out my hand, and when he climbs to his feet and links our fingers, I begin to walk toward the Virtutes Waterfall.

With the sound of the music, laughter, and talking fading into the distance, the calmness of the night settles around us.

The stars shine bright above us, and for the first time in a long while, I feel at peace.

When I spot flickering lights in the long grass, I ask, "What are those?"

"Fireflies."

A smile spreads over my face, and grinning at Raighne, I whisper, "Yes."

"Yes?" He asks.

"I'd love to become your wife," I explain my answer.

I'm yanked to a stop and wrapped up in his strong arms. His eyes sparkle in the dark as he stares at me. "Do you mean that?"

"Of course. I love you, and you're my home."

He looks deep into my eyes, then his voice sounds up in my mind. *"We are bound as one and will never live as two again."*

"Forever," I agree as I push myself up on my tiptoes and press my mouth to his.

CHAPTER 35

ALCHERA

S tanding on the stretch of beach of a lake that has an eerie mist creeping over the water, I stare at a great willow tree to my left. Its roots are covered in the greenest moss I've ever seen.

Looking to my right, my lips part and the air is ripped from my lungs. Beyond the forest, everything is dark. There are massive tunneling clouds looming overhead. The one nearest to me surges with bolts of lightning, ripping a tree from the ground, roots and all.

What's happening?

Unable to stop myself, I walk toward the darkness before I float into the sky, the pull unbelievably strong.

I stare beneath me at the landscape that's turning from green and colorful to dark and gray and soon find myself hovering over a barren land where a man is kneeling.

Ares.

His head snaps back, and he looks up at me.

"Leave this place, Luna!" He shouts.

Luna? I glance down at myself, and seeing the silver strands of hair billowing in the air and the balls of light forming in my palms, I gasp.

What is Luna doing here?

There's a rumble of thunder, and shadows begin to move, swirling around each other until Void takes on a shadowy form with a black cloak billowing in the wind.

"I've been waiting for you, child of the moon," he tells Luna, his tone eerie and hollow.

"Free her mind," Luna demands, her tone filled with aggression, "Or I will kill you right here and now."

Void's laughter fills the air, and it sounds so evil I shrink back.

His arm flies up, and a tidal wave of shadows rushes toward Luna, but she shoves her arms forward, and streaks of light race to collide with the advancing shadows.

The thunderous force of light and shadows colliding makes the air vibrate and the ground shudder.

Jerking awake, I shoot upright in bed while shouting, "Luna!"

TO BE CONTINUED...

NOTEWORTHY DETAILS ABOUT VAALBARA

Earth: Earth as we know it at this precise time.

Vaalbara: New Earth, where the chosen ten will begin a new life. Home to the Immortalis who watch over humankind.

Immortalis: The Latin word for immortal. The race that watches over humankind.

Virtutes: The Latin word for Virtue/Virtute.

Virtutes Waterfall: The entrance to Vaalbara and exit to other realms and planets.

House Regales: The Royal family of Vaalbara.

Infirmarius: Hospital. Also, the place where all potions are stored.

Sanitorium: Where they learn to make elixirs and cast spells.

Seminarium: The school where they learn about different powers.
-
Sepulturae: Burial rites for an immortalis to send their soul to Awo.

Shift: Moving from one place to another through a waterfall.

Shimmer: The power of moving anywhere at any time.

EYES:

Amethyst: Purple – Protection & healing.

Emerald: Green – A life-affirming stone. Promotes friendship, peace, harmony, and domestic bliss by enabling the wearer to both give and receive unconditional love.

Moonstone: Pearl – Represents inner clarity, cyclical change, and a connection to the feminine. It is a symbol of light and hope and also encourages us to embrace new beginnings.

Sunstone: Sunny/red/orange – Freedom and originality.

Amber: Orange or brown - Cleansing and renewal. Ancient energy.

Obsidian: Black - Grounding, healing, and protection.

Blue Lace Agate: Light blue - Tranquillity and calming an anxious mind.

Lapis Lazuli: Blue sprinkled with gold – Wisdom, knowledge, truth, and understanding.

Sapphire: Deep blue – Wisdom and virtue. Brings insight, clarity, and spiritual truth.

Ruby: Red – Royalty. Powerful protection, guarding against negativity, and dynamic leadership.

Bloodstone: Dark green with flecks of red – Warrior's stone. Courage and perseverance.

CHARACTER LIST

Alchera:

    -Meaning 'dream time.' (The remote period of time in which the ancestral spirits of aboriginal tribes in Australia walked the earth – The Oxford Dictionary.)

    -Talents – has visions of the future and the chosen ten and is a weaver of dreams.

    -Also known as Jane: This is Alchera's human name.

    -Youngest daughter of House Regales.

Raighne:

    -Meaning 'strength.'

    -Talents – As Alchera's guardian, he can heal her physically, mentally, and emotionally. He can hear her thoughts and feel what she feels. He can move objects.

    -Also known as Ryan on Earth.

Ares:

    -Meaning 'ruin & war.'

    -Son of Adeth and stepson of Void.

    -Talents – Shimmers (Teleport). He can read minds. He can burn you with a touch. Later, he attains the same dark power as Void and is able to control shadows. He has the ability to rip a soul from a body.

Adeth:
-Main villain in book 1 – Visions and Shadows.
-Powers – She can make poisonous vines grow. She can control minds. She can create agonizing pain by holding her hand over you.
-Ares' mother.
-Griffith's sister-in-law & Raighne, Finian, and Phoenix's aunt.

Brenna:
-Talent – warrior.
-Alchera's older sister.
-Middle daughter of House Regales.

Eryon:
-Head of House Regales and King.
-Alchera, Brenna, and Thana's father.

Finian:
-Meaning 'warrior.'
-Talent – As Brenna's guardian, he's able to heal her. He can shoot electric bolts from his hands that stun people.
-Raighne's older brother and twin brother of Phoenix.

Fleur:
-Talent – Potions and spell weaver.
-Alchera's aide and close friend.

Griffith:

-Meaning 'chief warrior.'
-Talent – Speed, stamina, and fighting. As King Eryon's guardian, he's able to heal him.
-Father of Raighne, Finian, and Phoenix.

Janak:

-Abba / High Priest.
-Oldest Immortal and wisest.
-He talks with Awo and is able to give destinies to immortals.

Aster:

-Ima / High Priestess.
-Mistress of potions and spells.

Luna:

-Talent– Her strength depends on the moon as she draws light from it, which she can use to stun or kill someone.
-Twin sister of Lucius.

Lucius:

-Meaning 'bringer of light.'
-Talent – He draws power from the sun and throws orbs of light that can stun or kill a person. He can turn anything he touches into lava or fire.
-Luna's twin brother .

Phoenix:

-Talent – As guardian to Thana, he can heal her. He can also levitate objects.
-Raighne's older brother and twin brother of Finian.

Mya:
-Wife of Eryon.
-Alchera's mother.
-Queen of House Regales.

River:
-Talent– Fighting and speed.
-Roark's Guardian.
-Raighne's best friend.

Roark:
-Power – Fighting.
-Alchera's older brother and next in line to be king.

Storm:
-Talent – He can control the weather and create any kind of storm.
-Trains everyone on how to use their powers.

Thana:
-Meaning 'death.'
-Talent – She can control fire, earth, water, and air.
-Alchera's oldest sister.
-Eldest daughter of House Regales.

Void:
-Meaning 'emptiness and hollow.'
-Powers – spreads darkness, mental ability to create delusions, spreads insanity.
-Ruler of the shadowlands.
-Where Awo is made of all the good souls, Void is made of dark souls.

Awo:
-Made up of all the good souls.
-Giver of life and talents.

CHOSEN ONES:

Jason De Nil:
-Chosen for his love of animals. Vet.
-From The Netherlands

Sarah O' Kelly:
-Chosen because of the pure love she shared with her brother, Doug.
-Amazing singer and songwriter.
-From Ireland.

Doug O' Kelly:
-Chosen for the pure love he shares with his sister, Sarah.
-Musician & Painter.
-From Ireland.

Dylan Hunter:
-Major in U.S. Army & Survival Skills. Great leadership skills. Will not leave someone behind.
-From The USA.

Matt Hunter:
-Degree in History – Historian USA.
-From The USA.

Sky Wong:
-Chosen for knowledge of cultures and psychic abilities.
-From Japan.

Lydia Newton:
-Chosen for doctor skills and unselfishness – with Doctors without Borders
-British, but found in DRC.

Silvana Cayo:
-Climate activist found near the Amazon forest. Cares about nature and every living thing.
-From Venezuela.

Pearl Tembe:
-Pediatrician and willing to die to help others.
-From South Africa.

Riccardo de Luco:
-Chosen for his selflessness. Police Officer.
-From Italy.

Teenage boy, three toddlers, and baby girl:
-Not chosen ones, but selflessly saved by Alchera.
-From Australia.

PUBLISHED BOOKS

In Reading Order:

FANTASY ROMANCE

THE VAALBARA SERIES

Visions and Shadows
To be released at a future date:
The Land of Shadows
A Light in the Shadows

MAFIA ROMANCE

THE KINGS OF MAFIA SERIES
Mafia / Organized Crime / Suspense Romance
(Can be read in this order or as standalones)
**This series is not connected to any other series I've written,
and there will be no spin-offs.**

Tempted By The Devil
Craving Danger
Hunted By A Shadow
Drawn To Darkness
God Of Vengeance

THE ST. MONARCH'S WORLD
(The Saints, Sinners & Corrupted Royals all take place in the same world)

THE SAINTS SERIES
Mafia / Organized Crime / Suspense Romance
(Can be read in this order or as standalones)

Merciless Saints
Cruel Saints
Ruthless Saints
Tears of Betrayal
Tears of Salvation

THE SINNERS SERIES
Mafia / Organized Crime / Suspense Romance
(Can be read in this order or as standalones)

Taken By A Sinner
Owned By A Sinner
Stolen By A Sinner
Chosen By A Sinner
Captured By A Sinner

CORRUPTED ROYALS
Mafia / Organized Crime / Suspense Romance
(Can be read in this order or as standalones)

Destroy Me
Control Me
Brutalize Me
Restrain Me
Possess Me

CONTEMPORARY ROMANCE

BEAUTIFULLY BROKEN SERIES
Organized Crime / Suspense Romance
(Can be read in this order or as standalones)

Beautifully Broken
Beautifully Hurt
Beautifully Destroyed

ENEMIES TO LOVERS
College Romance / New Adult / Billionaire Romance

Heartless
Reckless
Careless
Ruthless
Shameless

TRINITY ACADEMY
College Romance / New Adult / Billionaire Romance

Falcon
Mason
Lake
Julian
The Epilogue

THE HEIRS
College Romance / New Adult / Billionaire Romance

Coldhearted Heir
Arrogant Heir
Defiant Heir
Loyal Heir
Callous Heir
Sinful Heir
Tempted Heir
Forbidden Heir

Stand Alone Spin-off
Not My Hero
Young Adult / High School Romance

THE SOUTHERN HEROES SERIES
Suspense Romance / Contemporary Romance /
Police Officers & Detectives

The Ocean Between Us
The Girl In The Closet
The Lies We Tell Ourselves
All The Wasted Time
We Were Lost

STANDALONES
LIFELINE
(FBI Suspense Romance)
UNFORGETTABLE
Co-written with Tayla Louise
(Contemporary/Billionaire Romance)

ACKNOWLEDGMENTS

Visions & Shadows was the first book I wrote back in 2009. Fifteen years later, I decided to dust it off.

It all started when Sheldon was a toddler. I told him the story of Alchera and Luna, and over a span of twenty-six years, the story grew into the world of Vaalbara.

This has always been a passion project, and I hope you all will love it half as much as I do.

My editor, Sheena, thank you for putting up with me and always being honest with your feedback. I appreciate you so much!

To my alpha and beta readers – Leeann, Brittney, Sherrie, and Sarah thank you for all your time and feedback. I love getting your emails and messages!

Candi Kane PR – hands down the best PR in the world.

A big thank you to Yolly for making cover after cover until we found the right one.

My street team, thank you for promoting my books. It means the world to me!

A special thank you to every blogger and reader who has taken the time to participate in the cover reveal and release day.

Love,
Michelle.